Coma Girl
The Complete Daily Serial

STEPHANIE BOND

ISBN: 978-1-945002-10-6

DEDICATION

For June Ross, who is watching from the other side

INTRODUCTION

For as long as I can remember, I've had insomnia. I've always been a night owl and a morning person, surviving on five, maybe six, hours of sleep cobbled together in restless bouts. In hindsight, I realize all my life I sort of resented having to sleep. I suppose I was afraid on some subconscious level I'd miss something important or exciting or unrepeatable. Which makes my current predicament all the more ironic.

I am in a deep vegetative state... better known as a coma.

Other people refer to my situation as "sad," "heartbreaking"... even "tragic." I find all the attention rather strange considering before I landed in Bed 3 in the long-term care ward of Brady Hospital in Atlanta, Georgia, I was the girl no one paid much attention to. I was the middle child—middling pretty, middling smart, a middling achiever with a middling personality in a middling job at a middling company. My name is Marigold Kemp, but these days I'm more commonly referred to as Coma Girl. Apparently, I have a bit of a following. I've trended on social media. I have my own hashtag.

1

Since it appears I'm going to be here for a while, I thought I might as well start telling my story; there have been a few twists and turns as to how I got here, and doubtless more to come. The list of pluses of being in a coma is pretty darn short, but if I had to name the best thing, it's that you can learn a lot when people think you aren't listening. I am the ultimate eavesdropper, and friend, if I ever wake up, I'm going to write a tell-all.

Meanwhile, I'll tell you.

JULY

July 1, Friday

TODAY I CAME BACK from wherever I've been since the accident that put me here. Well, not back entirely, but just below the surface of wakefulness, close enough to process the audio inputs around me, yet not close enough to respond. But I'm starting to string together those gluey inputs, starting to make sense of things. From repeated muffled announcements over a public address system, I know I'm in Brady Hospital in Atlanta, Georgia. I recall Brady has a renowned trauma center, a fact that both terrifies and comforts me. And from the conversations between nurses and orderlies, I gather I've just been moved to this room. The fact that my situation is new to them is helpful to me because it's new to me, too.

"I see we have a fresh one," a male voice said.

"Right," another guy said. A rustle of paper sounded. "Chart says her name is Marigold Kemp."

"Ha! A marigold in the vegetable patch—that's funny."

The 'vegetable patch,' I realized, is the term given to the long-term care ward. And apparently, there are four of us veggies in the room.

"What happened to her?"

"TBI."

"Huh?"

"Traumatic brain injury."

"That explains the head bandage."

3

Ack—a bandage? I needed my thin, brown shoulder-length hair to frame my face just to be passably attractive. I'm pretty sure a bandaged head is not a good look for me.

"Head-on collision Memorial Day weekend. You know Keith Young?"

"The Falcons new hotshot receiver? Yeah, man."

"He was driving the other car."

"No shit? Is he okay?"

Of course they would be more concerned about a Falcons recruit than little old meaningless me.

"Physically, yeah, but they say he was driving drunk. He's screwed, big-time."

"Were there any witnesses?"

"Yeah, another girl in the car… a sister, I think."

Sidney? Oh, my God, was she—?

"But she walked away with only a few scratches."

Thank you, Mother Mary.

"Which means she can testify against Young."

"Yep."

"Damn, there goes any hopes of being in the playoffs." Their voices faded, then I heard a door open and close.

I've never heard of Keith Young, but then I'm not a football fanatic. How can someone grow up in the Southeastern Conference with an older brother playing college football and not be a fan? Let me clarify—I know the rules of the game and I cheered on my brother Alex as he pounded and got pounded for the University of Georgia Bulldogs, but I guess I just never saw the point. Ironic, huh, that my mother always fretted *he* would end up in the hospital with a head injury? Even more so now that Alex is in Afghanistan. He'd once joked with my parents that the traffic in Atlanta is more harrowing than a battlefield, and I guess he was right.

I backtracked and assimilated the information I'd overheard. My sister and I had been in a car accident caused by an inebriated professional athlete, and apparently I'd sustained the brunt of the impact. I had no memory of the event and, in fact, couldn't remember my last memory. There were wispy bits in the corners of my brain, but they remained elusive. According to the timeline I'd cobbled together, I'd lost the entire month of June. How is that possible? Where did it go? And how insignificant is my life that I could be absent from it for a month and the world had pretty much kept bumping along?

And I hate to start sounding like a whiney little vegetable, but where is my family? Because it's pretty obvious to me now that I can hear and understand what's going on around me, I'll be waking up any minute now.

July 2, Saturday

"THE TRUTH IS, she might never wake up."

My mother burst into tears, and my father made a sound like a wounded animal. My sister Sidney murmured soothing words to my parents while I sent hateful vibes toward Dr. Sigrid Tyson, who seemed to be the acting authority in the room.

"All along the hope has been Marigold would improve to the point that we didn't have to move her into this long-term care ward. The longer it takes for her to come out of the coma, the better the chance she won't."

I willed myself to open my eyes then and there, just to say, "Boo!" and freak her out.

But I don't... I can't. And it scared the hell out of me because ever since my parents and Sidney had come into the room, I'd been trying to move, whimper, blink—something to let them know I'm in here and I'm aware of what's happening around me. And hearing I might never wake up, well, that's just impossible.

This cannot be my life.

I mean, no one has to tell me my life isn't all that. Especially compared to my remarkable older brother who passed on a career in Silicon Valley to become a decorated soldier. Or compared to my bombshell younger sister who's in law school and could seriously be president of the world someday. They are both splendid specimens of their gender and the Kemp name, and I... am not. I've always pictured my starchy mother looking at the three of us and wondering what happened to her middle fetus. And my sweet, practical dad saying, "Two out of three isn't bad, Carrie."

In hindsight, I assumed the only role in my family I could. There simply wasn't room on the Kemp stage for three stars, so I became the stagehand and audience for my siblings. In between, I graduated from a tiny state college with a generic degree and landed a job managing a carpet warehouse. I don't mind the work—it pays for my half of the rent in an apartment in an artsy (i.e., "shady") part of town—but wrangling Berber isn't the kind of career my mom can brag about.

Plus I don't have a boyfriend and from what I can remember, no prospects, unless you count booty pings on Blendr and Tinder. But to be honest, I don't get a lot of those because I post an actual picture of myself, fully clothed.

I don't have any exciting hobbies, I'm not a big partier, and I have no useful talents.

Still... it's my life and as little as it is, I want to get back to it sooner rather than later. My boss Mr. Palmer won't hold my crappy job forever.

"There's no change in her condition whatsoever?" Sidney asked.

"We're going to run another series of tests to check for brainwave activity," the doctor said.

I cheered. Surely the tests would reveal I'm still here, listening and… well, just listening.

"Is there anything we can do?" my father asked, dear man.

"Talk to her," the doctor said, her voice growing more distant. Her footsteps indicated she was leaving.

"What are we supposed to say?" my mother asked, her voice elevated.

"Just talk to her the way all of you normally talk to her."

The door opened and closed. In the ensuing silence, I pictured my parents and sister looking pensive and coming to the collective realization they normally didn't talk to me.

A ding sounded over the P.A., then a voice announced visiting hours were over.

"We should leave," my mother said.

And they did.

July 3, Sunday

"SO WE'RE TAKING TURNS," Sidney said. "Now that you're out of intensive care and people can visit, Mom and Dad and I came up with a schedule so everyone won't be tripping over each other."

Everyone? My social circle would fit in a refrigerator.

The sound of a chair scraping the floor brought her voice closer. "It's nice to have some privacy, just the two of us." Then she made a thoughtful noise. "Well, the two of us and your three roommates, but I'm pretty sure they can't hear me." She sighed. "Can you hear me, Sis?"

I focus all my efforts on making my mouth move, on saying I'm so relieved she wasn't hurt in the accident. But since Sidney doesn't react, I assume I'm still inert.

A clinking noise sounded—something against metal.

"I brought you my favorite rosary beads. I'm hanging them on your bed."

I knew the one she meant—the beads were blue glass with a little yellow flower painted on each one, the Madonna and crucifix were silver. Sidney always had it with her. In addition to everything else, my sister had always been a better Catholic than me. But I'm touched by the gesture. Just knowing something familiar and beloved is nearby is comforting.

"I can't believe this is happening," she said, her voice breaking. "Are you going to wake up?"

The door squeaked open.

"May I help you?" Sidney asked, and I could tell from the tone of her voice she was addressing a man.

Did I mention Sidney is gorgeous?

"Pardon the intrusion," the man said. "I'm Detective Jack Terry from the Atlanta Police Department. Are you Sidney Kemp?"

"Yes. What's this about?"

"The accident you were in with your sister," he said in a tone that asked what else would it be about?

"I gave a statement the day after the accident."

"I have the notes here. I was hoping to clarify a few details."

"How did you know I was here?"

My sister is going to make a great lawyer.

"I stopped by your parents' home. They told me where I could find you."

"You work on Sundays, Detective?"

"Is it Sunday? I hadn't noticed."

"Can't this wait?"

"I suppose," he said agreeably. "But since we're both here, you'd do me a big favor by letting me tie up some loose ends. I'll try to be brief."

"Okay. Of course I'll help any way I can. Has Keith Young been charged?"

"No."

"Why not?"

"I can't speak for the district attorney's office, but I'm told Young's toxicology results aren't yet available."

"It's been weeks, how is that possible?"

"This isn't a TV show, ma'am... the state labs are so jammed up, we'll be lucky to hear back within another month."

"So much for the victim's right to a speedy trial," Sidney said dryly.

"Ah, yes, I read in the report that you're a law student."

"That's right."

"What year?"

"I start my third year at Boston U this fall."

"So you're almost done, good for you."

"Thank you."

"I'm really sorry about your sister."

He had a handsome voice and I wondered if he looked the way he sounded.

"So am I," Sidney said, her voice defiant. "What questions do you have about the accident?"

He cleared his throat. "If you don't mind, I'd like to start from the beginning. I understand your sister Marianne—"

"Marigold. Her name is Marigold."

"Right—sorry. I understand Marigold picked you up from the airport Memorial Day weekend, on that Saturday?"

I don't remember any of this, so I'm riveted.

"Yes. I came home for summer break."

"What time did the two of you leave the airport?"

"Around nine that evening."

"And your sister was driving a tan-colored 2010 Ford Escort?"

"That's correct."

"Okay. The report says you drove straight home?"

"Yes."

"I found a receipt in the Escort from a convenience store with a timestamp around the time of the accident."

"Oh, right. I forgot—Marigold wanted to stop and get a lottery ticket. It's silly... a psychic once told her she was going to win the lottery, so she was a little obsessed with it."

I wouldn't have used the word "obsessed"... *dedicated*, maybe.

"Was any alcohol purchased?"

"No."

"Did you make any other stops?"

"No. From the convenience store, we headed home."

"To 558 Northwind Drive?"

"Yes. We were maybe five miles from my parents' house when Keith Young hit us."

"Did you notice his car before the accident?"

"What do you mean?"

"Keith Young drives a yellow Jaguar—it stands out. You must've seen it coming toward you?"

"I... wasn't looking, I guess. Besides, it was dark."

"About that—do you remember if your sister had her car lights on?"

"I... would assume so. Marigold is a very responsible driver."

"I know. I ran her license—she's never had a violation."

"All the more reason to arrest Keith Young. He was driving drunk and he crossed the center line."

"I thought you said you didn't see his car."

"I didn't."

"So you didn't actually see him drive across the center line?"

"I saw the aftermath."

"So someone told you he crossed the center line?"

"I suppose."

"Or maybe you heard it on the news?"

"I don't remember," she said evenly.

"Okay. Do you know if your sister saw his car coming? Did she honk the horn or scream or try to swerve?"

"No… maybe… I can't remember, but no, I don't think so."

"Was your sister distracted, maybe using her phone?"

"No. By the way, when do we get our phones back?"

"I'll have to let you know. Unfortunately, confiscating phones at the scene of accidents is standard protocol now."

"You don't need our phones. The accident was Keith Young's fault—he was drunk."

"What makes you say Young was drunk?"

"I smelled alcohol on him."

"This was when he tried to administer aid to your sister at the scene?"

"Yes. But if you think that makes up for what he did to my family, Detective, think again. Look at my sister—because of Keith Young she might never get out of this bed."

"I'm very sorry for your family. And for your sister."

"Are you finished with the questions? Visiting hours are almost over."

"Yes, I'm done. I'll leave you." His footsteps sounded on the floor. "Ms. Kemp, I hope your sister wakes up soon."

Sidney didn't respond and after the door closed, I realized she's crying. I wanted to cry, too. I had been straining to remember, hoping some detail of the accident would open the floodgates of my memory, but nothing had changed. My mind is still like a giant blackboard that had been erased.

July 4, Monday

"AND AS SOON AS you wake up," my mom said, "we'll go to the laser light show at Stone Mountain. I know how much you enjoy watching it, and we haven't been in a while."

By my calculations, we hadn't been in sixteen years. Hey—the math part of my brain is still working. Now if only that part would nudge the 'lift your hand' part.

"We hate to go to the fireworks in Centennial Park without you," she continued, "but Sidney is devastated over your situation, and your father and I thought it would be nice for all of us to take a little break."

From me. I'm catatonic, and I'm still too high-maintenance for my family.

But I knew what she meant. My family loves me, they're just not used to worrying about me, accommodating me… dealing with me. And I understood they had their own lives. Since it's the Fourth of July, my dad has the day off from his job, so I'm getting them both at once. Plus I remembered the hospital is close to Centennial Park, so I'm on the way. Like Starbucks.

"Sidney went down early with a group of friends," my mother said. "After all, she's supposed to be on summer vacation. She works so hard at her studies, she deserves to have some fun before she has to go back."

I agreed, but I'm desperate for company. Still, my family is probably getting fatigued. Who knew how many hours they'd already spent at my bedside during my "lost" month.

"But before we leave," my dad said. "We have a surprise for you."

There was some fumbling, then I hear a muted bleeping noise.

"Go ahead," my mom said loudly.

"Hi, Sis."

Alex. His voice sounds tinny and distant, but it's my big brother, all right.

"We're Skyping," my mother said, apparently to me. "Can you see Marigold, Alex?"

"Yes, I can see her."

The anguished sound in his voice is jarring—nothing rattled my brilliant soldier brother. I can only assume I look ghastly. He, on the other hand, would be sharp-featured and tanned, muscular and vibrant.

"How's it going, Sis? Will you open your pretty green eyes and talk to me?"

My entire life I'd done anything and everything my brother asked just to please him. This time, I could not.

"Okay, I'll let you rest then. But I'll be home soon and I expect you to be awake and giving me a hard time, you hear me?"

In the silence that followed, I assumed my parents were scrutinizing me for movement or sound.

"Did she respond?" Alex asked.

"No," my dad said woodenly. "She's the same."

"Jesus, she looks so pale... and the scars."

I winced inwardly. Scars?

"What are the doctors saying?" Alex asked.

"Not much," my mom said. "No one seems to have any answers."

"They're going to run more tests soon," my dad added. "Hopefully we'll know more then."

A muffled horn sounded. "Sorry, that's for me," Alex said. "Gotta run. Happy Fourth!"

"You too, son. We're flying our flag at home."

"Bye, dear."

"Tell Sid hello for me. Bye, Marigold!" I pictured him waving his big hand.

When they disconnected the video call, my parents' disappointment was palpable in the room.

"Well, I guess you're not going to open your eyes today," my mother said, as if I were lying here motionless out of spite. "So we're going to leave."

"We'll be back soon," my dad promised.

They left and all I could hear was the beeping and whooshing noises of the machines in the ward, keeping us vegetables alive. But later I realized the room must have a window because I could hear the distant *pop-pop, pop-pop-pop* of fireworks. I imagined the canisters shooting high, then bursting with spectacular wheels of color before falling and fading into the night sky. I suppose some people might see the fireworks as a metaphor for life, but I don't. Because I'd missed out on the bursting-with-spectacular-color part.

At one point, I heard a sound from the show that seemed a little off from the others—instead of a *pop* within a symphony of other pops, it made a thick, thudding noise. *Fffp*. A dud, I realized.

Okay, there's my metaphor.

July 5, Tuesday

"GOOD MORNING, Coma Girl."

I slowly became aware of a nice male voice I didn't recognize. The fact that I don't recognize the person speaking isn't unusual—the number of people moving around in a hospital on any given day is pretty remarkable. What strikes me about this voice is the friendly familiarity, as if he knows me. But the volunteers—candy-stripers, retirees, students—have a way of making patients feel as if they're old friends. And for all I knew, this volunteer has been coming to see me regularly.

"Do you like poetry? I brought a book by Emily Dickinson to read from that I thought you might enjoy. This poem is called 'Dawn'." He cleared his throat. "When night is almost done, and sunrise grows so near... that we can touch the spaces, it's time to smooth the hair... and get the dimples ready, and wonder we could care... for that old faded midnight that frightened but an hour."

Inside I'm smiling. The words described how I'd always felt about the night. I'm twenty-eight years old and every evening I still face bedtime like a toddler—I procrastinate and whine and get a drink of water and pee and adjust the thermostat and the shades and... well, basically, I dread closing my eyes and going to sleep. I looked it up once—it's a thing, with an official name: *hynophobia*.

The article I read said the thought of going to sleep made me anxious because I saw it as losing control or sacrificing time that could be spent accomplishing things. I'm not sure I buy either of those explanations because I don't see myself as a controlling person, nor as someone who could set the world on fire if not for that pesky needing sleep thing. I confess as bedtime approaches, the more things I can think of that simply have to be done, but they fall a little short of what my mother would deem an accomplishment: tie-dyeing a skirt in the bathroom sink or organizing my CD collection alphabetically. (Yes, now you know the name of the one person in the world who still buys CDs.) And did you know if you stream Netflix at three in the morning, you pretty much have the service to yourself? No jerky interruptions just when you get to the good parts. But I digress.

In short, I've always suffered from insomnia. Which kind of makes my current dilemma seem like some kind of sick karmic joke, huh?

The nice volunteer reading to me couldn't know that about me, but he probably knows if I can hear him, I might be a little afraid my dawn will never come.

The truth is, I *am* afraid. None of this makes sense to me—how is my mind processing some sensory inputs, but not others? Do I have a big dent under the bandage on my head—is a chunk of my brain missing?

On an episode of *Forensic Files*—which fyi, plays all night until 6:00 am—a woman killed her husband by injecting him with a drug that paralyzed him, then setting a fire. The poor man lay there, knowing he was going to die, and could do nothing about it. I remember thinking that must be the most helpless feeling in the world.

Unfortunately, I can now confirm it is.

As the volunteer slips from the room, he can't know how grateful I am he took the time to read to me when, for all he knows, I'm already gone.

I hope he comes back soon and brings another poem with him.

July 6, Wednesday

"THEY'RE CALLING her *Coma Girl!*" Sidney shrieked.

My mom gasped. "*Who* is calling my daughter such a vile name?"

A man named David Spooner who is apparently vying to be my attorney coughed lightly. "Actually… everyone. It started on social media and now the mainstream media is picking up on it. But if it's any consolation, Mrs. Kemp, people seem to be using it as a term of endearment."

"It isn't," my mother chirped. "What am I looking at here?"

"These are mentions of hashtag Coma Girl across Facebook, Twitter, Instagram, et cetera."

"Oh, my God," Sidney said. "She's trending on Twitter on the east coast!"

"And gaining momentum," he said.

Wow… if I'd known a coma was the fast lane to popularity, I might've konked myself on the head in high school.

"This is why the phone is ringing nonstop at home," my dad said. "I finally unplugged it."

"You should change your phone number," David Spooner said.

A rap on the door sounded, then a man said, "Flower delivery for Coma Girl?"

"Her name is Marigold Kemp," my mother corrected. "But you may bring them in."

"All of them?"

"How many are there?" my father asked.

"Thirty-seven."

"Thirty-seven bouquets of flowers?" Sidney asked with a croak.

"And eleven planters."

"See what I mean?" David Spooner said. "Yes, bring them in for now. We'll sort them out later."

"But I don't understand why anyone would be interested in Marigold," my mom said. "She's nobody."

Thanks, Mom.

"Sometimes things in the media just catch fire," Spooner said. "And the fact that a professional athlete is involved in this situation makes it more juicy."

"Look at these Facebook posts," Sidney said. "A woman created a Coma Girl logo, and someone else created a Coma Girl cartoon character!"

"Oh, well, now that's just wrong," my mother said.

Actually, it sounded kind of cool to me.

"They're making a mockery of Marigold," Sidney said. "What can we do to stop it?"

"I don't think you can stop it," Spooner said. "I think it would be better to try to manage it. If you bring me on board, I'll help you."

"How?" my dad asked.

"First, you'll need a family spokesperson."

"A spokesperson?" my mom said with a laugh. "Why?"

"The public is clamoring for information about Marigold. Left to their own devices, they'll simply make things up. A family spokesperson can help to manage public opinion, which will be especially important if Keith Young is brought up on charges and goes to trial."

"You mean *when* Keith Young goes to trial," my sister corrected.

"You've heard from the District Attorney?" Spooner asked.

"Not yet," Sidney admitted.

"This case doesn't seem to be a priority," my dad added.

"If you bring me on, I'll apply as much professional pressure as I can to get things moving."

"You would be our spokesperson?" my mother asked.

"If you wish, but it would be best if it's a member of the family."

"Well, that would be Sidney, of course," my dad said.

"If she's willing, I think Sidney would be an excellent choice," Spooner said, and I could hear male appreciation in his voice.

"What would that mean, exactly?" Sidney asked.

"It means you'll keep the media and public updated on Marigold's condition, and let everyone know how much the family appreciates the concern and support. We'll hold periodic press conferences and you'll take control of Marigold's social media... with my help, of course."

"We're in over our heads," my dad said. "I suppose we do need some guidance here."

"Would any of that help to light a fire under the D.A.?" my mother asked.

"I believe so, yes," Spooner said. "The D.A. has to be concerned about public perception, especially in an election year."

There was a pause in the conversation where I imagined my family was trying to decide what to do about me.

"If at any time you want to suspend our relationship, that would be fine," Spooner added. "Or if Marigold wakes up, of course she can make decisions for herself."

"*If* Marigold wakes up," my mother said.

"Hush, Carrie," my dad said. "She's going to wake up."

"But meanwhile," Spooner said, "you need to take steps to protect her, and to protect your family. You can bet Keith Young has a dozen attorneys working on his behalf."

He's convincing, for sure. But I could sense my family's reluctance, their bewildered resentment for having to deal with this.

"Okay," my dad said, sounding exasperated. "You're hired."

"Good," the man said, then clapped his hands. "I'll need to know everything about Marigold, all about her job, where she lives, who her friends are."

A yawning silence descended—I visualized the expressions on my family's faces because they don't know anything about my life. Not only had they never been to my apartment, but I'm pretty sure they don't even know the physical address.

"Okay, we'll do that later," Spooner said, obviously trying to cover the awkward moment. "The first thing I'm going to do is talk to the hospital administrator about tightening security for this room."

"Do you think Marigold is in danger?" my dad asked.

"Not physically," Spooner said, "but this morning someone posted this picture of her."

My mother gasped again.

"That was taken in this room," my dad said. "You can tell by the machine behind Marigold's head."

"It's a very unflattering photograph," Sidney said.

Oh, great.

"Someone on staff probably took it," Spooner said.

A memory stirred, but lay there, quivering. Anxiety fogged my broken brain. All I knew was I had some idea of who might've done it, but I couldn't conjure up their identity.

July 7, Thursday

"READY FOR A BATH?"

Am I ever. Now that my sense of smell had returned, I'm pretty aware of my own body odor. This vegetable is getting ripe.

Despite my gratitude, the situation is more than a little awkward for me. Before I landed in the hospital, only a handful of people had seen me naked: my gynecologist, who had no other choice, my roommate Roberta, who had caught me a couple of times getting out of the shower, and two or three inept lovers—although in hindsight, I'm not sure they saw me entirely naked because various articles of clothing had been left on during our encounters.

And then there's Duncan, the love of my life. We met at some random party and it was love at first sight… at least for me. I'm pretty sure he wasn't attracted to me physically, but we had so much fun together and liked the same things that he eventually started hanging around. We had a few great months together before he left for the Peace Corps for two years, a commitment he'd already made before we met.

I was despondent because I had a bad feeling Duncan would meet someone else while he was abroad, and he did. Early in his tour we texted or Skyped constantly. But when he got more involved in his duties, the contact became more sporadic. And when we did talk, the name of a particular girl in the Corps kept popping over and over: Trina. She was also from Atlanta and they had bonded over being so far away from home.

Here's where I should say Duncan and I had only engaged in heavy petting and only when we were drunk, so in his mind, we weren't boyfriend and girlfriend and he was free to fall in love with Trina, which he proceeded to do, oblivious to the pain it caused me. Occasionally when he Skyped me, she would nudge her prettier face into the screen and wave as if we were old pals. Then one day she held up her hand and announced, "Surprise, we're engaged!" I tried to be happy for Duncan like the good friend he considered me to be, but between you and me, I was positively heartbroken.

Suddenly I wondered if Duncan knew about my accident and just as quickly realized there's no reason he would. He'd never met my parents or my sister and they had no reason to believe he was any more important to me than anyone else in my address book. If Duncan had tried to Skype me recently, he would just assume I was busy. One upside of being in this bed is I won't have to go to his wedding. When I don't RSVP, would he think I'm angry with him?

If so, good. How's that for passive-aggressive behavior?

"She has great skin," Nurse Teddy said. "It's a shame about the scars."

The scars again—am I a monster?

"I have some cocoa butter that will help them fade," Nurse Gina said. "She'll be pretty again when she wakes up."

"Have you ever seen anyone in this ward wake up?"

"No," Gina admitted. "But it's the least I can do."

"Poor thing," Teddy said.

"Yes, poor thing," Gina said.

"What did you bring for lunch today?"

"Tuna salad—you?"

"Leftover lasagna."

They moved away, and I was already forgotten. But at least they had left me smelling like cocoa butter. It was a gift.

July 8, Friday

TODAY IS TEST DAY. Early this morning my bed and I were wheeled to another part of the hospital. Sidney's rosary clicked against the bed in a rhythm that seemed to say, *I'm with you... I'm with you... I'm with you...*

I was psyched—at first. But ugh, the delays. Over what seemed like hours, I was put in an MRI machine and given a CT scan—both passive tests that simply look at the state of my brain. I heard Dr. Tyson say she wanted to assess the swelling. Then I was hooked up to an EEG—an electroencephalogram, a fancy name for a machine to measure what, if anything, was happening in my head. I heard Dr. Tyson talk to others about electrodes, so I assume they were attached to my head in some way, although I couldn't feel them. I tried to concentrate on what was going on around me, but I confess all the voices and noises and scents made for sensory overload… I could almost feel my brain misfiring. When the doctor addressed me directly, presenting me with words and phrases that were meant, I assume, to trigger a sensory response, I was fading in and out.

In school, I was known as someone who studied diligently, but who didn't test well. And here I went again.

From the snatches of conversation around me, I realized someone was touching different areas of my body with instruments ranging from brushes to sharp probes to see if I responded, ditto for heat and cold. I didn't feel anything at all, but I hoped my body was sending signals to another part of my brain that was responding, and I just didn't know about it yet. I was also subjected to a series of sounds ranging from soft buzzing to shrill sirens. And finally, scents of evergreen and ammonia and other chemical smells I didn't recognize were passed close to my nose. If I ever wake up, I'm going to suggest they add the scent of a cheeseburger to the lineup.

By the time they had wheeled me back to my room where my family waited, I was pretty sure I had failed the brainwave tests, and I was terrified of what that might mean. Would they remove my feeding tube? I had filled out a healthcare directive stating I didn't want to be kept alive by artificial means. What I should've checked on the form was the box for "Don't ever give up on me."

So if the time came for my family to order me to be starved to death, I had only myself to blame.

"What are the results of the tests?" Sidney asked. She's taking the role of my spokesperson seriously.

"Let's start with the good news," Dr. Tyson began. "Marigold is breathing on her own, and all her organs seem to be functioning well."

"Except for her brain," my mother prompted.

"Yes," the doctor agreed. "But today's tests indicated there is still substantial brainwave activity."

"Oh, thank God," my mother said.

"And Marigold exhibits localized response to pain, which is good… but not great."

"So she can feel pain?" my dad asked.

"Your daughter had an involuntary, localized response to pain. What we're hoping for is a more general response—a full-body response—to pain stimuli. That tells us more parts of the brain are communicating."

"I'm confused," my mother said. "Marigold is in pain, or she's not in pain?"

"The test involved external stimulus… we don't believe she's in pain on an ongoing basis."

"But you don't know?" my dad asked.

"We can't say for certain."

Sidney made a frustrated noise. "Doctor, is my sister going to wake up?"

"We just don't know. The brain activity isn't as vigorous as I had hoped, but there's still some swelling from the injury she sustained, so we won't know for sure until it's completely healed."

"And how long might that take?" my dad asked.

"Again, we don't know. You're going to have to be patient. Meanwhile, when you talk to Marigold, you might try talking about childhood routines and memories."

"Why?" my mother asked.

"It has to do with how the brain establishes and stores new and recent memories. It takes time for new memories to be recorded and hard-wired into the brain. Older memories are sometimes easier to recall simply because we've recalled them more often."

So that explained why I can't remember the events around the accident yet... and if my brain had been traumatized during the "recording" of the accident, maybe I never would.

"With that in mind," the doctor continued, "you might try calling to Marigold to wake her up the way you did when she was little."

"Okay," my mom said, although I had a feeling she would not want to reenact her trips to the bottom of the stairs where she would yell, "Marigold, get up already! Don't make me come up there!"

My poor detached family... the attorney had charged them with learning about my current life, and now the doctor wanted them to relive my childhood, too.

July 9, Saturday

I SMELLED MY ROOMMATE Roberta Hazzard before she announced her arrival. Roberta works at a bakery, so the scents of cinnamon and cocoa cling to her like DNA. I think this adds to her sex appeal because despite the fact that Roberta is a large woman, she has her pick of men. They literally follow her home. I kid you not—there have been times when I've left the apartment and found some lovesick guy lingering in the hall, hoping for a whiff of Roberta.

"Hi, Marigold, it's me, Roberta." Then she laughed. "Or should I call you Coma Girl? Girlfriend, you're a dang celebrity. I can't go online without seeing some mention of you."

The chair creaked as she settled into it.

"I brought one of the apple fritters you like. But since you're not awake," she continued thickly through a mouthful, "I guess I'm going to have to eat it myself."

As if she needed a reason.

"New room, huh? Well, this is better than ICU, I guess. They only let me step inside once to get a look at you, then shooed me right out again."

The sound of fingers being licked enthusiastically filled the ward. I can smell the glazed icing on the fritters. It's like a little sniff of heaven.

"They thought they were going to lose you, you know. Guess you showed them."

No one had told Roberta that being moved to a long-term care ward isn't really an improvement over ICU—it's only an improvement over death.

"Between you and me," she said, her voice sounding closer and lower, "you're the best-looking one in here. Your roomies seem a little... stale. Coma Girl, you gotta get out of here."

I'm working on it.

"Guess who came into the bakery today? Go on—guess. Okay, you'll never guess so I'll tell you—Marco. Remember Marco? The guy I dated last spring until I found out he was married? Well, he says he's left his wife for real, this time, and he wants to get back together. What do you think I should do?"

Run like the wind.

"I know you never liked Marco, but I think he's changed."

He hadn't... people don't change, not for the better anyway.

"Guess who else came in this week? Go on—guess. Okay, you'll never guess so I'll tell you—Duncan."

Duncan. The mere mention of his name nearly sent me back under—I could feel the fingers of deep unconsciousness pulling at me—the equivalent, I supposed, of a person in a coma almost passing out. I hated that even in this state of near-nothingness, he could still affect me.

"He's back in town, and get this—his fiancé is friends with the owner of the bakery. They came in to taste test cakes for their wedding. I mean, what are the chances they'd walk into the bakery where I work? If you ask me, it's kind of freaky."

Welcome to my life.

"He didn't know about the accident. When I told him you'd been injured, he was really upset."

I guess that made me feel a little better, but not less comatose.

"I wasn't nice to him, in case you're wondering. I wasn't rude, but I wasn't nice because no matter what you say, I think he treated you pretty shabbily."

And that's why I love Roberta.

"Oh, and his fiancé—who laughs like a barking seal, by the way—chose the pink grapefruit cake for the reception. I mean, yuck. Am I right?"

She's right. But pink grapefruit is trendy and sounded hip on Pinterest wedding boards. Not that I'd ever haunted Pinterest wedding boards. What reason did I have to look at Pinterest wedding boards? I could count on one hand the number of proposals I'd received in my life—*if* I put my finger and thumb together to make a big, fat "zero." If I could lift my hand.

"Anyway, I thought you'd want to know he was back in town."

And planning his wedding. To someone else.

The sound of wax paper being wadded up reached my ears and the chair creaked, indicating Roberta had stood. "Listen, Marigold, I hate to be a downer, but I have to know what to do about the apartment. I mean, your half of the rent is still being drafted out of your checking account, but I feel bad that you're paying and you're not even there. On the other hand, I don't want to find another roommate if you're going to wake up tomorrow."

I would do my best to oblige.

She sighed. "Okay, I gotta run. Marco is waiting for me in the lobby. Bye, Coma Girl."

July 10, Sunday

"I LIT A CANDLE for you this morning," my mother said.

"So did I," my aunt Winnie said, "although I don't have as much clout with the saints as your mom."

My colorful Aunt Winnie is my favorite relative, but because she lives four hours away in Savannah and she and my mom don't see eye to eye on pretty much anything, I don't get to see her as often as I'd like.

My mother made a disapproving noise, then said, "Marigold, remember the time you and Winnie and I went to see the show at the Center for Puppetry Arts?"

"She won't remember, Carrie."

She's right—I don't remember.

"The doctor said it would be easier for her to recall older memories than new ones, so we're supposed to talk about things we did when she was a child."

"Okay... except we didn't take Marigold, we took Sidney."

"No, we didn't."

"Trust me, we did."

"Oh... well, maybe so. Hm. Well, there was the time we went to the Swan House for tea."

"Also Sidney."

"What? No."

"Yes."

"Are you sure?"

"I'm positive. Marigold was already in school. But you and I once took Marigold to the Botanical Gardens."

"We did? I don't remember that."

I remembered it. I'd loved the butterfly center.

"She loved the butterfly center," Winnie said.

"I think you must be thinking of someone else," my mom said.

"And I think you've blocked out your middle child's childhood."

"That's ridiculous," my mother sputtered.

"I couldn't agree more."

I could picture my mother's face turning red, her pretty mouth puckering.

"Let's go," she bit out. "Visiting hours are almost over anyway."

"Go ahead. I want to have a private moment with Coma Girl."

"*Don't* call her that."

"Okay, okay—sorry. I'll be right out."

The clickety-clack of my mother's shoes told of her supreme irritation. When the door closed, my aunt chuckled.

"Listen, Marigold, my love, I totally understand why you wouldn't want to come back to those people—they haven't always done right by you. But they do love you in their own way, and I love you more than I love myself, so please wake up."

I tried so hard to open my eyes... but it didn't happen.

"Okay, then," she said. "You're on your own timeline. I can respect that. I'll come back soon by myself so we can visit. Goodbye, sweetheart."

When the door closed, I felt lighter. Aunt Winnie is a force of nature, so if she believes I'm still viable, that has to be good.

A few minutes later, the door opened and closed again. I thought either my mother or aunt had forgotten something.

"Hi, Marigold."

Holy pink grapefruit cake.

"It's me... Duncan."

As if he'd have to tell me. As if I hadn't memorized every creamy nuance of his caramel voice. And he still wore that smoky cloves cologne I loved.

He stepped close enough to my bed to ping the metal, and the pained noise he made is proof of how grim I must look with my bandaged head and scars apparently crisscrossing my face. And admittedly, when it came to grooming, I did the bare minimum. So my basic routine would be undone after a few weeks of neglect—my eyebrows were probably bushy, and my breath probably reeked. And was someone keeping the crusties out of my eyes and nose?

"I didn't know this had happened," he murmured. "I didn't know. I'm so sorry, Marigold."

Sorry for the condition I'm in, or sorry for breaking my heart?

Okay, technically, that last part isn't fair because he doesn't know he broke my heart. But he'd lost his chance to be with me forever, so if he was having regrets, he was just going to have to live with himself. Oh, and Trina.

"The nurse said I could only stay for a couple of minutes, but I just wanted to see you in person and tell you..."

Yes? I'm waiting. I have nothing but time.

"Goodbye."

After the door closed, I lay there and just... lay there. Duncan apparently had his closure. This coma thing isn't as satisfyingly vengeful as I'd hoped.

July 11, Monday

I KNEW THE NAMES of my unwitting ward roomies because the nurses often called out patient names to each other—I assume they were checking charts against wristbands—before they administered medication. Which I found amusing—did they think we were all playing possum and in the middle of the night, we switched beds just to mess with the staff?

Although that could be funny.

Bed one is occupied by Audrey Parks. She landed in the hospital two years ago because of a water skiing accident. The fact that she was having fun a split second before the injury seems especially cruel to me. I don't know how old she is, but I assign some youth to her just because she was on water skies. I tried to water ski once and the way I face-plowed into the wake, it's a wonder I didn't wind up in here then. So I have sympathy for Audrey and how quickly things can go bad going twenty-five miles an hour standing on two slivers of wood in deep water.

Karen Suh is in bed two. She fell off a ladder trying to clean gutters at her house. I find it terrifically sad that a woman who was attempting to do something for herself would take a tumble and is now in this place. For the record, if I ever get out of here, I will never climb any higher than a curb. Like Audrey, Karen has been here for two years.

Jill Wheatley is in bed four. She suffered a stroke while in surgery and never gained consciousness. I gather she's the oldest patient in the ward and has also been here the longest—going on four years.

I'm in bed three and the fact that I'm the new gal but my bed is out of sequence isn't lost on me. I wonder who was in bed three before me, and the circumstances of her exit. The fact that Nurse Gina said she'd never seen anyone in this ward wake up tells me the former bed three patient exited the ward either into the hereafter or into a nursing home… which, in my mind, is one and the same.

I'm wondering if Audrey, Karen, and Jill are each lying there trapped in their bodies like I am, slowly going mad as the days, weeks, months, and years crawl by.

The saddest part of my roomies' situation is none of them have gotten a single visitor since I entered the ward.

Until today.

"Hello, ladies, it's Sister Irene. Peace be with you."

And also with you. The response was automatic, like breathing. Sister Irene is, obviously, a Catholic nun.

"How are you Audrey? Karen? Jill?"

She paused after each name, out of courtesy, I suppose… or to leave room for a miracle should one of them decide to spontaneous respond.

"And who do we have here?" From the noise at the foot of my bed, I assumed Sister Irene was checking my chart. "Marigold Kemp. What a nice name."

I confess my experiences with nuns at my private high school had not been entirely positive, but I'm inclined to like this one. From the authoritative edge to her voice, I deduced Sister Irene had been around the block a time or two and was perhaps in her sixties.

"And I see, Miss Marigold, that you are a Believer, considering the lovely rosary hanging on your bed. Very good. What should we pray about today?"

Okay, that's where she lost me. Despite my Catholic upbringing, I'm not a very religious person. I have problems with God—I think he should be more open to my suggestions. I know that's a sacrilegious statement and some of you might think that's why I'm here, that I was struck down and sentenced to lie here until I've paid penance for my wicked independence. But this can't be my destiny.

If anything, my story and my ward mates' stories tell me that life is so random, no one is in control… not even God.

If I could talk, I'd tell Sister Irene to save her prayers for me and spend them on someone else. Because I'm going to get out of here.

On my own.

July 12, Tuesday

"SO I WAS THINKING," Sidney said. "If people want a picture of Coma Girl, let's give them a good picture. I brought my makeup kit and a head scarf to cover up that hideous bandage. Then we'll have something to push out into your social media streams. I ran this by David, and he thinks it's a great idea."

Wow, my sister had singlehandedly come up with a new genre: coma porn.

And why hadn't she thought of this before Duncan came to visit me in all my bedridden unsightliness?

Yes, of course I'd been thinking about him almost nonstop since his short visit to my room. I desperately wanted to call Roberta and ask her what she thought about it, but that's out of the question. Plus I knew what she'd say: *Girl, you're in a coma, and you're wasting what few brain cells you have left thinking about a man who doesn't want you? What are you, stupid?*

And she would be right.

Meanwhile, from all the zips and thumps and snaps and taps, it sounded as if Sidney was unpacking an arsenal.

"I've always wanted to do this, but you would never let me."

I don't remember Sid ever offering to make me up, but she's doing it now, and that's what matters.

"I only wish you would open your eyes so I'd have more to work with."

Except that would render the entire exercise moot.

"First I have to trim those eyebrows of yours. Honestly, sis, they look like mustaches."

Now there's an image that will stick with me.

"Okay, better. Next, a nice crystal scrub to remove all the dead skin cells. I'll be careful around the scars."

I can't feel anything, but I know my sister knows what she's doing.

"Now I'll use a wipe to remove the crystals. There, that's better already. I'm going to tell the nurses to exfoliate your skin at least once a week."

And I'm sure they will put it on the top of their list.

"Now moisturizer—with luminescence so your skin will glow. Oh, sis, you really do have nice skin... you should play it up more."

Duly noted.

"And you're dreadfully pale, but I think this foundation color might work. Hm... yes, that looks nice. And concealer for this scar... and that one... and that one... and that one..."

Jesus, my face must look like a jigsaw puzzle.

"Okay, that's the worst of it. Now a contouring stripe to minimize your nose."

Apparently my too-big nose is still intact—*check*.

"And powder to set... good. And a little mascara..."

I still have eyelashes—*check*.

"A touch of blush on the cheeks and eyebrows..."

Check, check.

"And lip balm."

Whew! *Check.*

"Now let me see about covering that bandage in front."

The muffled ring of a cell phone sounded. Sidney shifted in the creaky chair and fumbled while it rang a couple more times. The police must have returned our phones.

"Hello?" Sidney said. "No."

Her footsteps sounded as she walked away, in the direction of the window.

"I told you not to call me."

Her voice was lower, but I could still make it out. She sounded angry—was it a boyfriend? Sidney was never in want of male company, but neither had she mentioned one certain guy.

"My sister is in the hospital. I haven't been able to work on our project as much as I had planned."

Ah—it was obviously a fellow student.

"Can you cut me some slack? My sister is in a coma and my family is falling apart."

I don't think that's the case but if Sid is late on a project, it was because of my predicament, so she could use whatever excuse she wanted.

"Don't call me again. I'll call you when it's ready." She ended the call and cursed under her breath. "This isn't fair!"

I understood her frustration. She had arrived home from school anticipating a fun summer of partying with friends and instead is babysitting her comatose sister and holding my parents' hands. She's right—none of this is fair.

Sid inhaled and exhaled audibly, as if searching for a Zen place, then she came padding back to my bed. "Okay, let me take a peek at my handiwork," she said, her voice only slightly elevated. "Good. Now you don't look dead."

Always a plus.

"Say cheese, Coma Girl."

July 13, Wednesday

"GOOD MORNING, Coma Girl."

My toes curled... at least they wanted to. It's the silky-throated volunteer with a penchant for poetry. I had tried so hard to remember him, but I needed the live trigger of his voice to bring it all back. Just as Dr. Tyson said, forming new memories was harder than conjuring up old ones.

"Goodness, look at all these flowers... and balloons... and stuffed animals. Wow, you are one popular lady."

The flowers kept coming every day. David Spooner had arranged for most of them to be distributed throughout the hospital so other patients could enjoy them. And as much as I appreciated the gesture, the cloying sweetness of the live flowers was getting to me... it reminded me of a funeral, and that cut a little too close for comfort.

"It's going to be a beautiful day," he said. "Sunny with a blueberry sky and a magnolia breeze. Can you see it?"

I can see it... smell it... taste it...

"I found this poem in the Emily Dickinson book, and it seemed right for today. I hope you think so, too. It's called 'Angels In The Early Morning.' " He cleared this throat politely. "Angels in the early morning may be seen the dews among, stooping, plucking, smiling, flying... Do the buds to them belong? Angels when the sun is hottest may be seen the sands among, stooping, plucking, sighing, flying... parched the flowers they bear along."

Beautiful. I'd been lying here in the dark for so long, I'd almost forgotten how sunlight looked and what it felt like on my skin—with 50 SPF of course.

A soft thud indicated he'd closed the book. "What did you think? If you don't give me something to go on here, I'm going to have to keep winging it."

Fine by me.

"Okay. I appreciate a person of few words. I think everyone would benefit from talking a little less and listening a little more. It gives you leverage, you know—listening. As long as you really hear what the other person is saying."

I guess I hadn't thought about it like that, but my condition did put me in a unique position. Because even though people talked at me and to me and in front me, few people truly believed I could hear them. Which meant they usually relaxed their verbal filter.

"Hey, I saw someone posted a new picture of you online... it looked nice. Everyone is happy to see you're improving."

Was I improving? I think so.

The chair creaked, meaning he'd shifted... closer?

"What's going on in that bound up head of yours?" he asked softly. "You're not dead, but you're not alive. What's it like to be in limbo?"

Frustrating… maddening… scary… really scary. Which is why I had to find a way out.

"One day I'm hoping to walk in here and find you sitting up and talking, and then you can tell me."

Deal.

"Later, Coma Girl."

July 14, Thursday

"I'M SORRY it's been a few days since I've been by to visit you, sweetheart. I've taken off a lot of work since the accident, and my boss was leaning on me to get back on the road."

My dad, Robert Kemp, sells road signs… you know, the kind you see when you drive along the highway. He sells to local municipalities, county governments, state governments, and he even has some accounts on the federal level. If you've ever traveled throughout the Southeast, you've probably driven by one of my dad's signs. It's not a very glamorous job, but my dad is good at it, and he takes a lot of pride in his products. The garage, basement, and attic of the home I grew up in are stacked with samples and rejects—misprints and misspellings. Louisiana seems to give sign makers the most trouble, followed by Mississippi, although Tennessee is problematic, too.

"Mr. Boxer isn't a bad guy," my dad said. "He asks about you all the time. But this is a busy time of the year since so many governments' fiscal year ends in June, so new budgets are being set—and spent."

My dad has always travelled during the week and been home on the weekends, but there have been occasions when he's had to be on-site for a big install and was away from home for a couple of weeks at a time. When Alex was old enough, he travelled with Dad during summer breaks. Ditto for Sidney. I'm not sure why I didn't—maybe Dad was waiting for me to ask, and I was waiting to be asked. Anyway, Dad had always had an easy rapport with Alex and Sid, but he struggled more to talk to me.

"And even though Mr. Spooner is working on the contingency that Keith Young's insurance will pay for everything, there are still retainers and medical bills and—well, you don't need to hear all that. Just know that I'm going to take care of everything."

But I never doubted my father's love for me. And it pained me to think he would be working overtime to pay for expenses I'd incurred.

"I checked with the police impound lot and they agreed to release your car. It's a mess, but I think I know a guy who can fix it. I'm having it towed to his shop this week. Don't worry, by the time you get out of here, it'll be good as new and waiting for you."

Some people believe a person's wellbeing is reflected in their teeth. My dad believes a person's wellbeing is reflected in their vehicle. It made sense because he spent so much time in his SUV, which is always immaculate and in top running condition. There were plenty of times after I hit driving age when I'd missed a dental checkup, but my dad wouldn't hear of me missing an oil change. So I can't imagine what it did to him to see my little Ford Escort banged up.

"Hey, I got a new grill," he said as if it had just popped into his mind. "One of those nice egg ones. Sidney gave it to me for Father's Day."

I'd missed Father's Day, I realized. But I could never top Sidney's and Alex's gifts anyway.

"And Alex sent me cufflinks made from lapis mined in Afghanistan."

See what I mean?

"When you wake up, I'll make you a big juicy steak," he said, his voice cracking. "And I want to braid your hair."

Braid my hair? Maybe I hadn't heard him correctly.

"When you were a little girl, you came to me once and asked me to braid your hair. You were maybe six or seven. I was irritated, probably busy with something I thought was important. And I didn't know *how* to braid your hair. So I snapped at you and sent you away. I'm so sorry, Marigold."

I remember when that happened—only because my father is generally so sweet-natured, the few times he'd raised his voice to me had made an impression. But I hadn't been traumatized by the incident. He'd obviously thought a lot more about it than I had. And now he seemed afraid he wasn't going to have the chance to right what he perceived to be a grievous wrong. I wish I could reach out to my Daddy now and tell him it was fine, and I'm fine.

But I'm not fine, of course. Else I could tell him I'm fine.

July 15, Friday

"GATHER AROUND bed three," Dr. Tyson said. "Move some flowers if you have to."

From the number of footsteps that filed into the ward, I assumed the doctor was going to use me as some kind of show and tell segment.

"Patient is a twenty-eight-year-old female with a traumatic brain injury from a car collision approximately eight weeks ago. She was unconscious when first responders arrived on the scene. Upon arriving at Brady, she underwent surgery to relieve bleeding on the brain. She has not yet regained consciousness. Questions? Phillips, go."

"What is the state of the brain bleed?"

"Stable and healing, but considerable swelling remains. Gaynor, go."

"Did the patient have a brain incident before the crash, or was the bleed caused by the crash?"

"Patient was healthy before the crash, the brain damage is an impact injury. Tosco, go."

"Is the patient verbal?"

"No. Streeter, go."

"Does the patient exhibit brainwave activity?"

"How would you measure it?"

"EEG—an electroencephalogram."

"Correct. An EEG showed she does have substantial brainwave activity. Sayna, go."

"Does the patient respond to commands to blink or to move her extremities?"

"No. Goldberg, go."

"Does the patient respond to pain?"

"Patient responds locally when external pain sources are applied. Is that good, Goldberg?"

"A general response to pain would be preferable."

"Correct. Jarvis, go."

"Is this Coma Girl?"

The room fell completely silent. I wondered if she knew what he meant, although with the influx of flowers and with David Spooner lobbying the hospital for tighter security, she must.

"Yes," Dr. Tyson said finally. "This is the patient the media refers to as Coma Girl. Keep your phones stowed, people. And don't even think about touching your Google Glasses. Anyone who takes a picture of the patient even for their own use and records, will forfeit their residency. Understood?"

A chorus of yeses sounded.

"Kwan, what test is used to determine the severity of a coma?"

"The Glasgow index."

"Correct. And based on the answers to the previous questions, where would the patient land on the index?"

"In the 'severe' range."

"Correct again. Statler, go."

"Can the patient hear us?"

"I've told the family she can and encouraged them to keep trying to communicate with her."

"But?" Statler prodded.

"But between us, I doubt very much Coma Girl has any awareness of what's going on right now."

Not only am I aware, but I'm incensed. How dare the doctor just write me off like that.

"Jarvis, do you have a question?"

"But you don't know for sure the patient can't hear us?"

"It's my opinion based on the results of the EEG that she cannot."

"But you don't *know*?" he pressed.

"No," Dr. Tyson conceded. "I don't know for sure. Let's move on to the cardiac ward."

Okay, I kind of like that Jarvis guy.

July 16, Saturday

"GOOD MORNING, MARIGOLD. I'm Dr. Jarvis and I have a little something for you."

Oh, God, please don't let him be a pervert.

The door opened and from the bumping sounds and squeaking wheels, I got the impression of something sizable being wheeled into the room.

"Where do you want the TV, doc?" a man asked.

"Over there is good, let me move some of these flowers out of the way."

"We're supposed to take some of those with us," another man said.

"Right. Why don't you take a few to the maternity ward, and some to the chemo department?"

"Sure thing, doc."

A television? Terrific! I am having withdrawal from late-night shows. And if the hospital got the Discovery ID channel, I'd be set. Spouses conspiring to murder each other never gets old.

After some shuffling and more bumping noises, the door closed to relative quiet. The whooshing and wheezing of various machines hooked up to us veggies had become white noise. From the sound of Dr. Jarvis's footsteps and the rustle of fabric, I realized he was standing next to my bed.

"Marigold, can you open your eyes?"

No.

"Okay, then, can you wiggle your toes?"

Nope.

"Try again, please? Just one toe?"

Not happening.

"Okay, I'm holding your hand. Very soft, by the way."

Really, doc? Flirting with Coma Girl?

"Can you squeeze my hand?"

I tried to visualize him holding my limp hand and sent impulses toward it.

"Concentrate, Marigold, and squeeze my hand."

I'm trying.

"No? Okay, we'll try again later. Now then, just to let you know what's going on— I've arranged for a television to be placed in the ward, for the stimulation of all the patients, of course, but especially you, Marigold. I've reviewed your EEG results and unlike Dr. Tyson, I believe you can hear me, and hear things around you, too. To that end, I've asked that the television remain on and at an audible volume during daylight hours to provided sensory input when people aren't around."

In my mind, I was hugging him.

"I've done some research into what types of sounds are most effective in stirring responses in the brain, especially in the area where your injury occurred."

It was a full body hug.

"Fortunately, the hospital has an extensive lineup of channels, so I was able to find a few to experiment with."

HBO? CNN? HGTV? I love me some *Property Brothers*.

"As it turns out, music is the sound that stimulates the most areas of the brain."

Okay, that's a little disappointing, but I dig my CD collection and I'm down with Pandora. My tastes run the gamut from pop to blues to folksy acoustic stuff. I've been known to listen to country, although I prefer older country to the new. And I don't turn off hip-hop when it crosses my earbuds. Actually, I pretty much listen to all kinds of music, except classical.

"And tests show the most stimulating music is classical."

Crap.

With a couple of clicks, the strains of a violin-led symphony floated into the room, sucking all the joy out of the air.

"There. Now let's see what a steady diet of Bach will do for that bruised brain of yours."

I'm officially rescinding the hug.

July 17, Sunday

A RAP SOUNDED on the door, and from the sharpness and the force, I guessed the visitor to be a man. Sure enough, heavy footsteps sounded—the guy was wearing boots in the dead of summer in Atlanta. Whoever he was, he was alpha. The question is, which one of us turnips had he come to see?

"Hello, Marigold. It's Jack Terry from the Atlanta Police Department."

Oh, I remember him. He's the one who'd pumped Sidney for details on the accident. If he'd come back hoping to run into her again, he would be disappointed. Sid had breezed by earlier to retrieve the cards from the newly delivered batch of flowers, and although she said she was working on a school project today, I'd smelled suntan lotion.

Which is fine… good even. Sid deserves to enjoy a Sunday afternoon at the lake. She was spending lots of hours fielding questions about me and organizing our family "message," as David Spooner called it. I received occasional eye-popping (if my eyes could pop) updates: My Coma Girl Facebook page had over 250,000 likes, and Coma Girl Pinterest boards were the quirky trend of the moment—Things You Can Do While Bedridden, How to Jazz up a Hospital Bed with Throw Pillows. And Coma Girl T-shirts were all the rage.

Who knew comas were cool?

So Sid deserves a day off from me and my trappings.

"All alone today?" he asked.

Ha—just as I suspected.

"Me, too," he said. "I was told you hadn't woken up yet, but since I'm a detective and all, I thought I'd come and check for myself. I brought flowers."

He brought flowers?

"But I see you have a few dozen bouquets already…. and all nicer than mine, I might add. I only brought a handful of black-eyed susans that were growing around the dock where I live."

So the man who wore boots lived on a boat? Interesting. But if he has a boat, isn't the weekend the best time to be out on it?

"Someone told me you're an Internet sensation. I'm not really into all that, I must be the only person alive who doesn't have a Faceprint account."

LOL, Detective.

"I don't really like people that much in person, can't imagine taking the time to like them online."

Fair enough.

"I'm still investigating your case, by the way. The D.A. found some extra resources somewhere to get priority on the lab work, and they're going to recreate the accident—which isn't cheap. You, Coma Girl, are causing quite a ruckus."

He seemed impressed.

"I see you got a TV—nice. But what goober put on this awful music for you to listen to?"

He must've found the remote control because the music went away mid-note, thank God. He channel-surfed for a while, then stopped.

"Hey, the Braves are playing the Rockies. This could be a good game."

I heard a chair being dragged across the floor. "Mind if I hang out here for a while?"

I didn't mind—the man had picked flowers for me, after all. But I had to wonder... what was going on in Detective Jack Terry's life that he preferred to spend the afternoon with Coma Girl instead of going home?

July 18, Monday

ROBERTA HAD COME BACK to see me. This time she brought a bear claw for us to "share."

"Girlfriend, you are the biggest thing on the Internet since that whole is-the-dress-blue-or-white nonsense. Guess that accounts for all the watchdogs on this floor. I had to leave a dozen jelly doughnuts at the nurses' station just to get in to see you. Yuck—who turned on this horrid music channel? Oh, my... I wish you could taste this bear claw."

So do I. Roberta practically hums when she eats, so even comatose foodies get to enjoy. I hope I'm not drooling.

"Your mail at the apartment has piled up to the point that I had to do something. I mean, if I opened it on my own, that would be totally illegal, right? So I figured opening it here and reading it to you would be the next best thing to you doing it."

She licked her fingers noisily.

"Okay, let's see what we got. There must be fifty cards and letters here."

I heard the sound of paper ripping.

"This one's written on pretty rose-colored stationery. Dear Coma Girl..."

She proceeded to read to me messages written from strangers all over the country—all over the globe. I was amazed at the outpouring of sympathy and kindness. Some of the letter writers had a relative who was in a coma, and my story had given them hope by bringing new awareness to their relative's case.

That's cool.

"Oh my God, this one contains a ten-dollar bill! What am I supposed to do with it? Should I give it to your parents? By the way, I got a voice message from some guy named David Spooner. He wants to talk about the lease you and I signed, and he said your mother wants to come to the apartment and go through your things."

Ack.

"Look, I know she's your mother and all, but I also know y'all aren't particularly close, and I don't know what to do. I mean, if the roles were reversed, I don't think I'd want my mom rifling through my stuff. It just seems like an invasion of your privacy, you know?" Roberta sighed. "I really wish you'd wake up, Marigold, and tell me what to do."

Being in a coma gave me a glimpse of what things would be like if I'd died in the accident—or if I died still: My parents and the media sifting through the remnants of my limited life, wondering why I'd bought a certain knick-knack or kept a certain photograph... judging me.

"Oh, my God! This one is a marriage proposal—assuming you wake up, of course. Is that nice, or is that creepy?"

More creepy than nice, I think. But not as creepy as the second marriage proposal a few cards later from a guy who didn't mind if I never woke up. Now that's accommodation... and a felony.

"Hey, more cash! This woman sent twenty dollars... and a coupon for diapers. Wait—that's a little mean."

I'm sure the woman meant well, but yeah... *ouch.*

"That was the last one, but I'm sure they'll start piling up again tomorrow. Let's see, you have one hundred and twenty-five dollars in cash. Should I give it to your parents?"

Probably.

Roberta made a thought noise. "You know, I think I'll just save this and give it to you when you wake up."

I love Roberta and she has a good heart, but I had a feeling the cash was headed for her perpetually overdrawn bank account. And I'm okay with that.

"By the way, Duncan and his woman came back to the bakery yesterday. He didn't talk much—actually he didn't even make eye contact. Now that he's back and knows about the accident, I wonder if he thinks about visiting you?"

Not anymore.

"Anyway, forget about Duncan. You have admirers all over the world! Gotta run, I'll be back soon with more mail!"

Forget about Duncan. I'm trying.

July 19, Tuesday

"HELLO, LADIES. It's Sister Irene. How's everything in here today?"

Just peachy. I wonder if Sister Irene notices at a glance that her prayers from last time went unanswered?

"Oh, my, Marigold, look at all these beautiful flowers! Aren't you the lucky lady?"

That's me—lucky, lucky, lucky.

Sister Irene made a wistful noise. "You know I used to get my fair share of flowers when I was young."

Really?

"I'm sure that surprises you. But long ago, before I was a nun, I was a woman."

Academically, I knew that nuns didn't come out of First Communion with a habit and vows, but it was difficult to think of sisters going through puberty, attending prom, and reading *Teen* magazine.

Her footsteps moved away. "I had suitors and dreams," Sister Irene said in a faraway voice. "I was going to travel to exotic places and write a novel."

She must've been standing at the window because her voice sounded a little echo-y. I imagined her using a finger to doodle in the condensation on the glass while she reminisced. Then she cleared her throat, as if bringing herself back to the present.

"But I chose a life of service, and that's the life I've lived."

She made her way around the room, from bed to bed as best as I could determine, murmuring private greetings. When she got to my bed, she was so close, I could smell the lemony scent of her laundry detergent, and starch—she must be wearing some parts of her habit, probably only a simple head covering since she wasn't in church. It was the equivalent of Casual Friday dress code for nuns.

"I saw a picture of you on the news, Marigold, and a clip of the young man they say caused the accident. There's a great deal of animosity toward him… and standing here looking at you, I certainly can understand why people feel that way. You were innocent, with your whole life ahead of you. You were simply in the wrong place at the wrong time."

That's me—lucky, lucky, lucky. "But at a time like this, it's important to forgive this man. I don't know him, but I'm quite sure he never meant for anyone to get hurt, and would relive that careless moment if he could."

Blah blah, forgiveness, blah blah. The thing is, I'm plenty mad at Keith Young for driving recklessly, for putting me and Sidney in danger, and for smashing up my beloved little car, but I don't really feel as if there's anything to forgive. I'd be waking up soon, and then the star athlete would be off the hook. And the media would move on to the newest Kardashian kidlet or the latest politician who accidentally Tweeted his wiener to the world.

"Let us pray," Sister Irene said, and proceeded to ask Saint Aurelius of Riditio (the patron saint of head injuries, I recall obscurely from my Catholic indoctrination) to pray for us, to make a miracle out of our lives, then added 'if it is God's will.'

Ah, the Catholic caveat. If the prayer is answered, it's God's will, and if the prayer *isn't* answered, well, then, that's also God's will and we just have to suck it up.

But I don't believe my fate is in God's hands… I believe my fate is in my own hands. It's up to me to get out of this bed… and that's what I'm going to do.

If only someone would turn off that annoying classical music!

July 20, Wednesday

"HELLO, MARIGOLD. I'm Dr. Jarvis, remember me?"

Of course I remember him. He's the one responsible for the unending, nonstop, unrelenting trudge of chamber music that played in the ward ten to twelve hours a day. I know he said classical music is supposed to be the most stimulating to the brain, but I'm not so sure.

Unless the incentive is that the patient is so sick of listening to classical music, it drives them to rally atrophied muscles and leap out of the hospital bed just to change the damn channel. A few more days of this and all four of us veggies were liable to rise up and turn this floor into an episode of *The Walking Dead*.

"Okay, Marigold, I'm going to repeat some of the tests performed in your EEG, although this time you won't have electrodes attached. I'll be observing you for a physical response. Throughout the test I'll let you know what I'm doing and you just try to respond in some way, okay? Can you nod your head okay?"

He's a sneaky one, slipping in a possible breakthrough before the test even started. Alas, I can't nod.

"Marigold, can you open your eyes? Open your eyes, Marigold."

Not today, apparently.

"Okay then. I'm uncovering your feet. Ooh, nice feet."

I do have nice feet. I just dearly hoped someone had been clipping my toenails.

"Okay, Marigold, can you wiggle your toes? Tell your brain to wiggle your toes, Marigold."

I'm telling my brain, but apparently it's not listening.

"Okay, let's try something else. I'm going to pull a brush across the bottom of your right foot. Can you feel it? Even if you can't feel it, think about it hard and try to make your right foot move. I'm brushing... I'm brushing."

Nada.

"Let's try a different instrument. I have a metal probe that's not sharp enough to break the skin, but you should feel a pinch. I'm pressing right under the arch of your left foot, can you feel it? Concentrate hard and tell your brain to accept a message from your left foot."

But my brain is still pouting because it's not doing anything I tell it to do.

"Okay, I'm moving to your hands, Marigold. First, I'm holding your right hand. Squeeze my hand if you can. Tell your brain to tell your hand to move, Marigold. Try again, squeeze your right hand."

I guess it still isn't working.

"Okay, now I'm holding your left hand. Squeeze my hand, Marigold. Move your left hand. Try again, squeeze your left hand."

Again nothing.

He sighed, unable to hide his disappointment. "Don't worry, Marigold. I'm not giving up on you."

Before he left the room, Dr. Jarvis increased the volume of the television for good measure. The music channels on TV are apparently in a loop; they play a series of forty songs in three hours, then the whole thing starts over. And all commercial-free. I never thought I'd be starving to hear an insurance or dogfood commercial, but it would be a welcome break from the cello.

I'm not a total rube, so I do recognize a few Mozart, Bach, and Beethoven tunes, although I couldn't name them with any confidence. But after hearing the same songs over and over (and over), I've memorized the opening movements of each one and can predict which song is going to play next.

It's the only way I can keep from losing what little mind I have.

July 21, Thursday

"I'M VERY UPSET, MARIGOLD."

My mom is a part-time real estate agent. Actually, part-time might be a bit of an overstatement. In the decade or so since she took the exam, she's sold a total of three houses, all of them for friends. I think my mom likes the idea of being a realtor more than the actual footwork. For all her organization and drive, my mother was never a career-oriented woman. In truth, my parents had a very traditional marriage. My dad brought home the bacon… and my mom wouldn't let him eat it because of his high cholesterol.

Seriously, my mom was always busy with us three kids and my dad was happy she wanted to manage our home life. For the record, I love my mother. But Carrie Kemp sees the world through the lens of a sheltered suburban housewife. And when something is not to her liking, she simply ignores it.

Apparently I have not been to her liking since I was a toddler.

"I went to your apartment to check on your personal belongings, but your roommate—Roberta, I believe she said her name is—wouldn't invite me in. She said as long as you were still paying the rent, you were the only person she would let in. Which was a lie because a shady looking character named Marco answered the door. I told her I had a right to be there, but she slammed the door in my face."

I knew Roberta didn't plan to let anyone go through my things, but I'd never known her to be rude. And was Marco living with her now? Eating my Costco barrel of Chex Mix and using my stockpiled toilet tissue?

"And I have to say, Marigold, I was shocked at the state of the area of town you live in. People sleeping on the streets and graffiti everywhere. I suppose you never told me your address because you didn't want me to worry about you."

I never told my mother my address because she never asked.

"Your father and I have discussed it and we've decided that when you wake up, it would best if you come back home to live for a while. I know I turned your bedroom into a craft room, but you can stay in Sidney's bedroom. Or if she hasn't gone back to Boston yet, you can stay in Alex's bedroom."

Did you get that? Mom turned my bedroom into a room for gourd painting and soap making, yet Sidney's room and Alex's room remain intact. I'm sure a psychologist would have a field day with that one, but my mother would just say the lighting is best in my old bedroom.

"Meanwhile, Mr. Spooner has been a great advocate… he's going to see what he can do about getting a key to your apartment from management. He and Sidney are working together beautifully. He even got Sidney a membership to his gym at the country club so they can strategize while they're running."

Uh-huh.

"And he's been urging the district attorney to stay on your case. He promised to set up a meeting with us soon. We're determined to make sure that Keith Young pays for what he did to us."

Me. What he did to *me.* But whatever. I would let them fight that fight—I realized they needed something to focus on.

My mother cleared her throat. "I, um, also talked to your boss Mr. Palmer."

Now there's a surprise. And I would pay for that video—to see my prim, pristine mother have a conversation with my sweaty, hairy boss.

"He's hired a temp for your position until you are well again. He said you're the best employee he has ever had. He said there are two keys to his business and that he has one and you have the other. I confess I was surprised and proud at how much your coworkers think of you, Marigold. You've never really talked about your job."

Again—don't ask, don't tell.

"He gave me a collection that had been taken up among the employees—it's almost five thousand dollars."

Five thousand dollars? Most of the people who worked at the carpet business made barely above living wage. The fact that they had dug so deep into their pockets for me is both stunning and touching.

"I just want to say, Marigold, that I was doubtful about your job choice at first but it seems as though you made a good decision after all."

Mark this day on the calendar, people. My mother just said out loud I had made a good decision. Of course, the only witnesses to her statement were four comatose women.

"So you can see how upset everyone is. It's time to wake up, young lady, and stop worrying everyone to death." Her voice cracked. "If you're doing this to hurt me, Marigold, you win."

Then she left.

July 22, Friday

"YOUR SOCIAL MEDIA stats are improving every day," Sidney said. "David knows an online marketing whiz who offered to work with your brand pro bono."

I have a brand?

"He thinks Coma Girl has the potential to be a huge entertainment franchise—books, television, movies… maybe even a Broadway musical."

A musical about a girl in a coma?

"He's interviewing agents now. This is so exciting! Maybe I should consider going into entertainment law."

A cell phone rang. I heard Sid rummaging through her bag, then connect the call with a click. "Hello?"

From the sound of her footsteps, I could tell she'd walked away from my bed.

"I told you not to call me." Her voice sounded low and serious. "I'm busy. Yes, I'm working on the project, but I don't have enough to send you. I need more time." She made an exasperated noise. "I don't know when I'm coming back. This situation with my sister is taking longer than I thought."

I could hear her foot tapping in irritation, then it stopped.

"What? *No*, you can't come here. I'll call you when I've made some progress." The way she stabbed the phone to end the call told me she really wanted to throw it. "Dammit," she muttered.

I felt terrible Sid was so behind on a school project, but she'd been spending more time with David Spooner than with me.

The door opened and I recognized the sound of the hard soles of Spooner's shoes before he even spoke.

"I just gave the local networks a thirty-minute warning for the update on Marigold's condition. Dr. Tyson is standing by; she said she can't say Marigold is improving, but she can say she's not declining."

Not declining. That's supposed to be positive?

"So," David said, "I suggested to Dr. Tyson that instead she say Marigold is holding her own."

"Oh, that sounds much better."

"Doesn't it?"

It does, I conceded. The man could spin a phrase.

"Okay," Sidney said. "How do I look?"

"Amazing, as always," he gushed. "Wait—take a flower from one of the arrangements and put it in your jacket pocket."

"How about this pink rose?"

"That will look perfect. Touch it occasionally and if you have a chance, mention it's there to remind you of Marigold."

Oh, brother.

"Do you have my notes?" she asked.

"Right here, but try not to use them unless you have to. People want to see you speaking from your heart."

"But what if I mess up?"

"You won't, but if you do, just apologize and say you haven't had much sleep and the situation with your sister is wearing on you."

Not a stretch, but really?

"That's good. What if someone asks a question I don't know how to answer?"

"Just look at me. If it's appropriate, I'll step in. Or if I give you this 'cut' sign, tell them you're sorry, but you've just been called back to your sister's bedside."

Okay, that's a bit much.

"Hey, are you okay?" he asked. "You seem a little anxious."

"Just nervous, I guess. I just wish all of this wasn't happening."

When I heard the plaintive note in Sidney's voice, I forgave her for her earlier enthusiasm.

"I know," he soothed. "But it *is* happening, and the best way you can help your family is to keep your sister's case in the spotlight."

"You're right. Let's go."

"By the way, what's up with the incessant classical music?"

"Beats me," Sidney said.

The door closed behind them.

Don't mind me... I'll just be lying here building my brand.

July 23, Saturday

"HELLO, MARIGOLD. It's Dr. Jarvis again. How are you enjoying the music?"

I've memorized every note of all forty songs, but not out of love.

"What do you say we try a few more tests?"

I'm game, although I keep thinking about Dr. Tyson's declaration that I'm not improving.

"I'm going to be touching your face, Marigold. I hope that's okay. Feel free to speak up now if you don't like strange men getting so personal." He chuckled.

I didn't speak up.

"Okay, I'm using both hands to lightly touch your face, starting at your forehead and slowly moving down your nose... and out to your cheeks... do you feel that?"

I don't, but I can smell the strong soap he'd used to wash his hands. I wonder if he has nice hands.

"Okay, I'm moving down to your mouth. Do you feel that, Marigold? Do you feel me touching your mouth?"

Again, no. But I kind of loved thinking about it.

"And now to your chin. Do you feel my hands, Marigold?"

No, but I'm starting to feel panicky that I'm running out of time and maybe running out of people who believed I could get out this bed.

"Okay, I'm holding your right hand, Marigold. Do you feel my hand in yours? Can you squeeze my hand, Marigold? Can you? Marigold, tell your brain to tell your right hand to move. Do it, Marigold... please."

At the pleading note in his voice, I gave it all I had. I visualized my brain as a detached cartoonish image with arms and legs, looking down and wagging its finger at my hand, telling it what to do. And my hand meekly obeying.

I heard his sharp intake of breath. "Marigold, you did it!" His voice was jubilant. "You squeezed my hand—I felt it!"

Hooray! Inside I'm having my own ticker tape parade. This is the beginning of the way back.

"I have to find Dr. Tyson! Don't go anywhere, I'll be right back!"

He ran from the room, calling Dr. Tyson's name.

My family was going to be so happy! Not to mention all my Facebook fans and Twitter minions and Instagram followers and Pinterest boarders and—

The door burst open and footsteps rushed inside. "Which hand did she move?" Dr. Tyson asked.

"Her right hand," Dr. Jarvis said. "She squeezed my hand."

"Curb your excitement, Jarvis. You might not have felt what you think you felt."

"I didn't imagine it, Dr. Tyson. I asked her to squeeze my hand and she did."

"It could've been an involuntary response, or a spasm."

"But she responded to my request."

"Which could be a coincidence. If she did it once, she can do it again."

I sensed her leaning over me, and I recognized the click from a penlight. She must be holding open my eyelids and shining a light over my green irises. The click sounded again.

"Pupils are fixed. Ms. Kemp, can you move the fingers of your right hand?"

I tried, but could feel my brain fogging. What image had I used before? I couldn't recall.

"Ms. Kemp, try again. Can you move the fingers of your right hand?"

"Marigold, move your fingers," Jarvis urged.

"Jarvis, I've got this," Dr. Tyson said in a stern voice. "Ms. Kemp, squeeze my hand. Use your right hand to squeeze mine."

From the silence, I assumed my hand is not responding.

"Try again, Ms. Kemp," Dr. Tyson said. "Squeeze my hand."

Nothing.

Jarvis made an exasperated noise. "She squeezed my hand, I swear."

"Okay, first of all, what were you doing in here?"

"I... had some free time and thought I would work with Marigold—er, with Ms. Kemp."

"Really? So you just decided you're going to conduct your own little experiment?"

"I... uh..."

"Where did that TV come from?"

"The doctor's lounge," he said sheepishly.

"Put it back," she snapped. "And from now on when you have some free time, come and see me. I have a mountain of patient folders that need to be organized."

"Yes, Doctor."

"And not a word about this to anyone," she said, "including the family. I won't have you giving them false hope over something you probably imagined."

"Yes, Doctor."

Her irritation was evident from the way she stalked from the room. I imagined Dr. Jarvis standing there, alone and defeated.

You said you wouldn't give up on me, I implored. Don't fail me now.

He walked across the room. I hoped Jarvis would defy Dr. Tyson and once again take my hand. Instead, the volume of the TV went silent. Then I heard him gathering cords and roll it away, wheels squeaking. When the door closed, the silence was so... lonely. The sounds of the machines around our beds seemed louder now, more menacing.

I never thought I'd miss the cello, but I do.

July 24, Sunday

WHEN THE DOOR OPENED, I recognized the sound of Detective Jack Terry's boots. He stopped somewhere near the foot of my bed and I pictured him, hands on hips, looking down at me.

"Hello there, Marigold." He sighed. "Still not keen on coming back to this world? I don't blame you. Get some rest. The whole mess will still be here when you wake up."

This is a man who's been worn down a little by life. As a police officer, he'd probably seen it all, the worst of the worst. I, for one, am grateful to men like him who stand between the dredges of humanity and the rest of us.

"Hey, what happened to your TV? I thought we'd watch the Braves game again. They're playing the Rockies again this weekend, this time in Denver."

I'm really starting to miss that TV.

"Well, I guess we'll have to listen to it on my phone instead." A few beeps and clicks later, the sounds of the baseball game came into the room. "Yeah... that'll do in a pinch."

He dragged a chair across the floor. "I hope you don't mind, but I brought my lunch—a burger from The Vortex."

I could smell it... heaven.

"I brought you one, too, in case you pulled a Lazarus while I was sitting here."

A burger might just be worth waking up for.

"Your parents and sister probably told you, but they're meeting with the D.A. tomorrow."

They hadn't said a word.

"It's more of a publicity ploy than anything—the D.A. can't afford to look complacent even if all the evidence hasn't landed yet. And he wants to get a good look at you, see how much of a sympathy card he has to play. He's kind of an asshole, but he'll do what needs to be done. And if he takes this to trial, he'll take down Keith Young, no matter how many attorneys the guy has."

That would make my parents happy.

Jack gave a little laugh. "Your social media mob has already found the man guilty. By the way, my girlfriend—I mean, a girl I know—has one of your T-shirts. And she's a fashion diva, so it must be hip."

Hm... he had corrected himself pretty quickly on the girlfriend remark. Was she a former girlfriend? A friend who happened to be a girl? Or someone he wanted to be his girlfriend?

"Oh, come on ump, that was a strike!"

From the rustle of paper, I assumed he'd taken a bite out of his burger, and the rub of a straw against a cup cover indicated he'd brought a drink with him.

"The thing is, Keith Young doesn't have any traffic violations, and although he admits to drinking earlier that evening, he and his witnesses say he didn't drink enough to be drunk. Still waiting on lab results."

He took another bite and chewed.

"And he swears your car came into his lane. Your sister has her own version of what happened and although her statement is helpful, I don't think she was paying attention, and it's always best when you can talk to the other driver."

He took a drink through the straw.

"That's why I wish I could talk to you about this, Marigold, to get your story. I want to make sure you didn't swerve to avoid an animal, or drop a drink in your lap, or something that would mitigate the circumstances. Don't get me wrong—if Keith Young's bloodwork comes back and shows he was drunk, that's the end of the story and I won't mind seeing him go to jail. But if something else happened, I need to know."

He took another bite and chewed.

"You weren't texting and driving, were you, Marigold? Your sister's phone shows she wasn't using it at the time of the accident, but your phone was destroyed, so we had to subpoena the phone company and we don't have the records yet."

I wanted to tell the detective to relax, but even if I could talk, I couldn't say it. Because as much as I'd like to say I never text and drive, that's not true. I've been known to dash off a quick message if the traffic is light and I feel safe, although I realize it's never safe. And although I can't imagine texting or talking on the phone after dark while Sidney was in the car with me, maybe I did. I just can't remember.

Was Sidney covering for me?

July 25, Monday

"YOUR DAUGHTER'S DOCTOR said she hasn't shown any signs of waking up."

The District Attorney, Kelvin Lucas, sounded stooped and frowny. He must be intimidating since my parents had barely said anything, leaving most of the talking to David Spooner.

"That's correct," David said. "There's been no change in Marigold's condition for several weeks now."

I wanted to scream. Dr. Tyson should've told him and my family I allegedly squeezed Dr. Jarvis's hand, even if she didn't believe it happened.

Lucas made a mournful sound. "Unfortunately, even if the evidence points to Keith Young as the driver at fault, that leaves me in an awkward position. With your daughter in limbo, so are the charges."

"What do you mean?" my dad asked.

"It means," Sidney said, "they need to know if Marigold is dead or alive before they file charges. Am I right, Mr. Lucas?"

"As awful as it sounds, yes. Before a judge can pass sentence, we have to spell out what the damages are. And right now, no one really knows."

"You can't look at my daughter and see how she's been damaged?" my mom asked.

Go, Mom.

"Mrs. Kemp, I'm very sorry about your daughter," Lucas said, gentling his tone. "But if a jury thinks she might get up and walk tomorrow, they're not going to convict on a higher count. I'm not saying I won't file charges, I'm just trying to explain how tough the road ahead might be."

"I heard on the news," my dad said, "that Keith Young wouldn't submit to a blood test at the scene."

"That's correct. His blood was drawn when he arrived at the police station."

"After how much time passed?" David Spooner asked.

"About forty-five minutes."

"So unless he blows over the legal limit, there's no case," Sidney said.

"Not necessarily, but it does complicate matters."

"When will you get the phone records?" Sidney asked.

45

Oh, no… she sounded worried. Did she have a reason to be worried?

"We should get your sister's and Keith Young's phone records any day now."

"Why is everything taking so long?" my mother asked.

"Laws regarding data on phones and car electronics are complicated," Lucas said, "and when we get the information, it has to be processed by experts to ensure the accuracy. These days, cases are won and lost in the evidence-collecting and processing phase. We have to do everything by the book to make sure we have a strong case if and when we get to that point."

"Keith Young is as guilty as he can be," my dad said, his voice rising. "All these professional athletes think they can get away with anything. And he doesn't even have the decency to stay away from the cameras."

"In all fairness, the press seems to be chasing him," Lucas said. "The Falcons have to allow cameras in practices to drum up publicity for the season. And sure, the reporters are going to seek out Young because of this case."

"But that can be to our advantage," David Spooner said. "It keeps the public opinion on our side."

"No offense, Mr. Spooner," Lucas said, "but I need more than Facebook friends to win a case. I need solid evidence. So for now, we're in a stall pattern."

Welcome to my world.

July 26, Tuesday

YOU NEVER KNOW how much you love something until it's gone. Without the deluge of opera and orchestrals, the ward seemed deathly quiet.

Silence can work on a person, can mess with your mind. Hardly anyone had been through the door today, and in fact, it had been hours since a nurse had walked in and made her rounds. I assumed she'd checked to make sure nothing had come unplugged, gone dry, or overflowed.

So as I lay there listening to the machines wheezing and whirring, paranoia crept in. What if something had happened—a deadly virus unleashed—and we were the only four people left alive in the hospital, protected by our immobility? And as days went by and we lay starving and withering, the virus finally made its way into our ward. (It would have be a stinky virus in order for me to know it was coming.) Trapped, we would all inhale the putrid pathogen, and just as I was prepared to die, a miracle happened—the virus had the opposite effect on us, stirring our sleeping limbs and not only pulling us from our comas, but making us more healthy and powerful than before. And it was up to the Super Vegetables to corral and destroy whatever evil faction had released the virus city-wide.

It could happen.

I lay there and spun stories of doom and gloom until I put myself into a funk.

So when the alarm first sounded, I actually thought it was only my imagination.

But no, it was the fire alarm, as sharp and shrill as an ice pick to the ears. It sounded three times, then paused, then three times again... and kept sounding.

So now I was sure a terrorist incident had occurred in the hospital, and a hostage had broken loose to pull the fire alarm and summon help.

Actually, I was pretty sure the hospital was on fire.

That notion was confirmed when the first tendril of smoke tickled my nose. Let me tell you, nothing is more frightening than knowing danger is near and not being able to move away from it. I thought about the man whose wife had injected him with a paralytic, then left him to die in a fire. This was how he felt, unable even to flop out of bed and lie on the floor hoping the smoke would rise.

We would be tomorrow's headline: *Four Comatose Women Burned Alive in Brady Hospital Fire.* The orderlies would be making jokes about roasted vegetables.

The smoke was getting thicker and I wondered when my body would rebel. This wasn't how I wanted to die, and frankly, it seemed extra cruel to heap this new indignity on top of our old one. Blue on black.

So this was it, then. I was going to die alone.

The door burst open and people rushed in—firefighters, I assumed from the sound of the heavy gear. From the noises around me, I had the sensation of my bed being pushed out of the smoke and into a clearer area. We were on an elevator, then some sort of underground space—a parking garage? It made sense if they were going to put us in ambulances and take us to another facility.

But they didn't. By and by, the commotion died down and we were returned to the ward, accompanied by giant fans to blow away the lingering scent of smoke.

In the end, the source of the smoke wasn't a terrorist attack or biological espionage—just a plain old unattended microwave fire in the nurses' lounge compounded by a fire extinguisher that didn't work.

But I have to get out of here. There are too many things in a hospital that can kill you.

July 27, Wednesday

"IS MARIGOLD OKAY?" my brother Alex asked from whatever device my folks had Skyped him on—my dad's phone, I think.

"Her doctor checked her out and said she's fine," my mom said.

"But not better?" Alex asked.

"No, not better," my dad said. "The same."

"Does she have more color in her face?" Alex asked.

In the silence that followed, I assumed my parents were looking at me to check.

"No," my mom said.

Great.

"Ah... maybe the scars have faded some."

"No," my mom confirmed. "Same."

Great.

"Poor thing," my brother said. "She must've been scared to death. We gotta get her out of there."

"But it's the best trauma center in the Southeast," my dad said.

"And her doctor is world-renowned."

"I don't mean move her to another facility, I mean get her well."

"No argument there," my dad said.

"You said you had something to share that might be helpful?"

"Maybe," Alex said. "You know, the Army deals with more traumatic brain injuries than all other hospitals combined."

"Makes sense," my dad said.

"My captain pulled a few strings and I got to talk to one of the top neuroscientists at Walter Reed, Dr. Al Oscar." Alex laughed. "Believe it or not, he'd heard of Coma Girl. My sister is famous."

"Is he going to help her?" my mom asked.

"He said he'd be happy to talk to Marigold's doctor about some new treatments for TBI."

"What kind of treatments?"

"I wrote it down. He calls them 'multifunctional' drugs—they're a combination of hormones, statins, antibiotics, and heat shock proteins, among other things."

"And this Dr. Oscar thinks it will help Marigold wake up?" my mom asked.

"No guarantees," Alex said. "But he's willing to talk to the doctors there about his ideas."

"Repeat that," my mom said. "I'm writing it all down."

Alex, ever patient, did. It was so sweet of him to be thinking of me and doing things for me half a world away.

"I'll give this to Marigold's doctor before I leave today," my mom said.

"Thank you, Alex."

"Wish I could do more. How's Sid?"

"She's a trooper, taking care of all the media stuff and still working on a project for school."

"Sounds like Sid."

"When are you coming home?"

"Soon, I hope. Gotta get back to work. Talk to you soon. Bye, Marigold!"

They disconnected the call and I could hear my parents breathing into the silence, as if they were sitting, staring. Staring at me? Staring at each other? I could sense their mental and physical fatigue.

"I want to go home," my mom said.

"Okay," my dad said. "We'll call the doctor tomorrow."

When the door closed, I was despondent. I wanted to go home, too. Maybe Alex's Army doctor would be able to help me.

But what I really need is a mind-reader.

July 28, Thursday

"WE'LL KEEP this visit just between us," my Aunt Winnie said. "Your mother doesn't have to know."

My lips are sealed.

"Marigold, I brought someone with me. Do you remember my friend Faridee?"

The psychic who told me I was going to win the lottery! Six years ago. It hadn't happened yet, but I'd played every day up until the accident. Darn—wouldn't it be a bummer to get out and find my numbers had come up while I'd been lying here?

No wonder Winnie didn't want Mom to know she was here—my mother thinks psychics are bullshit *and* evil. I told her they couldn't be both, but that had not gone over well.

"Hello, Miss Marigold," Faridee said in a smooth, smoky voice. She smelled like incense. "Your Aunt Winnie thought you and I might have a chat."

I'm so excited! I can tell Faridee what I want my family to know!

"As long as it's a short chat," my aunt said. "We have to get back to Savannah tonight. And if your mother finds us here, I'm toast."

"Let's get to it, then," Faridee suggested. "I'm going to apply some special oils to your hands, Marigold. There now, doesn't that feel good?"

The scents of sandalwood and sage permeated the air. I couldn't feel her hands, but while she was holding mine, I tried to squeeze. Apparently, though, nothing happened.

"I'm going to simply hold your hands for a while, Marigold, until I feel our minds connect. You'll feel it, too, and when you do, know that everything you think will be apparent to me."

I didn't know what to do, so I just let my mind float, and tried to be ready to experience the mind connection she'd described. A minute passed, then another.

"There!" she exclaimed.

I'd felt nothing, sensed nothing... but I was open to going along for the ride.

Tell them I'm in here... that I can hear things... and smell things... tell them I'm in here... that I can hear things... and smell things...

"Marigold has a message," Faridee said.

"What is it?" my aunt asked in a hushed voice.

"She wants you to know... that she visited the spirit world."

"Oh, my," my aunt said.

What the freak?

"And she was taken in by a great androgynous spirit and given the secrets of traveling between the two worlds."

"I knew she'd been somewhere special!"

Aunt Winnie, I was upstairs in the ICU unit.

"Her dilemma, she says, is whether to go back to that magical place, or come back here to the people she loves, that's why she's in the coma."

"Oh, of course, that makes perfect sense," my aunt said in awe.

Mom was right—this is total bullshit.

"Is there anything we can do to help her come back?" my aunt asked.

"I'll ask her," Faridee said.

I'm mentally whistling.

"Here it comes... Marigold said if you want to help her come back...
"

"Yes?" my aunt asked, breathless.

"You should buy one of my scroll amulets to help pull her spirit back through the tunnel."

Oh, my God—really? That's the best she can come up with? My aunt will never fall for that.

"How much are they?"

"Two hundred fifty, so precious."

"I'll take two and sneak one to my sister as a gift—she'll never know and that way we can both pull at Marigold's spirit."

The only thing being pulled here is my aunt's chain. What a crock.

From the rustling and clinking sounds, I assumed my aunt was trading cold hard cash for cold hard trash. While Winnie exclaimed over the powerful amulet—she could feel it warming in her hand—I heard Faridee's sandals slap on her feet as she walked.

"What is it, Faridee?"

"One of these other women is calling to me."

Oh, brother.

"Which one?"

"I don't know yet. Hello... hello... talk to me. Hi, Karen."

Don't get excited—I'm sure she read the name on Karen Suh's wristband.

"You're lonely? For as long as you've been in here, I'm sure you are. But don't despair—he'll be here tomorrow."

An act for my aunt's sake. I'm so angry Faridee would use helpless ill people to make a quick buck.

"Goodbye, dear," my aunt whispered in my ear. "I'll wear the amulet all the time."

I hope it doesn't turn her neck green.

The women started to leave, but at the door, I heard Faridee's feet falter. "Marigold, something's coming to me."

Fraud charges?

"I'm supposed to tell you your message will be delivered."

Let me guess—by a winged creature from the spirit world? Right. May the force be with you, Crazypants.

July 29, Friday

WHEN DR. TYSON came in, I was sure she was going to announce she'd been in touch with the neuroscientist at Walter Reed and I'd been approved to receive the concoction of drugs my brother Alex had mentioned.

Instead, it appeared to be a routine check of my vital signs, probably for insurance purposes. I was weighed (how is it possible that I'm in a coma and I gained a pound?) and inspected for bed sores—delightful. My nails were clipped, my head bandage was changed, and I got a head to toe rub down with moist wipes. To complete the day spa treatment, I was dressed in a clean hospital gown.

All dressed up and nowhere to go.

"Everyone is rooting for her," a nurse said.

"Excuse me?" Dr. Tyson said.

"She's famous, Coma Girl. People all over the world are praying for her. That has to count for something."

"Let's hope so," Dr. Tyson said.

"There's nothing more to be done for her medically?"

"No. A colleague at another facility told me about a drug cocktail that's shown promise, but it's incredibly expensive and it's experimental. The insurance company refused to pay for it."

"Can you file an appeal?"

"I did… but the insurance company is already looking at enormous losses on this patient—they will never approve it."

"Won't she get a lot of money from that professional football player who caused the accident?"

"That's none of our business," Dr. Tyson said. "We can only deal with the present financial situation. Besides, even if the drug was free, the hospital board would have to approve the use of an experimental formula, and I can't remember the last time they did that—too much liability."

So the brain cocktail was not an option… *sigh*.

"Dr. Tyson… do you think she can hear us?"

"I almost hope not."

As they were leaving, another visitor was coming in.

"Excuse me, sir," the nurse said. "This room has limited visiting hours—who are you here to see?"

"Karen Suh. I'm her ex-husband, Jonas Suh. I haven't visited in a while, but I've been seeing all the news reports about that Coma Girl, and it sounds crazy, but something just told me I needed to come see Karen."

"May I see your I.D.?" the nurse asked.

"Sure… here's my driver's license."

"Okay, you have ten minutes."

"Thank you."

He walked over to Karen's bed and began talking to her, slowly at first, but then he picked up momentum. I heard him mention someplace he'd traveled to recently, and a mutual friend he'd spoken to. Small talk. He sounded as if he missed her. If my notoriety has played a part in his visit, I'm glad.

As he rushed to cram as much as possible into his allotted time, Faridee's parting conversation with Karen came back to me.

Don't despair—he'll be here tomorrow.

Hm…

July 30, Saturday

"HELLO, MARIGOLD. I'm back."

Dr. Jarvis—what a nice surprise.

"I've been banned from your room," he said. "But I'm taking a chance that Dr. Tyson has left for the day."

The chair next to the bed creaked.

"Now, Marigold, you and I both know that you squeezed my hand last Saturday, don't we?"

We do.

"So I'm going to give you an opportunity to show me again."

You gotta love a man who gives a woman a second chance.

"Okay, Marigold, I'm holding your right hand. Can you squeeze my fingers? Squeeze my fingers, Marigold. Concentrate. Tell your brain to tell your hand what to do."

In my brain I'm straining. I want to prove to Dr. Jarvis he was right to believe in me. If I'm ever going to get out of this bed, I desperately need a champion.

"Try once more, Marigold. Squeeze my fingers. Concentrate and squeeze."

Nothing. And the effort had left me hazy. And now I'd probably lost his support for good.

"Okay, well, that's disappointing. But we'll try again soon. Meanwhile, I brought a gift."

Something clanked on the bedrail next to my pillow. And suddenly, classical music filled the air.

"It's an old iPod," he said. "And a long playlist so you won't get too bored. I slipped one of the orderlies some cash to come by and turn it off at night and back on in the morning."

I wanted to kiss him. With tongue.

"Let's just hope Dr. Tyson doesn't find out. I'll be back soon."

He made a thoughtful noise, then the chair creaked again.

"Are you ladies passing notes around? You dropped one on the floor."

I don't know what he's talking about.

"Wait, what is this? 'Dr. Al Oscar, neuroscientist at Walter Reed… multifunctional drug shows promise.' "

The note my mother had written when she was Skyping with Alex. She must've dropped it.

"That's bizarre," Dr. Jarvis murmured. "But definitely worth looking into. See you soon, Marigold."

After he left my mind was still racing. And another one of Faridee's comments came back to me.

I'm supposed to tell you your message will be delivered.

Hm… the woman is definitely a scam artist… but maybe she isn't a total sham.

July 31, Sunday

"COMA GIRL, we need to talk. I brought éclairs."

Hopefully lemon—that's my favorite flavor of éclair to listen to Roberta eat.

"Okay, first of all, your mama is crazy. She came to the apartment and pounded on the door like she was the Big Bad Wolf and she insisted on coming in. And when I told her no, she got really snippy."

My mom can do snippy alright.

"I can see why the two of you don't get along. Is she your birth mother?"

Yes, and I'd seen the birthing video to prove it. When I was a teenager and vexing her more than usual, she'd made me watch it, from labor pains to afterbirth—ugh. But it was effective.

"So I brought more cards and letters. The super had to switch us to a bigger mailbox. He wanted to charge us more, but I told him Jesus Christ, my roommate's in a coma, and then he backed off."

She read me my mail in between wolfing down three eclairs. Lots of heartfelt wishes, another pervy offer from a guy wanting to be my "caretaker," and more cash.

"A hundred twenty dollars this time," she said. "I'll add it to your stash."

She licked herself clean, like a cat, then heaved a sigh. "Listen, I've been watching the news a lot lately. Marco likes to stay informed. And that guy who crashed into you, the Falcons football player, I mean the press is really tearing him up."

I wonder where this is going.

"Anyway, something's been weighing on my mind, so I'm just going to come right out and tell you."

I waited.

Another noisy exhale. "So the night of the accident, you called me from your car. You were with Sidney, heading home. We were talking, and then suddenly, I heard someone scream and then the phone went dead."

I had been talking to Roberta when the accident happened?

"I'm scared to death I was the one who distracted you and made you crash. I mean, we were laughing and cutting up, and then *boom*! And now you're... like this," she said, her voice breaking. "And I haven't told anyone because I don't want to get you in trouble. Everyone thinks Keith Young caused the accident, and maybe he did."

But maybe he didn't.

"Should I tell someone? I mean, your family has already been through so much. And how can the police tell exactly what time the accident happened? Maybe I should just keep my mouth shut."

A rap on the door sounded and it opened to admit heavy boot steps. Detective Jack Terry. *Yikes.*

"Can I help you?" Roberta asked.

"I was just looking in on Marigold, but I can see she's busy."

"Who are you?"

"The detective investigating her car accident. Who are you?"

"Oh... just a neighbor."

"Are you close friends with Marigold?"

"Not really. The super asked me to drop off some mail. Want an éclair?"

"No, thanks. I'll come back some other time."

When the door closed, I heaved a mental sigh of relief.

"That was close," Roberta muttered.

I knew it was only a matter of time til my phone records showed I'd been talking around the time of the accident, but Sidney had already said I wasn't on the phone when it happened, and if Roberta stayed quiet...

If Roberta stayed quiet, Keith Young could be wrongfully charged.

Or maybe not—maybe the bloodwork would show he was drunk... and maybe the accident recreation would show he'd crossed the center line and it wouldn't have mattered if I'd been talking on the phone or not.

But the bottom line is *I* know I was a distracted driver.

And that means I might've done this to myself.

AUGUST

August 1, Monday

"BLOOD PRESSURE is normal," Dr. Tyson said.

Dr. Tyson is giving me a maintenance checkup, but I can't stop thinking about Roberta's revelation that I was talking to her on my phone when the accident happened.

"Pulse rate, normal."

I mean, I have the public's sympathy... Coma Girl has become a cottage industry... Sidney is looking into having me incorporated.

"Temperature is ninety-nine," Nurse Gina said.

"A little high, but not unexpected. Still, I want her monitored every four hours for a change."

Was that my hot shame registering on the thermometer? Because what would my adoring fans think when they found out I'd been a distracted driver when my Ford Escort hit Keith Young's yellow Jaguar head on?

"Her cheeks do look pink," Gina said.

Dr. Tyson made a frustrated noise. "It's *blush*. Gina, explain to me why my coma patient is wearing makeup."

"Her sister occasionally puts makeup on her."

"I didn't ask who, I asked why."

"To cheer her up, I guess."

"To cheer up the patient, or the sister?"

Ooh, good one, Dr. Tyson.

"It's not hurting anything, is it? I think it's kind of nice."

"Skin color can be an indication of something abnormal, such as too little oxygen in the blood. Or a sudden bruise that could indicate a blood clot. Please arrange to have Ms. Kemp's face cleaned."

"Yes, Doctor."

Just to clarify, in Georgia, driving a car while holding a cell phone, eating a burrito, or putting on mascara isn't against the law. But the District Attorney might see my multitask chatting as a mitigating circumstance. At least I hadn't been texting while driving—which *is* against the law in the peach state, by the way. But I don't have Bluetooth, so it wasn't as if I'd had my hands on the steering wheel at two and ten o'clock position.

"What's this?"

"It looks like an iPod, Dr. Tyson."

"I know what it is, who put it on the bed?"

"I... don't know."

I was pretty sure Gina knew Dr. Jarvis had put it there, but she was protecting him. Good girl. Don't get me wrong—I am sick to death of his playlist of classical music, but it had taken on a certain painful familiarity... like Google Ads.

"Pupils are—" Dr. Tyson stopped. "Hm... pupils are dilating. That's... different."

"But that's good, isn't it?" the nurse asked.

It has to be good!

"Not so fast, Gina. You and Dr. Jarvis want so much for Ms. Kemp to wake up, you read too much into small things. The pupils are dilating, but they're sluggish, which is better than fixed, but far from good."

I was going to start calling her Dr. Downer.

"Respiratory rate, normal," Dr. Tyson continued, her voice crisp. "What's her weight?"

"Plus a half pound."

Not getting much cardio in the coma unit. Audrey, Karen, Jill and I could all use a Zumba class.

"So the feeding tube is functioning well," Dr. Tyson said. "Bowel movements?"

"Chart says every three or four days."

You were wondering, weren't you? Now you know. When you enter a coma, you say goodbye to every last shred of modesty.

"I.V. looks good. And urine looks clear, but let's test it for traces of blood to make sure the catheter is comfortable. We don't need a U.T.I. flare-up."

No, we do not. For those of you who've never had a urinary tract infection, it's like giving birth to a briar bush. Through your pee hole. I would be happy to coma through that.

"Make a note to change the urine bag more often, Gina. I have Ms. Kemp on diuretics to help with the swelling in her brain, and it's not good for her bladder to get too full."

"Will do, Doctor. How is the swelling?"

"No change, so let's keep her fluids flowing."

"I don't suppose the insurance company changed their mind about paying for the experimental drug cocktail?"

"No."

"What a shame."

"There's no guarantee it would work," the doctor chided. "Not every patient can be saved. Just look at Ms. Kemp's roommates."

"I know," Gina said. "But it's so sad. Especially since Ms. Kemp is in this bed through no fault of her own."

"We'll do all we can to get her out of here," Dr. Tyson said.

But after they left I wondered if word gets out that I might have contributed to the accident, would the staff treat me differently?

August 2, Tuesday

"I HAD TO MAKE A DELIVERY right near here, so I figured I'd pull off and say howdy."

My boss, Percy Palmer, was standing near the foot of my bed. I could visualize him dressed in blue coveralls, wringing his favorite Mohawk Carpet bill cap in his big, hairy hands. And I could tell from the sound of his voice he was on the verge of bolting.

Poor thing. He's gruff and single and baffled by the fairer sex. Any time a woman at the carpet company needs off for "lady reasons" he lifts his paw and says, "No details, just go." So seeing me lying there in a hospital gown in a veritable garden of pale, lifeless women must be hard for him. Especially since he's accustomed to seeing me with a bullhorn barking orders at the truck drivers.

"I hired somebody to fill in until you come back," he said. "But they're not as good as you at keeping everybody in line."

From our five years together, I'd learned Mr. Palmer was not good at dealing with change. I had replaced a woman named Tatiana, a factoid I know because he called me Tatiana for the first year I worked there. And God bless the unwitting temp he'd hired who is now having to respond to "Marigold." I dearly hope it's a woman.

"Everybody at the warehouse misses you," he blurted.

And I miss my job. Miss the sharp tang of carpet adhesive in the air that keeps everyone on a slight buzz. Miss going home every evening covered in a light fuzz of carpet fibers like an enormous piece of Velcro. Miss the ninety-minute commute there and back...

On second thought—

"We passed a hat for you at work, everyone feels so bad for you and your family."

The faces of my coworkers flashed through my mind. Unbeknownst to most, Mr. Palmer often hires ex-cons looking for a second chance because he'd done a stint in lockup himself when he was younger. And not to be stereotypical, but if you're conjuring up images of some rough looking dudes, you'd be right. But their loyalty to Mr. Palmer is evident, and the workers have been nothing but respectful to me. Still, as touched as I am by their donations, knowing what I know now about the accident, I wish they had kept their hard-earned money.

"When I brought the envelope by, I was surprised to meet your mother. A right proper lady. But I thought your mom was dead."

Oh, God, I hope he hadn't told her that.

"She seemed a little taken back when I told her that."

Inside I'm wincing.

"Not that you'd ever said she was dead," he rambled on. "It's just you only ever talked about your dad, so I just thought, well, you know...."

That she was dead?

"That she was dead."

My mother had omitted that little topic of discussion when she'd mentioned meeting Mr. Palmer. Her feelings must've been terribly hurt. She and I were good at finding each other's soft tissue.

"Anyway, she seemed really nice." He cleared his throat. "I thought you'd like to know I ordered a whole truckload of that silk blend carpet you told me to get. I had my doubts, but the salesmen said you were right, it's awesome carpet and it's already our number one seller."

That's good news.

"You really know rugs, Marigold."

Aw...aside from sounding a tiny bit X-rated, that is maybe the nicest compliment I've ever received, because Mr. Palmer is hard to impress.

"The carpet in the waiting room could sure use an upgrade. Commercial contractors put in the cheapest carpet on the cheapest pad, and in a high traffic area. What were they thinking? It's people like that who give carpet a bad name. It's why we're losing ground to hardwood, you know."

If Mr. Palmer had his way, every surface indoors and out would be carpeted. The man was evangelical when it came to fiber density, weight, and stain resistance.

"A nice wall-to-wall remnant would make it a lot nicer in here," he said. "I hate to see you like this."

I suspect all the vinyl tile is making him nervous.

"Well, I'd better go. I have the truck double-parked. We're all pulling for you, Marigold."

His voice cracked on my name, bending my heart.

His footsteps sounded and I sensed he'd come closer. "And don't worry," he said, his voice lower, "that football player is going to get what he deserves for what he did to you, one way or another."

As his heavy steps left the room, my mind raced. Mr. Palmer's heart of gold was outweighed only by his sense of justice. Had he just threatened to do or have something done to Keith Young?

August 3, Wednesday

"DAVID BLAH, BLAH, BLAH, David...whoop, whoop, David... and then David boop boop be-doo."

Sidney is doing our nails and talking about David Spooner so much, I've started substituting words, just to entertain myself.

"But it's not like we're having sex," she said.

They were *so* having sex. She is super animated, talking a mile a minute.

"But David's just so hidey hidey hoe." She sighed. "And so shoobie doobie do."

I'm sure he is.

"I'm putting baby blue polish on your fingernails, and orange on your toenails. Someone left a nasty note on your chart about no more makeup, but they didn't say anything about nail polish."

I have a feeling Dr. Downer will have plenty to say the next time she comes in to check my pupils. She might've downplayed my "sluggish" dilation to the nurse, but she'd been back in every few hours to give my eyeballs a lookey-loo. Since she'd ended each session with a disappointing click of her tongue, however, I assume my pupils haven't picked up their pace.

"Oh, I forgot to tell you David boogie oogie oogie!"

I'm happy to have the company, but I'm getting really irritated with Sid for acting as if nothing is amiss. If from the beginning she'd been truthful about the fact that I was talking on the phone when the accident happened, I wouldn't be lying here marinating in remorse. I know she did it out of love for me, and I appreciate the gesture, but I'm worried the lie is going to boomerang back and hit me in the face.

Then a sudden thought occurred to me—maybe she'd lied because she thought I'd die... and she was lying still because she thinks I won't wake up... or wouldn't remember what happened if I do wake up.

She had me there—I've played the scenes leading up to the accident over and over in my head just as Detective Jack Terry and Sid had discussed them, but I can't remember them. I can picture pulling up curbside to Hartsfield-Jackson Airport and waving to Sidney as she emerged from baggage claim with some hapless stranger carrying her suitcases in the hopes she'd give him her number. And I can picture us driving north on I-85 to midtown, then jumping onto Northwind, her chattering like a magpie the entire time. I can even picture us stopping at the convenience store to buy a lottery ticket and maybe pick up a half gallon of chocolate milk for Dad. I can picture all these things because I've done them multiple times. But I can't remember doing them Memorial Day.

Sid was blowing. "There. It's not a perfect manicure, but it looks pretty good, if I do say so." She gave a little laugh. "Remember Mom used to keep her nail polish in the refrigerator door? The bottles were lined up like pieces of candy, all different colors. When I was little, she would let me pick one and paint my nails, and I thought it was the greatest thing ever."

I do remember that—I used to watch them, green with envy. Mom didn't paint my nails because I chewed them to the quick, a nasty habit that made her crazy. And the more crazy it made her, the more nervous it made me and the more I gnawed on them. I'd stopped biting my nails about twenty minutes after I moved out of the house I grew up in.

A clinking noise sounded—Sid's rosary.

"It was just a little lie," she murmured, so low I could hardly hear her. "To protect us... to protect Mom and Dad. They were so distressed, I couldn't bear to pile on. You understand, don't you?"

I don't know if she's talking to me, or to God. But how could I be angry with her when she'd done something wrong for the right reason?

After all, if the tables were turned, I'd lie for her, too.

August 4, Thursday

"GOOD MORNING, MARIGOLD. It's Dr. Jarvis."

He's whispering. But then again, it's very early in the morning because the hospital is quiet. At the sound of a click and a slight buzzing noise, I gathered he'd turned on a light over my bed.

"Marigold, I'm holding your right hand. Can you squeeze my fingers?"

I concentrated on his voice, could smell the lingering scent of shaving cream.

"Marigold, tell your brain to tell your fingers to move."

I wondered if his hands were large or small, soft or callused, warm or cool.

"I felt that!" he said, his voice excited. "I felt you move your finger. I'll be right back!"

Oh, thank God. Maybe some progress.

He exited noisily, then came back with someone else, his words tumbling out. "She squeezed my hand again. I need a witness so Dr. Tyson will believe me this time."

"What do I do?" asked a woman whose voice I recognized as Gina.

"Take her right hand and be very still."

"Marigold, I need for you to move your fingers again, like before."

I'm trying... man, am I trying.

"Anything?" he asked.

"No," Gina said.

He urged me several more times to move my fingers, but apparently, I can't repeat my earlier feat.

"Thanks anyway, Gina," he said, his voice dragging.

"If it's any consolation, Dr. Tyson might not have taken my word for it either. She thinks both of us are being too hopeful."

"I didn't realize there was such a thing," Dr. Jarvis said dryly.

Gina made a thoughtful noise. "Dr. Tyson can be a little negative, but she's a good doctor, and I know she's taken an interest in Ms. Kemp's case."

"She's had to, Marigold is Coma Girl, the hospital's most popular patient."

"Maybe all the attention will convince the insurance company to reconsider approving the experimental drug."

"Maybe," he said.

The door opened and closed, but from Dr. Jarvis's sigh, I realized he was still in the room. I heard the scratch of the curtain around my bed being closed and wondered if he was going to perform some kind of test on me.

Then I heard the muted chirping of a Skype call being made. Had Dr. Jarvis decided to take advantage of the quiet to chat with his girlfriend?

"This is Dr. Oscar," a man's voice came from a device.

It took me a few seconds to recognize the name as the neurosurgeon at Walter Reed Army Research Institute my brother Alex had mentioned to my parents. Dr. Jarvis had found a piece of paper where my mother had written the information.

"Dr. Oscar, good morning, this is Dr. Jarvis at Brady Hospital in Atlanta. I talked to your assistant yesterday."

"Yes, he gave me the message. I understand you're calling about the comatose patient Dr. Tyson is treating."

"Th-that's correct."

"I understand the patient's insurance denied the claim for the experimental cocktail."

"Yes, sir, but we've filed an appeal."

The man made a thoughtful noise. "That's a longshot, unless the hospital board is behind you."

"We're optimistic," Dr. Jarvis said, then cleared his throat. "I wanted to talk to you about the treatment protocol so once we receive approval, we can administer the cocktail as soon as possible."

"I already briefed Dr. Tyson."

"My apologies, sir. Dr. Tyson asked me to step in, and considering what's on the line, I wanted to get the information directly from you."

"Alright then. For my own information, I'd like to see the patient's updated Glasgow stats."

"I'm with the patient now," Dr. Jarvis said. "I can give them to you real time."

"I'm ready," Dr. Oscar said.

I listened as Dr. Jarvis moved around my bed, checking and reciting my vitals in response to the neurosurgeon's questions. When the remote doctor asked if I responded to commands, Dr. Jarvis didn't hesitate.

"Yes, the patient moves her fingers when I ask her to."

"Pupils?"

"The pupils are dilating."

He didn't add "sluggishly."

"The pupil dilation and response to commands shows improvement. I'll work up a new protocol. Shall I email it to Dr. Tyson?"

"Er, no," Dr. Jarvis said quickly. "Send it directly to me."

While he gave the doctor his private contact information, I was smiling inside. Dr. Jarvis was going rogue.

August 5, Friday

"COMA GIRL, our little secret is really eating me."

Roberta was back. And if our little secret was eating her, she obviously was keeping pace by eating everything in the bakery case. Since she'd arrived, she'd wolfed down a vanilla bean cupcake, a butterscotch brownie bar, and was working on her second honey bun.

"But I've decided to keep my mouth shut," she said, licking her fingers. "I looked it up online and you weren't breaking the law, so it doesn't matter. But did you know it's against the law to text and drive in this state? How did I miss that? And how do they expect you to let your boss know you overslept and won't make it in on the dot? I mean, if I stopped to do that before I got in the car, I'd be even more late."

I can almost see her logic.

"I forgot to bring your mail, but it's piling up again." She sighed. "Marigold, when are you going to wake up? It's so sad to see you like this. And it's sad to see all your stuff around the apartment. By the way, I hope you don't mind, but I borrowed your ladybug scarf to wear to a dinner party. I got a lot of compliments on it."

I don't mind.

"And um… there's another thing. A reporter from a local TV station was waiting outside the apartment this morning. He asked me a lot of questions about you. I told him I was late for work—which was true—but he left me a card, asked me to call him."

Uh-oh. Reporters have a way of weaseling info out of people.

"I don't intend to call him, but girl, he was *cute*."

Double uh-oh.

"Not that I'm interested. I've got my Marco, you know." Then she sighed again. "Although he's been scarce lately because he's been busy moving things forward with the divorce and all."

Uh-huh. Leopards don't change their spots. My guess is Marco is bouncing back and forth between his wife's bed and Roberta's. But that's for Roberta to figure out. And who am I to give out romantic advice? The only man I've ever cared about is happily planning his nuptials to someone else.

She cleared her throat. "Duncan came by the bakery today."

Right on cue.

"He put down a deposit on the wedding cake and the groom's cake."

Blackberry, I'll bet. It's his favorite.

"The groom's cake is blackberry, with caramel icing. I told him that was a good choice, and it wasn't too late to change his mind about the pink grapefruit wedding cake. He said that was his fiancée's idea, and I got the feeling that he's completely whipped."

That hurt. It's hard to imagine Duncan being so mesmerized by someone that he'd just go along, but isn't that the way love is supposed to be?

"In case you're interested, the wedding is in November. Sounds like it's going to be huge. The cake is five freaking tiers."

Wow. Most of the wedding cakes on Pinterest wedding boards are three layers, sometimes four. Five is… impressive. Repeating, not that I've ever haunted the Pinterest wedding boards.

"I thought your name would come up," she said. "But it didn't."

Of course it didn't. Why would it?

"Gotta run. Later, Coma Girl."

August 6, Saturday

"ALEX SENDS HIS LOVE," Mom said. "He's hoping to get leave soon for a visit home, but he doesn't know when that will be. I told him Dr. Tyson said the experimental drug isn't going to work out for you, and he's really disappointed."

I wondered if Dr. Tyson had found out what Dr. Jarvis had done and shut him down. But if he'd been reassigned, he hadn't come back to reclaim his iPod which still played classical music… and played… and played…

It's to the point now where I can almost see the notes on a sheet of music. I learned the basics of reading music in middle school, but haven't used it since. Still, those long-dormant lessons are coming back to me—the staff, the clef, the parts of a note, and acronyms to help remember the notes: Every Good Boy Does Fine, and FACE. I can recognize a C note, so I'm building from there.

"And Winnie calls every day to ask about you. She sent me the oddest gift—a pendant she found somewhere."

Ah—the amulets the psychic had conned Winnie into buying to help "pull my spirit back through the tunnel." Winnie had purchased one for my mom.

"Anyway, I suppose she meant well, but it's too ugly to wear."

So apparently my mom can't even be tricked into faux helping me.

"Your father sends his love, too," she said. "He was called away on business. One of his municipal accounts in Georgia is a town called Climax and apparently they were the victim of some prank because all the town's signage disappeared overnight."

Okay, that was kind of funny.

"We're still waiting to hear from the district attorney's office on what charges will be filed against Keith Young." She made a frustrated noise. "He's all over the news, tossing around a football and hamming it up for the camera like he doesn't have a care in the world."

The chair creaked as she shifted her weight.

"Sometimes I get so furious, I think I'm going to lose my mind!"

My mother rarely gets emotional, so I'm riveted.

"I just want this to be over," she cried.

Over, as in me waking up, or over, as in me going the other direction?

A knock on the door sounded, then it squeaked open.

My mother sniffed, then asked, "Can I help you?"

"I was hoping to see Marigold Kemp?" a woman asked.

I know the voice, but can't place it.

"I'm her mother. Are you a friend of Marigold's?"

"Not really. My name is Tabitha. I'm a student of hers."

Oh, of course—Tabitha!

"You must have the wrong Marigold Kemp," my mother said. "My daughter isn't a teacher."

"She teaches me at night, once a week."

"Teaches you what?"

I wish my mother would let it go—she was going to embarrass Tabitha.

"Um… I'm not the best reader. But I have a good job, and my boss said he could promote me if my reading and writing skills improved. I went to an agency and they connected me with Marigold."

I can almost hear that info settling into my mother's mind.

"Oh. I didn't know Marigold… did that."

"She's a volunteer," Tabitha said. "And she's a great teacher."

But she's being generous. She's an eager learner, and she made my job easy. I'm ashamed I haven't thought of Tabitha and how my absence might have affected her progress.

"It's very kind of you to stop by," my mother said. "Unfortunately, Marigold is… asleep."

"I understand. I just wanted to drop off this card. When she wakes up, will you give it to her? I picked it out myself."

"Of course."

My mother can't appreciate how long it must've taken Tabitha to read through a section of greeting cards and choose one. But I can. Of the adults I'd tutored, she'd come the farthest, and she'd had the most to learn.

Tabitha said goodbye, then my mother fell silent. I could picture her staring at Tabitha's card. She had probably written my name in neat block print using a ruler.

"Marigold, you never told me you were a literacy volunteer."

It simply had never come up.

She made a pensive noise. "What else don't I know about you?"

And maybe it's me, but she sounds a little... *angry*?

August 7, Sunday

I KNOW IT'S SUNDAY from the rounds of church bells ringing outside my window... and from the sound of Detective Jack Terry's boots on my floor.

"Hello, Marigold, it's your favorite detective."

That's true.

"I see it's just us today—good. I brought chili dogs from The Varsity and a couple of frosted orange shakes. If you don't wake up in the next ten minutes or so, I'm going to have to eat your share, too."

This man has good taste in food.

"Braves are in St. Louis today, are you with me? We probably don't stand a chance, but we might get a miracle. Actually, we could use a couple of miracles today, couldn't we? Are you about ready to get out of that bed?"

Am I ever.

He gave a little laugh. "If Carlotta was here, she'd make a crack about this being the first time I tried to get a woman *out* of bed."

Ah... the fashionista with the Coma Girl T-shirt had a name.

"But," he added under his breath, "Carlotta is not here."

I wondered where she was.

"So, I've been looking into your background. Carpet, huh? I've been thinking of recarpeting Serena, so maybe when this is all over, I'll pay you a business call."

He's talking in man-shorthand, but if my mushy brain is connecting all the dots, his boat is named Serena, and she needs new carpeting. We don't sell marine-grade stock, but Mr. Palmer could hook him up with a wholesaler. But the really interesting part of the whole spiel is his boat is not named after fashionista girl. So who was Serena?

He dragged a chair across the floor, then set about tearing into paper bags, releasing mouth-watering smells of the four basic food groups— grease, preservatives, salt, and sugar.

"Your older brother is a war hero, and your younger sister is in law school. That's a lot of pressure on both ends. No offense, Marigold, but it looks like landing in this coma is the most interesting thing you've done."

With that smooth tongue, no wonder Carlotta was elsewhere.

"Seriously though, you're a sensation. Are you going to wake up and enjoy some of this attention... or are you going to milk it a little longer? Couldn't blame you. How often does someone get to hide out from life?"

A few beeps later, the tinny roar of a crowd surged into the room.

"Game's starting."

Okay, who does this philosophical cowboy think he is, crashing my coma with fast food and baseball and metaphysical questions?

Because he's a little bit right, darn him. As long as I'm asleep, I'm Coma Girl. But if and when I wake up, I'll go back to being Marigold Kemp.

And no one really cares about her.

August 8, Monday

"DID YOU MISS ME?" My volunteer poet gave a little laugh. "Or were you hoping I wouldn't come back?"

Not at all. Now that I'm getting back into culture via the classical music looping on the iPod Dr. Jarvis left me, I'm even remembering some of the poetry I learned in school—Robert Frost, T.S. Eliot, Sylvia Plath. When our teachers had made us memorize the poems and recite them in class, I thought I would die of stage fright. I was a gawky kid and did not like being on display. Every word had been torturous, but the experience must have woven the words into the fabric of my brain because as soon as the first phrases of "The Hippopotamus" came back to me, all nine stanzas had unwound. I'm eager to hear more Emily Dickinson, and try to commit it to memory, too.

Although so far, Dr. Tyson has been right... my childhood memories are surfacing more readily than what had happened yesterday. My mind is operating on a first-in, first out method of recall.

"I had some medical appointments of my own," he said.

Maybe that's why he volunteers—because he spends a lot of time in the hospital himself. I hoped it isn't something serious. Some people just get dealt a bad hand.

Yes, I'm feeling sorry for myself. Sue me.

"How are you doing, Coma Girl? Are you getting better in there? Figuring things out?"

Not really. When you have a lot of time to think, you analyze things too much, start scrutinizing and dissecting and second-guessing. Before you know it, everything has folded back onto itself.

"Believe it or not," he said, "there are a lot of people who would trade places with you because from where they stand, your life is peaceful by comparison."

He is probably right. How many people numb themselves to life with alcohol and drugs and other mind-altering substances? Aren't they, in a sense, seeking a coma-like state?

"I'm going to read to you now. This is from a poem titled 'A Prayer.' "

He has such a nice voice I wonder if he's an actor... or maybe in broadcasting.

"I meant to have but modest needs, such as content, and heaven; within my income these could lie, and life and I keep even. But since the last included both, it would suffice my prayer; but just for one to stipulate, and grace would grant the pair. And so, upon this wise I prayed, Great Spirit, give to me; a heaven not so large as yours, but large enough for me."

I repeated the words after him, but they got away from me quickly. Still, even after he left, the sense of the poem stayed with me, like a toothache.

Life has a way of getting out of hand, especially in a country of abundance. Before the coma, I had been content with my small life. But as Coma Girl, I've received more attention from my family and friends and total strangers than I've ever gotten in my life.

And I like it.

And I'm getting pretty irritated at the implication from some that I'm being greedy.

Then again, perhaps my dormant Catholic guilt is kicking in. Because just as the childhood memories were flooding back, so were the emotions from that precarious time I thought I had successfully squashed.

August 9, Tuesday

I'VE BEEN THINKING a lot about my three ward mates lately, but not particularly good things. Like when you're relegated to a group you don't want to be in, such as the team of scrubs in P.E. (Yes, life is all about high school.) But instead of bonding with the scrubs, you get mad at them for even being there? Because if they weren't there, you wouldn't have to be lumped in with them.

I'm angry at the other vegetables for being vegetables in the first place. At what point had they simply given up and submitted to the limbo? It makes me angry to think about them, because they are ever present reminders of what I might become.

I eavesdrop on their checkups because I'm morbidly curious. Audrey Parks, who is in bed one, had apparently at one time been a good candidate for recovery after her water skiing accident. She had responded to verbal cues and had even vocalized a few times before sliding into a deeper coma. After two years, she now scores straight ones across the Glasgow Coma Scale for pain response, eye movement, and vocalization. Three is the lowest score possible on a scale of 15.

In bed four, Jill Wheatley is about the same, with a four on the Glasgow scale, but with the added insult of a ventilator—which, can I just say, is noisy as hell. She has been here an astonishing four years, which I gather isn't normal, but there's some dispute about a possible Do Not Resuscitate order violation and a legal challenge over who should serve as her medical guardian, so she's in legal purgatory. I get the general feeling everyone has forgotten about her, poor thing, because she hasn't had a single visitor since I became oriented. Dr. Tyson is trying to find her a bed in a nursing home.

In bed two, Karen Suh is faring a little better, with no vocalization and no eye movement, but a clear response to pain that earned her a total score of seven. She's the one who fell off a ladder cleaning her gutters. Her ex-husband Jonas has been visiting her more regularly, although for only a few minutes here and there. Still, it's something and I dearly hope she can hear him.

Today, however, Audrey Parks has a visitor, and I'm intrigued.

"Hello, Sweet Audrey, it's Dad."

His voice was deep and warm and kind, like a TV Dad. I guessed him to be around sixty, which meant either Audrey was a little older than I had assumed, or her parents had had her later in life.

I heard the kiss he gave her, probably on the cheek or forehead. "I'm sorry it's been so long since I came to visit. Your mom has needed me, so I've had to get my hours in at the store in between."

Ack—the man's wife is sick, too?

"It's Alzheimer's, sweetie. Tests confirmed it this week. She's fretted so over the fact that she's not well enough to visit, is afraid you'd worry because we haven't been by. I promised her I'd stop by to tell you we think about you and pray for you every day. We love you, Sweet Audrey."

My heart is breaking for this man. How much can one family take?

He kissed her goodbye and I pictured him dabbing at his damp eyes with a handkerchief as he exited.

And my heart is breaking for Audrey, too. Because what if she, like me, could hear him? I'd thought nothing could be as scary as knowing the hospital was on fire and not being able to move, but what if you knew a loved one was slipping away, and you wouldn't even get to say goodbye?

August 10, Wednesday

IT'S BATH DAY AGAIN, which always makes me happy, but I also look forward to the entertainment because, I've learned, Nurse Gina is dating Gabriel, one of the orderlies.

"So how was the second date?" Nurse Teddy asked.

"Better even than the first date," Gina gushed.

"Look at you, you're blushing."

"Stop it. And don't tell anyone. I don't want it to be a problem at work."

"There's no policy against it."

"But I don't want it to be grist for the gossip mill."

"So that must mean you're going to go out with him again?"

Gina giggled like a little girl. "Yes. He's a great guy. And he loves kids, said he's really looking forward to meeting my son."

"Does he have kids?"

"No. And he's never been married."

"Sounds promising."

"I'm trying not to get ahead of myself," she said, "but this is the most excited I've been about a man in a long time."

"Good. You deserve a great guy."

I'm happy for Gina. She spends a lot of time at the hospital. I've heard her volunteer for extra shifts, so I gather she's a struggling single mom.

"Oh, poor Marigold. She's starting to get that smell."

What smell?

"What smell?" Teddy asked.

"Kind of moldy, you know?"

Teddy sniffed. "Yeah, I think I smell it."

Oh, dear Lord, more vegetable analogies?

"They all get it," Gina said. "It's from lying still all the time."

"I have to admit, this is one of the most depressing wards to work in."

Thanks... thanks a lot.

"Imagine how it must be for them and their families," Gina chided. "Besides, Dr. Jarvis thinks Marigold is improving."

"How so?"

"He says she moved her finger on command."

"Did anyone else see it?"

"No. He pulled me in to witness, but she didn't do it again."

"Hm. Dr. Jarvis has a reputation for being a little 'out there.' "

"I think he really believes she did it."

"Just because he believes it, doesn't mean it happened. Of course he wants to be credited with helping to wake up the famous Coma Girl. All I'm saying is be careful about letting him pull you into the middle of something."

"Okay, I'll be careful." Then she *tsked, tsked.* "Oh, this nail polish has to go before Dr. Tyson sees it."

"I think we have some remover here—you do her fingers, I'll do her toes. Wow, she has pretty feet."

73

When I get to the afterlife, I'm going to ask God why he wasted my pretty on feet. The sharp ammonia scent of the remover floated up to me.

"Her scars look better, don't you think?" Gina asked.

"Yes, the cocoa butter is helping. When do you think she'll be able to lose the head bandage?"

"In a few weeks maybe. Then it'll be easier to wash her hair."

"When it grows back in," he added.

What? Okay, now I'm pissed—why didn't someone tell me underneath the bandage, I'm bald? I mean, honestly—

I stopped bitching because I was distracted by something… strange. What *is* that?

"Wow, I need to ask her sister what kind of nail polish she used," Gina said. "This stuff is stubborn."

There it is again…

"Try the gauze pads—they have more texture than the cotton."

"Okay. Yes, that's much better."

Wait—*I feel that!* I can freaking feel her putting pressure on the tips of my fingers!

"Her sister is a looker, huh?"

"Yes, she's very pretty. The mom, too."

Yeah, yeah—my family is gorgeous and I'm a troll. Shut up already because *I feel that!*

I remember reading somewhere a person's nailbeds are so sensitive because of the concentration of nerve endings. And a few times I'd been tested for pain response, I recall Dr. Tyson instructing the person to push on my nails. So it made sense that the pressure and the chemical stimulation of the polish remover would stir up dormant sensations.

Hallelujah! I focused like a laser on the ends of my fingers, and the sensations became stronger. Soon I could feel faint pressure on my toes, too. God bless Sid and her industrial nail polish. I know enough to know the more they massage my nails, the stronger the connections to my brain will become. I readied myself for a rush of physical awareness in the event my body came alive, knowing full well acute pain might be one of the first things I registered. *Bring it on.*

"All done," Gina said.

"Me too," Teddy said, and the sensations ended.

No! Don't stop now!

But they were busy putting their bath cart back together. I listened to the bangs and squeaks, feeling utterly helpless.

"Ready for lunch?"

"Sure."

"Whad'ya bring?"

"A Lean Cuisine. You?"

"Chicken salad…"

August 11, Thursday

"WE'RE BAAAACK."

It's Aunt Winnie and her scammy psychic sidekick Faridee.

Well, okay, so a couple of things she'd said had come about, like Karen Suh's ex-husband coming to visit the next day, and my 'message' being delivered when Dr. Jarvis had found the note my mom had written about the Army neurosurgeon, but I was still perturbed over the way she'd conned my aunt into buying those bogus amulets.

"How are you, dear? I visit your Facebook page every day—people all over the world know about Coma Girl. Your mother has been keeping me updated—when she's not working. I understand her real estate business is booming from all the exposure."

What? I didn't know Mom's business had taken off. And while some part of me knows Mom is probably concerned about paying the bills I'm accumulating, another part of me feels a little used.

"Well, you look wonderful," my aunt lied.

"Yes, so ethereal," Faridee added. "Like an angel."

Mental eye-roll.

"Faridee wants to see if she can connect with your thoughts again," my aunt said. "I've been wearing my amulet every day. I hope you're closer to coming back to us."

I'm just hanging out here in the spirit tunnel, waiting for a nudge.

But out of love for my aunt, I played along as Faridee instructed my aunt to rub her amulet and recited a chant to help our minds find each other. Just in case her brain stumbled upon mine, I settled on an empirical plea to get someone to stroke my response center: *Polish my nails… Polish my nails… Polish my nails…*

"There she is," Faridee announced.

"Oh, how amazing," Winnie said.

Polish my nails... Polish my nails... Polish my nails...

"Hello, Marigold... thank you, it's good to see you again, too."

Oh, brother, here we go.

"I'm here with your Aunt Winnie. She wants me to help you come back to your family."

"Tell her she's a celebrity," Aunt Winnie said. "I always knew she was the special one."

Aw, Aunt Winnie.

"You are a celebrity, Marigold. The entire world is calling you Comma Girl."

"That's 'Coma Girl'," my aunt corrected. "You know, because of the coma?"

"Oh, right."

Really, just... really?

"The entire world is calling you Coma Girl," she said. "I can see you are still enjoying the spirit world."

Lady, would you shut up and listen? *Polish my nails... Polish my nails... Polish my nails...*

"Is she closer to coming back through the tunnel?" my aunt asked, her voice hushed. "I have a blister on my thumb from rubbing the amulet."

"Marigold," Faridee asked, "are you ready to come back to this world?"

Polish my nails... Polish my nails... Polish my nails...

"Wait—she's speaking to me. She says to thank you, Winnie, for believing in the power of the scroll amulet to escort her home."

Argh!

"What else can I do?" Winnie asked.

"She says... she says she'd like to talk to you directly."

"How can she do that?"

"If you take my upcoming seminar on communicating in the next dimension, you can learn."

Oh, for Pete's sake.

"Of course I'll take it," my aunt said. "How do I sign up?"

"I can take your reservation now. It's only four hundred dollars."

"Will you accept a credit card?"

"Yes, but I offer a ten percent discount if you pay with cash."

"I'll stop by the ATM on the way out."

Are you hearing this?

"Wait," Faridee said, her voice low and dramatic. "I'm getting something else from Marigold."

"What?" my aunt asked.

The finger, if I could lift my hand.

"This is strange. Is your family... Polish?"

"No, neither her mother or father."

"She keeps saying the word 'Polish.'"

Holy crap, the kook *could* hear me, but she couldn't get the word right? *It's "polish," you thief, not "Polish."*

"Hm... I wonder what she could mean?" my aunt mused.

"There's Polish sausage," Faridee suggested.

"And Polish rye bread. Maybe she's hungry."

"Does she like Polish dancing?"

"The polka? Not to my knowledge."

"Wait—there was a Polish pope, wasn't there?"

"John Paul, I think, the Second. And he died."

Faridee snapped her fingers. "That's it—she's with Pope John Paul II in the spirit world."

Wow... what a whopper.

Winnie inhaled sharply. "She's with a Pope? Jesus, Mary, and Joseph, I have to get back to church."

I give up. Things had gone completely off the rails.

"She said to come back soon," Faridee said. "And she will have more to tell. Marigold's story is far from over."

I hope that much is true.

August 12, Friday

"I HAVE BAD NEWS," my dad said.

He sounds so anguished, I'm worried something has happened to Mom or Sid or Alex.

"The Escort is in worse shape than I thought."

Ah... of course—my car.

"I was sure the guy at the shop I use could fix it, but he said he can't."

Hm, well it has a hundred fifty thousand miles on it, so it's probably time for a new car anyway.

"But I'm not giving up. I called around and found another mechanic who's supposed to be great and he agreed to take a look at it. I'm going to have it towed there in the next few days."

The car isn't worth saving, but fixing it seemed important to Dad for some reason... I suppose it gives him something to focus on.

"I know your mom talked to you about moving back home for a while when you get out of the hospital, and I figure you might like to take some time off to recover fully before you go back to work. So I was thinking... maybe you could go with me on the road for a few days. How does that sound?"

It sounds as if he's trying to hit the rewind button... and it's a sweet gesture. But I'm already wondering what we'd talk about for hours and hours in the car.

"It wouldn't be all sales calls," he said. "We could stop off and see some museums and maybe hit a few flea markets. Do you still collect books?"

I'm more into eBooks these days, but I still wander into bookstores occasionally. Tabitha and I meet for tutoring sessions at a public library, and it had reignited the luddite in me. Dad isn't much of a reader, but it's nice he remembered I am.

"Maybe stop at a casino to play the slots and see a show? Would you like that?"

Who wouldn't?

"And there are lots of state parks along my route. We could go hiking. How does that sound, sweetheart?"

It sounds nice, Dad.

"I said, *how does that sound?*"

It sounds nice, Dad.

"I said, HOW DOES THAT SOUND?"

He's shouting now and banging his fist on something, which, if you know my quiet father, is uncharacteristic and rather terrifying.

The door burst open and a voice I recognized as Nurse Teddy's said, "Is everything okay in here?"

"Yes," my dad said, sounding more like himself. "I'm sorry. I... don't know what came over me."

"It's okay," Teddy said, but his voice was tentative, as if he were scanning my father for signs of another outburst. "Would you like to talk to someone, Mr. Kemp?"

"What do you mean?"

"A chaplain, perhaps, or maybe a family counselor?"

"You mean a shrink?"

"Not necessarily, but someone who understands what you must be going through."

"No one understands what I'm going through," my dad said in a low voice. "And we're not the kind of people who talk about our problems."

"Okay," Teddy said gently. "But visiting hours are over, so maybe you should call it a night. The patients need their rest."

"Right," my dad said, sounding utterly defeated. "I'm not helping. I'll go."

When he left, I wondered how things were at home between him and Mom. They hadn't visited together in a while—were things strained?

If their relationship is strained, I'll never know. We aren't the kind of people who talk about our problems.

August 13, Saturday

"IF YOUR MAIL KEEPS ROLLING IN AT THIS RATE, one of us is going to have to sleep with the super."

Roberta heaved a sigh as she dropped into the chair next to my bed.

"And seeing as how you don't seem inclined to get out of that bed, I guess I'm going to have to take one for the team."

Her laugh cheered me considerably. I'd gotten so worked up over not being able to signal anyone about feeling my fingers and toes, every little thing set me off. I was angry at the unending classical music rotation, angry at the useless rosary hanging from my bed rail, angry at the machines beeping around me.

I totally understood my dad going off when he visited, because inside, I, too, was railing at God. *Why did this happen to me?*

And like most of the men in my life, God is leaving me hanging.

"I brought a brownie cake milkshake for dinner," she said, slurping.

"Brought one for you, too. Want a sip?"

Since I can smell the rich chocolate, I assume she's holding the straw near my mouth. I tried to make my lips move, but my brain was like sludge—maybe I'd fried it from all the internal tantrums.

"No? Okay, more for me."

Another hearty slurp sounded, then she tore open an envelope and described the sweet card signed by a classroom in upstate New York. Their words of encouragement humbled me and made me regret my peevishness. As she continued reading notes from strangers (and counting cash), I softened more and more, especially when I heard the grief-stricken words from relatives of coma patients.

"I hope someone is reading these words to you and you are hearing them," Roberta read. "Just as I read to my son Amos every day with the hope he can hear me." Roberta sniffed, then blew her nose. "That one got to me."

It got to me, too. Because as hard as a coma is on the patient, it's worse on family and friends because they don't know what to do, and how long to hold out hope.

"Hm, this one seems personal—do you know a Joanna Fitz?"

Joanna! She and I had met in a college literature class and become fast friends. She lived with her doctor husband and twins in Pennsylvania. I hadn't seen her in ages, but we stayed in touch through social media and the occasional phone call.

"She says she's so sorry to hear about your accident and will come to visit when you wake up."

Roberta went on to other cards and letters, but I confess I only half listened. I was too busy coveting Joanna's life. She had made it all seem so effortless—attract a great, ambitious guy who wanted a true partner in life. Be so synergistic that instead of having one baby, you produce twins. Then immerse yourself in motherhood while your husband pulled in enough money to set you up in a country club mansion. Don't get me wrong—Joanna deserved every bit of her good life. But why didn't I? What made women like Joanna the kind of people who were most likely to succeed, and people like me most likely to wind up in a coma?

And just like that, the slow boil started again. I'm tired of everyone's sympathy and good wishes. I resent the cash contributions, as if people are dropping money into a beggar's cup to assuage their own guilt enough that they could go on living their coma-free lives feeling as if they'd done their duty.

I've never been an angry person, but now it seems like the only thing I have to hang on to.

August 14, Sunday

"IF WE KEEP MEETING LIKE THIS," Detective Jack Terry said, I'm going to have to give you my class ring."

Ordinarily, his remark would make me smile, but I'm holding out, determined to stew over my predicament. Look where playing nice has gotten me in life.

Besides, I'm not going to become one more in what I suspect is a long line of women who think Jack Terry is all that.

"Braves versus Nationals, we need a win. So what do you think about the Braves moving to the burbs?"

What was it with men and sports? Personally, I think baseball is boring. The game needs some kind of wildcard, like drawing a name from the stadium spectators to play first base. That I would tune in for.

"I agree," he said, "leaving Turner stadium is proof the entire world has gone completely insane."

Assumption of agreement—so typical.

Although I sort of agree, if only from a practical standpoint.

"Tacos from Uncle Julio's," Jack said. "I didn't know if you'd like chicken, beef, fish, or pork, so I brought one of each." He sighed. "Please wake up, Marigold, and save me from myself."

I know he's referring to the fast food, but as always, it seems that Jack Terry says one thing and means another. Does he need to be saved from himself? He's obviously beating himself up over something, but what?

Despite his proclivity for high-caloric food, I had a hard time picturing an overweight guy living on a boat. Darn, I wish Roberta had told me what he looks like. Roberta is the equivalent of the guy hanging out in front of the Marta station, giving the once-over to every female who walks by. The fact that she hadn't described Jack Terry in precise feminist detail told me she had been scared witless at their brief encounter in my room. So I'm guessing he's the kind of guy who walks into a room and owns it.

But those men come with a boatload of ego and emotional thorns. Woe to the girl who falls for Detective Jack Terry.

"So just a quick update before the game starts," he said. "The re-creation of the crash was inconclusive, which sucks considering all the resources that went into it. Also, the phone records came back."

He has my full attention.

"You were talking to your roommate Roberta either right before or at the time of the crash. Careless, but not illegal. And, hey, I can't be a hypocrite—I've been known to talk and drive, too."

He tore into the bags of food. I'm on pins and needles.

"So did you swerve into Young's lane like he said? I guess we'll never know… and fortunately for you, it doesn't matter. Your and Young's lab results are back. Yours were clean—good girl. And Young blew .01 over the legal limit, which isn't much, but it's enough to charge him with driving under the influence."

So without proof to the contrary, I can assume the accident wasn't my fault. *Phew.*

"The press is going to have a field day when the results of his blood test are released. Your family will be told tomorrow, but I wanted to tell you first." Then he made a rueful noise. "Although really, does it change anything for you?"

There he goes being philosophical again. But while he unwrapped tacos and brought up the game, I felt a keen sense of satisfaction. Because it's good to have a confirmed, if faceless, target for my seething resentment: Keith Young.

August 15, Monday

"THIS ROOM MUST BE the most peaceful place on Earth," the poet volunteer said with a sigh.

From his footsteps, I can tell he's going from bed to bed. I can't make out the words, but he's greeting each of my roommates as if they are old friends. I wonder how long he's been coming to the ward. He seems especially warm today, which makes me wonder if his own diagnosis has taken a turn for the better. Since he visits in the very early mornings, I've decided he makes his rounds before some sort of treatment.

Chemotherapy? Kidney dialysis? Physical therapy?

Or perhaps his situation has taken a turn for the worse? I recalled his previous comment that some people would be happy to trade places with me. It seems clear he's at some sort of crossroads. I've even wondered if he's a doctor or hospital administrator who visits patients anonymously for his own insight.

If so, I wondered what he's learning from reading to the vegetable patch?

"Hi, Coma Girl. How's it going in there? Solving the world's problems? I hope so."

So if and when I wake up, I'm supposed to emerge with some kind of wisdom? Like people who are struck by lightning or who report being kidnapped by aliens?

The crackle of pages sounded. "This poem by Dickinson is titled simply 'Life.' I think it captures the uniqueness and fragility of our existence. 'Each life converges to some center, expressed or still... exists in every human nature a goal. Admitted scarcely to itself, it may be too fair for credibility's temerity to dare. Adored with caution, as a brittle heaven to reach... were hopeless as the rainbow's raiment to touch. Yet persevered toward, surer for the distance... how high unto the saints' slow diligence the sky! Ungained, it may be, by a life's low venture... but then, eternity enables the endeavoring. Again.'"

The pages rustled, signaling he'd closed the book.

"Well, what did you think?"

My life is certainly "still." But overall, I think Dickinson was saying if we don't get to do everything in this life we want, we get an eternity to try other things. Which sounds appealing... but I'm not ready to throw in the towel just yet.

"Alright," he said. "You think on it for a while, and so will I. Bye til next time."

Darn it—now he had me thinking I should be lying here dwelling on something important, like how to measure the universe, or if a comatose state is some sort of dimension between life and the afterlife. Instead I'm whiling away the hours with thoughts equivalent to how many licks to get to the center of a Tootsie Roll lollipop.

Jesus, can a girl not escape the pressure of expectation even when she's in a coma?

August 16, Tuesday

"THE HOUSE HAS SIX BATHROOMS—six. It's an amazing place and I'm so lucky to get the listing."

Carrie Kemp, Real Estate Agent, is on a roll, it seems.

"My broker says if I sell half the listings I've picked up, I'll make the Million Dollar Club for sure. They have their sales conferences in Hawaii! I've always wanted to go to Hawaii."

Ditto. Send me a postcard.

"It's so exciting to see how the other half lives, Marigold. It's a real eye-opener. All this time I've settled for run of the mill, but there's a whole other level of luxury out there, and it's within reach."

Someone had kidnapped my mom and replaced her with Tony Robbins.

"Your father simply doesn't understand, but he's always been an under-achiever."

Okay, there's my confirmation that all is not well on the Homefront. Something else to feel guilty about because I know my situation has introduced untold amounts of stress between my parents, and they appear to be dealing with the upheaval in their own way rather than together. Dad is on an extended business trip, and Mom has a whole new vocabulary with terms like "fee simple estate" and "deed-in-lieu."

My coma had sparked my mother's mid-life crisis.

"This is what he always does, you know. When things get tense, he goes on a business trip."

He does? I'm not sure I want to know these things.

"I called him last night to tell him the blood tests prove Keith Young was driving drunk. I told him he should've been here."

Well, in all fairness, we've been waiting for the results for a long time, and Dad couldn't just hang around. On the other hand, Mom shouldn't feel as if she's holding down the fort single-handedly.

"Anyway, the District Attorney asked us not to make any public statements about what a lowlife that Keith Young is. But Sidney did write a special Facebook post to say the rumor you were talking on the phone when the accident happened isn't true." She sighed. "I hope you know your sister is really looking out for you."

I do. And I hope Sidney's telling the truth, I really do. Maybe Roberta got it wrong—maybe our call simply dropped because I'd driven through a dead zone.

The door opened.

"You wanted to see me, Mrs. Kemp?"

It's Dr. Tyson.

"Yes," my mother said, and from the creak of the chair, I knew she had pushed to her feet. "Someone has been sneaking more photos of Marigold to the press, and I want it stopped."

They have?

"I apologize," Dr. Tyson said. "Everyone on staff knows they will be terminated if they compromise the confidentiality of a patient. And the staff seems very fond of Marigold—I don't believe the leak is anyone who works here."

"Then who could it be?"

"It could be one of your daughter's visitors, or a visitor of one of the other patients. We try to monitor traffic in and out of the ward, but short of a full-time security guard, we can't watch the door twenty-four seven. Do you know when it happened?"

"The photos showed up on TMZ yesterday."

"And you're sure your other daughter wasn't involved?"

Ooh, a direct hit.

"Yes, I'm sure," my mother bit out. "Sidney would never let such an unflattering photo of her sister be released. She's very protective of Marigold."

"I'm sorry for the added stress this must be putting on your family."

"If it happens again," my mother said, "I'll get the police involved."

"I understand. I'll remind the staff to keep a close eye on who comes in and out."

But I can think of someone who isn't on staff and technically, isn't a visitor. And now that my brain is working more efficiently, I remember the first time a photo had been leaked, I suspected it was someone who'd recently been in the room, but I couldn't remember their identity. But now I remember, and once again, the timing is right: the volunteer who reads to us.

I'd thought he was visiting to be a nice human being, but while I was soaking up the poetry, was he snapping photos of me to sell to the highest bidder?

Who is he, exactly?

August 17, Wednesday

"PEACE BE WITH YOU, ladies."

And also with you.

Sister Irene stopped by each bed and murmured a prayer for my ward mates, and for me. But I confess I blocked out the words—God and I are not on the best terms of late. I'm pretty perturbed at being trapped like this, and to have glimpses of hope snatched away... it's inhumane. And it goes against everything I was taught in school about a loving God. What possible good could come from me lying here? From all of us lying here? It's starting to feel as if we're being toyed with.

"I see the flowers are still coming in, Marigold."

Yes, the scents I'd once found comforting were now cloying. But she made a show of sniffing and cooing over the arrangements.

"I heard on the news the young man involved in your accident is going to be charged with DUI. And it sounds as if other charges are pending related to your condition."

Rightly so.

"I don't know what God has in store for you, Marigold, but in the event he chooses to take you home, you should use this time to confess your sins, and offer forgiveness to your enemies so you will meet Him with a pure heart."

Ack—I hadn't thought of that. Am I so wicked that God is giving me a chance to come clean before taking the rest of me?

Leave it to a nun to put it all back on me.

"If you can hear me, Marigold, try to put yourself in this young man's shoes—imagine the guilt he has to lie down with every night. This incident will taint the rest of his life."

Sister, I'd love to put myself in Keith Young's shoes—because he's walking around, talking, and feeding himself. He wasn't thinking of anyone but himself when he drank and then got behind the wheel, and now I'm going to be selfish, too.

"You will feel better if you forgive him."

I'm not listening… la la la… la la la.

"At least that's what they all told me," she murmured.

I stopped. Huh?

"They all told me I'd feel better if I forgave the man who killed my sister," she said quietly, almost to herself. "But actually, the only thing that made me feel better was imagining gouging out his eyeballs with a snail fork."

Wow. Wait—there's such a thing as a snail fork?

"So I told everyone—Mother Superior, the priest, and even the bishop that I forgave the murdering scumbag, but I didn't. That would have been a betrayal to my dear sister, and to me, that was a bigger sin."

I'm with you, Sister.

Then she made a rueful noise. "You want to know something?"

There's more?

"He's out on parole, the animal. And ever since I found out, all I can think about is finding him and killing him."

What? She couldn't mean that.

"Not just killing him, but torturing him… filleting him like a fish, then cutting him up, piece by piece, like he did to my sister."

Okay, maybe she did mean it.

"I know where he lives," she whispered.

If I could feel anything, I'm pretty sure the hair would be standing up on my arms.

Then a mewling sound escaped her, like a wounded animal, grating against my ear drums. But in that one guttural noise I sensed a tiny bit of how she had suffered. Her footsteps sounded quickly in the direction of the door. She stopped suddenly.

"Peace be with you," she said in a rush, then left.

And also with—wait… holy crap, had a nun just confessed to planning a murder?

August 18, Thursday

YOU MIGHT THINK ALL COMA patients sleep all the time, but that's not true. I sleep mostly at night, when the hospital is quiet. But just as I was pre-coma, I fight sleep, because now I'm afraid I'll never wake up again.

Eventually, though, my mind shuts down on its own, and then I sleep. And sometimes, I dream. So far, my dreams have all been about doing things I used to do—simple things, like brushing my teeth and walking up and down stairs. I've heard it's common for people who are wheelchair bound to dream about running and jumping.

And sometimes I dream about people I know, most often Duncan, Roberta, and Mark Ruffalo.

Okay, I don't know Mark Ruffalo, but I'd like to.

Anyway, I was having this nice dream about Mark Ruffalo when suddenly someone's voice rudely cut in.

"Mom."

Confused, I resisted leaving my dream, but the voice cut in again.

"Mom."

So I left the dream behind and lifted myself to the most conscious state I could, where I was aware of what was happening in the ward.

"Mom."

I don't recognize the voice, but it's female. My first thought is one of my ward mates has a visitor, a child I haven't heard about. But from the sounds around us—or rather, the lack of sounds—I realize it's the middle of the night, hardly the time for visitors.

"Mom… Mom… Mom…"

So the only other explanation is… one of my roomies is talking?

"Mom…. Mom… *mom*! MOM! MOM! MOM!"

The door burst open, admitting two sets of feet.

"What the heck?" said one voice.

"Oh, my, God," said another. "One of them is awake!"

"Which one?"

"Let me check—Parks… Audrey Parks."

Audrey had been hollering throughout and continued to yell, "Mom! Mom! Mom!"

"Call Dr. Tyson, stat. I'll try to calm her down."

But Audrey was still yelling for her mother when Dr. Tyson arrived twenty minutes later.

"Audrey," Dr. Tyson said loudly, "I will get your mother, but first you have to quiet down."

That shut her up—a good sign, I realize, because it means she hears and understands.

"My name is Dr. Tyson. I'm going to stay with you until your mother and father arrive. Let's get her to a private room," she directed in a lower voice, "where we can examine her. And contact her family immediately."

"It's a miracle," one of the nurses said.

"I'm sure there's a medical explanation," Dr. Tyson was saying as they moved the bed out into the hall.

Then I remembered Audrey's father's visit last week and his announcement that her mother has Alzheimer's. I believe Audrey had heard him and somehow, internalized the realization she might never see her mother again if she didn't get out of that bed. After two years of apathy, it had taken several days to get her brain synched up with her mouth, but there was no doubt in my mind, love had been the impetus, and sheer will had carried her out of her stupor.

So no matter what explanation Dr. Tyson manages to put on it, it *is* a miracle.

I'm in awe, and so happy for Audrey, even though she probably has a long road ahead of her.

And I'm also sick with jealousy. I wanted to be the one to spring up and startle the staff, make a fool out of Dr. Tyson. And I know the chances of two miracles happening back to back are nearly nil.

Audrey stole my miracle.

August 19, Friday

"DONNA SAID SHE JUST sat up like effing Lazarus and started talking."

"Man, that would've freaked me out."

Two orderlies, Nico and Gabriel, whose voices I now remember as being the first ones I heard when I became aware of my surroundings, were in the ward cleaning and removing equipment that had been adjacent to Audrey's bed.

"Wonder what made her wake up after two years?" Nico asked.

"Who knows? Donna is convinced it's a miracle. She said a nun was in here the day before."

Little did they know, instead of asking God for a miracle, Sister Irene was plotting a thrill kill.

"How are things with you and Donna?"

Gabriel's laugh was the kind guys share when they kiss and tell. "Great. She knows how to make me happy."

Hm… wasn't Gina dating Gabriel?

"Happier than Gina?" Nico asked.

Gabriel gave another laugh. "They both make me happy in different ways."

"You're playing with fire, dating two women who work here. One is bound to find out about the other."

"Not if I'm careful, and I intend to be."

"Man, I'm telling you, Gina's going to want you to put a ring on it."

"No way am I getting married again."

Hadn't Gina said he'd never been married?

"The third wife did me in," he added.

What a rat.

"Hey, over there's the one they call Coma Girl," Nico said. "I heard Keith Young blew a lousy .01 over the limit."

"So they're going to charge him with DUI?"

"Yeah, and maybe worse, depending on what happens to CG."

"Man, he's been looking good in practice, too. Damn shame."

"Hey, maybe CG will wake up, too. Then he can pay a fine and do community service for the DUI, and we get a respectable season of ball."

"Let's try," Gabriel said.

"Let's try what?"

"Let's try to wake her up."

"Are you crazy?"

"We'd be heroes, think of it."

"Okay, as long as you don't touch her."

Thank you, Nico.

They walked closer to my bed and I wondered what Gabriel had in mind. A loud clap sounded near my face. Then another.

"Hey, Coma Girl, wake up," Gabriel said.

I don't.

"Wakey, wakey, eggs and bakey."

Cute.

"That's enough, man," Nico said. "We're done, let's go."

"Hey, my sister said there are places that will pay good money for a picture of her. She's famous, like Pokemon Go."

What the heck is Pokemon Go?

"Forget it," Nico said. "Dr. Tyson ripped everyone a new one a few days ago over some leaked photos. It's not worth getting canned over."

"You're probably right," Gabriel said. "I wish she'd wake up, though."

Don't we all.

The door opened and closed. One less bed changed the acoustics in the room. I can feel Audrey's absence, and I wonder if Karen and Jill are aware she made her escape.

And then there were three.

August 20, Saturday

"UGH, THE D.A.'S OFFICE asked us not to make a statement about Keith Young's lab results."

Sidney is wound up today—she's talking so fast I can barely understand her, but I almost don't care what Sid is saying—I'm ecstatic because she's doing my nails again. Which means the nurses will take it off again, and I'll get to feel the sensation of touch again.

"David is irritated, but says for now it's best to comply. The good news is the piece I posted that you were *not* on the phone when the crash happened has two hundred thousand likes."

So if everyone else believes it, I probably should, too.

Then she made a sound of frustration. "But how dare that Audrey girl steal your thunder by waking up first?"

I totally agree. Although I heard the nurses say Audrey was making good progress through physical rehab and speech therapy, and I'm happy for her.

"We got a little mileage out of it, though, by saying your presence has brought a new energy to the ward, with all the flowers and stuff people are sending. That allowed us to thank your fans and ensure the arrangements keep coming, which gives us more pictures to post on Instagram."

That explained the spike in flower deliveries.

"I talked to Mom and Dad, and I've decided to sit out this semester."

Oh, no—I don't want Sid to postpone her education because of me.

"David's going to need help with everything and I just don't feel comfortable turning it over to someone else."

Ah, so David is the reason.

"One semester is no big deal. Hopefully, you'll wake up soon and everything will get back to normal."

A phone rang and Sid answered, "Hello."

She pushed up from the chair and walked toward the window.

"Yes, I have good news. The project is finished, I just need to find a way to get it to you."

I was glad to hear Sid had completed her school project in between handling the Coma Girl media.

"I'll get back to you when I work it out," she said, then ended the call.

When she came back to the chair, she was humming, so I assume the project had been weighing on her mind.

"This time I'm putting yellow on your fingernails and blue on your toenails," she sang.

The door opened and I smelled Roberta's sugary sweet presence.

"Who are you?" Sidney asked.

"I'm Roberta, Marigold's roommate. Who are you?"

"I'm Sidney, Marigold's sister."

I can sense them sizing each other up and deciding they don't like each other.

"I brought her mail," Roberta said.

"Oh, you can just leave it, and I'll go through it."

"No, actually, I like reading it to her, so I'll come back another time."

"No, actually, that wasn't a question," Sidney said, and I imagined her smiling.

I hear Roberta's footsteps, then the sound of something being dropped on the floor—a bag of mail, I presume.

"Thank you," Sidney said. "Why are you carrying my sister's purse?"

"I'm not."

"Yes, you are. It's a Chloé bag. I know because I bought it for her."

It's true—Sid said she was tired of seeing me carry a backpack and for Christmas, had given me the purse. It was beautiful, but unpractical for all the crap I had to carry around. Still I liked opening my closet and seeing it there.

"She gave it to me," Roberta said. "I guess she didn't like it."

Not true. Roberta has been shopping in my closet.

"What did you say your name is?" Sid asked.

"Roberta. I was talking on the phone to Marigold when the accident happened."

"No, she'd already hung up when the accident happened."

"I don't think so."

"But I know so," Sid said firmly. "Thanks for stopping by."

"Don't mention it," Roberta said, her voice menacing.

The door opened, then closed.

And Sidney started humming again.

August 21, Sunday

"WE'RE PLAYING THE NATIONALS AT HOME," Jack Terry said. "I'm eternally optimistic."

Detective, give it up—even I know there will be no post-season.

"Hey, I see you're minus a roomie. When I heard on the news a comatose patient at Brady had woken up and started talking, I was sure it was you."

Sigh...

"But I see you've decided to extend your nap a little longer. I brought pizza from Nancy's and root beer. You're missing out."

I heard the metallic click of a soda can opening.

"Whoever painted your nails did a pretty terrible job. I'm a moron about stuff like that and even I can tell."

Hm... Sid is usually so particular. The encounter with Roberta must've distracted her.

"Carlotta wears a pink color I like."

I wonder if he's ever told her.

"Guess I should've told her," he muttered.

Ah... past tense.

"But hey, enough about me... I want to know about Esmerelda."

I froze. How did he know?

He gave a little laugh through a mouthful of food. "I wouldn't have taken you for a burlesque dancer."

93

It's not as risqué as it sounds. I took a class, and we all had a recital of sorts. And okay, I performed in a handful of shows at small venues, but always incognito, ergo the stage name. Even Roberta doesn't know—so how did Jack Terry find out?

"I found the suitcase of costumes and a few handbills in the trunk of your car, and did a little investigating."

Oh, right. My family would freak *out*.

"Don't worry, I'll keep it safe until you wake up. No one else has to know."

I owe him one. When I wake up, I'll sign his girlfriend's Coma Girl T-shirt, if she's still in the picture.

"Feels good in here. I can't remember when we've had such a hot summer."

Sounds like a good day to be on the lake... in a boat.

"Weekends are impossible at Lanier," he offered, as if he'd read my mind. "Between the cigar boats and the cruisers, you get tossed around just sitting in a slip at the marina. Drop in every redneck in three counties with a pontoon and a cooler of beer, and it's a freak show."

He's chatty today.

"I'm going to have to move anyway," he added with a heavy sigh. "Find a proper place to live."

I wondered what had prompted the change in his living arrangements.

"Hey, maybe I'll give your mom a call. I saw her billboard on Georgia 400."

Billboard? She must be going gangbusters, which explained why she'd been so scarce. Well—partially explained.

"Damn, my battery's almost dead. Let me find an outlet for my phone charger."

He must have found one because a few minutes later, he was streaming the game from his phone and munching on pizza, his life decisions postponed for the time being.

I wish I could talk to him and ask him what was going on in his life. And tell him about Sister Elaine. And the phony psychic ripping off my aunt. And that Mr. Palmer might be planning to hurt Keith Young. And that a guy posing as a volunteer might be working for a tabloid.

But I can't. So I'll just lie here and silently scream.

August 22, Monday

"LOCK THE DOOR," Dr. Jarvis instructed.

"Why?" Gina asked.

"Just do as I ask."

I heard the click of the lock.

"Dr. Jarvis, what's going on?"

"I asked you to be here because I know you've taken an interest in Ms. Kemp."

"It's hard not to grow fond of certain patients," she agreed.

"So I'm sure you want for her the best possible chance at recovery."

"Of course," she said, but her voice sounded suspicious. "What's this all about?"

"Dr. Tyson and I spoke with a neurologist at Walter Reed Army Institute about a new drug the military is using to help TBI patients recover."

"I know. Dr. Tyson told me. But she said the insurance wouldn't cover it."

"An appeal was filed… and I secured the formulary."

"The drug is in that syringe?"

"Yes."

"But that's great news. Why the secrecy?"

"The board hasn't yet signed off."

"Then why are we talking?" Gina asked, her voice suddenly stern.

"Because I need your help. The sooner Ms. Kemp gets this drug, the sooner she might get better. If we wait for the board, it could take weeks. By the time they say yes, she could already be on the road to recovery."

"What if they say no?"

"She's a public figure now—they won't say no."

"But if they do, I could lose my job, and you could lose your license."

"If this goes sideways, don't worry—I'll take full responsibility. No one will know you were involved."

I feel for Gina. No matter what he says, she knows if things go wrong, she might be implicated. And she has a child to support.

"I'll administer the drug," he said. "I just need you to watch and make sure I follow procedure."

"Except for the getting approval part," she said dryly.

Touché.

"You know I wouldn't do this if I didn't believe it would help Ms. Kemp," he said.

"Did you administer another motor response test?"

"Yes, this morning."

"And?"

And I couldn't respond.

"And she didn't respond to my commands. But she did twice before, I swear to you. I want to give her the drug now because I'm afraid she's losing ground."

"This is unethical, Doctor."

"Is it? Look at her, Gina. She's twenty-eight and she could spend the rest of her life like this. I think if Ms. Kemp could talk to us, she'd tell us to try."

Darn tootin', I would. Come on, Gina!

Gina sighed. "Okay. Follow my instructions."

"Thank you, Gina."

"Don't thank me. Put on gloves... then clean the IV port with an alcohol pad."

They were really going to do it!

"Okay, now insert the syringe."

The doorknob rattled, then a hard rap sounded on the door. "Hello? Why is this door locked?"

"That's Teddy," Gina whispered, her voice panicked.

"Relax," Dr. Jarvis said. "This will take only a few seconds."

"Flush the syringe slowly."

The knock sounded again. "Gina, are you in there?"

"Just a minute!" Gina called.

"Almost done," Dr. Jarvis said. "There."

"Hide the syringe," she hissed.

Her footsteps sounded, then she unlocked the door.

"What were you doing?" Teddy asked.

"Physical exam," Dr. Jarvis said. "I didn't want the family to come in and be startled."

"Ah," Teddy said, then he grunted. "Looks like someone painted her nails again."

"We'll get that tomorrow," Gina said and even to me, she sounded flustered.

"Dr. Jarvis," Teddy said, "I believe Dr. Tyson is looking for you."

As Scooby-Doo would say: *Ruh roh.*

"Why?" Gina asked, sounding panicked.

"She didn't say," Teddy said slowly.

"Thank you," Dr. Jarvis said. "I'm just going to check Ms. Kemp's vitals again."

"Good idea," Gina said, too loudly.

The door closed. Dr. Jarvis checked my pulse, blood pressure, respiration, and temperature, and seemed satisfied.

"All seems to be well, Marigold. I'll be back to check on you. In the meantime, cross your fingers."

Ah… coma humor.

August 23, Tuesday

"HER SISTER MUST'VE been in a hurry," Teddy said. "It looks like a preschooler painted her nails."

"Uh-huh," Gina said.

"Why do you keep looking at her?"

"I don't."

"Yes, you do, every few seconds."

"I… I don't mean to."

"You've been acting strange since yesterday."

"No I haven't."

Yes, you have, Gina. Even I can tell.

"What were you and Dr. Jarvis doing when the door was locked?"

"Nothing," she said, but her voice squeaked.

"I think I know."

"What?"

"You were fooling around, weren't you?"

"What? No!"

"Then why are you acting so funny?"

"I… I guess I'm just spooked about the other patient waking up. That's why I keep looking at Ms. Kemp—I keep hoping she'll open her eyes."

I hope I do, too. I feel the sensations in my fingertips and toes like before and thank goodness for Sid's sloppy nail-painting job because it's taking longer and they're applying more pressure. The repetition has to be good for my brain.

"I'm sorry for giving you a hard time," Teddy said. "Not that anyone would blame you for tossing over Gabriel for a doctor."

"I'm not tossing over Gabriel. We had a great time the other night." Her voice was giddy. "I will deny this if you repeat it, Teddy, but I think he's the one."

Uh—no, he's not, Gina. Unless you mean the one who is already lying and cheating.

"Don't fall too hard yet. You hardly know him."

"I know, but can you ever really know a person?"

"These days with social media, I feel like I know too much about people."

"My son lives on social media, it's taken over our lives."

"I went out to look at the Coma Girl Facebook page and Instagram," Teddy said. "She has close to a half million followers."

That's... kind of scary, actually.

"And there's all this merchandise," Teddy added. "T-shirts and sleep masks and pillow cases and tote bags... it just seems like people are celebrating the fact that she's in a coma. I mean, do people even understand that she's *in a coma?*"

"I doubt it. I believe most people think it's romantic, like some kind of mystical state, you know?"

"That's because people only remember the reports where patients wake up from comas—they don't remember the stories where people wither away for years before their bodies give out."

Yikes.

"That won't be Ms. Kemp," Gina said. "She's going to wake up."

"What makes you so sure?" Teddy asked suspiciously.

"I just am, that's all."

"I hope so, poor thing. Don't you think it's strange that her family doesn't visit more often?"

He'd noticed that, too?

"You noticed too, huh?"

"Yeah. It's like they don't want to interact with her, but they're happy to build this Coma Girl franchise around her."

Yes, it's kind of exactly like that.

"Shh," Gina said.

"What?"

"She might be able to hear us, that's what. And who wants to hear their family doesn't want anything to do with them?"

Not me, that's for sure.

August 24, Wednesday

"WE CAN SEE YOU," my dad said.

"Speak up so Marigold can hear you," my mother added.

"Hi, Sis!"

It was good to hear Alex's voice, good to know he was safe.

"How are you doing, Marigold? You look good."

Liar.

"You've got a big fan club over here. Someone ordered a bunch of Coma Girl T-shirts—I see them all the time. You're famous!"

"Can you believe it?" my dad said. "Our little Marigold is known all over the world."

"How is she?" Alex asked.

"The same," my mom said. "We keep hoping to get a call that she's up and walking around, but she's still unresponsive."

"What are the doctors saying?"

"More of the same," my dad said. "Be patient, her brain is still healing."

"We haven't given up hope," my Mom said.

Whew.

"Yet," she added.

"I'm really sorry the medication Dr. Oscar suggested isn't a good fit for Marigold's case," Alex said. "I'm going to send him a thank you card anyway."

Hm... that could trigger questions...

"That's nice," Mom said. "It was good of you to take the time out of your busy schedule to do something for your sister."

"Gosh, Mom, it wasn't much. I'm going a little crazy over here knowing she's in this state."

"Oh, don't worry about her, sweetie. She has good care here. How are you?"

Wow... she'd skimmed right over me.

"I'm fine. Although I was pretty upset when I heard Keith Young was definitely driving drunk when he crashed into Marigold."

"We were going to tell you," my dad said, "but you already heard?"

"One of my Army buddies in Atlanta called me. He's been following the case in the news. In fact, he offered to dispense a little street justice if I want him to."

"What's that, dear?"

"He's offering to rough up Keith Young," my dad said.

How chivalrous.

"You know how these athletes get away with murder," Alex said. "I wouldn't mind seeing him banged up a little."

"Let's leave it up to the police," Dad said.

"Yes, we don't want you to get in trouble over something that was Marigold's fault."

Wait—my fault?

"But it wasn't Marigold's fault, Mom."

"She was late picking up Sidney at the airport. You know how slow she is. If she'd only gotten to the airport on time, none of this would've happened."

Wow.

"Mom, you can't blame this on Marigold."

She sighed. "You're right. I'm sorry. I've just had a long day and I'm tired."

Translation: Her filter isn't in place.

"Your mother is a full time real estate agent now," Dad said, and I detected a little sarcasm in his voice.

"Really? Go, Mom."

"Thanks," she said, sounding pleased at Alex's praise.

"She has a billboard on Georgia 400," my dad said. "Her face is as big as a panel truck."

Hostile much?

"Business must be good," my brother said. "That's great. Listen, I gotta run. Let's do this again soon, okay?"

"Okay, bye, dear."

"Bye, Marigold!"

My mother disconnected the Skype session, and my parents sat in charged silence.

Three, two, one…

"Did you have to make a dig at me in front of Alex?" my mother demanded.

"You mean the obnoxious billboard? It's the truth, Carrie!"

"You're just angry, Robert, because I didn't go through you to get it made."

"Well, it does beg the question why, if you needed a sign, you didn't ask your husband, who sells signs for a living!"

"Because I wanted to do something on my own." From the squeak of the chair, I could tell my mother had stood up. Hands on hips, I visualized. Her footsteps moved toward the door. "My world doesn't revolve around you, Robert."

My dad's footsteps followed her. "You have a gift for stating the obvious, Carrie."

The door opened and closed, and I heard their angry footsteps fading.

Bye… don't forget to write.

August 25, Thursday

"HI."

It was one of those rare times I was napping during the day. My sleep patterns were off lately, and I wondered if it had something to do with the drug Dr. Jarvis had administered.

"Are you dead?"

A child is standing next to my bed. I don't know any children, so I'm confused.

"Hey, lady, are you dead?"

It's a girl and if I had to guess, she's about six years old.

"You look dead. But if you're dead, why aren't you in a casket?"

The little girl knows something about death if she knows about caskets.

"What happened to your face? Did someone hit you?"

And she knows something about being hit if that's where her mind went first.

She sighed. "When someone hits you, you're not supposed to hit them back... but I would anyway."

Good girl.

"There's a mean boy at school I'd like to hit. His name is Jeremy Hood. He calls me names like fattie and fatso and fathead and fatbutt. But my name is Christina Ann Wells. And one day I'm going to whomp him good... I'm just waiting for the right time."

I'd buy a ticket to that show.

"Do you like ice cream?"

Who doesn't?

"I love ice cream," she said wistfully. "I love chocolate and strawberry the best. My mama gets the striped kind."

Striped? Oh, neapolitan.

"But I eat the chocolate and strawberry first. Vanilla is the one I eat last, and it's okay. Just not as good as chocolate and strawberry."

The girl had her priorities straight.

"I have new shoes," she announced. "They're shiny with a bow."

Then she proceeded to stomp and jump around the room in her hard sole shoes which I suspected were patent leather.

"I can't run in them, though."

We start hobbling our girls young in the South.

"I like your turban."

Ha—she thinks my head bandage is a turban.

"Are you magic?" she asked, her voice awestruck.

If only.

"Can you make my mama better? She's sick in her belly. She can't eat, not even ice cream."

I hope it's something minor.

"She gots the cancer."

Oh, no.

"I need for her to get better because I can't tie my shoes."

Kids are nothing if not practical.

"Can you try to make her better, lady? I'll be good... after I whomp Jeremy Hood."

The door opened and a man's voice boomed, "Christina! I told you not to leave the waiting room. Come here and quit bothering sick people."

"She's not sick and she's not dead. She's a magic lady," the little girl explained, breathless. "I asked her to make mama better."

"Then I'm sure she will," the man said, his voice more gentle. "Come on, baby."

The door closed and I felt some of the anger that had built up over the past month subside. And for the first time in years, I prayed.

That Christina would have some magic in her life.

August 26, Friday

"THANK YOU. You won't regret it. I'll touch base again next week."

David Spooner stabbed a button on his phone, then hooted. "We did it, Sid. You, pretty lady, are booked as a guest on *The Doctors*!"

She exclaimed her delight, then from the smacking and moaning, I assumed they were either licking each other or kissing.

"This will be huge exposure," she said. "Nationwide!"

"The producers said they'd gotten more mail about comas and Coma Girl than any single subject in the past year."

"This is so exciting! I've always wanted to go to L.A."

Ditto. Send me a postcard.

"You're going with me, aren't you, David?"

"Of course."

"Oh, my goodness—what am I going to wear?"

"Relax. We'll get you something spectacular for your TV debut."

More licking ensued.

"Okay," David said. "This has to be a homerun, so we need to get prepared. Let's start thinking of things we'll need to gather. They'll want visuals, for sure."

"We'll take lots of pictures—maybe you can take some of me and Marigold together?"

"Sure."

"And maybe one of us Skyping with Alex. That will appeal to the military families."

"How about some family pictures of you all growing up? You know, Olan Mills type stuff?"

"Er, I'm sure I can find something," Sidney said.

I'm sure she can't. But there's always Photoshop.

"And pictures of Marigold before the accident, you know happy and smiling."

"Let me work on that," she hedged.

"And maybe some pictures of you and your parents working with Marigold, reading to her, massaging her limbs, doing things to help her recover."

Yes, let's stage all those pictures of fake family rehab.

"Sure," Sidney said. "Wait—I paint Marigold's nails."

"That'll make a *great* picture."

I couldn't care less about the photo opp, but if that's what it takes to get my nails painted again, terrific.

"What we really need is something exclusive for the show," David said.

"Like what?"

"Some inside scoop on Marigold's condition."

"Yeah, that would be great," Sid said. "But so far, her doctor just keeps saying there's no change, no improvement."

"With the other woman in her room waking up, we need to toss the producers a bone or Marigold will be upstaged." He snapped his fingers. "Hey, what if we arrange to live stream video of Marigold from her bed. And maybe have someone ask her to open her eyes. I mean, think of it—if she opened her eyes for the first time on a live stream, the ratings would go through the roof!"

This guy didn't leave anything on the table.

"I'll get Mom to do it," Sid said. "In fact… who would question Mom if she said Marigold squeezed her hand?"

"I love the way you think," David gushed.

I don't even know how to respond to that. I want to say Mom would never go for it, but I'm sure Sid could convince her it was in the family's best interests.

"Oh, and we need to talk about the money," David said.

"What about the money?"

"The producers have already asked what's being done with all the donations."

"We'll tell them they're for Marigold's medical bills."

"I'm afraid that won't be good enough. We might need to come up with a foundation of some kind to share some of the donations with other causes."

Sid made a frustrated noise. "Do we have to?"

"Trust me, a foundation will bring in enough incremental donations to more than pay for itself. And you'll be named the executor, of course."

"Okay, then!"

"So we have everything we need to get started?"

"I think so, yes," Sid said.

"Then let's go."

After the door closed behind them, I realized if I inconveniently croaked between now and the show, they would probably put me on ice and bring me out to thaw during the sound check.

No one would know the difference.

August 27, Saturday

THE DOOR OPENED and from the banging and clanging, I assumed a new piece of equipment was being wheeled in.

Maybe it's time for more tests. Dr. Jarvis has been stopping in regularly to check me for motor reactions, but so far, I haven't been able to respond. And at some point I know Dr. Tyson will be checking my brainwaves to make sure they're still flapping.

"Hello, r-roomies."

It took me a few seconds to realize the slow female voice belongs to Audrey Parks.

My heart took flight. For all the grousing I've done about Audrey getting what I want, I'm so happy for her.

"They tell me I was in this room for two years," she slurred, obviously still working on her speech, "but I don't remember very much."

The wheels squeaked on the floor.

"I never knew there was a window... nice view, too. I can't believe how things have changed in two years. You can watch anything on TV anytime you want. I've been watching the news nonstop. *Crazy* election, and all the things going on in the world are a little scary."

Her voice trailed off, as if she's worried about re-entry. That makes sense, I guess. You miss good things when you're in a coma, but on the flipside, you don't have to experience the bad things. She's been sheltered from the world for over two years.

"My mom doesn't recognize me." She heaved a sigh. "I finally wake up, and now I'm losing my mother to dementia. It's not fair."

She wheeled closer to our beds.

"I had a sense of other patients in the room, but I didn't know your names."

I heard the scrape of clipboards being removed from the footboards.

"Karen Suh... Jill Wheatley... and Marigold Kemp." She gave a little laugh. "So you're Coma Girl... everyone is talking about you. And I see you're the source of that awful classical music."

Technically, I'm a reluctant third-party distributor.

"It's annoying, but it was one of the few things that cut through the fog, gave me something to concentrate on, like a beacon."

Dr. Jarvis will be happy to know his scheme worked. Although it doesn't make the music less maddening.

"Except now that I'm awake," she said softly, "I don't even recognize myself. My body is different. My personality is different. This isn't me."

Silence fell in the room, then suddenly I realized Audrey was sobbing.

The door opened. "Audrey?" Gina asked. "How good to see you. I was your nurse when you were in the ward. Are you okay?"

Audrey is clearly not okay.

"My therapist thought it would be good for me to come back here," Audrey said between gulps of air. "But I wish I'd never come, because I don't want to see what I used to be." She was wailing now. "Get me out of here, please."

After a noisy exit, I lay there thinking I'd been jealous of Audrey for no good reason. Her brain injury and two years of isolation had left her melancholy and emotionally fragile and a shell of her former self.

I hadn't considered that if I ever wake up, I might not be the same person I was before.

August 28, Sunday

"THANKS FOR MEETING me here, Detective Terry."

"No problem, Ms. Spence. Since Lucas handed you the Kemp case, I thought it would be good for you to meet Marigold."

"You sound as if you know her," she said in a silky voice.

And you sound as if you're flirting. Assistant District Attorney Spence also sounds skinny. And blonde.

"Never met Marigold," Jack said. "But I'm starting to feel as if I know more about her and her family. They're eager for Keith Young to be prosecuted. Where do things stand?"

"Well, since his blood alcohol level was over the legal limit, we could get him on DUI."

"And?"

"And technically, you know he can be charged with reckless driving, driving to endanger, and assault."

"So why hasn't he?"

"Can she hear us?"

"She" meaning me.

"I honestly don't know," Jack said.

Her footsteps moved toward the window, and he followed.

"Well, between you and me," she said, her voice lower but perfectly audible. "Lucas has consulted with several neurosurgeons on this case. And they told him most patients with this type of brain injury will expire within a few months."

Expire... like a Walgreen's coupon.

"So he wants to wait to see if she dies so he can up the charges to murder?"

"Or see if she wakes up." The ADA sighed. "Look, Lucas already explained to the family why proving damages in a coma case is difficult. And Young's blood alcohol level was barely above the limit. His attorney has already insisted on retesting. And even if the results are verified, no jury is going to find Young guilty if they think she's going to wake up. And frankly, this Coma Girl social media blitz is doing just that—people are convinced she's Sleeping Beauty and she's going to open her eyes any minute."

Jack made a frustrated noise. "So everything is on hold."

"For now. Unless there's a change in her condition one way or another. If she doesn't improve within a few months, the hubbub will have died down and it'll be easier to convince a jury that she's not going to wake up. Trust me, it's in the best interests of her family to wait."

"And meanwhile, the Falcons get to start their season with their hotshot receiver."

"I know Keith Young is cocky, but I talked to him, and he's not a bad guy."

"I thought the same thing when I saw his interview. But it just seems so unjust for that young woman to be lying in that bed, and no one is held accountable."

I don't know what I've done to gain a champion in Jack Terry, but I'm grateful.

"I understand," ADA Spence said. "But just because a situation is tragic doesn't mean it's criminal. That why it's called an accident, Detective."

I'm tragic?

"Say, didn't you used to date Liz Fischer?"

He coughed. "Liz and I go way back."

Aha—and the plot thickens with yet another woman.

"You know she's pregnant?"

"I'd heard that, yes. Are we through here?"

"Yes. Actually, I was just on my way to get a drink if you'd like to join me."

Ooh, smooth.

"Sorry," Jack said. "I have another commitment."

"Okay, maybe another time."

"Maybe."

The woman's heels clacked on the floor as she left the room. I'm disappointed Jack has somewhere else to be.

Then he dragged a chair closer to my bed. "It's Braves versus the Giants in San Francisco. We really need this one, Coma Girl. Are you with me?"

I'm with you, Detective.

August 29, Monday

"YOU'RE STILL RUNNING a temperature," Gina said to me. "But Dr. Jarvis assures me that's okay." She sighed. "I hope he's as good a doctor as I think he is."

That makes two of us.

A knock on the door sounded, then it opened.

"May I help you?" Gina asked.

"I'm here to visit Marigold Kemp," the woman said. "I'm an old friend of hers."

The voice tickled a memory chord.

"Did you leave your name at the desk?"

"Yes. I'm Joanna Fitz."

Joanna—my college friend who now lives in Pennsylvania. After receiving a card from her, I never dreamed she'd visit in person.

"Visiting hours are over, but you can have fifteen minutes."

"Thank you. Can she hear me?"

"We don't know for sure," Gina said. "But assume she can."

When Gina left, Joanna was silent. I knew she was studying me.

"Oh, Marigold," she said on a sob.

She'd last seen me the summer I'd met Duncan. I'd been happy and bouncy and flush with possibilities. I'm sure my slack, scarred appearance is a shock to her. She, on the other hand, is probably still beautiful, slim and tanned from all that tennis.

Joanna dropped into the chair next to my bed, sniffling.

"I decided on an impromptu visit to Atlanta to see my folks," she said, "and thought I'd stop by. Brian and the twins are good... his practice is good... everything is... good."

She broke off on a sob, and I wanted to reach out to her. Compared to her life, I probably seemed—how had the ADA described me? Oh, yeah—tragic.

Joanna cried for a little while, then sniffed. "Marigold, I lied. My life isn't good—it's awful. I came home to stay with my parents because Brian is having an affair and the twins have behavior problems, and I'm drinking too much."

Whoa—what ever happened to breaking bad news gently?

She blew her nose noisily. "Nothing has turned out the way I thought it would."

A bed in the vegetable patch wasn't on my list, either.

The door opened. "I'm sorry," Gina said, "but it's time to say goodnight."

"I'll be right out," Joanna said.

She took a few deep breaths to compose herself, then pushed up out of the chair.

"Why can't we hit the rewind button and go back to the last time we saw each other? We were both so happy. Now look at us. You're in this bed, and I'm just going through the motions."

Both comatose.

"When did life get so hard?" she whispered.

As she walked to the door, I noticed her steps were wobbly. The sound of the door closing behind her seemed like a gong heralding the end of our youth.

And while I'd always been envious of Joanna's life, now I wouldn't trade places with her for a king's ransom. Because my chances of waking up from my stupor are probably better than hers.

August 30, Tuesday

I'VE DECIDED WHEN I wake up, I'm going to learn to play the cello.

I can read music now, from hours of listening to the classical tunes playing on Dr. Jarvis's iPod, and translating it from sound to notes. And I visualize my fingers on the strings of the cello, turning the notes back into sound. In my mind I picture a symphony, with my hospital bed sitting to the rear of the cellos, between bassoons and trumpets.

I'm bored today, but I take it as a good sign, that my brain is looking for something new to do.

In other words, I take it as a sign the drug Dr. Jarvis administered is working.

Something is definitely different. Whereas before my mind was chugging along evenly, now it seems to ebb and flow, but the extremes are more... more. I'm napping more, but when I'm not sleeping, I seem to be firing on more cylinders.

And the range of my emotions seems to be ever-widening... and sometimes ever-changing. Sometimes I think Keith Young should be punished for his wanton carelessness... other times I wonder if I did swerve into his lane. With Sidney chatting on her phone and Roberta laughing in my ear...

Wait, was that a flash of memory, or simply a manufactured scenario?

I tried to zero in on the image, but it slipped away.

Hopefully, though, it will come back tomorrow.

I didn't have any visitors today, and it makes me long for even the melancholy of Audrey's company. And while Joanna's visit still plagues me, I recognize the encounter as yet a different stimulation that I need to process.

And the realization itself is progress.

I'm getting better, I can feel it.

August 31, Wednesday

"THANK YOU FOR ARRANGING to be here today. I know you all have busy schedules."

Dr. Tyson has asked my parents and Sidney to come in. I'm so excited because I'm sure Dr. Jarvis came clean about administering the experimental drug, and Dr. Tyson is going to tell my parents I'm improving.

"I wanted to talk to you about some changes in Marigold's condition, and I felt it was important to tell you all together, since what happens to Marigold affects all of you."

The door opened and closed.

"Nice of you to join us, Dr. Jarvis," Dr. Tyson said. "You will be interested in this development, too."

"Sorry for the tardiness," he said, sounding contrite.

"As I was saying, Marigold's situation has gotten more exposure than the typical patient, so what happens to her affects all of you on many levels."

"That's exactly why I wanted David Spooner here," Sidney said, sounding defensive.

"You're free to share updates with non-family members as you see fit. But I hope you'll keep Marigold's best interests in mind."

"That's a given," Sid said, still annoyed. "Can we get on with this?"

Dr. Tyson seems to be taking her time, choosing her words carefully.

"As you know, Marigold has shown very little change since she was placed in the long-term care ward two months ago. And even though she's shown no motor response, I've always been encouraged that her organs are functioning well and her brainwave activity is strong. And my hope

111

remains that as the brain injury continues to heal, her condition will improve."

"So she hasn't improved?" Sidney asked.

"Not exactly."

"She's getting worse?" my dad asked, sounding distraught.

"No," Dr. Tyson said. "She's not getting worse, but there is a new wrinkle."

"What is it?" my mother demanded.

"Marigold is… pregnant."

Okay, I did not see that coming.

SEPTEMBER

September 1, Thursday

MY MOTHER AND Sidney have been in my room for a half hour tapping their feet and heaving labored sighs.

Labored—get it? *Ha*—pregnancy humor. I'm trying to adjust to Dr. Tyson's announcement yesterday that I have a fetus growing inside me, but I confess I'm still reeling... along with my entire family it seems.

"I can't believe this is happening," my mother kept repeating.

"I know," Sidney kept responding.

But the pregnancy explains why I've been feeling so different lately, and why my moods have been swinging like a pendulum. Oh, and the weight gain.

The door opened.

"Good morning," Dr. Tyson said.

"Not from where I stand," my mother said.

"I think we can all agree this is about the furthest thing from a good morning," Sidney added.

"Er, sorry. I understand you have some questions for me about Marigold's... condition?"

"That's right," Sidney said. "Yesterday, I think we were all too shocked to think straight."

"I'm glad you came by. I was planning to reach out to you after you'd had time to digest the news. Will Mr. Kemp be joining us?"

"No," my mother said. "Sidney and I decided this is too delicate of a matter to involve Marigold's father. As you can imagine, he is very upset."

Inside I'm cringing. Yes, I'm a grown woman, but I'm still sensitive to how my dad sees me. Now he knows I've had S-E-X.

"I understand," Dr. Tyson said. "This is quite unexpected."

"That's an understatement," my mother snapped. "Exactly how far along is she?"

"We're going to perform an ultrasound tomorrow, but my best guess is around fourteen weeks."

"And we're just now learning about this?" Sidney asked.

"Rigorous tests were run when Marigold was first admitted, and at that time, no hCG was detected in her urine."

My mother gasped. "Someone impregnated her after she was admitted?"

"I'm calling the police right now," Sidney declared.

Oh, Jesus.

"That's not what happened," Dr. Tyson said, her voice elevated. "It takes about ten days from conception for the hormone to show up in a urine test. The timing indicates Marigold was newly pregnant when she was admitted, but not far enough along to test positive. Lately we've been checking her urine for blood, and I noticed the hCG was elevated."

"Okay," my mother said on an exhale, as if she was striving for calm. "So what happens now? I assume she will miscarry."

Because that, in my mother's eyes, would solve everything.

"It's possible," Dr. Tyson said. "It could also be an ectopic pregnancy. But if not, a healthy fetus could come to full term even if Marigold remains in the coma."

"How can that be?" Sidney asked.

"I don't mean to sound crude, but Marigold's body is a perfect incubator. A comatose patient giving birth isn't unprecedented."

"That sounds positively wretched," my mother said, her voice choked.

Dr. Tyson cleared her throat politely. "We're still within the guidelines for termination."

My heart stopped. What?

"An abortion?" my mother asked.

"We're Catholic," Sidney bit out.

"I'm only providing you with all the options," the doctor said. "This is a very unique situation. I assume you'll want to consult the father of the baby."

The silence was palpable.

"Ah. You don't know the father of the baby."

"Marigold never mentioned a boyfriend to me," my mother said.

"Me either," Sidney said.

"Maybe a friend would know, or a coworker?" the doctor suggested.

"I don't see why it's necessary to involve anyone else," my mother said. "We're Marigold's family, the decision is up to us."

"How can you be sure the baby wasn't injured in the car crash?"

Sidney asked.

I hadn't thought of that. I was already a bad mother.

"We can't be," the doctor admitted. "Why don't we meet again after the ultrasound? I'll have more information for you then."

"Okay," my mother said, sounding relieved to postpone the discussion.

Dr. Tyson said goodbye and left the room. I could visualize my mom and Sidney staring at each other, feeling helpless.

"You can't tell David," my mom said. "Or anyone... not until we figure this out."

"I haven't said anything to David. Actually, I've been avoiding him because I was afraid he could tell something was wrong. But," she added, her voice rising an octave, "he might be able to give us some advice on how this will affect Marigold's case."

And my brand. My social peeps will go bananas when they find out I have a bun in the oven.

"Let's hold off for now," my mother said, her voice low and thoughtful. "Until we know what we're dealing with."

So, Catholic cornerstones notwithstanding, apparently no options were off the table.

"I have to run," my mom said. "I'm showing the Hershey house in forty minutes."

"Oh, the contemporary house with the roof garden?"

"That's the one."

"I'll walk out with you," Sidney said. "By the way, David arranged a session for me with the top media trainer in the city...."

They left, and left me wondering what I'd have to do to get my family's full attention.

September 2, Friday

"WON'T THE RADIOLOGY Department miss the ultrasound machine?" Nurse Gina asked.

Gina and Dr. Tyson had appropriated a piece of equipment for a private viewing in my room.

"Not if we hurry," Dr. Tyson said. "At this point, I can't afford for anyone else to find out about Ms. Kemp's condition. The family is under enough pressure without word leaking to the press."

"I understand," Gina said. "Um... does Dr. Jarvis know about the pregnancy?"

"Yes, he was present when I told the family the day before yesterday.

Why?"

"No reason," Gina squeaked.

Poor Gina. She was probably feeling so guilty about helping Dr. Jarvis administer the experimental cocktail.

"Please turn off that music," Dr. Tyson said irritably.

Gina obliged, and the sound from the iPod ended abruptly between movements of Arcangelo Corelli's *Concerto Grosso No. 8 in G Minor.* (See how cultured I'm getting?)

The door opened.

"Speak of the devil," Dr. Tyson said. "What brings you by, Dr. Jarvis?"

"I wanted to talk to you about Mari—about Ms. Kemp."

"You'll have to talk to me while I administer the ultrasound."

"Okay. Gina, would you give us some privacy?"

"Gina is Ms. Kemp's nurse," Dr. Tyson said. "Whatever you have to say, you can say it in front of her."

"I'd rather not, um, involve anyone else," he said.

Good—he was going to protect Gina.

"Okay," Dr. Tyson said, her voice suspicious. "Gina, you may leave."

Gina's footsteps sounded. The door opened and closed.

"What's this about?" Dr. Tyson prompted.

"I, um, have a confession to make."

"I'm not a priest, Dr. Jarvis."

He must've looked anguished because she added, "Okay, spit it out."

"It's about the experimental cocktail Dr. Oscar is using at Walter Reed."

"How do you know about that?"

"I... found out about it."

"And?"

"And... I contacted Dr. Oscar."

"Excuse me?"

"It gets worse," he said morosely. "I told him I was working with you and I got the formulary protocol."

"And?" Dr. Tyson's voice was steely.

"And... I administered the drug."

"You did *what?*"

"I know it was wrong—"

"It's *way* past being wrong," she said, her voice shaking. "What you did is criminal, Dr. Jarvis."

"I know," he said. "I didn't know about the fetus."

"Yes, there's that, too!" she snapped. "This is why there's a protocol for doing things around here, Jarvis! What the hell were you thinking?"

"I was thinking it wasn't fair that Ms. Kemp be denied the drug simply because her insurance refused to pay for it."

"And now the hospital will have to eat the cost, and you might have done much more damage than good."

"What can I do to make it right?"

"You're assuming it can be made right."

"As soon as I found out about the baby, I contacted Dr. Oscar and asked if anything in the drug posed a danger to the fetus."

"And?"

"And he said not that he was aware of."

"Because the drug probably wasn't tested on anyone who was pregnant," she said grimly. "And you know the fetus is most vulnerable in the first trimester."

"If it's any consolation, I believe the drug is helping. I've kept a chart of my verbal command tests with Ms. Kemp, and the times and dates she responded by moving her right fingers."

A rustle of paper sounded.

"She moved her fingers yesterday morning?" Dr. Tyson asked.

"And this morning," he said. "I came in before rounds."

"Did anyone else witness her movement?"

"No."

"Well, let's try again now, shall we?"

She sounded falsely cheerful, as if she fully expected me not to respond.

"Ms. Kemp, I'm holding your right hand and I need for you to move your fingers if you can. Can you move your fingers, Marigold? Can you move the fingers on your right hand?"

I'm trying so hard to make Jarvis look good.

"Anything?" he asked.

"No," she said, as if she hadn't expected anything different.

"It seems as if she responds better in the morning versus later in the day."

"And yet, you have no witnesses to confirm she responded at all."

"No."

"It's clear to me, Dr. Jarvis, that you're projecting what you want to happen onto the patient to justify your unconscionable actions."

"Can we try one more thing?"

"*No.*"

"You hold her hand and let me give the command. What could it hurt?"

She sighed. "You have thirty seconds."

From the shuffling of feet, I assumed they had changed places by my bed.

"Hello, Marigold, it's Dr. Jarvis. I need for you to squeeze my hand,

Marigold. Tell your brain to tell your arm to tell your hand to move your fingers, Marigold. Try really hard, it's very important. Move your fingers, Marigold."

I visualized each step he described, picturing the command forming in my brain, then traveling down my arm to my hand and instructing my fingers to move.

"I felt something," Dr. Tyson said, her voice hushed. "Tell her again."

"Good job, Marigold," he said excitedly. "Do it one more time. Move your fingers, Marigold."

"Yes," she said. "I definitely felt her fingers move."

He whooped. "I told you! See, the drug is working."

"Not so fast," Dr. Tyson said. "We have no proof that the drug is working. It could be elevated hormones from the pregnancy causing metabolic changes. Don't think for a minute this excuses you breaking almost every medical protocol this hospital has in place."

There was another rustle of paper.

"I typed up a memo detailing what I did to exonerate you and the hospital from liability."

"Unfortunately, it doesn't work that way. I'm on the hook for you, Jarvis. We might both lose our license to practice over this."

"Tell me what to do."

"You can shut the hell up while I run this ultrasound and pray I find a fetal heartbeat."

He shut the hell up and I held my mental breath.

"There," she said, relief shading her voice.

"Is it strong?"

"Yes. And it's where it should be, so not ectopic."

So at least my unconscious reproductive system is working properly.

"Now what?" he asked.

"You don't get to ask that question," she said, her voice low and lethal. "Give me the memo."

From the sound of paper tearing, I deduced she had yanked it from his hand.

"Now go home, Dr. Jarvis, and don't set foot back into this hospital until you hear from me, is that understood?"

"Yes, doctor."

Dr. Jarvis's footsteps sounded, then the door opened and closed.

Dr. Tyson uttered a long, frustrated noise. "For someone so quiet, Marigold Kemp, you are causing quite an uproar."

Suddenly, the classical music resumed in bombastic glory.

Was Dr. Tyson coming around to Dr. Jarvis's unorthodox treatments?

September 3, Saturday

"THANK YOU FOR COMING today to talk about Marigold," Dr. Tyson said.

"You don't have to thank us," my dad said, sounding cranky. "She's our daughter."

"I know," Dr. Tyson said calmly, "but you would be surprised how difficult it can be to get a patient's family to engage in a patient's care in a meaningful way."

She let that sentence hang in the air for everyone to absorb, although I'm pretty sure it bounced off my Teflon-coated family.

"I don't understand why we can't have these meetings in your office," my mother said. "It's unnerving to have these conversations over Marigold's body."

As if they're talking over a corpse.

"I like to think that Marigold can hear us," Dr. Tyson said, "and would want to know what's going on with her recovery."

I forget why I ever had bad feelings toward Dr. Tyson.

"In fact, I have good news—yesterday, Marigold responded to a command to move the fingers on her right hand."

Exclaims of surprise sounded.

"So she's getting better?"

"Can she hear us?"

"Why didn't you call us?"

"Some movement is definitely better than none. I don't know that she can hear all the time, and even if she can, it doesn't mean she understands what's being said. Reacting to a command to move fingers is a very basic response... but it's cause for optimism. And I did call and leave a message on your home phone."

"Oh," my mother said, "we haven't been home that much lately. My business has become so demanding."

"And I've been on the road," my dad explained.

"And I never check the land-line phone," Sidney added.

"Well then," Dr. Tyson said.

Which pretty much said it all, really.

Sidney was the first to recover. "But what great news!" A few digital noises sounded. "And I just posted it to Facebook. Coma Girl's followers will be thrilled!"

Dr. Tyson cleared her throat. "Now... as for the fetus. I want to begin by telling you the ultrasound revealed a strong fetal heartbeat, and confirmed it's fourteen weeks along."

"And is the baby okay?" my dad asked.

"It's impossible to say for sure, but for this stage, everything seems normal."

"Thank God," he said.

"So you've decided Marigold will carry the baby to full term?"

"Of course we have," my dad said.

"We haven't decided," my mom said at the same time.

Oh, no. More dissention.

My dad sputtered. "What are you saying?"

"Marigold is my first priority," my mother said. "I want to know more about what this pregnancy will do to her."

It's hard to be angry at her for feeling that way. Actually, it's kind of touching.

"That matters to me, too," he said, his voice rising.

"Why don't we hear what the doctor has to say," Sidney suggested.

"It's a valid point," Dr. Tyson conceded. "The fetus will take whatever it needs. Our challenge will be to keep Marigold nourished to the point that there will be enough stores for them both to draw on."

"But the baby will tax her body," my mother said.

"Yes, the baby will consume resources."

My mother made a thoughtful noise. "Won't that impede her own healing?"

"It might," Dr. Tyson agreed. "We were already facing an uncertain situation, and this development complicates things further. I can only assure you that we'll have the best team possible looking after Marigold and the baby, if the decision is made to continue with the pregnancy."

"We want the pregnancy to continue," my dad said.

"No," my mother said, her voice sounding robotic. "We will discuss this and get back to you, Dr. Tyson. If Marigold is showing signs of improving, I don't want this to be a setback."

"There is one other thing to consider," Dr. Tyson said. "Mr. and Mrs. Kemp, I'm sure you recall the information you passed to me about the experimental drug the physician at Walter Reed has had some good results with."

"Yes," my mother said. "The military research doctor our son reached out to."

"Right."

"You said the drug wasn't right for Marigold's situation," my father said.

"There was a… reconsideration. And the window to administer the drug was narrow, so I made a decision to give it to Marigold."

Ah, she was covering for Dr. Jarvis.

"Without consulting us?" my mother demanded.

"I, um, left a message on your home phone to please call me as soon as possible," Dr. Tyson said.

Ooh, good one, Dr. Tyson, to turn their disinterest back on them, even if it was a fabrication.

"When I didn't hear back," she continued in a rush, "I had to make a unilateral decision I thought was in the best interest of my patient. And since you were the ones to bring Dr. Oscar and his experiment to our attention, I assumed you would approve."

"When was this?" my father asked.

"Two weeks ago."

"And this is the first we've heard of it?" Sidney asked, sounding litigious.

"There was some miscommunication between me and Dr. Jarvis. I only just became aware that you weren't informed. My sincere apologies."

"So the drug is the reason Marigold moved her fingers?" my father asked.

"We believe so," Dr. Tyson said.

"I knew it would work," my mother said. "My son Alex is brilliant."

"*Our* son," my dad corrected.

Oh, good grief.

"Yes, well," Dr. Tyson said, "what I'm trying to say is the drug was administered before we knew about the fetus."

"Will it cause problems for the baby?" Sidney asked.

"We don't know. The drug hasn't been tested on a pregnant comatose patient."

"But it's a drug for neural stimulation," my dad said. "So for all you know, it could be *good* for the baby."

"That's possible," Dr. Tyson admitted. "But typically a fetus develops best in an unadulterated environment."

"What's the window for terminating the pregnancy?" my mother asked.

"Twenty weeks, so there's still time. You need to prepare yourselves for a range of outcomes regarding both Marigold and the fetus. If you like, I can recommend a therapist who will help you reach a decision that's best for your family."

"That won't be necessary," my mother said briskly. "We've never needed a therapist to help us make family decisions before, and we're not going to start now."

Right, I thought. Why ruin a winning streak?

"We'll get back to you," my mother said, "as soon as we decide the best course of action. Meanwhile, I want your personal assurance that this information will be kept completely confidential."

"Don't worry," Dr. Tyson said evenly, "I don't have a Facebook account."

September 4, Sunday

WHEN THE THIRD SET of church bells rang, I realized Detective Jack Terry had forsaken me today.

I hope it's for something fun, like tickets to a Braves game or fishing, versus something gruesome, like a murder. Or maybe he'd decided to spend the day with a woman who walked and talked. He seemed to have a surplus of ambulatory females to choose from.

Okay, so it's just us. I guess now's as good a time as any to tell you about the father of my fetus. I'm chagrined to tell you, it's none other than the engaged Duncan who's destined for a five-tier-pink-grapefruit-cake wedding in two short months.

Here's the way things went down:

When Duncan returned from his tour in the Peace Corps, we got together for old times' sake and tossed back a few too many brews—he because he was happy to see American beer again, me because I was happy to see him again. We picked up right where we left off, it was a great evening and neither one of us mentioned his fiancée. He was too drunk to drive, so he crashed at my apartment, and sometime during the night, had migrated from the sagging couch in the living room to my bed. Shame on me, I knew he was in love with Trina, but I reasoned she would have him for the rest of their lives, so having him for one little night didn't seem so wrong. After all, I'd seen him first.

But if you're thinking the encounter was a drunken grabfest, you'd be wrong. Duncan's lovemaking was sweet, but surprisingly intense and purposeful. It was such an emotional experience for me, I convinced myself he felt the same way about me and the engagement would be unwound. We fell asleep with our hands intertwined... and I woke up alone. While I was wiping the sleep from my eyes, I'd gotten a text from Duncan.

Last night was my mistake. I value your friendship, but I'm marrying Trina. Please don't hate me.

I was crushed. And mortified that something that had meant so much to me, he considered to be a mistake. By the time I brushed my teeth, I realized how sadly unoriginal the whole story was and resolved to act as if it hadn't happened. I deleted his text without responding, and I didn't tell a soul, not even Roberta. When she found his San Antonio Spurs cap in the living room and demanded to know who it belonged to, I convinced her one of her sniffing admirers had left it behind. She had hung it on a peg in the entryway with a plethora of other hats and coats and umbrellas. Every morning before I left the apartment I touched the cap.

The morning-after text was the last time I'd heard from Duncan until he visited my room. I wonder if he'd stood there and congratulated himself for not ending his engagement and getting involved with me because then he'd feel obligated to the vegetable in bed 3.

Anyway, the bottom line is I'm fourteen weeks pregnant, and I have a laundry list of problems. The only person who knows who the father is can't talk or move. The medicine Dr. Jarvis gave me might have harmed the baby. If I don't wake up, who will raise the child? And if I do wake up, how well will I be, and what kind of mother would I make on my own?

I'm scared to death my family is going to take my baby. And I'm scared to death they won't.

September 5, Monday

"I'VE ALWAYS FELT GUILTY for having Labor Day off," my dad said. "I know my job contributes to the economy, but it's not like I'm working a jackhammer every day."

From his footsteps, I deduced he was pacing.

"But I do keep a mallet in my trunk in case I see a road sign that's fallen over. Did I ever tell you that's how I got the business for a country club in Peachtree City?"

Only a dozen times… but I'm happy to hear it again. And picture him acting it out.

"I was driving down the road and noticed a school sign was leaning way back. Those are reflective signs so they need to be standing straight or headlights can't catch them, and then what's the point? So I pulled over to straighten it, and a guy in a pickup truck stopped to help me. Looked like he didn't have a hundred dollars to his name. Turns out, he was developing a big country club down the road—the guy was a millionaire. He said he drove by that crooked sign every day and had been meaning to fix it. When he found out I was in the sign business, he gave me the account for the project without so much as a quote, just on a handshake. Said I was the kind of man he wanted to do business with."

He gave a happy little laugh at the memory, then he sighed. "I know most people don't give signs a second thought, but signs are critical to everyday life… and to law and order. Without signs, how would people know where they are or what to do?"

It's true when you think about it. Without signs, there would be total anarchy.

He walked back toward my bed and from the scrape of the chair, I knew he was sitting. "I wish I had a sign now to tell me what to do," he whispered, his voice anguished.

It pains me to be putting him through this. My father is not built to deal with emotional conflict.

"Your mother says I should stay out of the decision... and maybe I should. Otherwise she might oppose my opinion just to spite me." His voice broke off on a sob.

"What's wrong, Mister?"

The presence of another voice threw me for a few seconds. A memory chord stirred, but I couldn't place the child's voice.

My dad sniffed. "My daughter won't wake up."

"The magic lady is your daughter?"

Oh—it's the little girl who visited before.

"The magic lady?"

"See her pretty turban? She's magic."

He gave a little laugh. "You think she's magic, huh?"

"Uh-huh. She's going to make my mama better."

"Your mama is sick?"

"Uh-huh." She sighed. "I'm scared sometimes."

"I'm sorry. I'm scared sometimes, too."

I'd never witnessed my dad interact with a child before. It bore no resemblance to his standoffishness when I was little. But it gave me a glimpse into how he would be with a grandchild.

"What are you scared about?" she asked, her voice solemn.

"That my daughter might not wake up."

"Maybe that's how she does the magic," the little girl reasoned. "And then when the magic is all done, she'll wake up."

"I'll bet you're right," he said, and I could hear the smile in his words.

"Christina!" came a booming voice from the hall.

"I gots to go," she whispered. "Bye! Bye, Magic Lady!"

The patter of her departing footsteps blended with the rumble of Dad's low chuckle, then he sighed.

"Marigold, can you hear me?"

The chair squeaked.

"Marigold, I'm holding your hand. If you want me to fight for the baby, squeeze my hand."

I panicked. Did I want him to? Did I have the right?

"Sweetheart, if you can hear me, squeeze my hand if you want to keep the baby."

What if I were responsible for bringing a fatherless, disabled child into the world, and my family would have two of us to deal with?

"I didn't feel anything," he said.

Good. This was not the time for my brain to be sending involuntary signals to my fingers.

"Okay, squeeze my hand if you *don't* want to keep the baby."

Because in truth, even if I were well, I might be struggling with the decision to keep the baby. The fact that Duncan was marrying someone else could make things pretty unpleasant for everyone involved.

To squeeze or not to squeeze? If I even could.

"I guess you can't hear me," he said. "Okay. Goodbye for now. Keep doing your magic, Marigold."

September 6, Tuesday

"HEY, YOU'RE DOWN a roommate."

Our poet volunteer is back.

"I heard one of you dream girls got up and walked out of this place. So it was Audrey, huh? Go, Audrey. Are the rest of you giving her a head start before you bounce out of here, too?"

He couldn't know that Audrey's post-escape visit had been a downer to the point that if her old bed had been setting there, she might've crawled back into it.

"I like the new head scarf, Coma Girl. Pink and yellow and orange flowers, kind of a seventies vibe. Nice."

It sounds nice. I'm grateful he described the scarf. Sidney had brought the first wrap to cover up my bandages for a picture, and after she posted the photo on social media, scarves started pouring in. Store bought, handmade, and hand-me-downs. Now once a week, nurses gather up the extras, launder them, and take them to the chemotherapy department. And although someone or another usually changes my scarf every day, they usually don't think to describe it to me.

"If you ask me, women should wear scarves more often. It allows you to concentrate on a person's face, you know?"

Except I know my face is a cross-hatch of scars. He's being very kind... which makes me very suspicious. Because I suspect my kind visitor is the person who's been leaking photos and other information to the tabloids. I'm worried he can tell I'm pregnant... that I have a tummy bump showing through my hospital gown, or a nurse had unwittingly written it on my chart.

I heard the sound of pages being turned.

"I think I'll read this Dickinson poem. It's called 'A Charm Invests a

Face.'"

He shifted in the chair—was he using the book of poetry to hide his phone in case someone walked in while he was taking pictures?

"A charm invests a face, imperfectly beheld, the lady dare not lift her veil, for fear it be dispelled. But peers beyond her mesh, and wishes, and denies, lest interview annul a want, that image satisfies."

Damn… why does he have to pick such good poems, the ones that mean something?

"So are you hiding behind your veil, Coma Girl? Going to just lie there and be mysterious and pretty?"

According to Dickinson, it was better than opening one's mouth and dispelling the fantasy. Or as my boss Percy Palmer would tell his guys, "If you're an idiot, keep your dang mouth shut and no one will know for sure."

I heard a clicking noise… a camera? Or the book closing?

Then the door handle jostled and a rap sounded. "This door isn't supposed to be locked." It was Nurse Teddy. "Is someone in there?" More jostling sounded. "Hello? I'm getting security."

"I might not be able to visit again for a while," the visitor whispered. "Take care of each other."

Ah, so he *is* the source of the leak—why else would he lock the ward door when he came in? His hurried footsteps sounded and I heard the door open and close. But he must've locked the door behind him because when Teddy returned with someone I assumed was a security officer, they had to use a key. When they burst in, I could hear Teddy searching the room, pulling back curtains, and opening cabinets.

"Maybe one of the patients locked the door," the officer said with a little laugh.

Teddy wasn't amused. "Someone on staff must've accidentally locked the door as we left. But can you keep a closer eye on this room? We have a VIP in here and the press has been relentless."

"Sure thing," the guy said. "Hey, is this Coma Girl? My wife loves her. Can I take a selfie?"

September 7, Wednesday

"IT'S NOT TOO LATE to enroll for the semester," my mom said.

"We've been over this, Mother," Sidney said. "I'm needed here."

"I don't want this incident to derail your life. It's bad enough that Marigold might never get out of that bed, but I don't think I can bear it if this keeps you from graduating law school."

"Mom, nothing is going to keep me from graduating law school. And you heard Dr. Tyson—Marigold is getting better."

"She allegedly moved a finger, but we only have the doctors' word for it. I've asked her to squeeze my hand every time I've been here since they told us, and she hasn't squeezed my hand once. Watch."

Mom walked to my bed. "Marigold, can you move your fingers? Can you squeeze my hand?"

I'm trying.

"See? Nothing. It makes me wonder if they made it up."

"Why would they make it up?"

"To cover their butts and make it seem like the drug they gave her is working."

"I don't think—"

"And now on top of everything else, she's pregnant? What on earth was that girl thinking?"

I was thinking I wanted all of this to happen, Mother.

"I'm sure Marigold didn't mean to get pregnant," Sidney chided.

"No, but she was being careless, just like the night of the crash."

"Mother, Keith Young was driving drunk, remember?"

"Well, maybe if Marigold hadn't been talking on the phone with that dreadful roommate of hers, she could've avoided the crash."

So Sidney had told Mom I was distracted when the accident happened.

"Don't repeat that, Mother. I lied to the police to protect Marigold, and they can't prove otherwise."

"I won't. But the point is, Marigold isn't the one dealing with the fallout of her poor choices—we are."

Hello? I'm in a coma. That's not punishment enough?

"Mom, Dad's right—we can't terminate the pregnancy. It's wrong."

I admire Sidney's conviction. I don't know if I could be so sure if I were making this decision for someone else… or even for myself.

"More wrong than bringing a possibly damaged baby into the world?" my mother asked. "I don't mean to sound selfish, but I have to consider the worst-case scenario. What if Marigold doesn't recover? I don't know if I can deal with raising a child at this stage of my life, especially a child with special needs."

She's right. It's not fair to expect her to take on that responsibility.

"I could take it," Sidney offered.

My heart swelled.

"Absolutely not. You have to graduate law school and someday you'll have babies of your own. I'm not going to let you ruin your life by taking on someone else's problem."

Okay, that stings. But neither can I argue with her points.

"Mother, I think the best thing to do is to let nature take its course. If the baby isn't well, she'll miscarry. Or if we learn in the next few weeks the baby has grievous defects and won't survive, or is putting Marigold's life in danger, then we can ask the doctors to intervene."

"You're right," my mother said. "But we still haven't addressed what to do with the child once it's born if Marigold can't take care of it."

"We don't have to make that decision right now," Sidney soothed. "But in the short term, announcing Marigold is pregnant will help her case and put more pressure on the A.D.A. to prosecute once the result of Keith Young's blood alcohol content test is confirmed. And we need to be ready to file a civil suit."

"You think?"

"Definitely. Keith Young has celebrity on his side, so we need an ace in the hole to get his legal team to settle quickly. Now we're facing not only long-term medical bills and care for Marigold, but also a child."

"When will you make the announcement?"

"David and I will work that out. Until then, no one can know—not even Aunt Winnie. And I'm going to have another talk with Dr. Tyson— another photo of Marigold was leaked to the tabloids this morning. That's bad enough, but this piece of information can't get out before we're ready."

"What about the father? If we announce Marigold is pregnant, what if he comes forward and wants to be involved somehow?"

"That could complicate things," Sidney agreed.

"What if he's unbearable? What if it's her hairy boss, for God's sake?"

I could do worse, Mother.

"I'll see if I can find out who it might be before we go public with the news in case we need to do some damage control," Sid said. "The police still have our phones, which is making me crazy. I'll visit that detective with the swagger. Maybe he'll help me get them back. He seems to have a soft spot for Marigold."

"Okay. So, we're going public with the news, and we're letting nature take its course."

"I think that's best," Sidney said.

I am beyond relieved. Because I don't know if I would've had the courage to make the right decision on my own.

My mother sighed. "Well, you're always right, Sidney, so I trust you now, too."

Her voice was soft and I imagined her cupping my sister's face with her hand. I've tried not to be envious of their closer bond, but I confess it's still hard to witness.

"Hm, are those new earrings?"

Sid gave a little laugh. "David bought them for me."

"Wow, first the watch, and now the earrings. They look expensive, too."

"He has good taste."

"He likes you, so yes, he does have good taste."

They had another mother-daughter moment, then Mom announced she had to get to a closing. That billboard on GA-400 must be working.

"I'll stay and say goodbye to Marigold," Sid said.

That's nice of her. And I hope she takes my hand because I want to try to let her know how much I appreciate what she did for me and my baby.

But once the door closed, I heard her rummage in her purse, then make a phone call. Since the police still had our phones, Sid must've purchased another phone after the accident.

"David, it's me. You know that exclusive announcement we talked about for my appearance on *The Doctors*? We've got it, babe, and it's going to blow everyone away."

Within a few hours, we'd gone from a possible abortion to announcing my pregnancy on a nationally syndicated television show. So Sidney had made the right decision... but for the wrong reason?

September 8, Thursday

"COMA GIRL, what's going on?"

Roberta floated into the room on a coconut-scented breeze and fell into the chair next to my bed.

"I mean it—what's going on? Your sister showed up at the apartment this morning and asked if we could have a chat."

Sidney? Where is this going?

"I don't have to tell you after she accused me of being a thief when all I did was *borrow* your Chloe purse, I wasn't too keen on chatting. But since she brought breakfast from The Flying Biscuit as a peace offering, I let her in. French toast is a weakness."

Roberta has lots of weaknesses.

"Anyway, she said she's going on that television show *The Doctors* to talk about your coma and she needed some recent photos of you. I think it's kind of strange that your own sister doesn't have pictures of you, but now that I think about it, maybe it was a ploy to get in the apartment and look around."

The sound of a bag ripping rent the air. "I brought us a cinnamon coffee cake to split, does that sound good?"

Indeed it does.

"So like I was saying," she said through a full mouth, "your sis walked around the apartment looking at pictures of you in frames. I let her take some of them and I gave her some pictures from my phone because I want you to look good on TV, you know? Don't worry, I didn't show her the ones where we drank too much sangria and drew mustaches on each other with Sharpies." She laughed. "Do you remember how long it took for those to wear off?"

I remember. I'd resorted to wearing Band-aids over mine until the permanent marker grew off.

"She took the one of us singing karaoke, said she didn't know you could sing. I told her you were a hit that night, that people kept asking you to come back up and do another song. Girl, you missed your calling, shoulda tried out for *American Idol*."

Roberta is being kind, but I do enjoy singing. Funny how reciting a poem in front of class left my knees knocking with stage fright, but put a microphone in my hand, and get out of my way.

"But looks like you're going to make it on TV after all. *The Doctors* is a big honking deal. I'll bet you get so much fan mail, the super will have to move our mail to a separate box all on its own. He's still complaining, but I've been dropping off day-old cookies from the bakery, and the last time he brought the mail by, I answered the door in my bra and that seemed to grease his wheels."

I'll just bet.

"Your sister asked me if you had any family photos, but I don't remember seeing any."

Because they were scarce. Apparently Sidney hadn't been able to find any at home, either. Roberta took another big bite of cake and kept right on talking.

"And she asked me all kinds of questions about if you dated and who you dated and if you were seeing anyone special. I told her no, that you'd met up with a few guys on line, but it hadn't amounted to anything. I didn't mention Duncan because the two of you were never really an item and besides, he's getting married."

Good girl.

"Get this—she asked if anything was going on between you and Mr. Palmer—that made me belly laugh. And she asked me if you'd hooked up with anyone right before the accident. Nobody came to mind, but I asked her why. She said she and your parents just wanted to make sure they had contacted all the people who were important in your life."

It sounds plausible.

"She asked for your mail, said they were going to post some of the letters on your Facebook page, so I thought it was okay to give her the ones I'd already opened and read to you. Things got a little touchy when she asked me if anyone had sent cash. I told her I was keeping it in an envelope for you in the freezer. I thought she'd make a fuss, but she just said thanks for being such a good friend, and promised to bring me back an autographed picture of that yummy popsicle Dr. Travis from the show. I mean, honestly, what doctor looks like that?"

I'm glad Sidney was cordial to Roberta.

She licked her fingers. "Oh, and Marco is back and guess what? He bought a new big-screen TV for the living room! You're going to love it. It's humungous, one of those curved models. He has a new job and is making great money. He filed the divorce papers, so we're good. He's even been talking about us getting married, having a family of our own. I've never thought about having a baby before, have you?"

I want to belly laugh.

September 9, Friday

"PEACE BE WITH YOU, ladies."

And also with you. I was happy to see Sister Irene hadn't been arrested for murdering the man who killed her sister.

Yet.

"So it's true, then," the nun said, her voice high and sunny. "Audrey did wake up. What a glorious miracle. I wish the same for you, Karen, and you, Jill, and you, Marigold."

She prayed over each of us, stopping at my bed last. And since I've been contemplating the miracle of the life growing inside me, I actually listened this time and even joined in the prayer Sister Irene uttered.

You see, I've been negotiating with God lately. Okay, I realize He's holding all the cards, but I'm prepared to do just about anything if he will take care of my baby. Here's what I'm offering:

I will stop taking His name in vain—although it's such a habit, it might take some time.

I will strive to forgive people who have wronged me, including Keith Young. Although I'm a little conflicted between not wanting him to suffer, but hoping he can cough up enough cash to cover my medical bills and the repairs on my car.

I will stop fornicating. Okay, that one's only applicable if I get out of this bed. But now I totally get the monumental potential of creating a human being every time I have sex. My hormones have been scared straight.

I will try to mend my family. I don't know where things went wrong, but I know there is much disharmony among the Kemps. I've always had the feeling I was at the heart of my family's discontent, maybe even the cause. But I realize that's a selfish point of view—it's not about me. And now that I'm an adult, I share some of the blame if my family is in disarray.

I want a chance to fix things. And if I don't wake up, I hope my child will be the conduit for love I haven't been.

For the record, God hasn't let me in on whether it's enough, or how long he'll make me wait to find out.

"How are you, Marigold?" Sister Irene asked. "You look especially peaceful today, like someone who has forgiven trespasses." She sighed. "You might be wondering where I am on my own path of forgiveness."

I *so* am, considering the last time she visited, she talked about filleting her sister's paroled murderer and cutting him up into chunks.

"Sadly, I'm not there yet," she whispered. "But I've been reading the Bible every day."

That sounds promising.

"You know, Ecclesiastes 3:3 says there is a time to kill."

Uh-oh.

"So I bought a big knife."

Yikes.

"Shhhh," she said close to my ear. "Don't tell anyone."

As if.

September 10, Saturday

I NEVER KNOW what Saturdays will be like. Sometimes we have many visitors because people are off work, and sometimes we have few visitors because people are off work and would rather do just about anything other than visit the vegetable patch.

Today all my people are obviously out doing more fun things. But over in bed two, Karen Suh has a visitor. Her ex-husband Jonas is back, and he brought flowers.

"Hi, Karen," he said. "I've been doing some work at the house, and the jasmine bushes were so full, I thought I'd cut some for you."

The scent is heavenly.

"I hope you don't mind," he said. "But I drove by the house a couple of weeks ago and noticed there were a few things that needed to be done, so I've been going over after work and taking care of things. I, um, still have a key."

So it was the house they have lived in when they were married.

"I let Mrs. Baxter know I'd be in and out so she wouldn't think I was a burglar." He gave a little laugh. "She wanted to know if my name is still on the deed and I told her it is, that we hadn't gotten around to filing a quitclaim before you—" His voice broke off, then he recovered. "Before your accident. But she was nice and asked about you. I told her you're still recovering and will be waking up soon."

He sounded wistful. The man obviously still had a lot of affection for his ex-wife.

"The back yard was a mess," he continued. "Lightning got the pear tree, split it in two. Branches were on the ground, and debris everywhere. I repaired the swing and fixed a couple of loose boards in the fence."

He dragged a chair across the floor. "Inside, there was a leak in the master bathroom, so the floor will need to be replaced. And there's some damage to the dining room ceiling, but it won't take me long to fix it. But some of the pictures that were sitting on the sideboard are ruined. Not sure why you still have pictures of us sitting around anyway, after what I did to you... to us."

Ah... a story.

"If I could rewind the clock, I would in a minute," he said, sounding like a broken man. "If I hadn't cheated, we wouldn't have gotten divorced, and you wouldn't have climbed that ladder."

To clean the gutters, I recall. Only to fall and wind up in this bed. A freak accident, and Jonas Suh felt responsible for setting in motion the series of events that led up to it.

"If I'd done the right thing, this wouldn't have happened. I wish God had punished me instead of you."

Although it sounds as if he is punishing himself plenty.

"If you can hear me, Karen, please forgive me. And come back to me."

If my Aunt Winnie's rinky-dink psychic is to be believed, Karen Suh is still aware. What was it Audrey had said? That she'd needed something to latch onto to bring her back. For Karen, I hope it's the voice of someone who still cares about her.

September 11, Sunday

"BRAVES AND METS at home," Detective Jack Terry said. "It doesn't get better than that."

He's baaaaaack.

"I brought burgers and sweet potato fries. Are you hungry?"

Ugh, no. It must be the baby, because food doesn't smell as good as it used to.

"Did you miss me last Sunday? Come on, Marigold, I'll bet you did."

Okay, maybe a smidgen.

"Trust me, I would've rather been here watching the game with you. I went house-hunting."

Wow.

He ripped open a bag. "I know—I can't believe those words came out of my mouth. And yes, it was just as awful as it sounds. More, even. It's a damn project. There's trying to decide what part of town to live in, then what kind of house, yard, garage you want, in what kind of community. How the traffic flows, the crime rate, what school system you're in."

School system? Jack has children?

He groaned and I visualized him pulling his hand down over his face. "I'm not cut out for domesticity."

Was he getting married? Moving in with someone?

"I guess that's why people pay agents like your mother to do the legwork for them. I'm kind of obligated to call this one agent who's a friend of a friend, but I dread it because… well, you don't want to hear my problems."

Oh, but I do. Don't stop now.

"The Falcons play today, too," he offered, changing the subject. "First game of the regular season. Keith Young is supposed to start. He's allowed to play until results of his blood alcohol test are confirmed, then we'll see. But by then, he'll have two or three games under his belt."

And if he racks up stats, he will be harder to prosecute.

"On another note, your sister came down to the station yesterday to see me. Wanted your phones back, said she had to find the phone numbers of some friends of yours to let them know what happened. I can't release them while the case is still open, but against my better judgment, I let her go through your phone."

No worries—Sidney won't find anything on my phone that will lead her to Duncan—no racy selfies or sexts, no chummy IM's or flirtatious Facebook posts. I don't think his last name—Wheeler—is even listed on his contacts page.

"I feel as if I violated your privacy, even though she's your sister." He sighed. "Did I do the right thing?"

I'm touched Jack is worried he did something to upset the girl in the coma. Is he usually this sensitive? Or is he projecting onto me because I can't interact with him and I'm safe?

September 12, Monday

"DOES MARIGOLD SEEM different to you?" Nurse Teddy asked.

"No," Gina responded in her high 'I'm lying' voice.

"Come on, spill. What's going on?"

"I don't know what you mean."

"Okay, I guess you'll tell me when you're ready," he groused. "How are things with you and Gabriel?"

"Couldn't be better," she said happily. "So well, in fact, I think I'm going to introduce him to my son next week."

"Ooh, so the nookie is good?"

"I wouldn't know," she said primly. "My rule is no nookie the first ninety days."

"Damn, really?"

"If a guy can't wait ninety days, he's not worth keeping around."

How very refreshing.

"How many men fail the ninety-day test?"

She sighed. "So far, all of them."

How very depressing.

"But I think Gabriel is different," she added.

"I hope you're right."

The door opened.

"Dr. Jarvis," Gina exclaimed. "You're back."

My hero has returned from exile.

"Were you away?" Teddy asked, sounding confused.

"Um, just for a few days," Dr. Jarvis said. "Teddy, would you mind to get me another lab coat?"

"Okay," Teddy said, his voice suspicious. "Be back in a jif."

When the door closed behind him, Gina said, "You're not in trouble anymore?"

"Tyson let me out of jail, but I'm still on probation. I understand the family wants to keep the baby?"

"Yes. But the pregnancy is top secret, even from the rest of the staff, so the family can make the announcement when they're ready."

"Mum's the word."

"Thanks, Dr. Jarvis, for not mentioning that I helped administer the drug."

"I told you I'd take full responsibility."

"No offense, but people don't always do what they say."

"You're obviously spending time with the wrong people," he said.

I can't feel anything, but even I detect electricity in the air.

The door opened and Teddy returned. "One lab coat."

"Thank you," Dr. Jarvis said. "Have either of you asked Marigold to respond to commands this morning?"

"Not yet," Gina said. "We only just finished her bath. And fyi, Ms. Kemp hasn't responded to Dr. Tyson's commands in three days."

Jarvis made a concerned noise. "Okay, let's test her. Marigold, it's Dr. Jarvis. I need for you to do something for me. I need for you to blink. Can you blink?"

135

I tried. How hard could it be to blink?

"No? Then Gina, will you take her right hand, and Teddy, will you take her left? Hold her fingers lightly and let me know if you feel any movement, no matter how small."

I readied myself mentally.

"Okay, Marigold, let's repeat something you've already done. Move the fingers on your right hand. Can you move your fingers, Marigold?"

I played the brain-bone-is-connected-to-the-finger-bone song in my head.

"Anything?" he asked.

"No," Gina said.

"Marigold, now try to move the fingers on your left hand. Can you do it? Can you move the fingers on your left hand?"

Again, I focused like a laser.

"Anything?" he asked.

"Nothing," Teddy said.

Dr. Jarvis sighed. "Okay, we'll try again tomorrow."

But the disappointment in his voice is loud and clear. I try not to let my lack of response bother me, but I remember the conversation between Dr. Tyson and my mother about the baby consuming resources. Was it the cause of my setback?

September 13, Tuesday

"GUESS WHO?"

I recognize Aunt Winnie's voice, and the slide of Faridee's sandals. I guess that makes me psychic.

"Your mother won't return my calls," Winnie said. "So I thought I'd come and check on you myself."

Mom is probably afraid she'll inadvertently spill the beans about the baby ahead of Sidney's TV appearance this Friday.

"Faridee is with me," my aunt said. "But I completed the workshop on communicating in the next dimension, so I'm going to try to make contact with you, too."

"Don't forget to call on the power of the amulet," Faridee whispered.

"Oh, right," my aunt said.

Oh, brother.

The sounds of hands clapping and rubbing filled the air, followed by the scent of sage and cloves. "Hello, Marigold," Faridee said. "Move toward me and I will move toward you."

The previous attempts to send an empirical message to the woman had failed miserably, so this time I decided to just hang.

"Where are you?" Faridee sang.

Right here. See? I'm waving.

"Oh, there you are," Faridee said. "Have you made contact, Winnie?"

"I don't believe so," my aunt said. "I don't feel anything yet."

"It's not a feeling—it's a sensing."

"A sensing," Winnie repeated.

"Do you sense Marigold's spirit? She's reaching out to us."

"Reaching," Winnie whispered.

What, no sales pitch, Faridee?

"Because Marigold's spirit has ascended so high, you might need to take my advanced seminar in order to connect with her," Faridee said.

And there it is.

"When are you next giving the advanced version?" my aunt asked.

"Tomorrow."

How convenient.

"I'll be there. Is Marigold any closer to coming back to us?"

"Yes, I believe so."

"Is she still hanging out with the Pope?"

Yes, Winnie. Pope John Paul and I are thick.

"She's—"

"Faridee? What do you see?"

"I see... two Marigolds."

Oh, here we go. More vague metaphors.

"Two? You mean one here and one in the spirit world?"

"No."

How about a good Marigold and a bad one? A fat Marigold and a thin one?

"One Marigold is young, and one Marigold is old."

Wait—a big me and a mini me? Does Faridee see my baby?

"What does that mean?" my aunt asked.

"I don't... know." Faridee grunted. "I lost her."

"Darn it! I totally missed out."

"We'll try again soon, after the seminar," Faridee assured her.

"Okay."

My aunt sounded like a disappointed child.

"Goodbye, Marigold, my love. We'll be back whenever I can sneak another visit past your mother."

"Wait," Faridee said.

"What is it?"

"Someone else in the room is trying to reach me."

I listened as her sandals moved away from me.

"Yes, Karen, I hear you," she said in an odd voice. "Yes, I'll write it down." Then she whispered, "Winnie, do you have something to write with?"

Winnie carries a huge bag of oddball stuff. She'd be the one in the audience of *Let's Make a Deal* who could pull a gerbil out of her purse on command.

"Here's a pen... and a notepad."

"Okay, I'm ready," Faridee said. "Okay.... okay.... okay... okay.... okay. Got it."

"What's the message?" Winnie asked in a hushed voice.

I'm skeptical, sure it's a missive from "beyond" for Winnie to hand over the PIN number to her debit card.

"Dear Jonas," Faridee said. "I never liked that pear tree."

"What does it mean?"

"I have no idea. But I'll pin it to her gown, and maybe it will make sense to someone."

Okay, y'all... I'm a believer.

September 14, Wednesday

"WHEW, NOW EVERYONE has clean sheets," Gina said. "Thanks for helping me, Gabriel."

"You're welcome, baby. I'm looking forward to seeing you tonight."

Gina gave a little laugh. "Same here. But it's 'Gina' at work, okay?"

"Sorry. You just look so beautiful today, I forgot myself. But I'll save it for tonight."

"Okay," she said, her voice fading as she walked toward the door, "but you know my ninety-day rule. See you at seven."

"Uh-huh."

When the door closed, he grunted like a man denied a treasure. Then he walked around the ward gathering up discarded bedclothes, whistling under his breath.

"What's this?" he murmured.

Paper crackled.

"'Dear Jonas, I never liked that pear tree.' Huh?"

Ack—the note Faridee had written for Karen Suh yesterday and pinned to her gown. It must've fallen off when they shuffled us around to change the sheets. I was hoping Jonas would be back to visit before it was lost.

The sound of paper being crumpled into a ball tears at me. I wonder if Karen can hear it, too.

The door opened.

"Oh—hi, Gabriel."

"Hi, Donna," he said, his voice rich with innuendo. "Just the person I was hoping to see."

What an indiscriminate flirt.

"Are we still on for tonight?" she asked.

"Yeah, but it'll be nine before I can get to your place."

So an early date with Gina, then a late date with Donna?

"I'll make it worth the wait," she promised.

He gave a deep laugh. "How about a little preview now?"

Kissing noises sounded.

"Stop, Gabriel, we can't."

"Why not? No one will be looking for me for another thirty minutes."

"What if someone comes in?"

"Into the vegetable patch? No one comes in here. These patients don't have to be fed, they never push a help button, and visitors are few and far between. It's a pretty depressing place."

More kissing noises.

"Still… it doesn't feel right."

"Oh, baby, it feels right to me. Come on. You got me so hot and bothered, it's not going to take long."

"Okay," she relented. "But hurry."

Oh, my God—they're not really going to have sex right in front of me.

Thirty seconds later, moans and groans sounded, then a distinctive rhythmic thump.

They really are having sex right in front of me.

I'm caught between fascination and horror, admiration and disgust. Having sex in a coma ward is akin to having sex in a cemetery. But worse, because we're not dead yet.

Although I have to admit, it's the best entertainment I've had all day. And it's the closest thing to getting laid we veggies have experienced in months, and in some cases, years.

True to his word, Gabriel did not take long. I was hoping Gina would walk in at the event's climax, but alas, it didn't happen. The couple disengaged with a sucking noise of unknown origin, then quickly said goodbye "until later." Donna left first, and Gabriel, the cad, took his time gathering linen and reorganizing the cart.

The door opened and I was afraid Donna had come back for another round.

"Oh, you're still here," Gina said.

"Guess I was daydreaming about you," Gabriel gushed.

She laughed. "You're making me impatient to see you tonight. Let me help you with that cart."

After they left the room, I lay there marveling at how lopsided relationships can be. And how the person who cares the least always has the upper hand.

September 15, Thursday

"DO YOURSELF A big, big favor," Joanna Fitz said. "Don't ever have kids."

I wish I could tell her the ship has sailed on that one, but even if I could talk, she doesn't seem to be in a mood to listen... only in a mood to drink.

"First, it wrecks your figure. Your ass gets wide and your boobs get long—it ain't pretty. Then your hormones get out of whack and you have mood swings like a human pendulum. You want to bite the head off of everyone you meet, and wash it down with a bottle of wine."

The mention of wine must've reminded her she'd brought a flask of rum, because she took a hearty drink. Joanna has been here for thirty minutes and she has to be near the bottom.

"And your husband starts seeing you as this mother-blob. He's not attracted to you anymore because he's seen what goes on behind the curtain, if you know what I mean. Not that you want to have sex anyway because you're scared to death you're going to get pregnant again."

That's nice.

"And then you start to hate your children," she slurred. "The sound of them crying is like an icepick to your eardrums, and the only way hearing them yell *mommy* works is if you turn it into a drinking game."

Which reminds her to take another drink.

"So you get together with all the other wide-assed, long-boobed mothers and start betting on the age of your husband's next girlfriend. And when you win the pool, you buy yourself a diamond watch. See?"

I can't see it, but I get the gist.

"And then you start fantasizing about ways to murder your husband, and how you could get away with it. I could smother him... shoot him... poison him... stab him... cut his brake line... or push him off our houseboat and run over him with the propeller and say it was an accident."

Okay, that last one seems a bit more well-thought-out than the others.

"I could do it... I've seen every last episode of *Forensics Files*."

Me, too! But I've never considered it a tutorial.

The door opened.

"Sorry, ma'am," Gina said, "but visiting hours are over."

"Okay," Joanna slurred. "I'm leaving." I heard her screw the top back on the metal flask, then the chair creaked, indicating she'd stood.

"Whoa, there." Gina rushed over, presumably to steady Joanna. "Why don't I call you a cab?"

"Probably a good idea, since I'm not supposed to be driving. My license was suspended over two lousy DUI's, can you believe it? I should've driven over my husband's dick." She laughed at her own joke.

"Okay, steady," Gina said. "One foot in front of the other. I'll get you a cup of strong coffee while you wait."

"Don't have kids, Marigold," Joanna shouted. "Don't ever have kids!"

September 16, Friday

"THIS IS SO EXCITING," my mom said.

She had convinced Teddy to filch a television from the doctors' lounge and invited Aunt Winnie to watch Sidney's live segment on *The Doctors* from my room.

"Except for the fact that Sidney's TV debut is to talk about Marigold being in a coma," Winnie added lightly.

"Well, yes," my mother agreed sourly. "Sidney's just trying to make the best out of a bad situation."

"I guess I'm still not sure what this is supposed to accomplish," Winnie said.

"If you're going to talk the whole time, you can go."

"Okay, I'm being quiet."

The volume increased and I could hear applause.

"Welcome back to the show for a special live segment of *The Doctors*. In our studio today is Sidney Kemp, sister of the young woman many of you may know as Coma Girl. Please welcome, Sidney Kemp."

Applause and cheers sounded.

"Oh, there she is!" my mom said. "Doesn't she look beautiful?"

"She does," my aunt agreed.

"Thank you," Sidney said, her voice modulated and pleasing.

"Sidney, your sister Coma Girl has been in a coma in an Atlanta hospital since a car accident over three months ago. How is she doing?"

"She's doing well, considering the circumstances. She's responding to commands to move her fingers, so we have reason to believe she's getting better and will hopefully wake up soon."

Applause sounded.

"And you were in the accident with your sister, is that right?"

"Yes," Sidney said. "It could've just as easily been me in the coma and my sister sitting here talking to you."

"Except Marigold would never go on TV to talk about her comatose sister," Winnie said.

"Shhhh!"

"And on the large screen behind you, Sidney, are some pictures of Coma Girl before the coma, right?"

"Yes, this picture was taken of Coma Girl when she was singing karaoke with friends. She had a great singing voice."

"And this picture?"

"That's Coma Girl in her hospital bed, and me painting her fingernails. It's one way I can interact with my sister."

"Our hearts are breaking for you," the host said. "I know we can't talk about the accident that put your sister in a coma because it's still an open case."

"That's right," Sidney said. "And since I'm in law school, I can't plead ignorance of the statutes."

"Oh, you're in law school?'

"Yes, third year at Boston. Well, I'm sitting out this semester to help with my family's situation."

"Well, she got in a good plug for herself," Winnie said.

"Shhhh!"

The host made a mournful noise. "I can only imagine what you and your family have been going through."

"And Marigold," Winnie muttered.

"Shhhh!"

"We're doing the best we can," Sidney said. "All the great cards and social media posts to hashtag Coma Girl have been a real boon to our spirits."

More applause sounded.

"But you're here today," the host said, "for a special update on Coma Girl exclusively for our viewers. What can you tell us?"

"Even in the darkest situation," Sidney said, her voice wavering, "a beacon of light can appear."

"What is she talking about?" Winnie asked.

"Shhhh!"

"And our beacon of light is finding out that Coma Girl is pregnant."

Exclamations sounded from the TV, then the audience erupted into wild applause.

"Look, they're giving her a standing ovation!" my mother said.

"Oh, poor Marigold," Winnie murmured.

"A reminder," the host said, "that Coma Girl T-shirts and scarves are available on the Coma Girl website and Facebook page. All proceeds will go toward medical expenses and to the Coma Girl Foundation."

Aunt Winnie gasped. "The baby—that's what the psychic meant by two Marigolds!"

"Psychic?" my mother asked. "What psychic?"

While the two of them bickered over the closing credits of the show, I contemplated the fallout of the announcement. I'd counted the number of times they'd said Coma Girl and the number of times they'd said my name.

Coma Girl: 11, Marigold Kemp: 0.

September 17, Saturday

"I ALMOST SWALLOWED a biscuit," Roberta said.

Roberta had been eating when she watched Sidney's announcement—shocker.

"I called in sick to work so I could watch it. Then I was like, 'Did she just say Coma Girl is *pregnant*?' Last time I checked you have to have sex to get knocked up, and I thought we had an agreement that you would tell me if you ever got yourself laid."

In fairness, *she* had agreed I would tell her, not me.

"So that explains why your sister was asking all those questions about if you were seeing anyone right before the accident. They don't know who the baby-daddy is."

Bingo.

"Okay, you gotta wake up and tell me. Right now—wake the hell *up*."

She said it with such force, I'm kind of surprised I didn't just snap out of it.

Roberta heaved a sigh. "Now I have to speculate. Since you didn't tell me you got some sausage, that means you're embarrassed or ashamed. Is it your boss, Mr. Palmer? If it is, that's gonna be one hairy baby."

Really, Roberta?

"Is it someone you met online for a hookup? I think not, since you and I both watched the YouTube video about what you can catch from one unprotected date-site wiener—ugh. Herpes? MRSA? Zika?"

Right. A girl might as well ride the door handle of a porta-john.

"Is he married?"

No, but you're getting warmer.

Suddenly she snapped her fingers. "It's hat guy! I found that hat in the living room a week or so before your accident and you said you didn't know whose it was. You little liar. You lie like the carpet you sell, Marigold Kemp."

She was right. I lied.

"What was on that hat? Some NBA team logo. The Houston Rockets?"

The San Antonio Spurs.

"Golden State Warriors?"

The San Antonio Spurs.

"New York Knicks?'

The San Antonio Spurs.

"Well, anyway, it's still hanging on the rack in the entryway. I bet if I can find a guy to claim the hat, he's the one."

A big if.

"I'm gonna get a cute detective outfit and get right on that case. Roberta Hazzard, P.I.—how does that sound?"

Pretty good, actually.

"And every detective needs a prop—Colombo had his cigar, and Kojak had his lollipop. Mine will be a bear claw. *Grrrr.* Okay, I gotta run."

Her footsteps headed toward the door, then she stopped.

"By the way, remember that cute reporter I told you about? He contacted me again, wants to have lunch, said he would pay me a co-writing fee for a story about our friendship, said it might even lead to a book deal—imagine that. I told him I don't think so. But it sure sounds exciting. Later, Coma Girl."

A story about our friendship? More likely, he wants the inside scoop on the father of my child. Which makes me wonder if this reporter is the driving force behind Roberta's 'detective' work?

September 18, Sunday

"WELL, WELL, WELL," Jack Terry said when he strolled in. "Marigold, you know how to keep a secret."

Inside I was squirming a little. I'm not sure why this man's opinion of me mattered. If not for the accident, our lives wouldn't have intersected. I didn't mind what the world at large thought of me, but I didn't want the detective to think ill of me, to think I was just another careless young woman who'd gotten liquored-up and slept with the first guy who crawled into her bed.

Well... okay, so the liquored-up part is true... and Duncan is the first guy who'd crawled into my bed. But... but... but...

Never mind. I have no moral ground to stand on.

"So that's why your sister wanted to go through your phone—your family doesn't know who the father is. Your family doesn't know much about your life, do they?"

It doesn't take a detective to figure that out, Detective.

"I've never seen so many balloons and flowers... is one of them from the father?" He gave a little laugh. "This one is from Elton John, so I'm going to say no. I heard your sister made the announcement on a national show, so I guess this is what she wanted to happen."

He made a rueful noise.

"I got a call from the A.D.A.—she feels a little blindsided. But maybe that was part of the plan, too? You at least got her attention."

It's Sidney's plan... and it sounds as if it's working.

"I brought you a bandana."

Really?

"It has little teddy bears on it," he said, sounding sheepish. "I'm not good at this stuff, but I thought it was cute. I'll tie it on the bedrail next to the rosary. You don't have to wear it, or even keep it. I'm sure you have nicer stuff."

But not from a nicer guy.

Since Friday I've been thinking about Duncan nonstop. Sidney said the ratings for the show were through the roof, and the segment has been viewed online almost ten million times. I have a new hashtag, ComaGirlBaby, and my story is on the top fold of every national newspaper, next to election coverage. Everyone is rooting for me, and I'm being held up as a victim of a drunk driver, a victim of pro athlete elitism, even a victim of a healthcare system that has no good place for long-term care patients with short-term needs. Coma Girl seems to have captured the imagination and the heart of most Americans... except for Duncan Wheeler. Unless he's been living under a rock, he has to know about the baby, has to have done the math in his head and know it's his. The fact that he's staying away sends a message loud and clear that he doesn't want anything to do with me, or the baby.

"Braves and Nationals at home today," Jack said, but he sounded distant and distracted.

I was thinking about a baby and how my life is forever changed. I wonder what has his mind occupied?

September 19, Monday

"I WOULD'VE APPRECIATED a heads up," ADA Spence said, "before you made the announcement on national television."

"It wasn't my idea," my father said.

"Everyone knows that," my mother said, and not as a compliment.

"You know about the baby now," David Spooner said. "So what are you going to do?"

"I can't do anything until Young's blood alcohol content lab results are confirmed."

"And if they come back again at .01 above the legal limit?" Sidney asked.

"If the results are the same, or higher, then we have two victims instead of one, and we'll go after him with all the might of the D.A.'s office."

"Good," my mother said. "All we want is justice for Marigold and the baby."

"How will the Falcons play into this?" my dad asked. "Keith Young is having a great season so far. I can't turn on the news without seeing his face."

"It'll be touchy, but the owners and coaching staff want to do the right thing. Just keep in mind that allowing Young to play might be the best thing for Marigold and the baby."

"How's that?" my dad demanded.

David Spooner coughed politely. "If Keith Young continues to play, his net worth will be higher."

"Which means," Sidney added, "the monetary award from a civil case would be higher."

"But only if the criminal case is successful?"

"We can still file a civil suit regardless of the outcome of the criminal trial, or even if charges don't go forward," Spooner said. "But it'll be stronger going in with a conviction on our side."

I noticed his sly insertion of "we" and "our."

A gonging noise sounded, sending a strange vibration through my brain.

"Sorry," Sidney said, rummaging noisily through her bag. "I need to take this call."

"Now?" David asked.

"It concerns school," Sidney said evenly. "I'll take it in the hall."

She left the room, and the discussion resumed, but I tuned it out.

Something about the gonging ringtone had seemed familiar, but the memory that went along with it remained tantalizingly out of reach. And the more I chased it, the farther it receded.

September 20, Tuesday

"CROWD IN AROUND bed three," Dr. Tyson said. "Move the balloons aside."

Ah, time for show and tell.

"Patient is a twenty-eight-year-old female recovering from a traumatic brain injury received in a car accident approximately sixteen weeks ago. She was unconscious when she arrived at Brady. She underwent surgery to relieve bleeding on the brain. She has not yet regained consciousness. Also, the patient is sixteen weeks pregnant. Questions? Gaynor, go."

"What is the state of the brain bleed?"

"Stable and healing, some swelling remains. Streeter, go."

"Is the patient verbal?"

"No. Sayna, go."

"Does the patient still exhibit brainwave activity?"

"Yes. Goldberg, go."

"Does the patient respond to commands to blink or to move her extremities?"

Tyson hesitated.

"Sometimes," a voice piped up.

Dr. Jarvis, my hero.

"I've got this, Jarvis," Dr. Tyson said. "Sometimes," she repeated.

"More often than not?"

She didn't respond at first. "Go ahead, Jarvis. She's your patient as much as mine."

"The answer is… no," Dr. Jarvis said, speaking more slowly. "More often the patient doesn't respond, and in fact, her responses are declining."

"When was the peak response time?"

"Two weeks ago," Jarvis said.

"Could the fetus be negatively affecting the patient's neural recovery?"

Dr. Jarvis didn't answer.

"Yes, indirectly," Dr. Tyson said, her voice dragging. "We believe the increased volume of fluids and more circulatory demands could be stalling the brain heal… or even eroding it."

Eroding? That's not good.

"Tosco, go."

"What are the chances the baby will be brought to full term?"

"Good to very good."

Whew.

"Gaynor, go."

"And what is the prognosis of the patient?"

I'm waiting… and waiting…

"Um… let's move on to the maternity ward."

Is she running late, or avoiding the question?

"But before we leave I'd like to remind everyone this patient is receiving a lot of media attention and as such, you might be approached by reporters or others for information on her condition, or the baby's. If that happens, keep your mouth shut and call the police. Are there any questions?"

"I have a question."

"Go, Tosco."

"Can you address the rumor going around that this patient is receiving special treatment?"

"Such as?"

"Such as experimental drugs?"

I held my breath.

"Since you brought it up, yes, Dr. Jarvis has administered an experimental treatment to this patient that was completely unauthorized. Dr. Jarvis, please step forward."

His footsteps sounded as if he were headed to the gallows.

"Please take a few minutes to explain the idea behind the iPod's continuous loop of some of the worst music ever perpetrated on the human ear."

Rounds of laughter sounded, then Dr. Jarvis launched into an enthusiastic explanation of his research on the effects of classical music on the brain.

I silently applauded Dr. Tyson. But at the same time I realized she'd had time to answer the question about my prognosis, but had deftly dodged it.

September 21, Wednesday

"HELLO, MY DEAR."

It's Aunt Winnie. But why is she whispering?

"I know it's early, but I had to bring Faridee when I was sure your mother wouldn't be around."

"Good morning, Marigold."

Faridee sounds groggy.

"Carrie fairly threatened me the other day, refuses to believe in the power of the mind, nearly blew a gasket when I told her the amulet I gave her is to help pull you back to this world."

I'm with Mom on that one.

"Anyway, after I thought about her distress that no one knows the identity of the baby's father, I realized this is the perfect time to call in Faridee! She can connect with you and then you can tell her who the father is, and then we'll find him. It's brilliant, and I can finally convince Carrie there are more things in the world to explore than shopping malls."

Because, of course, if two crazily dressed women go to Duncan and tell him they communed with his comatose non-girlfriend on another dimension and I told them he is the father of my baby, he will totally believe them, end his engagement, and devote his life to a vegetable and our child.

Besides, I've already gone over this in my head a thousand times. If Duncan simply read a newspaper, he knows about the baby, and if he were remotely interested in being involved, he would've already come forward. And he hasn't.

"Do your thing, Faridee. We don't have time for a lot of ceremony."

"I forgot to bring the sage."

"Let me see what I've got in my purse. Here's a packet of vanilla flavored Stevia—will that do?"

"I can try."

Great—a bad idea magnified by a half-assed psychic. This can't go wrong at all.

"Are you ready, Marigold?" Faridee asked.

Someone tore open the paper packet, then gasps sounded.

"*Agggg*—it went up my nose!"

"You threw it in my eyes!"

Fits of sneezing ensued, and much slapping of clothes. I waited while Lucy and Ethel composed themselves.

"Okay, Marigold, can you meet me halfway?" Faridee asked.

Sure. Let me coma right over there.

"I'm coming toward you," she said. "Closer... closer..."

The thing is, I'm still not sure how to play this because with Faridee's hit or miss "powers," she might interpret Duncan Wheeler as Dunkin' Donuts. Then some poor shmuck at the corner shop would be assaulted by these two loons.

"There you are, Marigold. Congratulations on being a mother! Now, what can you tell me about the father of your child?"

I try to blank my mind or think about something else, but my mind keeps bouncing back to Duncan and the night he crashed at my apartment.

"I'm getting something," Faridee said.

"What is it?" Winnie whispered. "What is she telling you?"

"Wait for it... Wait for it.... Yes... He's a cowboy."

Oh, brother.

"Hm, that doesn't seem like Marigold's type. Are you sure?"

"Yes. I'm going to snort Stevia more often because this is the clearest signal I've ever received. No question—I see spurs."

Sigh. Spurs... as in San Antonio Spurs.

September 22, Thursday

"I CAN'T STAY LONG," Roberta said. "Just came by to read you some mail—it is flooding in again. I guess everyone and their neighbor saw your story on television."

She tore open the first envelope. "Dear Coma Girl, You're going to burn in a pit of hellfire—wait, that one's not very nice."

A thick ripping sound filled the air.

"Goodbye, Creepy Jesus Freak," she sang.

She tore open another envelope. "Let's see, Coma Girl, ba, ba, ba... illegitimate devil spawn... okay, *goodbye*."

Another hearty rip sounded.

"What is wrong with people?"

She tore open a third one. "Okay, here's a sane person... Dear Coma Girl, I saw your story on *The Doctors*, and... no, wait—this lady wants to buy your baby for three hundred dollars. *Goodbye*. Oh, wait—she sent a ten dollar deposit. That, we will keep." She heaved a sigh. "I don't like opening your mail, Marigold, but maybe I should go through them at home and weed out the perverts, lunatics, and devil worshippers. What do you think?"

I think that sounds good.

"By the way, I've started my detective work. I called your office and told your boss I found a man's San Antonio Spurs hat at the apartment and did it belong to anyone there? I have to say, I was very relieved when Mr. Palmer didn't lay claim to it. He said he'd ask around the office and call me back."

Then she cleared her throat. "Actually, Marigold, it crossed my mind that it could be Duncan, although to my knowledge, you two never did the nasty. But just in case, this morning I looked up his phone number from the cake order and called."

I'm in agony. I want to know what he said, but I don't want to know what he said. I need closure, but I don't want it.

"Anyway, his fiancée answered. Duncan left the States over a month ago to work in refugee camps and won't be back until the wedding. I made up some lame excuse about the order. But while I had her on the phone, I told her someone had left a San Antonio Spurs hat at the bakery, and I wondered if it belongs to Duncan. She said no, that Duncan is notorious for dissing professional basketball."

It's true, he prefers college basketball. He'd said there was a story behind the hat, but he never got around to telling me, was too busy impregnating me.

"So that's that, Duncan is not the father of your child." She sighed. "Pity though, I bet the two of you would have decent-looking kids. Not gorgeous, mind you, but really decent-looking. And sturdy."

Aww. I hope she's right.

So Duncan is traveling overseas. Which means he might not know

I'm pregnant, or if he does know, he might not be able to reach me.

Women do that—we make excuses for our men… it blunts the pain.

Because the more likely scenario is Duncan left the country to get away from me.

September 23, Friday

IT'S BEEN A WHILE since Sidney came to visit by herself. I'm happy to hear her jabber on about the Coma Girl brand, but I'm really excited that she's painting my nails again. I know Dr. Tyson and Dr. Jarvis are worried I'm losing ground, and I want to prove to myself I still have working connections to the tips of my fingers and toes.

"Peacock blue for your fingers," Sid says. "And sunshine yellow for your toes." She yawned noisily. "Ack, I need a nap."

She does seem tired today, but I know she's been working nonstop on building a support system for Coma Girl fans and followers.

"Do you know that some newspapers are offering a bounty for the name of your baby's father?"

No, I hadn't heard. That's… weird.

"Everyone wants to know who is the father of the Coma Girl baby."

She was blowing, I assume on my nails to dry them faster.

"I'm curious, too. I mean, you've never really had a serious boyfriend."

That she knows of.

"And no one has come forward to say it's his. I'm thinking it was just a one-night stand—at least that's what I hope."

She hopes?

"I mean, I hope it wasn't an attack or something."

Ah. No, thank goodness.

"There are all kinds of conspiracy theories floating around out there."

There are?

"Some people are saying the baby belongs to Keith Young, and when he found out about the baby, he put you in a coma."

Okay, that's… impossible.

"And some people are saying it's an alien baby."

Okay, that's… more impossible.

She yawned again. "And some people are saying it was immaculate conception and you're carrying a messiah."

Okay, who are these people and are they wearing white jackets with sleeves that tie in back?

The gonging ringtone sounded, stopping me mid-thought. By the time Sidney removed the phone from her bag, it had rung five times. Long enough to echo in my head again… and again… and again.

"Hello? Yes. I told you the project is done, but I can't give it to you all at once. Did you get the first part? Well, it's going to have to do until I can make arrangements to get another segment to you. What?" She pushed up from the chair and walked toward the window, turning her back. "Don't you dare threaten me."

Threaten? That sounds a bit extreme for a class project. On the other hand, we're talking about lawyering. She might be working on a project for a firm where a lot of money is at stake.

"Are you crazy? You can't come here. You'll ruin everything. No, don't—hello? *Hello?*"

Sidney cursed, then cursed again. She strode back to my bed, then started slamming things into her purse. "I have to go, Marigold. Mom and Dad are visiting tomorrow—good luck with that."

Good luck with that… Good luck with that… Good luck with that…

Why was the phrase oddly familiar… and at the same time, repulsive? And strangely, I sensed it had something to do with the gonging sound.

September 24, Saturday

"SO CATCH ME UP," Alex said. "Marigold is *pregnant?*"

"I'm afraid so," my mom said, somehow managing to marinate all three words with disapproval, condemnation, and dismay.

"She doesn't look pregnant from here."

"Really? Her cheeks don't look puffy?"

Thanks, Mom.

"No, she looks great. Who's the lucky guy?"

"Nobody seems to know, except Marigold, and she isn't talking. I don't suppose she mentioned a boyfriend to you?"

"No. She mentioned a guy in the Peace Corps a couple of times, but she said they were just friends."

"Do you remember his name?" Mom asked.

"No, but I'll look back through the letters I got from her and see if she mentioned a name."

Ack—I'd written a lot of letters to Alex—had I mentioned Duncan?

"How is Sis doing?"

My mom heaved a sigh. "At the beginning of the month, the doctors were optimistic she was improving with the experimental drug, but as the baby grows, she seems to be losing ground."

"That doesn't sound good. Should I ask for time off to come home?"

"We'd love to see you, of course, but don't come for Marigold's sake, Alex. She probably won't even know you're here."

Thanks, Mom.

"*I'll* know I'm there," he said. "I'll see what I can do. Meanwhile, what's going on with the case?"

My parents hesitated.

"No good news there either," my dad finally said.

This is the first I'm hearing of it.

"The ADA called this morning." My mom's voice was tight. "Keith Young's blood alcohol content test came back measuring less than before."

"It dropped from .09 to .08," my dad bit out. "The legal limit."

"So he wasn't drunk?"

"So it would seem," my dad said. "But there's more. About an hour ago, a news blog reported they'd received an anonymous tip that the lab was paid off to return a lower result."

"Do you think it's true?"

"The ADA said they were looking into it, but unless they can track down the tipster, they don't have much to go on."

"Unbelievable. And he's starting in Monday night's game against the Saints. It's going to be beamed in for the entire base." It sounded as if Alex slammed his fist down. "This isn't over."

"Don't let it distract you from your duties," my mom said. "We'll keep you posted."

"Okay, bye. Bye, Marigold!"

They disconnected the Skype call and I felt my parents' anguish like a pungency in the air—sweats, tears, adrenaline. They sat completely still, as if they were too burdened to stand up. A minute... three minutes... five. Finally one of them moved, and the other followed.

And they left the room without saying a word.

September 25, Sunday

"BRAVES AND MARLINS, in Miami," Jack Terry said as he strode into the room. Then he stopped. "Oh—hello."

If I could've posted a flashing sign warning Jack to stay away, I would've. He has no idea what's coming.

"Hello, *cowboy*," my aunt Winnie said haughtily. "And you are?"

"Um... Detective Jack Terry, ma'am, Atlanta PD."

"So you're a *cop* cowboy?"

I only wish I could see this.

"Er... no, ma'am. Just a plain old cop."

153

"Really? And how do you explain those boots?"

"Um... I bought them? I'm sorry, are you a friend of Marigold's?"

"I'm her aunt, her mother's sister, although Carrie and I are nothing alike."

"Okay," he said carefully. "I didn't mean to intrude on your visit. I sometimes stop by and watch the Braves games with your niece."

"And I understand that's not all you do with my niece."

"Excuse me?"

"You gave her this scarf?"

"Yes, that looks like the one I brought as a gift."

"It has teddy bears on it."

"Uh-huh." He was talking slowly, like someone would speak to a child—or to someone who's unstable. "Because of the baby."

"Okay, now we're getting somewhere," Winnie said.

"Huh? Listen, I thought it was cute, but I don't know much about these things, so if it's Godawful, you can toss it. My feelings won't be hurt."

"So this is your first child?"

Oh, God. (Sorry God, I'm not supposed to be taking your name in vain, but this is *so* good.)

He grunted. "Yes. How did you find out about it?"

What? Okay, now I'm confused.

"A-*ha*!" Winnie shouted, and I'd heard her say it enough to know she added a flourish with her finger. "So you admit it!"

"Yes. Believe me, it's not something I'm proud of, but I'm not going to turn my back on my responsibilities."

Why is the girl in the coma the only one in the room making sense?

"Well, it's a good thing, cowboy, because her family expects it!"

His feet shifted. "Do you know Liz?"

"Who?" my aunt asked.

"Liz... Fischer. The mother."

"I'm sorry, whose mother?"

"The mother... of my child."

Oh, I get it—Jack got somebody knocked up, too!

Winnie gasped. "You're having two children with two different women?"

"What? Wait—*no*." I pictured him holding up his hands. "What woman are you talking about?"

"Marigold, of course."

Please God, let me open my eyes for this.

A strangled noise sounded. "You think I'm the father of *Marigold's* child?"

"Yes, I do."

Jack scoffed. "No offense, ma'am, but where did you get a cockamamie idea like that?"

"She... told me."

"Marigold told you?"

"Actually, she told a friend, who then told me."

"Did she wake up and start talking and no one told me?"

"No. I have a friend who's a psychic... and she... talked to Marigold."

"While she was comatose?"

"That's right. And my friend asked Marigold the identity of baby's father, and she said.... spurs."

"Spurs? Is that supposed to mean something?"

"Spurs—cowboy. And when I started asking around, you were the only cowboy type in her life."

"Seriously? That's how you made the leap that I am the father of her baby?"

"And the nurses said you come to visit every Sunday, and it just seems... strange." She sighed. "It made sense at the time. Why *do* you come to visit Marigold?"

"I investigated—am still investigating—her accident. I came in one Sunday and it was quiet and I put the Braves game on and... I don't know, it just felt good being here. I've heard that having activity around is good for coma patients. I thought having the game on was better than the quiet. And that terrible music they always have playing. But I'll leave you alone so you can visit with your niece."

"Oh, no," Winnie said. I heard the familiar rustle of her humongous purse. "I've done enough damage here for one day." She sighed. "I hope Marigold didn't hear her aunt make a fool of herself. I'm sorry, Detective Terry. Enjoy your game."

When the door closed behind Aunt Winnie, Jack exhaled noisily.

"Whew, Marigold, that was interesting."

He dragged a chair over and began setting up for the game. When he was settled, he popped open a can of soda. "Did you get that? I have a kid on the way, too."

I got that, Detective.

"Scary as hell."

Yep.

He sat and listened to the first few plays and when the game broke for a commercial he grunted. "Talked to the ADA yesterday. Tough break about Young's results coming back lower. But if he wasn't drunk, I don't want to see him charged."

Neither do I.

"I heard about the anonymous tip that the lab was paid off. I don't put much stock in anonymous tips—it could be anyone who has a beef with Keith Young. But the DA's office will look into it. Don't worry about it. You just need to get well and be there for your baby."

Roger that, Detective. You're going to be a good dad. I feel for the mother, but the kid's got it made.

He sat and listened to the game, occasionally offering commentary, but mostly just listening. In the top of the ninth inning, his phone rang.

"Terry," he said. "You don't say... I'm at Brady now. Oh, just visiting a friend. I'll find him and take his statement. Later."

He disconnected the call and stood up with a sigh. "Gotta cut it short. Someone assaulted Keith Young, beat him pretty bad from the sound of it. Ambulance brought him here, so I'm back on duty. Later, Coma Girl."

It sounds as if someone believed the rumor that the lab was paid off, and decided Keith Young was going to pay.

My boss's parting words during his last visit came back to me: *That football player is going to get what he deserves for what he did to you, one way or another.* Mr. Palmer had plenty of ex-cons on the payroll to do any side job he deemed necessary.

And in a previous Skype call my brother Alex had mentioned an Army buddy of his in Atlanta had offered to "dispense a little street justice." Had Alex called in a favor?

Or maybe a vigilante had taken it upon himself to right what he considered to be a wrong?

Except what if Jack Terry was right—what if Keith Young hadn't been driving drunk, and the anonymous tipster was someone with a beef against him? Another player, for example, or a jealous ex? The person could've set things in motion with a phone call, then sat back and watched things happen.

September 26, Monday

THE SILKY-THROATED volunteer is back... but now he makes me nervous. I'm sure he's the one who's been leaking photos to the tabloids, and I feel betrayed. Because I want to enjoy the poetry without feeling like I'm being exploited in exchange.

Sure enough, he locked the door before he came to sit beside our beds.

"Summer's fading," he said. "The change in temperatures makes for some beautiful sunsets. I wish you could see them."

So do I. My and Roberta's apartment isn't all that, but we have a Juliet balcony facing Alabama that, if you overlook the dumpsters and the graffiti just below and beyond, afforded us spectacular sunset views. I took them for granted, assumed I had many sunsets left.

Do me a favor, friend, and if you can get to a window this evening, watch the sun set for me?

"So I picked this Dickinson poem for you ladies today. It's called 'I Know a Place Where Summer Strives.'"

He shifted in the creaky chair.

"I know a place where summer strives with such a practiced frost, she each year leads her daisies back recording briefly, 'Lost.' But when the south wind stirs the pools and struggles in the lanes, her heart misgives her for her vow, and she pours soft refrains."

He coughed lightly—to cover a succession of camera clicks?—then resumed.

"Into the lap of adamant, and spices, and the dew, that stiffens quietly to quartz, upon her amber shoe."

See? That makes me hate him a little. Why can't he just leave me with the visual of an amber shoe, instead of taking a piece of me with him?

He coughed again and I distinctly heard the buzz of a mechanical gadget.

"Have a nice day, ladies."

Then he unlocked the door and left.

September 27, Tuesday

"PEACE BE WITH YOU, ladies."

And also with you.

But are you sure you don't mean "pieces," Sister Irene? Are you carrying around that big knife under your habit just waiting for the chance to gut someone who reminds you of the man who killed your sister?

"Let me count heads lest one of you decided to get up and walk out of here since the last time I visited—one, two, three. Yes, you're all still here," she said merrily. "Hello, Karen. Hello, Jill. Hello, Marigold."

Then she exclaimed. "And Marigold, what's all this I see? Balloons and flowers. You're going to have a baby? That's quite unexpected. But a baby is always a happy occasion. Children are our second chance at fulfilling our life's promise to God."

Uh-huh. That all sounds great, Sister, but it's hard for me to relax when I know what you're really thinking.

"I don't fully understand why I'm so drawn to talk to you, Marigold. Maybe it's because your face bears the mark of so much sacrifice."

The scars again—ugh.

"Maybe it's the sight of your lovely rosary. I've been praying the rosary with devotion to push through my crisis of faith, and I've finally reached a point of reconciliation. I know what I have to do, even though it's going to be hard. I've invited the man we talked about, George Gilpin, to my home to perform some repairs. My sister had a different last name, so he doesn't know who I am and really, it's better that way. You'll see. God has a plan for each of us, and I must follow mine."

She walked between our beds and offered up a prayer to the patron saint of head injuries, Saint Aurelius of Riditio. As she uttered the words, however, I realized Sister Irene has her own head injuries that need to be addressed. She is basically planning to invite a man to her house so she can skin him.

She stopped at the door. "Peace be with you, ladies."

And also with you. Seriously.

September 28, Wednesday

WHEN MY MOM WALKED into my room, I knew something was wrong.

Not wrong in the sense that something else had gone south with the case or that someone had died. But wrong in the sense that she needed to get something off her chest and she wasn't going to hold back.

I was about to get a lecture, but good.

She didn't say anything for a few minutes, just paced and drank coffee. I could smell the caramel flavoring she liked, and hear the jangle of her bracelets. This pacing, silent treatment phase was part of the punishment. It was the part I'd hated most when I was young because you had to sit there and wait until she was good and ready to blast you. I was pretty sure what the topic would be and frankly, was a little surprised it had taken her this long to dole out my well-deserved tongue-lashing.

She was going to tell me I disrespected myself by lying down with a man who obviously doesn't care about me and conceiving an unwanted child.

And that even if I get well, I barely make enough money to support myself, much less a baby and how am I going to do both?

That this unplanned child is simply another in a long line of poor decisions and haphazard life design and when am I going to grow up and be as smart and mindful as my siblings?

She walked over and set down her coffee cup with a bang and I mentally steeled myself to be stripped down to my tendons with her acid tongue.

Instead, the bed creaked and moaned and I was suddenly beset by fragrances I didn't even know I'd missed—my mother's tea tree oil shampoo and lavender body lotion, and the fabric softener freshness of her blouses. She had crawled into the hospital bed with me and wrapped herself around me and my baby.

I can't feel her, but I can smell her and hear her breath in my ear. I feel loved and I know my child will be loved, too.

September 29, Thursday

"JARVIS, COME in and lock the door," Dr. Tyson said.

"What's going on?"

"You know Ms. Kemp's progress continues to slide."

"Yes."

"At the rate she's slipping, we'll be lucky to get the fetus to a viable stage. And once the fetus is born, I'm afraid Marigold would be in a persistent vegetative state."

I'm so terrified at her proclamation, I can't think.

Jarvis expelled a frustrated sigh. "Are you going to ask the family to terminate the fetus?"

No, please...

"I considered it."

"And?"

"And instead I acquired another vial of the experimental cocktail."

"Acquired?"

"Don't ask. Ms. Kemp's responses and overall health were best right after you administered the first vial. I think we should try a second dose."

"But that's never been done."

"No... but it's never been tested on a pregnant patient. I figure we're dealing with two neural patients—the mother and the child. I think the baby took most of the first dose and Marigold got what was left over. This second dose will be for her."

"How much trouble can we get into?"

"No more than we're already in," she said. "If we don't, we're going to lose them both."

"Are you going to ask the family?"

"I have a better idea," she said. "Let's ask Marigold."

Oh, wow... no pressure.

"And since she seems to respond better to your voice, I need you to ask her."

"Okay," Jarvis said. "Do you have her hand?"

"Yes."

"Marigold, I need to ask you a very important question and I need you to tell me yes or no. Dr. Tyson and I want to give you a second dose of the experimental drug. We think it's the best chance for you and your baby. Do you want us to give you the second dose? No is default. If you don't move your fingers, we won't administer the dose. If yes, move the fingers on your right hand."

I'm trying so hard.

"Marigold, your baby's life depends on it. If you don't move your fingers, we won't administer the dose. If yes, move the fingers on your right hand."

Oooooooooohhhhhhhhhhhh.

"I felt that!" Dr. Tyson said. "She moved her fingers."

He exhaled. "Thank God."

"But I'm giving you a chance to walk out now, Jarvis, if you don't want any part of this."

"I'm staying," he said evenly.

"Okay," she said. "Let's do this."

September 30, Friday

I CAN ALMOST feel the experimental medicine they gave me filtering through my body. Last night I had the most vivid dreams I can remember since the accident. Everything seems louder, more colorful, more vivid.

But the dreams are more than dreams—they're memories… things that actually happened. It's been the one part of my brain that was chugging along more slowy—making new memories, and remembering things that happened around the time of the accident. They're close to the surface, as if they've been lying dormant and are bursting to break through….

I pull up to the curb at the airport and see Sidney emerge like a beautiful flower. It's hot, and the A/C in my car isn't working. I feel like a wet sponge, but Sid always looks cool and collected.

On the drive home, we have the windows down. Sid is smoking a cigarette, which I've never seen her do before. She says she smokes occasionally to keep her anxiety at bay. I say I didn't know she had anxiety, and she says I have no idea how hard law school is. She is right—I don't.

When we get off the interstate, I ask if she minds if I stop to get a lottery ticket. She teases me about it, but we stop. I run in to get a ticket and a half-gallon of chocolate milk for Dad. As I come back out…

Sid pulls up in my car. *I'm driving… you're too slow.*

I climb into the passenger seat and hold up my lottery ticket.

Good luck with that...

I don't need luck. Aunt Winnie's psychic told me I'm going to win.

My phone rings and it's Roberta. She wants to talk about a hot new guy at our apartment building. We're laughing and talking.

Sid's phone rings, a loud gonging ringtone. She reaches into her bag, rummaging for the phone. She's all over the road. I try to help her so she can drive, but her purse spills and...

Watch out!

OCTOBER

October 1, Saturday

WHEN THE DOOR opened and I heard my mother's voice, I tensed, hoping she'd brought my dad or Aunt Winnie... or was talking to one of the nurses or security guards... or was on the phone closing a deal on a McMansion in a part of Atlanta I wasn't familiar with.

"... can't understand why she wants to meet us here," my mom said.

My sister Sidney's long-suffering sigh is unmistakable.

"ADA Spence said it would draw less attention if she came here than if we went down to her office."

I retreated from the sound of Sid's voice. I was awake all night playing my recalled memories of the car crash over and over. Part of me wants to magically realize the scenes in my head are false memories or bad dreams. Instead I keep remembering small details and nuances that reinforce the realization I wasn't driving when my tan Ford Escort hit Keith Young's yellow Jaguar head-on.

Sidney was.

And she'd lied, had let everyone—including me—believe I was driving.

"What do you think she wants to talk about?" my mother asked.

Another sigh. "Marigold's case, I assume."

Sid sounds preoccupied—with her own guilt?

"Maybe the D.A.'s office found out there was a payoff to the lab to alter the results of Keith Young's blood tests."

"That would be such good news," Sid agreed.

"Is David coming?"

"Um, no. He had a commitment he couldn't get out of."

162

"Well, this *was* last minute. I had to postpone showing a penthouse condo, and my broker isn't happy."

"Couldn't Daddy have come instead?"

My mother snorted. "You mean actually participate in our family?"

Their conversation was cut short by the arrival of ADA Spence. I can tell from her curt greeting that she isn't delivering good news.

"I thought this would be the most private place we could talk," the woman said.

"About?" Sid prompted.

"If either of you know anything about the assault on Keith Young, I need for you to come clean."

"What?" my mother said. "That's preposterous."

"What makes you think we know something?" Sid asked, in a voice that makes me think she knows something.

"I'm not saying you do," the woman said carefully. "But Marigold has a lot of supporters, including a big social media following, and it's come to our attention that threats were made against Keith Young."

"People go on social media to blow off steam," Sid said.

"Maybe," Spence said. "Maybe not. Also, Keith Young told us his attacker seemed to be well-trained. 'Professional' was the word he used, maybe military or ex-military."

I recalled my brother Alex's comment to my dad that one of his buddies in Atlanta had offered to deliver 'street justice' to Keith Young.

My mother and Sid were silent.

"We know your son is in the Army," Spence added. "Is there something you want to tell me?"

"No," my mother said, her voice firm.

"I'm trying not to suspect your husband isn't here because he knows something—or because he did it."

My mother scoffed. "Robert isn't physical enough to pull off something like that."

How does my mother manage to make a denial of a criminal act sound like an indictment on my father's manhood?

"We don't know anything about the assault on Keith Young," my mother added. "And while we're not happy he was injured, you can't expect us to lose sleep over it, either."

"I understand how you must feel," the ADA said. "But if you know something and you don't report it, this could go bad for you."

Sid guffawed. "*Bad* for us? If you and the D.A. haven't noticed, things are already bad for us."

"I'm sorry. I misspoke. Of course things are not good."

"And we have no interest in making things worse," my mother said evenly.

"Okay," the woman said, sounding mollified. "If you do notice anything relevant in Marigold's social media stream or if you learn of who is behind the assault, even a rumor, you will call me immediately?"

"Yes," my mother said.

The woman's shoes clicked on the floor in retreat, then the door opened and closed.

"Of all the nerve," my mother sputtered.

"I know," Sid said, sounding more upset than I realized. "I wish David had been here." Her voice broke off on a sob.

"Oh, honey. Is everything all right between the two of you?"

"I'm having... second thoughts."

"About David?"

"No, not about David."

"What then?"

Perhaps about lying to the entire planet?

Sid sighed again. "I'm having second thoughts about sitting out this semester."

"Absolutely, you should go back to Boston," my mother said. "I never wanted you to interrupt your studies."

"But I hate leaving you and Daddy to deal with Marigold alone."

Deal with me—ouch.

"We'll manage. And David will still help, won't he?"

"Yes, of course. And I'll still be able to lend a hand with the social media accounts."

"Then *go*."

Sid sighed yet again. "Maybe I'll go back to talk to my instructors and see if the semester can be salvaged. I've only missed a couple of weeks' worth of classes."

"We'll book the next flight," my mother said, as if it were decided. "Walk with me to my car."

"I'd like to stay," Sid said, "and say goodbye to Marigold."

"Oh, okay," my mother said, as if she just remembered I am still in the room. "You're such a good sister."

I picture Mom squeezing Sid's shoulder and bestowing her with a look of parental pride and adoration. My turn to sigh.

My mother left. I wondered if Sid was just trying to get rid of her to make a phone call under the pretense of saying goodbye to me.

So I was surprised to hear the clink of the rosary my sister had hung on my bed, and the fervent words of prayer, so fervent I began to soften toward my sister. And I remembered something she'd uttered on a previous visit.

It was just a little lie. To protect us... to protect Mom and Dad. They were so distressed, I couldn't bear to pile on. You understand, don't you?

I understand now what she'd meant. And darn it, I have to agree that having one daughter in a coma, and one under suspicion for causing the accident might've been too much for my fractured parents to handle. And Sid had shouldered a lot of the responsibility for making the best out of a terrible situation.

The rosary beads clinked against my bed rail.

"Goodbye, Marigold. I'll be praying for us."

For *us*.

Earlier, when I'd thought Sid was lying to the police about me talking on the phone when the accident occurred was to cover for me, I conceded if the tables were turned, I'd lie for Sid. And in a way, I am doing that now.

So how can I be angry?

October 2, Sunday

"TIGERS AND BRAVES at home," Detective Terry said as he walked in. "This is the last regular game of the season, Marigold. I know it's been ugly, but I still hate to see it end."

So do I. It's been our thing, me and the detective. Will he stop visiting?

"It's cooling down outside. Where did the summer go?"

Indeed. I've missed an entire season of brutal Atlanta temperatures and off-the-charts pollen count. It's depressing. Is this how it's going to be? Me lying here while seasons slide by, like my roommates Karen Suh and Jill Wheatley? If so, would I be better off not to have a sense of time passing?

"I brought wings from Taco Mac," Jack said. "I figured you for the adventurous type, considering your double life as a burlesque dancer. So I got them with Three Mile Island spice."

Ooh, good choice, Detective. I do like spicy food.

He dragged the chair over to assume the watching position and brought up the baseball game on whatever gadget he had with him—I assume his phone. Detective Terry did not strike me as an iPad kind of guy.

"Falcons play today, too," he said. "At home. I heard Keith Young wanted to play to show everyone he's recovered from the beating, but the coaches didn't think it was a good idea."

He popped open a soda can. "I'm afraid I'm going to have to talk to your brother about his possible involvement. The D.A. wants this put to bed to squash some of the controversy."

I know Alex was angry on my behalf, but I don't think he'd ask someone to beat up Keith Young. Granted, if he were here, he might do something like that on his own, but I can't see him asking someone else to risk getting hurt.

"I heard your sister went back to Boston. She came by the station and asked for your cell phones again, but I had to tell her no because the investigation is still open."

With a start I realized Jack Terry had been suspicious about the accident from the beginning. Had he sensed Sidney wasn't telling the whole truth? And would he figure out what really happened? Although, with Keith Young's blood alcohol content at the legal level, it seems likely the investigation will be closed soon.

"Meanwhile," Jack said, "I've been reading through your social media posts to see if anyone threatened Keith Young. No offense, but people are kind of crazy. I mean, I understand why they'd be interested in your situation, but I'm blown away by the number of followers you have and the things people say." He gave a little laugh. "Do you know how many marriage proposals you have waiting for you when you wake up?"

And none of them are the marriage proposal I want. Poor little Coma Girl. Knocked up with a baby by a man who is marrying someone else. It's so *Melrose Place*.

He tore into a bag, and the strong scent of the hot wings filled the air.

"But it's been a good exercise for me," he continued. "I'm a dummy when it comes to social media. Carlotta keeps saying I need to join the rest of the world."

Carlotta again, not the mother of his baby, Liz... hm.

"I'm not a complete Neanderthal. I text, dammit, and it's hard when you have big fingers."

The scent of the wings grew stronger, and I heard him licking his big fingers, so I assumed he was chowing down. A sneeze sounded—the spicy food is getting to Detective Terry.

"Marigold?" he said in an odd voice. "Was that you?"

Wait—was it me? Did *I* sneeze? Is it a good sign? And more importantly, do I have snot all over my face?

"Hold on," he said, then his footsteps sounded and the door opened. "Could I get a doctor in here? She sneezed! Coma Girl sneezed."

October 3, Monday

"WHEN WAS THE LAST TIME a sneeze made national headlines?" Gina asked.

"This could be a first," Dr. Jarvis agreed. "If Marigold sneezed."

"The Detective swears he heard her sneeze yesterday."

"You were the first person in the room. Do you believe him?"

"Yes."

"Then why hasn't she done it again?" Jarvis sniffed, then gave his nose a hearty blow. "We've tried pepper and smelling salts and all we've managed to do is clear our own sinuses."

"Doctor, if Marigold did sneeze, what does that mean, exactly?"

"Hard to say." He made a thoughtful noise. "It's unusual, for sure. Being in a coma is like being in a deep sleep. When you're asleep, so is the part of your brain that affects involuntary responses, like sneezing and yawning."

"So if she sneezed, that would mean a part of her brain is waking up?"

"If she sneezed," he agreed.

"But I'm confused... she responds to pain—that's involuntary, isn't it?"

"The pain response is more primal, and more complex. It's controlled by as many as three parts of the brain."

"Wow, the brain is so complicated."

"And there's still so much we don't know about the brain, compounded by the fact that everyone's brain is different. It's why we're never a hundred percent sure of a coma patient's prognosis. Sometimes I think neuroscience is part science, and part science fiction."

"Is there anything else you want to try to trigger a sneeze?"

"Not for now," he said. "But do you have time to help me administer a motor sensory test?"

"My shift is over, but I'm happy to stay," she said.

"That's nice of you, Gina. You don't have anyone at home waiting for you?"

Ooh, sly, Dr. Jarvis.

"Just my son," she said. "But he's at my sister's house with his cousins, and I'm sure he won't mind if I'm a tad late."

"Something tells me the best part of his day is when he sees you," Dr. Jarvis said.

Gina cooed.

He cleared his throat. "Okay, then, let's see if Marigold has improved." The click of his penlight sounded. "Pupils are dilated and fixed. Heart rate is slightly elevated, but that's probably due to the baby."

He continued to check and report on my vital signs, and everything seemed normal. Then he went through a full battery of touch tests to my hands and feet, using a probe, a brush, and his hands.

The good news: I could feel sensations when he said he was holding my fingers and toes, like the pings I felt when Teddy and Gina removed my nail polish. The bad news: I couldn't seem to make my appendages move in response to his commands. In my mind, I'm gaining ground, but I know Dr. Jarvis was disappointed.

"How is the baby?" Gina asked.

"As good as can be expected," he said. "We'll administer another ultrasound soon. Thanks for staying Gina. Go home to your son." He sounded tired.

"Don't give up on Marigold, Dr. Jarvis. She needs us."

"I know," he said.

They left the room. I was so touched by their words, I wondered if my eyes were watering.

Then I heard myself sneeze.

Yes!

October 4, Tuesday

"I TOLD YOU NOT to have kids," Joanna said, her voice accusing. "Dammit, Marigold, you were the person I looked to for hope that women could live fearlessly and independently."

Let that sink in for a minute… a woman who's married to a doctor and is the mother of beatific twins is living vicariously through Coma Girl.

Joanna sighed as if the world was sitting on her liver. It also gave me a good nose full of the bourbon she was nipping from the flask that has apparently become her go-to accessory. Knowing Joanna, it's Dior.

"But maybe you'll be better suited to it than I am. I'm a terrible mother, as my husband often reminds me. And a terrible wife." She laughed. "But I'm a good drinker." She took another drink to prove her point.

I'm worried about Joanna. I can't see her, but I still don't recognize this person I'm hearing. I can't reconcile her to the happy, confident woman I knew in college. What happened to her?

"I have a confession to make, Marigold."

Oh, please—no more. I can't take it.

She scooted the chair closer and whispered, "I slept with my father-in-law."

Oh, Joanna, just… *yuck*. What the hell were you thinking?

"I know—I'm a horrible daughter-in-law, too."

Well, to your mother-in-law, anyway. Your father-in-law would probably give you a thumbs' up.

"It only happened twice."

Stop.

"Okay, two and a half times, but that's *all*."

STOP. Wait—what constitutes half a screw? Never mind, all I can think about is Joanna's father-in-law toasting his son at their wedding on his marvelous choice for a bride. Ew.

"So now you know why Stuart has filed for divorce. Yes, he cheated, but I suppose I took revenge sex to the next level."

You think?

"He's filing for full custody," she added in a barely audible voice. "I might not get to see my kids."

The kids she seems to resent, begrudge, and loathe? I have to admit, unless Joanna gets her act together, I think she needs a break from motherhood.

Joanna sighed, then screwed the top back on her flask. "Whew, it feels good to get that out. Secrets will eat you alive."

But what about the damage to the person you puked them on?

"You're better than an AA meeting, Marigold. And way cheaper than a therapist." She laughed, then trailed off into a wistful sigh. "I need a friend, Marigold. I wish you would wake up."

But for my sake... or for hers?

October 5, Wednesday

"YOU'RE HAVING A BABY, now isn't that just grand?"

My boss at the carpet place, Percy Palmer, has stopped by and his sweet greeting cheers my heart.

"If that's not a reason to wake up, I don't know what is."

He has a point. What had Audrey Parks said? She'd needed something to latch onto. I confess this thing with Sidney lying about who was driving my car has me distracted. What I should be doing is focusing on my baby and how to get out of this bed.

The door opened. "Hello... are you Mr. Palmer?" a woman asked.

From the swishing noise, I knew he'd removed his hat.

"Yes, ma'am."

And from the dip in his voice, I gather she's attractive.

"I'm sorry to interrupt your visit."

"I'm just saying howdy to Marigold. She works for me."

"How nice. Everyone in the hospital knows who Marigold is—she's our celebrity patient."

"She's just plain old Marigold to me, ma'am."

Ah, the adjectives every girl yearns to hear: Plain *and* old.

"I'm Sophia from the Materials and Maintenance Department, and I wanted to thank you in person for the donation of new carpet in our waiting rooms. It's a very generous gift, sir, and I don't have the words to thank you properly."

Sophia's voice is like honey dripping off a spoon. And my boss has a sweet tooth.

"It's my pleasure," he said, and I pictured his ears turning red. "It's the best commercial carpet money can buy... the pad, too. Most people don't realize if you don't put down a good pad, the carpet's going to wear out no matter how good it is."

"Really? I didn't know that."

"There's a lot of science behind carpet, ma'am. This one is antimicrobial. Figured that would be good with all the germs in this place."

"Um, yes."

"Tell your maintenance crew all it needs is a good vacuuming every day, and shampooing maybe once a year."

"I will."

"And I'm leaving a case of spray deodorizer—New Car smell. It's my best seller."

"How thoughtful. You know, I've been thinking about recarpeting my house. I'm on my way to lunch. Maybe you'd like to join me and give me some advice?"

"I'd... like that."

I'll bet he'd turned his hat inside out.

"Good. Why don't I grab my purse and let you say goodbye to Marigold? I assume she's the reason behind your donation. She must be special to you."

"Yes, ma'am. I'd do anything for Marigold. I thought new carpet in the waiting rooms would be a nice tribute."

"It's so kind of you to do something in her memory. Take your time, Mr. Palmer. I'll wait for you in the hall."

"Okay, ma'am. But I ain't dressed very nice."

"You look good to me," she said.

He made a noise that sounded like a cross between a cough and a giggle.

The door closed and I could picture him rocking back and forth on his heels, nervous and pleased. But mostly nervous.

Good for Mr. Palmer—he's a swell guy and he deserves a good woman in his life. I hope Sophia isn't schmoozing him just because of the donation he made.

In my memory. Ack—as if I'm already dead.

But if I do croak, it's nice to know I'll live on through the antimicrobial carpet in the Brady hospital waiting rooms that reek of New Car. I mean, who else has that?

October 6, Thursday

"PEACE BE WITH YOU, ladies."

And also with you.

Sister Irene sounds more cheerful than usual as she stops to say a prayer over my ward mates Karen Suh and Jill Wheatley. I dearly hope it is the cheerfulness of a clear, forgiving mind versus the cheerfulness of a spider with a fly in its web.

"Hello, Marigold. How are you today?"

Maybe she won't linger if I don't make eye contact.

Then I heard the sound of the chair being dragged closer to my bed. Darn.

"What a pretty head wrap—pink smiley faces. Your family must be very attentive."

They're not, but the nurses are good about changing my head scarf regularly. I had hoped to be rid of the bandages covering my surgery scar by now, but there was some concern about a skin infection blah, blah, blah, and more shaving and I still have the bandages.

"And how is your baby? Now it's clear why you survived, Marigold— to bring this child into the world."

It was a very nunly thing to say, and nicely meant, I'm sure. But I confess the feminist in me rails against the implication that I'm little more than an incubator. Is God going to pluck me up when the oven timer rings? On the other hand, for the baby's sake, I'm grateful my uterus was spared in the accident. On the other hand...

Sigh... I'm starting to comprehend the push-pull of being a mother. Is this how my mother felt when she was pregnant with each of us—happy a new life was starting, yet sad her life as she knew it was ending? Loving toward the baby growing inside her, yet resentful that it was literally consuming her?

Sister Irene sighed. "Motherhood is one of the great joys of life a woman gives up when she becomes a nun. And sex." Another sigh.

TMI, Sister.

"I've always wondered what sex would be like. I've read a thousand romance novels about it, and it sounds positively marvelous, all the moaning and the thrusting."

I can testify it's not always marvelous—most of the time my post-coital assessment puts the act on the pleasure scale somewhere above painting my bathroom and somewhere below a sale at IKEA.

"I once rented a porno movie."

I don't want to hear this.

"I figured it was the safest way to find out what really happens."

Uh-huh. Because UPS delivery guys, tow-truck drivers, and new next-door neighbors really look like that.

"It was kind of awful, but maybe I got a bad one. I mean, sex has to be more like it is in books for people to want to keep doing it."

La, la, la, la, I can't hear you, la, la, la, la.

"But enough of that. I thought you might want an update on my plan."

Now I'm riveted.

"George Gilpin is supposed to come to my place next week to look at the repairs I described over the phone."

She sounds giddy. But at least she's leaving a documentation trail so if something happens to him—

"I didn't call him on my phone, of course. I bought a throwaway cell phone for that—with cash. Anyone who watches *Forensics Files* knows that much."

I stand corrected. And apparently my friend Joanna isn't the only one taking copious notes during the show.

October 7, Friday

"HI, KAREN. IT'S JONAS. How are you today?"

When I realized Karen Suh's ex-husband had come back to visit, my heart sank. I'd hoped he would return in time to see the note Faridee had transcribed from Karen to him about the pear tree, a message that would convey she could hear him. But the note had fallen off where it was pinned to her gown and discarded, with no comprehension of its significance.

"You look pretty, like always." He chuckled. "I'm wet. It's pouring down rain and I couldn't find a covered parking place. I drove your car over, I hope that's okay. It's been sitting in that dusty garage since—for a long time. It needed a new battery and spark plugs, so I thought driving it would be good for the alternator. It took me a while to get here. You know traffic is always bad on Friday, and when it's raining…" He trailed off as if he suddenly realized he was rambling to someone who couldn't respond.

In the silence, only the sounds of our machines could be heard, and the unending dirge of my classical music, which sounded especially somber today with rain pinging against the window.

The vegetable patch is a pretty depressing place in general.

Today, it's purgatory.

The crackling of paper sounded.

"I received a letter yesterday," he said, "from the hospital. It says it's time to apply for a bed in a nursing home—they want to move you to a place where you'll receive long-term care."

They're giving up on her.

"I'm still listed as your healthcare proxy, but I called your cousin Sonya in Alaska and asked her opinion. She said she would leave the decision to me... although I guess the decision has been made. The letter says it might take a while to find an available bed, but I think it's time for me to do some things I've been putting off, like sell the house, and your car. The nursing home is going to be expensive, and in order to qualify for Medicaid, your assets have to be liquidated."

His wet shoes squeaked on the floor, as if he were pacing.

"But I know how much you love that house, and all your mother's antiques. The thought of them going to strangers...."

More squeaking, more pacing.

"There's more." He sighed. "I've been offered a job in London. Actually, it was offered to me before, but I didn't take it because... I wanted to stay close by. But now..."

Now he's giving up on her, too.

"I don't know what to do, Karen. I feel like this is all my fault and I want to be here for you. But maybe you waking up is just wishful thinking on my part. What should I do?"

His voice was hoarse with anguish and unshed tears. It gave me some insight into the decisions my parents might have to make for me someday, if I lingered here. And after a nursing home, then what? The decision to be kept alive through artificial means? Only to someday be forced to make another decision to pull the plug or withhold nourishment?

Ack—if only Jonas had seen the note, he'd realize Karen is still here.

Then a sobering thought hit me—just because I'm still here and Karen is still here doesn't necessarily mean we will wake up. What if we simply can't cross the barrier Audrey had managed to cross?

October 8, Saturday

ROBERTA WAS LICKING the remains of a pecan tart from her fingers and humming to emphasize its gooey goodness.

"Girl, you have to wake up so you can help me eat the leftovers I bring home. I'm going to get fat."

Hm... does that mean Marco is no longer around to scarf up my half of the freebies?

She sighed. "Marco split again."

Of course he did.

"And I'm just sick about this, Marigold, but the money I was saving for you from your cards and letters that I kept in the freezer? About a thousand bucks. It's gone, too." She made a mournful noise. "I'm so sorry. I just can't believe he'd steal from me." She blew her nose. "I mean, from you."

Poor Roberta—she always falls for the wrong guy. She reminds me of me.

"But I started saving all over again today when I sorted through your mail. Eighty dollars in the oven. Lord knows, Marco would never look there if he came back. And if he did, all he'd see are the sweaters I store in there."

That's Roberta—after slaving over an oven all day at the bakery, she never cooks at home. And the closest I come to cooking is watching chef Alain Allegretti YouTube videos on a loop. (Do yourself a favor and Google "YouTube Alain Allegretti Cod." I'm not ashamed to admit half of those Views are mine.)

Suffice to say, the sweaters and the cash are safe in our oven.

"But before I read your mail to you, I thought you'd want an update on The Case of the Mystery Hat Man. That's what I'm calling it—kind of catchy, huh?"

Roberta figured out the father of my baby left a San Antonio Spurs hat at our apartment, and is determined to find out who he is. You and I know it's Duncan Wheeler, who is engaged to be married and conveniently out of the country, but Roberta has already dismissed Duncan as a candidate because his fiancée Trina said he doesn't own a hat like that.

Since Roberta doesn't realize she already solved the case, she's still chasing down leads.

"Mr. Palmer called me back and said the hat doesn't belong to anyone at your office, so coworkers are off the list. Then I decided to put an ad on Craigslist for the owner with the title 'Did you leave this hat at my apartment?'"

Okay, that's only the setup of every slasher movie.

"But that turned out to be a bad idea because I got ninety-four pingbacks, including two from the Philippines."

Only ninety-four?

"So I'm kind of back to the drawing board. But I'll think of something. No baby daddy is going to outsmart Roberta Hazzard, P.I."

Which is kind of what I'm afraid of. Because honestly, what good could come from Duncan knowing he's the father? Enough lives have been plowed through.

"So here's my favorite letter of the week. Get ready to laugh. Dear Coma Girl, my name is Otto. I want to spread Dijon mustard all over you and lick it off… "

October 9, Sunday

WHEN JACK TERRY WALKED into the room, his bootsteps were slower than usual.

"I'm depressed, Marigold."

Really, Detective? Let's review—I'm in a coma, and you're the one who's depressed?

"Baseball season is over—for us anyway. And the Braves are leaving Turner Field. It just seems like an end to an era, you know?"

Why do I get the feeling he's talking about something other than baseball?

"And I know there's always next season, but by the time spring training rolls around, everything will be different."

Ah. The end of an era for *Jack*—bachelorhood?

He sighed. "I guess I don't have to tell you that life can turn on a dime."

Don't I know it. If I hadn't stopped at the convenience store that night for a lousy lottery ticket and jug of chocolate milk. If I'd insisted on driving the rest of the way to our parents' house. If Keith Young hadn't been traveling along the same stretch of road at the same time. If Sid's phone hadn't rung at that precise moment. And if she'd resisted the urge to answer.

A thought ribboned through my mind… who had been calling Sid? Not that it really mattered. It could've been Mom or Dad, wondering if we were getting close. But she had seemed so frantic to answer. In hindsight, it wasn't like Sid to behave so irresponsibly. Was the gonging ringtone specific to a particular acquaintance?

"I'm not supposed to tell you this," Jack said in a lowered voice, "but the DA is considering charging Keith Young anyway, even with a blood alcohol level below the legal limit. He thinks he can make a case that if Young had been tested on the scene instead of later at the station, he would've blown over the limit. But only if we can find out who's behind the assault on Young. Your brother seems clean, but the DA wants to make sure your family wasn't involved. Juries don't usually find in favor of people who take the law into their own hands."

Oh, no… here we go again, except this time I know even if Keith Young had been drinking, Sidney had some culpability, too, and wasn't being truthful. If I could speak to Jack, I'd tell him to drop the case before things went sideways. What if the convenience store cameras had caught us on video, with Sidney driving away? Or what if someone at the scene remembered? I'm no attorney, but even I know she could be charged with reckless driving, filing a false report and obstruction, and maybe a lot more.

And with that in mind, why had Sidney persisted with the lie, knowing it could be revealed by a random video on a passerby's phone?

"But you didn't hear it from me," the Detective said. "Got it?"

Got it.

"Hey, they brought the television back."

It was Dr. Tyson's concession to Dr. Jarvis's plan to expose me to as much stimuli as possible. Unfortunately, no one had turned it on today.

Jack was already flipping through the channels. "With baseball season over, how do you feel about Nascar?"

Ugh, Detective. Cars going round and round in a circle? If I wasn't already in a coma—

But he'd already found what he wanted on a channel and zoomed up the volume. Loud *vroom, vroom* noises filled the ward.

"And since everyone was so excited about your sneeze last week, I brought more wings."

The sound of paper ripping rent the air, and I waited for the spicy scent of the hot sauce to waft my way, hoping it would indeed trigger a sneeze or two.

Instead, I smelled... nothing.

And it dawned on me I hadn't smelled anything this morning when nurses had come and gone from the room—not the faint scent of lotion on their skin, or the odors of food or fabric softener that normally clung to their scrubs.

With dismay I realized one of the senses I've come to rely upon so heavily to take in the world around me has abandoned me.

This can't be good.

October 10, Monday

BY THE TIME DR. TYSON and Gina arrived the next morning with a handheld ultrasound device, I was a nervous wreck. I didn't sleep well, worrying about losing my sense of smell. I'm scared it means my health is deteriorating, that perhaps something is wrong with the baby.

"There it is," Dr. Tyson said. "Strong heartbeat... correct size.... everything looks normal."

Thank you, God.

"Can you tell the sex?" Gina asked.

I wasn't sure I wanted to know. I want a girl—no, a boy. No—a girl. Or a boy.

"Not the way the baby is angled. Maybe next time."

Oh, good. I don't want to be one of those mothers who already has a name picked out before the baby takes its first breath.

Although I've always liked the name Lauren. And maybe Kyle if it's a boy.

Ack—I guess I am one of those mothers.

"This never gets old," Gina said. "I remember how excited I was to see my first sonogram."

"I can imagine," Dr. Tyson said.

"You don't have children?"

"Um... no."

"I'm sorry, Doctor, I didn't mean to pry."

"It's okay. My husband and I have talked about it... it's just never seemed like the right time."

"I understand—you're so busy. What does your husband do?"

"He's a professor at Georgia Tech."

"Oh, nice."

"Uh-hm. Gina, why don't you print a picture of the sonogram for Ms. Kemp's family? Maybe it will help to... maybe it will help."

"Sure thing, Dr. Tyson. I'll be right back."

The door opened and closed and I was aware of Dr. Tyson hovering near my bed. I wondered what she was doing when I heard a sniffle, then a gulping noise. She was... crying?

My first thought is something is wrong with me or the baby after all... but I quickly registered Dr. Tyson wouldn't have told Gina everything is okay if it isn't, and wouldn't get emotional over a patient. It must be personal.

"You have to get a grip," she murmured, and I realized she was talking to herself. Then she gave a laugh. "Look at me, Marigold. I'm the most senior female physician on staff, and my colleagues look up to me. As far as my career is concerned, the sky's the limit."

I sensed a "but" coming on.

"But my husband of seven years just announced he wants an open marriage."

Yikes.

"Can you believe it? I thought we were going to talk about starting a family. Instead, he wanted to talk about starting a harem." She made a sound of disgust.

The door opened and she sniffed hard to regain her composure.

"Here you go, Dr. Tyson. Are you okay?"

"Yes. I think someone just cleaned back here. My eyes are watering."

"I'll take the ultrasound machine back," Gina offered. "Why don't you get some drops?"

"Good idea. You'll get that sonogram to Ms. Kemp's family?"

"Absolutely. As soon as they… come back."

Hanging unsaid in the air was the sentiment of when that might be.

"Maybe you should call the family," Dr. Tyson suggested.

"Good idea," Gina said.

October 11, Tuesday

"WHAT ARE THOSE?" my aunt Winnie asked.

"I brought the kids' baby albums, to reminisce. I thought it would be fun to look at their sonograms next to the sonogram of Marigold's baby."

It is a sweet gesture. Especially since I didn't even know I had a baby album.

"Yes, here's Alex's first sonogram," my mother said.

"Wow, it was pretty clear you were having a boy," Winnie said.

"I know. Alex came out well-endowed."

"I so did not need to know that, Carrie."

Ditto, Mom.

"Well, it's true. Oh, and here's Sidney's sonogram." She hummed with affection. "She was such a good baby, even in the womb. She hardly kicked. And her birth was the easiest."

"By the third one, you were stretched out," Winnie said.

"That's not how it works," my mother said hotly.

"Where's Marigold's sonogram?"

"I'm looking… I'm sure it's here somewhere."

"It's not as if there are that many pages to flip through," Winnie noted. "Marigold's album looks a little skimpy."

My mother made an exasperated noise. "With the first baby, you're excited and you take tons of pictures and document everything. And when the second one comes around, you're just too tired."

"I see you rebounded by the time Sidney was born," Winnie added dryly.

"By that time, I'd learned how to juggle everything. Plus we'd just gotten a digital camera… and Sidney was such a little doll, you couldn't help but take her picture."

"Uh-hm," my aunt said.

"Wait—here's Marigold's sonogram."

"No. That's another one of Alex's."

"No, it isn't."

"Did Marigold have a penis in utero?"

"Oh. You're right. That's Alex. Here's Marigold's."

"No... that one's for Sidney. Look at the year."

"Hm. Maybe I wasn't given a copy of Marigold's sonogram."

"Maybe. What else is in here?"

"Oh, the usual stuff, when they started crawling, their first word. Alex's first word was 'da-da,' naturally. And Sidney's first word was "ma-ma."

"Hm... do you remember Marigold's first word?"

"I didn't write it down?"

"No. It's blank."

"That's odd."

"Carrie, don't you see a pattern here?"

"Of what?"

"Of ignoring Marigold!"

"Don't be ridiculous. Marigold got more attention than anyone because she was in the middle. And she was needy."

"No, she wasn't."

"Yes, she was. She always needed attention. I remember once I told her not to bother me unless she was bleeding. So she took a red marker and made marks all over her leg, then told me she was bleeding."

Ha—I remember doing that.

"That's sad!"

"No, it's not... it's manipulative."

"Carrie, you need help."

"That's a terrible thing to say!"

"But it needs to be said. How are things at home?"

My mother made a dismissive noise. "Robert is off doing his own thing, as usual."

"And from the looks of that obnoxious billboard I saw driving into the town, so are you."

"I finally have a career—so sue me."

"You and Robert had better get your act together."

"You can leave now."

"Fine," Winnie bit out. The chair squeaked, then her footsteps sounded in retreat. "Carrie?"

"What?"

"Marigold needs you right now more than she's ever needed you."

"Did your whackadoodle psychic tell you that?"

"No," Winnie said, her voice even. "It doesn't take a mind reader to see your entire family is in crisis."

The door opened and closed. My mother sat in huffy silence and turned the crackly pages of a baby album.

Not mine, I assume.

October 12, Wednesday

IT'S BATH DAY and while I'm sorely missing my sense of smell, I'm happy to have the nurses in the room and listen to their easy banter as they give us vegetables a good scrubbing.

"Nice haircut," Teddy said.

"Thanks," Gina said, a little nonchalantly.

"Did you get highlights?"

"Some… is it too much?"

"Not at all. It's a nice pick-me-up for fall. Is it for Gabriel?"

"It's for me," Gina said defensively. "Oh, look—Marigold is starting to show."

"Oh, poor Coma Girl. Wish she would wake up."

"Dr. Jarvis is working on it."

"What do you mean?"

"I mean… nothing. Just that he's working with Marigold a lot, doing physical therapy, talking to her a lot. He even had the television brought in."

"Still the classical music channel—ugh."

"Dr. Jarvis says it's the best stimulation."

"Well, if Dr. Jarvis says so, it must be right."

"I believe her scars are finally starting to fade, don't you?"

"Yes, I can tell a big difference lately."

Finally, some good news.

"The prenatal vitamins are helping her skin and nails," Gina said. "I'm going to start filing down her nails every day."

"Are we changing her head bandage?"

"Yes, let's do."

"So… by my estimation, it's getting close to the ninety-day mark with Gabriel."

"Twenty-five more days," Gina said.

He laughed. "Not that you're counting. So he's been a good boy all this time?"

"Yep."

Because he's been a bad boy all this time with Donna.

"The skin around the incision still looks irritated," Teddy said.

"Dr. Jarvis said the swelling is keeping the incision from healing. It's just going to take a while."

"Shouldn't the swelling in her brain have gone down by now?"

"Dr. Jarvis says it's residual blood from the brain hematoma, and it has to be reabsorbed by her body. He says it's a positive sign."

"How so?"

"In Marigold's case, the doctors think the swelling in her brain is causing the coma, and when the swelling finally subsides, she might recover."

"Might?"

"Dr. Jarvis says for a coma patient, 'might' is the best-case scenario."

"I'm sorry, but this is like a horror movie to me. I mean, what if right now, Marigold can hear everything we're saying, but she can't let us know—how awful would that be?"

Pretty awful.

"Even Dr. Jarvis doesn't believe she's that fully aware."

I hope I get the chance to set him straight.

"But she still responds to commands to move her fingers, doesn't she?"

"Intermittently... and only for Dr. Jarvis."

"Maybe Marigold has a crush on Dr. Jarvis, too."

"Stop it," Gina said, then she groaned. "Is it that obvious?"

"I was talking about me," Teddy said. "But you're so busted."

October 13, Thursday

LIKE A BLIND PERSON, my hearing has become acute. So when an unfamiliar set of shoes and footsteps enter the room, I'm on alert. These feet are male, shod in stiff dress shoes, and the footsteps are heavy and pronounced—almost arrogant.

David Spooner.

"Hello, Marigold," he shouted. "How are you?"

Still in a coma, thanks. But not deaf.

"Are you awake?" he yelled.

Coma. Still.

I heard a few tapping noises. "Sid? Yeah, I'm here. She looks the same to me. Scarf? Looks like some kind of Aztec design. Damn, it's depressing in here. Yeah. Security is good, which is probably why we haven't seen any leaked pictures lately."

My poet volunteer hasn't visited in a long while. Maybe someone was on to him and he'd been banned from the ward.

"Sure, let me take one of her to send you." He repositioned himself. "Say 'comatose'!" A click sounded.

What an asshole.

"Sid? Yeah... I just sent it to you. How are things there? You gotta hang in there, Babe. Just get through this, then we'll be home free. Okay, talk soon."

Since he'd ended the call, I expected him to leave. Instead, he sat in the chair and placed another phone call.

"Hello, my name is Dean Bradley. B-R-A-D-L-E-Y."

Hm... a family name?

I need to arrange a wire transfer, please. From one of my accounts here in Atlanta to another bank account of mine in Panama." He rattled off the bank account numbers, then a long alphanumeric password. "Yes. One hundred thousand. I'll hold until you confirm."

He stood and turned the TV from my classical music to channel surf, stopping on a reality show about bungled plastic surgery procedures. From the rather explicit audio, I gathered a woman with gigantic knockers wanted to bump up another cup size, and from his snickers and guffaws, I assumed there were lots of visuals to go with the audio.

After several minutes of language that would singe a whore's ears, he said, "Yes, I'm here. Confirmation number, please? Okay, thank you."

He ended the call, then left the room, leaving the television on the embarrassing channel.

And why do I have the feeling that what I'm listening to on the television is less slimy than what I'd just overheard on the phone?

October 14, Friday

THE LAST TIME Audrey Parks, our former ward mate, had come to visit, she'd been in a wheelchair, and she was not a rolling ball of sunshine. This time, she was on what sounded like metal crutches, and I hoped she was in a better place.

"Hello, veggies," she said, sounding cheerful enough, but I was wary.

"No new roomie to take my place yet? Don't worry... I saw a couple of goners in ICU that looked like good candidates for the patch—if they make it."

I see she had moved from depressed to depressed and snarky.

"You'll be happy to know that traffic still sucks, the weather still sucks, and the economy is in the crapper. The company I used to work for went out of business. Not that I could get my old job as a bookkeeper back anyway—apparently my I.Q. has dropped fifty points."

Her speech had improved a bit, but her breathing sounded labored as she made her way around the room. "But I'm still smart enough to know to keep my ears open when I made the rounds in physical therapy, speech therapy, and head therapy. And guess what? I know more about each of you than you probably do. You know the doctors and nurses are never straight with you or your families."

"Karen, do you want to know what you have ahead of you? If you ever wake up, you'll probably never walk again. Did anyone tell you your spinal cord was crushed when you fell? No? Well, now you know."

That seemed unnecessarily cruel.

The crutches scraped across the floor as she moved to Jill's bed next. "Jill, if you ever wake up, you'll be on a ventilator the rest of your miserable life. And it will be miserable because you need a kidney transplant and a heart transplant, which you're never going to get because your lungs don't work. The doctors say your body is already gone, and you need to just give up your mind, too, and die already."

She was getting louder now, and breathing harder as she clunked over to my bed.

"And you, Coma Girl. I saw your picture on TMZ today—aren't you special with your baby and your headscarves? But you know what they're not telling you?"

What?

The door banged open. "Audrey," Teddy said in a calm voice, "you shouldn't be in here. Come with me."

"You know what they're not telling you, Coma Girl?" she shouted.

WHAT?

"That's it," Teddy said.

"If you ever wake up—"

The rest of her words were muffled with a large hand. And from the sound of it, Teddy had picked her up, crutches and all, and carried her from the room. The door banged closed, leaving the echo of her verbal assault.

And leaving me to wonder if there is some horrific thing the doctors and nurses aren't telling me.

October 15, Saturday

"I CAN HEAR YOU, Dad, but I can't see you and Marigold."

"Wait a minute. I'm not as good at this as your mother."

"Where is Mom?" Alex asked.

"She had to *work*."

The way he said it, I suspect he added air quotes that neither Alex nor I could see.

"Well, it's the weekend, Dad. That's when real estate agents are supposed to be busy."

"Uh-huh."

"Still can't see you."

Dad sighed. "What do I do?"

"Tap the bottom of the screen until a group of icons show up, then tap the video camera with the line through it."

"Okay."

"Now I can see you. Hi, Marigold! Good to see you, Dad."

"Good to see you, son."

"Any change in Marigold?"

"Not that we can see. The doctors say she's plateaued."

"So no better, no worse?"

"I guess so."

"Dad, are you talking to the doctors? Are you asking questions?"

If they are, they're doing it out of my earshot.

"Of course we are. But all they say is 'we don't know' or 'we can't say for sure' or 'time will tell.'"

"After we hang up, I'll call Dr. Oscar to see if he can shed any light on the situation."

"Great," my dad said, happy to offload the responsibility.

"How's the baby?"

"Fine, as far as we know."

"That's good. Do you know if it's a boy or a girl?"

"If your mom knows, she didn't say anything to me."

"Dad, this is your grandson or your granddaughter, you can be involved, too."

"Well, you know how your mother is."

My parents communicate in soundbites and one-liners.

"Any news on the county's criminal case against Young?" Alex asked.

"Some. The DA is considering charging Young anyway, even with him blowing below the legal limit, but they want to clear up the assault on Young first."

"Ah, so that's why the detective contacted me again."

"What did he want this time?"

"He rattled off some phone numbers, wanted to know if I recognized any of them, which I didn't. Then he asked me if I recognized a couple of names."

"What names?"

"I wrote them down. Gary Fortune... Cameron Kitt... Dean Bradley."

I perked up. Dean Bradley, aka David Spooner?

"I don't recognize them either," Dad said. "Are they suspects?"

"The detective wouldn't say. And I don't care as long as they can't be connected to the Kemps."

Uh-oh.

"Dad, if it turns out we can't sue Keith Young for damages, how will Marigold's medical bills be paid?"

"Thank goodness Sid has that covered. She and that Spooner guy hooked up with a company to fulfill all the T-shirts and mugs and whatever, and all the profit goes straight to the foundation they set up in Marigold's name. Then the foundation pays the medical bills."

"So the foundation is doing well?"

"Oh, yeah. The last time Sid showed me a statement, it had almost a half million dollars in it."

My mind went to the phone call David Spooner had made. But for how long would the account have a half million dollars in it?

"Oh, Dad, by the way, I went back over the letters Marigold wrote to me to see if she mentioned any one guy in particular."

"And?"

"There was the guy in the Peace Corps she mentioned a couple of times, but she said they were just friends."

"Did she mention a name?"

"Yeah. His name is Duncan."

October 16, Sunday

I WAS BARELY AWAKE when Detective Terry walked into my room. He's wearing new boots, I register vaguely. For a few seconds, I thought I'd slept later than normal because of the mental tossing and turning all night. But then I realized church bells are still ringing around the city. I'm not late—he's early. By several hours.

"Good morning, Marigold. It's Jack Terry. I can't stay long, I'm on my way to Vegas."

Vegas? Jack doesn't strike me as a Vegas guy, but maybe he's a gambler. Or maybe he's getting married!

"I have a murder case out there."

Even better!

Hm. Out of his jurisdiction—normally. But from watching *Forensics Files*, I know that means either the victim is from Atlanta, or the perp, or the murder is related to a crime committed in Atlanta.

This is so exciting! Maybe it's a real live serial killer.

"My girl—I mean, my friend Carlotta is in trouble."

Carlotta again. Well, well, well. She's from here, so I'm guessing she went to Vegas on vacation. But how does someone go on vacation and wind up involved in a murder?

I've obviously been playing it way too safe in life.

"It's complicated," Jack said, then added, "As always, where Carlotta is concerned," almost to himself. "I just wanted to let you know I might be out of pocket for a while. But ADA Spence knows where I'll be if something happens on your case."

You mean, like finding out my sister was behind the wheel instead of me?

Or if I can connect David Spooner to the Dean Bradley you're looking for in the assault on Keith Young?

Or if I suspect David Spooner is siphoning funds away from the foundation?

"I'll drop in when I get back," he said. "Stay out of trouble."

I'm already *in* trouble, Detective. About four months. And so are you, remember?

And if you're going to Vegas to rescue a girl you can't stop talking about, while another woman is having your baby, well, then you're *in* something else altogether.

October 17, Monday

"GOOD MORNING, MARIGOLD. It's Dr. Jarvis."

While I have nothing but gratitude toward Dr. Jarvis, I'm also wary—and a little angry. I haven't forgotten about Audrey's outburst and I'm worried about what she was trying to tell me. Have all of my limbs been amputated and the reason I can't feel anything is because there's nothing to feel?

Am I some kind of medical experiment? Has my brain been placed in a robot and still trying to assimilate with my man-made body?

Okay, so deep down I know these conditions are impossible, but when left to wander, my mind tends to spin fantastic catastrophes.

"Today, I brought in a friend. Say hello, Tag."

A cheerful bark sounded.

A dog in the hospital? Instantly my mood lifted.

"Tag is a Jack Russell Terrier, a certified therapy animal, and he's been trained to diagnose certain diseases. But today I think he just wants to lick your face. I hope that's okay, Marigold?"

I probably can't feel it, but knowing he's doing it will make me feel good.

"Okay, Tag is resting on your chest. I'm going to let you two get acquainted while I check your vital signs."

Tag barked a couple of times, as if he was trying to get me to respond.

Dr. Jarvis laughed. "He likes you. Can you feel him licking your face, Marigold?"

No... but something... is... happening. I heard myself sneeze.

"Excellent," Jarvis said. "Go, Tag!"

The dog yapped happily, and I heard myself sneeze again.

"Very good," Jarvis said. "And wow, I'm literally watching your blood pressure go down a couple of points."

A pungent odor suddenly assailed me—the unmistakable scent of DOG. My sense of smell was back!

"Okay, Tag, that's enough, boy. I'm setting Tag back on the floor, Marigold. He'll visit another time. I'll be back later, too."

The door opened and closed and I was peaceful for a while, breathing in and enjoying the faint odors in the room—food, cleaning supplies, cologne... it was all heavenly.

But then as quickly as it came, it went away again, like the tide going out. And I started to feel blue again. Why couldn't I seem to gain ground? What was it Dad had said? I had plateaued—no worse, no better.

Flatlining. And as far as I'm concerned, not getting better means I'm getting worse.

October 18, Tuesday

TODAY EVERY TIME the door opens, my hopes buoy. But when instead of hearing the voice of my mom or dad or Winnie, or even Roberta, I hear the shuffle and quick rapport of nurses, orderlies, and other staff, my heart squeezes again.

It's my birthday, and as the day I turn twenty-nine slides away, it becomes clear no one remembers.

Granted, it's also Tuesday and non-comatose people are busy. I'm sure my dad is on the road. My mom spends Tuesdays visiting new listings of other agents to scope out the best properties early in the week. I remember that Sid goes to the courthouse on Tuesdays, to observe trials. On the other side of the world, Alex is probably saving a village.

So I'm a Libra, which means I'm gracious (a pushover), diplomatic (a pleaser), and cooperative (malleable). I'm also indecisive, I avoid confrontation, and I'm prone to self-pity.

Not a bestselling singles profile.

And apparently, my biggest dilemma is when I have to choose sides because I choose *all* sides. Everyone in my household picked up on that fickle trait early on because I can't count the times I felt as if I was being drawn and quartered by the other four people in the house who demanded I come over to their side and support their cause. While I ran around trying to please everyone, I pleased no one, and at the end of the day, the one thing they all seemed to have in common was a resentment toward me; as a result, I would often find myself standing alone while the four of them walked off, arm in arm.

Don't get me wrong— our home wasn't a constant state of warfare. Not overtly. But grudges were quick to cut and long to heal. And I felt as if I was always being punished for some unwitting transgression.

So being a Libra, I'm lying here feeling bad for expecting people to remember it's my birthday and at the same time, indulging in a little pity-party. The argument could be made that it's been my day every day since the accident.

Still, as visiting hours draw to a close, I'm secretly hoping my family is huddled out in the hallway with noisemakers and confetti to surprise me.

The door opens, and I hold my breath.

"It's just me, Marigold," Gina says. "Dr. Jarvis asked me to take your blood pressure every two hours.

I fight disappointment, but honestly, why would anyone make a fuss? No one knows I know it's my birthday. It's like any other coma day.

"Okay," Gina said. "Your blood pressure is on the high side of normal, but that's common for expectant women, especially when you're not getting any exercise."

I heard the scrape of her removing the chart at the foot of the bed to record the reading.

"Oh, my goodness, Marigold, I see on your chart that today is your birthday."

She returned the chart, then left the room. A few minutes later, she was back. "I'm tying a Happy Birthday balloon to your bed. Happy

Birthday, Coma Girl."

Inside I'm smiling, if a teensy bit sad that I'm so forgettable. I mean, how does my Mom not remember the day she gave birth to me?

The door opened and I wondered if she or Dad had remembered at the last minute.

"Hello, lady."

It's my young friend Christina with the sick mother.

"Is it your birthday? It must be, you have a pretty balloon. Did you have cake and ice cream?" She sighed. "I love ice cream."

I remember.

She cleared her throat, then began singing in a sweet, pure voice. "Happy birthday to you... happy birthday to you... happy birthday, dear la-dee! Happy birthday to you."

She clapped for herself and for me. I've never been so touched by any gesture my whole stinking life. She's such a giving little thing.

"If you had a cake, this is when we'd blow out the candles and cut a big piece to eat. With ice cream."

"Christina!" boomed her father's voice from the hall.

"Don't forgets to do the magic for my sick mama," she said in a rush. "Happy birthday!" Then she scampered out of the room.

How can I possibly feel sorry for myself after that?

October 19, Wednesday

"HELLO, DEAR, it's Winnie, and I brought Faridee with me."

"Hello, M-Marigold."

Faridee sounded tense. I wonder if she's getting tired of my aunt dragging her all the way from Savannah to Atlanta to see me. I strained to smell the smoky herbs that always clung to Faridee, but alas, my olfactory apparatus still isn't cooperating.

"I'm sorry I missed your birthday, dear, but your mother is on the warpath with me, and I was afraid I'd run in to her here."

No chance of that, as it turned out. But I was pleased to know that Winnie remembered.

"I brought you a new scarf in all your colors—aqua, green, and turquoise. Let me tie it around your head. Sweetie, your hair is growing in nicely where they haven't shaved your head."

That's quite a caveat.

"Oh, yes, she looks lovely, doesn't she, Faridee?"

"Uh-huh."

The woman's voice sounded far away.

"Faridee, are you okay?"

Something crashed to the floor—a tray?

"Sorry," Faridee said. "Winnie, we have to go."

"Why? We can stay a few more minutes before we get in the car to drive all the way back home."

"We have to go now!" Faridee's sandals slapped against the floor as she beat a retreat to the door.

But my aunt must've caught up with her before she fled. "What on earth is wrong?"

"Death is in this room," Faridee whispered. "Say goodbye to Marigold."

"Wait—is Marigold okay?"

"Say your goodbyes, Winnie. Say your goodbyes."

The door opened and closed in a whoosh.

Holy crap—what was that all about? Am I dying? Is my baby okay?

"Goodbye, my dear," Winnie's voice sounded tremulous. She gave me a boisterous kiss somewhere close to my ear. "Don't be afraid. Just do whatever you need to do whenever you need to do it."

And with that bit of potty-training advice, she left.

I feel as if I've been sideswiped, until I remember that Faridee's readings are hit or miss at best.

"Death in this room" could mean an unfortunate fly in the window.

I have nothing to worry about. Probably.

October 20, Thursday

I WAS AWAKE when the morning nurse came in to check charts and get the day's routine underway.

"Rise and shine," she said.

It's Donna, Gabriel's other girlfriend.

I don't dislike her, but it's hard to respect someone you heard climax against a hospital laundry cart.

She went around the room hitting wall switches that set off small hums in the room. Lights for the people who aren't vegetables. Suddenly she gasped and came up short.

"Shit! Oh, shit, oh, shit, oh, shit!"

She sprinted to the door and flung it open.

"Help! Get a doctor!"

Feet stampeded into the room, but it was apparent from the mournful noises and gasps of recoil, they were already too late.

"Oh, she's been dead for a while."

"Yeah, probably gave it up right after midnight."

Who? Who's dead? Karen? Jill?

Me?

If I'm dead, would I know it?

The noises in the room sounded the same—the bubble of I.V.'s the rackety noise of Jill's ventilator.

"You just don't know, do you?" someone said. "One day a vegetable sits up and starts talking, and the next day the vegetable right beside them up and dies."

Who? Will someone please tell me who's dead?

"Step aside," Dr. Tyson said. "Donna and Gina, stay, please. The rest of you, get back to work. Teddy, will you call the morgue and let them know?"

"Sure thing," he said.

I'm going to die if you don't tell me who's dead!

"Time of death, between midnight and three a.m. Gina, will you read the name on the wristband to crosscheck with the patient's chart?"

"Jill R. Wheatley, date of birth... "

I don't hear the rest of what she says. I'm so giddy with relief I'm not dead, it takes me a few seconds to feel sad for Jill.

A heavy switch was thrown, and Jill's ventilator stopped.

"What do you think happened?" Donna asked.

"Probably her heart," Dr. Tyson said. "Her body has been so weak for so long, I'm surprised she lived as long as she did. She must've just given in."

Audrey's hurt words of less than a week ago came back to me.

The doctors say your body is already gone, and you need to just give up your mind, too, and die already.

And Faridee, bless her crooked heart, had actually sensed something real and terrible in the room last night.

Dr. Tyson and the nurses left, gloves snapping and paper scrubs being torn away. A few minutes later, Gabriel and Nico arrived to transport the body to the morgue.

"Ugh, this one's ripe," Gabriel said.

At the moment I was very glad my sense of smell was absent.

"Poor lady," Nico said. "Lying in this bed for years and then just dies, all alone."

"She wasn't alone," Gabriel said as they banged and clanged their way out the door. "The other vegetables were here."

The door closed on his mean chuckle.

And then there were two.

October 21, Friday

"WELL, IT DANG NEAR scared the poop out of me," Roberta said. "My reporter friend called at five-freaking-o'clock in the morning, wanted to know if Coma Girl had died." She made a dismissive noise. "I told him, you had good manners—no way you'd die at such an indecent hour."

Going forward, I will try to time my demise for a lady-like time of day. If it's a weekday—ten a.m., when everyone is already out of bed. And for weekends—noon at the earliest.

Roberta sighed. "I gotta tell you, I'm running out of ideas on how to find the guy who belongs to this San Antonio Spurs hat. And can I just say, it's an ugly-ass hat." She made a thoughtful noise. "It's a large, so I'm trying to think of the guys you know who have a big old head. Or a lot of hair."

Duncan had neither an enormous head nor a lot of hair. It had been big on him, but he'd worn the hat anyway. I gathered someone must have given it to him for it to mean so much that he'd wear a too-big hat for a franchise he didn't even follow.

"Well, I'm going to have to eat a bear claw and think on it more."

The chair creaked.

"Meanwhile, I want to talk about something serious. The other day I was in your desk looking for a stamp—"

Uh-huh.

"When I came across this big important looking envelope, and I decided to take a look inside."

From the rustle of papers, I realized she'd brought it with her.

"It's your will, and an advance healthcare directive. I assumed your family had a copy, but after that scare this morning, I thought I'd better get in touch with your sister and find out. She said no, she'd never seen it."

True. I'd had the documents drawn up through a benefit on my job close to a year ago, and I thought I had all the time in the world to tell my family about it. Since I'd made Sidney my healthcare agent, I should've at least told her.

Although knowing what I know now about Sid, I'm not sure I'd make the same choice. I wish I could wake up and yank those documents out of Roberta's hands.

And if I wake up, I won't need the documents anymore. Win-win.

I zeroed in on Roberta's voice and tried to move toward it.

"....so that's what I'm going to do."

Wait—what is Roberta going to do?

"I'll come back soon and bring you some more freaky mail from those freaky freaks who want to dress you up like a doll and put you in a giant cradle. Bye, Coma Girl."

Wait! Come back!

October 22, Saturday

"HI, SWEETHEART, it's Dad."

Yeah, Dad… after twenty-nine years, I recognize the voice.

Something pinged against my bedrail.

"Did someone bring you a San Antonio Spurs hat?"

Ah… Roberta must've forgotten Duncan's hat.

He sighed. "I've been out of touch… for a long time. But that's going to change. *I'm* going to change."

I want to give him the benefit of the doubt, but I've heard that before. And besides, I don't want to feel like an obligation. I'd love for things between me and my dad to be less awkward, but I don't expect for us to work things out while I'm in a coma.

"This whole situation has really thrown me for a loop. First the accident, then the coma, then the baby."

His voice sounds hollow, and my heart squeezed. My dad isn't built for drama. He's the most low-maintenance, by-the-book, squeaky clean guy you'd ever want to meet. I hate that I'm putting him through this. Frankly, I'm not surprised it's pushed him farther away.

"I'm going to fix this," he said. "I'm going to fix all of this."

Now I'm confused.

"I'm done dragging your car around to these lame mechanics. I had it towed to the house. I'm going to fix it myself."

Oh, my car—of course. But my dad isn't a mechanic—no way can he fix it. Although it's very sweet of him to try.

"I don't know if you can hear me, Sweetheart. I'm pretty sure you can't. The doctors are telling us you're getting worse."

Wait—I am? I mean, my sense of smell still hasn't returned, and I haven't been able to respond to Dr. Jarvis's commands for a while, but I'm still here. I'm still aware of everything going on.

"I realize our family is broken… and it's all my fault."

Whoa—where is this coming from?

"If your mother seems distant, it's because I drove a wedge between us with a lie." His voice broke off on a sob.

Now I'm getting a little freaked out.

"Before you were born, when Alex was little, twenty-five thousand dollars in cash was stolen from our safe."

I vaguely remember the story. They'd assumed a contractor working for them had stolen it, but he was long-gone by the time they discovered the money was missing.

"That money was every penny your mother and I had saved for ten years. It was supposed to go toward a down payment on a house your mother had her heart set on."

Ergo my mother's pervasive sense of dissatisfaction with every house we'd lived in. Which had emasculated my dad, and it was no secret my mom thought he was too passive.

"We weren't robbed," he said. "I took the money to pay off gambling debts and let your mother believe it had been stolen." He exhaled heavily. "There, I said it."

I so wish he hadn't. My dad is a gambler? And a liar? And a thief? This is a bad country song. I feel disoriented.

"But I'm going to fix our family," he said solemnly. "And I'm going to fix this situation with Keith Young."

What does he mean by that? Can someone tell me what just happened?

October 23, Sunday

JUST WHEN I was wondering if Jack Terry was going to show, or if he was still in Las Vegas, the door opened.

But when I heard the click clack of high heeled shoes instead of low-heeled boots, I realized it wasn't Jack.

"Hello?" ADA Spence said tentatively.

In my direction, I believe. Although I'm not sure what part of "coma" she doesn't get.

She sighed with exaggerated irritation, then paced over to the window, then paced back to my bed, then made another loop.

The door opened and I heard the familiar squish of the shoes of someone on staff.

"Hello," Gina said tentatively. "Can I help you?"

"I'm from the DA's office. I came to visit Marigold Kemp."

"Then you're in the right place," Gina said, and since her voice swung in my direction, I assume she gestured toward my bed.

"Yes, I know that's her. I—" The woman faltered. "I just don't know how to do this."

"Do what?"

"Talk to someone who's in a coma."

"Just sit down and talk to her."

"But can she hear me?"

"We do believe Marigold can hear us. We're just not sure how often, or how much she comprehends."

"So she doesn't communicate back?"

"No, ma'am. She has occasionally responded to her doctor's commands to move her fingers, but that hasn't happened in a while."

"She's getting worse?"

"You should make an appointment to talk to her doctors, ma'am."

"Just yes or no, is she getting worse?"

"She's slipping some, yes, ma'am."

"And the baby?"

"Is healthy as far as we can tell."

"Thank you," ADA Spence said.

When Gina left, I wasn't sure what to expect. I still wasn't sure why the woman had come to see me.

She sat in the chair, and from the sound of it, slipped off her high heels.

"I hate my job," she said finally.

That's a hell of an opener for someone you're supposed to be helping.

"I work for a boorish, misogynistic toad, and he tosses me all the bad cases. For example, I get the case with the comatose client, which sounds like a sympathetic case, but in reality, is proving damn hard to prosecute. And frankly, I'm tired of spinning my wheels."

I'm pretty sure no response is required from me.

"Marigold, do you know what attorneys do really well?"

Lie?

"We lie. So here's what I'm going to do. I'm going to tell Keith Young's defense attorney that you can communicate and are going to testify in a taped interview about what happened in the accident, and we're going to see if he will plea to a lesser charge to avoid going to trial. That gets me a conviction, and that gets you and your family an almost guaranteed civil judgement."

She repositioned in the chair.

"The risk of course, is they call our bluff. If that happens, we'll just fold and say your health has declined to the point that you can't testify. But by doing things this way, we have a lot to gain, and nothing to lose."

She made a pensive noise in her throat.

"And I'm sorry to say this, but if your health is failing, the sooner I extend the offer, the better. Plus I'll go ahead and get things moving as if we're going to tape your interview for say, November 1. That way our story will check out if the defense digs a little."

The woman is good… she reminds me of Sidney.

"I'll try to touch base with your parents to give them a heads up, but they're difficult to pin down. Worst case scenario, I'll inform them if we get a plea deal and before we settle."

ADA Spence pushed to her feet.

"I have no idea whether you can hear me or understand me, Marigold, but it's been nice talking to you."

I believe I'm supposed to feel good about the plan, but between you and me, I'm having trouble concentrating. I hope I'm just tired, and not…. something else.

October 24, Monday

"I THINK YOUR father has lost his mind," my mom said, her voice elevated. "He put a punching bag in the garage, and all he does is 'spar' and do pushups. He's eating grilled chicken every two hours. I caught him flexing and posing in our bathroom mirror."

Oh, brother. Is this what he meant by fixing things with Keith Young? Getting buff and roughing him up? Really Dad? On what planet and in what time machine?

"It gets worse," my mom said, her voice breaking up. "He got a tattoo on his shoulder—a *tattoo*. Then he tore the sleeves off all his T-shirts."

Sigh… maybe it's just a generic mid-life crisis.

"And he's listening to hip-hop music!"

That's not bad, that's just *weird*.

"Wait a minute—why do you have a San Antonio Spurs hat on your bedrail?"

Why are you asking the girl in the coma questions?

"Never mind. I told him I cannot deal with this right now. I have too much on my plate. I'm worried sick about you, I'm worried sick about the baby, and my job is so demanding. The last thing I need is for him to… change!"

Except only for my entire life, my mother has been begging and pleading with my dad to change.

"I'm not kidding, Marigold, I'm hanging on by a very thin thread."

She gasped for air in a wheezing breath. "Ack… I can't breathe."

Mom, hit the nurse call button.

She wheezed. "Marigold, I can't breathe."

Hit the nurse call button.

She wheezed. "Marigold, I can't breathe!"

Seriously, Mom, is this a trick? Are you trying to get me to wake up to *hit the nurse call button for you?*

I heard the squeak of a mattress and realized with mortification she had climbed into the bed that had been wheeled into the ward in preparation for a new patient. In between the wheezing, I heard flailing, then the ping of the nurse call button.

Several seconds passed before the door opened because the veggies don't press call buttons.

"Ms. Kemp, are you okay?"

She wheezed. "A panic..." Another wheeze. "Attack."

A flurry of activity followed to administer oxygen and ply her with Xanax. Within a few minutes, she was chatting and laughing, enjoying the attention and the promise of a prescription.

I am mentally shaking my head. Only my mother could find a way to upstage her comatose daughter.

On a deeper level though, I'm worried about my parents. They seem to be spinning off into their own orbits. And I sincerely hope my dad doesn't confess to Mom what he confessed to me. I have a feeling my mother will not be quite as forgiving or forgetting. Because my mother has never done anything illegal or immoral in her life. Ever.

That I know of.

October 25, Tuesday

"PEACE BE WITH YOU, ladies."

Oh, no. Not today... Please, God. I can't take it.

"Oh, ladies, I heard about dear Jill... let's say the Lord's Prayer, shall we?"

I tried to mentally recite the words, flubbing most as they floated back to me a couple of beats too late. Plus I'm already steeling myself against what was to come.

Sister Irene lingered over Karen, giving me time to sweat, I presumed. But eventually she made her way over to my bed.

"Hello, Marigold, oh, my goodness, you're definitely showing. Motherhood becomes you. Your skin is positively glowing."

Yeah, yeah, skip the small talk and get down to brass tacks, Sister.

"I'm sure you're wondering how things went with my new handyman, Mr. Gilpin. Unfortunately, he took a spill."

She threw him down the stairs. Or tossed him off the roof.

"He fell off a ladder changing a light bulb, and broke his leg, of all things."

With the help of a baseball bat?

"So he's spending a few days at my place, recuperating."

She has him tied to a bed, torturing him. Or hogtied in her basement.

"It's definitely not what he expected," she said merrily.

Hey, I won't be crying any tears over a half-human like the man who murdered her sister being toyed with—or even hurt. I can only imagine how I would feel if Sidney were taken away from me in such a brutal fashion. But I do worry about what's going to happen to Sister Irene when she gets caught. Is there a special prison for nuns, like the military?

"Don't judge me too harshly, Marigold. I've been a good person and sacrificed a lot for God. I think I've earned a pass, don't you?"

I'm not a religion scholar, but I'm pretty sure that's not how it works.

"Anyway, I've been very astute in who I've confided in. You're the only person who knows, and you're not going to tell anyone, are you, Coma Girl?"

No, ma'am.

"What a beautiful day God has given us. I have to move along, ladies, so I can get back to my houseguest. Peace be with you."

God help us all.

October 26, Wednesday

"HELLO, COMA GIRL. Remember me?"

The honey-throated poet is back after a long absence. I'd decided he'd been barred from coming into our room, that someone had caught him taking pictures and leaking them to tabloid sites.

"Sorry I've been away. Aw, I see you lost another roomie. That has to be hard. I imagine there are only a few people who've had the same experience. I suppose people either get better, or they get worse. I pray you both get better.'"

But maybe I'm wrong about him… I hope I'm wrong.

"Nice hat, Coma Girl. Spurs fan, huh? That's cool."

I heard the swish of pages as he opened a book.

"I found this poem by Emily Dickinson, and it's about how all the people you meet change you, and I thought it would be appropriate. It's called 'Experiment to Me.'"

He cleared his throat politely. "Experiment to me, is every one I meet.

If it contain a kernel? The figure of a nut, presents upon a tree, equally plausibly. But meat within is requisite, to squirrels and to me."

That's me, a little squirrel busily storing nuts when people throw them at me. I'm starting to feel like my cheeks are getting full. People who are comatose are repositories for whatever anyone else wants to dump on us— medicine, confessions, even abuse. It's a scary, vulnerable place to be… especially when you know you might be in this limbo for months, years… decades.

"Coma Girl, you're going to be a mother, how about that?" He gave a little laugh. "You've got to wake up to see that little face."

Yes, I'm hoping if childbirth doesn't kill me, that it jars my body enough to shock me out of this malaise. What if years from now I'm like this still, and my child is visiting, will never know me as anything other than a living corpse?

I don't want my mind to go there, but I can't help it. Depression is pulling at me. Every day I'm fighting harder and harder not to succumb.

"I don't know when I'll be back," he said. "Take care of yourself and your little one."

He slipped from the room so quietly I barely heard the door close.

But then my hearing is starting to fail me, too. Dr. Jarvis hasn't been in to see me in a while… or if he has, I've forgotten.

I feel myself being erased, like a pencil drawing, and I'm utterly terrified.

October 27, Thursday

"CAN I HELP you?" Gina asked.

"I came to see a patient," a female voice said. "Marigold Kemp?"

"Are you a friend?"

"My fiancé is a friend of Marigold's. We used to Skype with her. He's out of the country, so I came in his place."

"What's your name?"

"Trina Gold. I signed in at the desk, and I don't have a phone or camera."

"Ten minutes," Gina said. "It's bedtime for the patients, and Marigold especially needs her rest."

My brain is moving sluggishly these days, especially as the day goes on, but I realize with some amazement that Duncan's fiancée Trina is here. I rally all my resources because I'm curious as to why she would come to see me. And I feel completely exposed because I wonder if she knows, or does she suspect the baby is Duncan's?

"Hello, Marigold," she said. "I'm Trina, Duncan's girlfriend. This is a little strange because we've never met in person. I don't know if you remember, but we did Skype a few times."

I'm trying to recall what she looks like... all I can remember is pretty blonde hair.

"Duncan is still working with refugees in Germany, although I'm not sure where since he moves around so much. I haven't talked to him in weeks, but he promised to be home before our wedding. I know he was hoping you could be there."

I was hoping I could be at Duncan's wedding, too, but not as a guest.

She gave an awkward little laugh. "I used to be jealous of you. Because you knew Duncan first, I felt like the intruder. I know how much you mean—*meant* to him."

Past tense.

"I hope you and your b-baby recover soon. And I know Duncan wishes it, too."

I wish I could hate her, but I don't even have the strength. And except for the unfortunate choice of a pink grapefruit wedding cake, she seems perfectly lovely.

"I'll go now," she said. "I'll tell Duncan I saw you."

Then her footsteps faltered and she gave a little laugh. "A San Antonio Spurs hat. That's so strange... someone asked me recently... no, I can't recall. Goodbye, Marigold."

Goodbye. Take care of Duncan.

October 28, Friday

"WHAT'S WITH the empty bed?" Nico asked.

"Planting a new vegetable next week," Gabriel said. "To replace that expired cabbage we moved to the morgue a couple weeks ago."

Jill... her name was Jill.

"I remember," Nico said. "Hey, how's it going with Gina?"

"Grrreat. Get to sample the honeypot soon."

"Yeah? What does Donna think about that?"

"Donna's cool. She knows I'm not a one-woman man."

"But does Gina know?"

"No, and you better keep your mouth shut."

"Man, you don't have to worry about me. One of the girls will get wise and burn you down."

"Better to go out smoking than stokin'."

"Uh-huh."

"Hey, man, take my picture with Coma Girl."

"That's against the rules."

"Oh, come on. We could make a lot of money selling the pictures to the tabloids, people are crazy for her. We could say I'm the baby daddy."

"You're insane."

"Okay, but I'm going to take a picture of just her, and get that big belly in it. No one will know who took it. Be my lookout, I'll pay you half."

"No way, you're on your own. Tyson will have your job and your scrawny neck."

I heard the camera click three times.

"See, already done, and no one the wiser."

"Whatever."

"Hey, I like this hat. Spurs are playing great. I think I'll make it mine."

No, don't take the hat... the last connection I have with Duncan. Please.

"Man, that's stealing."

"Veggie ain't gonna miss the hat, man. Let's *go*."

No... please...

October 29, Saturday

"THANK YOU, Dr. Oscar, for joining us in this case review. Dr. Jarvis and I really appreciate it."

Drs. Tyson and Jarvis are talking over my bed, and beaming Dr. Oscar in via Skype.

"Happy to help a soldier's sister, Dr. Tyson. Is this the patient?"

"Yes, this is Marigold Kemp."

"Hello, Marigold. I'm Dr. Oscar."

I wish I could respond. I hope the doctors have good news for me.

"I've reviewed Ms. Kemp's scans and MRI and I have to say I agree— you need to operate again and remove the dried blood and other debris from the first surgery. The pressure is too much, it's leaning on vital areas of her brain waiting to come back to life. And you're definitely in danger of killing the optic nerves."

I'm no physician, but I know what that means—blindness. I wonder if that's what Audrey was going to tell me that the doctors were keeping from me?

"The first surgery was tricky," Dr. Tyson said.

"This one will be twice as complicated," Dr. Oscar said. "If you like, I can scope in."

"It would be an honor, sir."

"The honor would be mine," the man said. "For the chance to save this young girl and her baby. You don't get many opportunities like that. When are you planning to do it?"

"We want to operate as soon as possible, so we'd like to schedule it for Wednesday."

"November 2?"

"Yes."

"Looking forward to it," Dr. Oscar said. "Let talk on the first to go over a game plan."

The Skype call was disconnected with a bleep and Dr. Tyson exhaled audibly. "We need to make sure the family knows how risky this surgery is. If her brain starts to swell and we can't control it, we'll lose her and the baby."

"But if you don't do the surgery," Dr. Jarvis prompted.

"We'll probably lose them both anyway."

What was it ADA Spence had said? We have a lot to gain, and nothing to lose.

"But let's hold off telling the family until we confer with Dr. Oscar on the first," Tyson said.

"That late?"

"I don't want to get their hopes up in case we find something unexpected. And I want to tell them exactly what we're planning to do so they can make an informed decision. We took two big risks by administering the experimental drug. I want this surgery to be completely by the book. If we decide we can do it, and they need a couple more days to make up their mind, we'll push the surgery out."

"Okay, November first it is."

October 30, Sunday

"HI, MARIGOLD, IT'S Jack Terry. I understand you're not doing so well."

Ah… ADA Spence must've brought him up to speed on my marked decline. But Jack nor the ADA, not even my family knows yet about the Hail Mary the doctors are planning to throw up next week. I am buoyed by their optimism, wish they could perform the surgery tomorrow, but I understand the need for planning and tests, especially considering the shortcuts they took earlier on my behalf.

"Hey, I'm planning for you to be around to meet my first child when he or she is born."

His voice is cracking and I realize he thinks I'm a goner. I'm touched this big alpha guy could be moved by my situation. I'm sure he's seen every sadsack predicament under the sun.

"I just want to say that coming here on Sundays has meant a lot to me. It might sound silly, but it's been nice to get away from work and other situations that were pulling on me and clear my mind enough to make some grown-up decisions. Watching what you've gone through has given me perspective."

Wow... I had no idea anyone was analyzing my situation with such scrutiny.

"And I think it's fair to come clean about the situation I've been wrestling with. Some of it you already know. The mother of my child didn't plan to get pregnant."

Let's see, that would be Liz.

"It was carelessness on both our parts. What makes the situation especially difficult is I'm in love with someone else."

That would be Carlotta.

"But there are some extra complications that would make it impossible to be with the woman I love while raising the child with its mother. Not that she would have me anyway."

Carlotta again.

"In fact, she's probably going to marry someone else."

Gee, Detective, and I thought my situation was bleak.

"But hey, I'm the one who messed up everything. And it'll probably all work out for the best because this girl makes me absolutely crazy and that's not sustainable in a relationship. And now she can be with a guy who can make her happy in a way I never could."

Sounds like he had it all figured out.

"Right," he said, as if to bolster his own argument to himself.

"Anyway, I'll be here next Sunday, Marigold... and I expect you to be here, too." The door opened and closed with a bang.

October 31, Monday

THE HOSPITAL is doing what it can to make Halloween fun for the kids who are stuck here. Spooky music is playing over the intercom in between announcements. The staff are wearing costumes and passing out candy, and there's a general sense of fun in the air.

Roberta dropped by earlier to describe her zombie outfit, and to bring me a scarf covered with sugar skulls and spider webs. She proclaimed me gloriously spooky before she bounced out of here to go to a party.

I'm tired, and fatigue is pulling at the corners of my mind, but I'm excited about the doctors conferring tomorrow and the possibilities that surgery offers to me and my baby. I might not get much sleep tonight.

The door opened and closed. I don't recognize the shoes or the footsteps, but I assume it's a nurse wearing a costume.

So I'm surprised to hear the rosary beads on my bedrail clink together.

"I'm sorry, Marigold."

The voice sounds slurred, but familiar. Recognition shoots through me. Sidney!

But before I can register the pleasure of her surprise visit, my brain starts going haywire, misfiring and fogging. I am falling headlong, tumbling over and over into a deeper, darker place. I'm not getting enough oxygen.

And it dawns on me that my sister is smothering me.

NOVEMBER

November 1, Tuesday

"…SORRY… so sorry…"

Slowly I became aware of a muffled voice, but was it Sidney apologizing even as she smothered me, or St. Peter at the pearly gates saying sorry, he can't let me in?

"I'm sorry, Marigold. Please forgive me." The glass rosary beads clicked together in a way that made me think she's holding them.

It's Sidney, and she's crying. Am I dead and hanging in some kind of other limbo that's more hellish than being comatose?

"I haven't been a good sister, but I'll find a way to make it up to you."

Either I'm still alive, or she's promising to deliver one heck of a eulogy for me.

"Roberta gave me your living will, and in it you wrote you didn't want to suffer. And you named me as your agent."

I named you my healthcare agent, not my executioner.

"Anyway, I… thought it was best to end your suffering." She sniffed. "But I wasn't thinking straight. God, what have I done?"

Oh, no—I must be dead.

The door opened and the sound of soft footsteps faltered. "Who are you?"

Nurse Gina is making rounds.

A rustling noise sounded.

"I forgot I was wearing a mask. It's me, Sidney—Marigold's sister."

"Oh. Hello, Ms. Kemp." Gina sounded wary. "But it's after midnight. Why are you here?"

"I came earlier to visit Marigold." Sid's voice is barely above a whisper. "And I... stayed. I hope that's okay."

"You're family," Gina said. "Of course it's okay."

"Will you check Marigold's vital signs? I thought I heard her struggling to breathe when I first arrived."

Because you had your hands over my airways. Did you just pull off the perfect crime, Sid? If so, you must be watching *Forensics Files*, too.

From the nearby sounds, I assume Gina is tending to me. Wait for it...

"Her pulse is normal."

Oh, good—I'm still kicking. Well, not kicking, but alive.

Sid exhaled audibly. "Good. The baby, too?"

A pause, then, "Yes, the heartbeat is strong."

"Oh, thank God," Sidney said, relief coloring her voice. "Thank you, Blessed Mother Mary, for answering my prayer." Her hoarse voice bordered on hysteria.

"I heard you'd gone back to school," Gina said, her voice still guarded. "Boston, isn't it?"

"Yes, and I did. I just came back to—"

Murder me.

"—visit Marigold. I m-miss her."

She actually sounds believable.

"I imagine you wanted to see her before the surgery."

"Surgery?" Sid asked. "What surgery?"

Either Gina doesn't know or had forgotten the doctors weren't going to talk to my family about the risky surgery scheduled tomorrow to reduce pressure in my brain until they had satisfied their own requirements for proceeding.

"Er, I... misspoke. You should talk to her doctors."

"Please tell me. I was planning to go back to Boston, but should I stay?"

"Perhaps," Gina said. "The doctors are planning to talk to your parents today about performing surgery to release the pressure on Marigold's brain."

"That sounds dangerous."

"It is," Gina confirmed. "It's very dangerous."

"She could die?"

I expected Sid's voice to sound hopeful, but instead she sounded... scared.

"Yes," Gina said, her voice grim. "She could die."

The chair scuffed against the floor. "I have to go," Sid blurted.

"To your parents'?"

"No. To take care of some things. Please don't tell anyone I was here."

"I won't," Gina said, sounding perplexed.

After the door opened and closed, Gina expelled an exasperated sigh. "What a strange family you have, Marigold."

Lady, you don't know the half of it.

November 2, Wednesday

"DO YOU HAVE ANY last-minute reservations?" Dr. Jarvis asked.

He and Dr. Tyson were walking alongside my bed as it's being rolled toward an operating room.

"Only a dozen or so," Dr. Tyson said.

Is that a tremor in her voice? Is she worried, or still sleepy? It's early, after all. Although neither boded well for someone who would soon have her hand in my brain.

Jarvis grunted. "I confess when I woke up this morning, I hoped we'd come in to find Ms. Kemp miraculously improved since our final consult with Dr. Oscar yesterday."

Bless him, prior to Tyson's arrival, Dr. Jarvis and Gina had gone through a full gamut of sensory tests, asking me over and over to respond to stimuli by moving a finger or a toe. I couldn't. Indeed, I feel weaker now than any time since I'd become aware of my surroundings in July. And my sense of smell has not returned.

"Agreed, the best surgery is the one we don't have to do," Dr. Tyson said. "But even your perpetual classical music will only take her brain so far, Jarvis."

"I know," he said. "If Marigold's going to get better, we have to intervene."

"Jarvis," she said in a chiding voice. "My goal is to keep Ms. Kemp alive until the fetus is viable. Anything more than that will be a gift. At this point, the concept you have of her getting better is almost certainly off the table."

Wow. To hear the best I might ever be is trapped in this state of nothingness is a blow to my soul. Right now I almost wished Sidney had followed through on her intention to put me out of my misery. Except, of course, there is the baby to think of.

Jarvis's expression must've mirrored how I felt because Dr. Tyson made a comforting noise. "Let's just get through the surgery, okay?"

"Right," he said, then cleared his throat. "Are her parents here?"

"Um, no. I told them the surgery could take several hours. They asked me to call when Marigold is in recovery."

Mighty big of them.

Jarvis cursed. "Don't they realize she might not make it to recovery?"

"We shouldn't judge them too harshly," Tyson said. "My guess is they already feel as if they've lost their daughter. Being elsewhere might be their way of distancing themselves from more emotional trauma."

"What about Marigold's trauma? She's alone and pregnant and if she has any inkling of what's happening to her, she must be terrified."

"They can't do anything for her anyway," she said lightly.

"They could at least be here for her."

My bed was being banged against something—a doorway?

"It's better for us if they're not here. I don't like the pressure of knowing the family is in the waiting room, pacing. We don't know what we might find when we open her up."

Ack—she made it sound as if they might find a tube of Chapstick in there. Or a sock.

Other voices sounded in the background. Dr. Tyson and Jarvis said hellos all around, then video-conferenced in Dr. Oscar, who would have his own scope to watch what happened in my brain and even assist remotely if necessary. Dr. Tyson ran through what everyone is expected to do.

I'm astounded at the number of people who will be attending little ole me. An obstetric nurse will be dedicated to monitoring the baby, with an obstetrician on call. The anesthesiologist asked a few questions. Dr. Tyson went through a surgical precheck verbally. Everyone seems to be ready.

Except me. I'm utterly petrified. What if I don't wake up? Or at least get back to this place?

"Here we go, Marigold," Dr. Jarvis whispered close to my ear. "Three, two, one…"

Wait, I'm not—

November 3, Thursday

"I TOLD YOU, you were going to hurt yourself with that Kung Fu nonsense, Robert."

"Yes, Carrie, I heard you every time. And just now, too."

"Well, a lot of good it did. There's barely room for us in here, much less those crutches. Don't trip over a cord or a tube or something."

"Do you think you can stop fussing long enough for us to get a good look at Marigold? The nurse said we only get ten minutes with her."

So I made it through the surgery. I never thought I'd be happy to hear my parents bickering at each other, but right now their snippy voices sound glorious. And near me I hear a monitor pinging with regularity, which I assume is my heartbeat.

"Oh, they shaved her head again," my mother said.

Crap—I forgot about that. But a small price to pay to be restored to... this.

"She looks so pale," my dad said, his voice breaking. "She's been through so much."

"Shush, Robert. The doctors said the surgery was successful, so let's focus on that."

"And the baby is okay?"

"Yes. Dr. Tyson said everything went better than planned. Weren't you listening?"

"Did you call Sidney and Alex?"

"Of course. Sidney was at church, praying for Marigold."

Praying for me, or her own soul? Wait—that's a little bitter from someone who just made it through brain surgery.

"And Alex was out on patrol, but he left word to be radioed as soon as we called."

"They're such great kids," Dad said.

I know he doesn't mean to exclude me, but there it is again, the sensation that I'm the outsider. Then I scolded myself—a few hours post op is not the time to be examining my emotional responses to small talk in ICU. I am probably still under the influence of all kinds of drugs.

"When I called Winnie, she said that crackpot psychic of hers had predicted Marigold would come through the surgery with flying colors." Mom snorted. "Get this—she asked if the doctors had found a *sock* in her brain."

Wow, Faridee—impressive. And long-distance, too.

"Carrie, your sister has lost her mind."

"I know, right?"

"That reminds me—the police detective working Marigold's case called to ask about her."

Jack Terry had called? Aw.

"Don't you think it's strange that he visits her?" Mom asked.

"Maybe it's his way of connecting with victims. He asked if he could come by the house to take a look at Marigold's car."

"Whatever for?"

"I assume it has something to do with the accident."

"The accident," my mother murmured, sounding faraway. "When everything changed."

"Yep," my dad said.

They took turns sighing until a chime sounded.

"That's our cue to leave," Mom said.

"When can we come back?"

"In two hours, family members can go in for another ten minutes, but

I have a closing, so I need to take you home now."

"But I can't drive. How am I supposed to get back here on my own?"

"You should've thought of that before you jump-kicked a concrete column."

"It's called a roundhouse kick. And I'm trying to better myself, Carrie."

"Well, stop it, Robert. Let's go—we'll come back to visit Marigold tomorrow."

"Okay, tomorrow."

As their voices faded, I marveled how their indifference actually gave me a sense of peace. It's comforting in its sameness.

I'm back, y'all.

November 4, Friday

"SO THE ASSISTANT DISTRICT ATTORNEY was scamming Keith Young's attorney when she said Marigold was going to respond to yes and no questions about the accident."

I mentally tensed when I recognized the voice of David Spooner, the attorney who had cozied up to Sidney and is, I'm afraid, up to no good.

"Right," Sidney said. "It seems the ADA was scamming all of us."

Ah. So that's why Sid had tried to off me—because she was afraid I was going to expose her in the ADA's interview as the driver.

"Do you think Young's people fell for the story?"

"I haven't heard."

"Well, let's keep our fingers crossed. And hey, since the surgery was successful, maybe she'll wake up and testify after all."

"Maybe," Sid said.

Ah, so she hadn't even told Spooner that she'd been behind the wheel at the time of the accident.

"No offense, Sid, but you don't look so good. Hey, you're shaking."

"I'm just tired," she said, but her voice was tremulous.

"No wonder—you have so much on your plate with school and all of this, too. I saw a mention of Coma Girl's hashtag on HLN yesterday for top social media campaigns of the year."

"Yes... I believe that popped up in my media alerts. I've been a little distracted."

"Maybe it's time we brought someone on to help with the media demands. I'll get Alicia in my office to step in so you can concentrate on your studies."

"She's a little young, isn't she?" Sid's voice was tinged with jealousy.

"Alicia's twenty-one. And into all the latest mobile tech, including international apps that most Americans haven't heard of. She could be a big help."

"That might be best," Sid agreed. "I do have a lot going on right now."

"Nice earrings, are they new?"

"Uh-hm."

"Should I be jealous?"

"No," she murmured. "I just needed a pick-me-up."

"Wow, when I was in law school, internships didn't pay enough for diamond earrings."

"I put these on a credit card until I get my first check for managing Marigold's foundation. When will that be, by the way?"

"Any day now. I'll look in to it when I add Alicia to the payroll. What's with the rosary?" he asked, neatly changing the subject, I noticed.

The familiar clink of the glass beads sounded. "I'm Catholic."

"I know, but you've been carrying it around since I picked you up from the airport."

Sid had taken it with her when she'd left my room after... you know.

"I'm just worried about Marigold," she said vaguely.

"You said she'd be out of ICU soon, so things are looking up."

"Still, a little faith doesn't hurt."

"You're so good," he gushed. "There's my phone—I need to take this and they don't allow calls in here."

"I'll be right out," Sid said.

At the sound of Spooner's retreating footsteps, my mind raced. Something had made Sid change her mind a few nights ago when she had her hands over my face... but she could change her mind again. With me gone, her life would go back to normal, and she could play the bereaved sister.

At this very second, is Sid looking for a plug to pull?

She began reciting a prayer to the Virgin Mary for forgiveness, but even after she finished and left, my fears don't ease. Because some people believe in storing prayers in the Bank of God, then taking a withdrawal in one lump sum.

November 5, Saturday

LAST NIGHT I was moved back to the long-term care ward and, I heard a nurse say, assumed my regular position in bed three. I wonder if over in bed two Karen Suh missed me, or even knew I was gone.

Since I know from Faridee's bumbling psychic episodes that Karen is conscious to some degree, I wonder if she thought I'd died, like Jill Wheatley in bed four, or had woken up, like Audrey Parks in bed one. If being in a coma is lonely, being the only person in a four-bed coma unit has to be the bottom of lonely. I gave her a mental wave and tried to metaphysically make myself known to her.

Before spending a couple of days in ICU, I hadn't known it was possible for me to have a sense of place, but I realize now how accustomed I'd become to the sounds in the ward—the muffled sound of distant city noise from the lone window to my left, the frequent P.A. announcements in a muted monotone from the hallway, and the familiar swish of the door opening and closing, admitting an array of nurses, doctors, staff, and visitors to the vegetable patch, as we are fondly referred to.

Oh, and my iPod playlist of classical music. Someone—Dr. Jarvis, I presumed, since the constant barrage of symphonious music was his idea—had hit the 'scramble' button, and I'm enjoying the surprise of which song will be next. It occurs to me Karen probably knows I'm back from the crashing symbols of Tchaikovsky's Symphony No. 4.

It also occurs to me that my hearing seems more acute than prior to the surgery. Hooray!

The door opened and since it's still early, I assume it's Gina coming to welcome me back. But even though the shoes are soft-soled, the footsteps are too heavy for Gina. Teddy, maybe?

"Hi, Coma Girl."

It's my poet volunteer with the satiny voice.

"New bandages? Did they cut you open again? Hm... I didn't hear anything about that on the news."

Meaning he wishes he'd had the scoop on my surgery, so he could've leaked it himself?

"Still just the two of you, huh? I guess that's good. This isn't really a place anyone aspires to be, is it?"

The chair creaked, indicating he'd settled himself.

"I found this poem the other day and marked it because it made me think of what you two ladies must be going through. It's Dickinson again, this one is called 'Escape.'"

The swish of pages sounded as he found his place.

"I never hear the word 'escape,' without a quicker blood, a sudden expectation, a flying attitude. I never hear of prisons broad, by soldiers battered down, but I tug childish at my bars, only to fail again."

He closed the book with a soft *thwack*.

"Is that how you feel, Coma Girl?"

You nailed it. Or rather—Dickinson did.

The chair creaked and I heard him creep closer to my bed, so close I

212

can smell the minty aroma of something clean—the soap he used? Chloroform?

After the episode with Sidney, I'm a little paranoid, and at this point, I hope the only thing he has in mind is snapping a picture for the tabloids. So when I hear the faint *click, click* of his phone camera, I actually relax.

It was only after he stealthily opened and closed the door to make his exit that a realization hit me—my sense of smell has returned. Hooray!

November 6, Sunday

WHEN THE DOOR OPENED, I was hoping to hear the sound of Jack Terry's boots on the floor. Instead it was the clackety-clack of ADA Spence. She was talking on the phone.

"Dad, I'll try to make it home for Thanksgiving, but I can't make any promises."

Her voice was low and patient, but from her quick body movements, it was clear she was stressed.

"I know. I miss her, too," she murmured. "I want to visit, it's just that right now my workload is overwhelming. Maybe we'd better shoot for Christmas instead."

I wondered if I'd be home for the holidays. Or alive.

"Don't get upset, Dad, please. I'll see what I can do, okay? I'll call you in a couple of days. Okay, bye."

She expelled a heavy sigh just as the door opened again to admit booted feet.

"Hello, Detective Terry," she said.

"ADA Spence," he said, and I imagined him giving her a courtesy nod. "Nice flowers. Black-eyed Susans?"

"Uh, yeah. These are for Marigold, but I see a lot of other people had the same idea—only nicer."

Since word had leaked that I'd had another surgery (thanks to my duplicitous poet, no doubt), more flowers had poured in. From my bed, I can smell the pungent scents of fall flowers, with herbs thrown in for greenery, I suppose—mums and sage and rosemary.

"Did you pick these?"

"They grow wild around my... place."

A new earthy scent reached me—the wildflowers smelled like freshly-cut hay.

"Well, isn't Liz Fischer the lucky one?"

"Um, thanks. What's the latest on Marigold's case?"

She made a regretful noise, as if she didn't want to talk business, then dragged the chair away from my bed (and closer to Jack?) and from the sound of it, dropped into the seat.

"Last week I met with Keith Young's defense team and told them not only can Marigold communicate, but she already testified from her bed about the accident through a taped interview. I told them a pregnant coma patient reaching out from beyond along with the sister's testimony that Young smelled like alcohol at the scene will probably be enough to convict him, even if he didn't blow over the legal limit."

"That was a pretty bold lie."

"Bolstered by a DVD I placed in a clear, locked storage case on the table between us."

"Which did not contain an interview with Marigold."

"No, it was a recording of my niece's ballet recital, but they didn't know that. I told them if he pleads guilty to reckless driving and vehicular assault, we won't go to trial."

"What was their response?"

"They're going to talk to their client. They called today and asked for sixty days to decide."

"Long enough for Young to finish the football season."

"Right. I gave them until the end of this month, but told them if Marigold's condition changes, the deal could be withdrawn."

Meaning, if I croak before Turkey Day.

"I assume you're keeping the Kemps in the loop?"

"As much as they want to be. They're... "

"Disconnected?"

"Yes. Family cuts both ways, doesn't it?"

"I suppose."

"You'll find out soon enough," she said slyly, alluding to Jack's baby on the way. "Anything new on your end of the investigation?"

"No. But I might be getting close on a couple of things."

"Something you want to share?"

"Not really—just following up on a couple of hunches."

The chair creaked and it sounded as if she was gathering her things. "Okay, keep me posted."

"I will."

"And say hi to Liz for me," she added lightly.

He didn't respond, and she was gone in a clatter.

Jack grunted, as if he's glad the encounter is over. He made his way back to my bed.

"Hi, Marigold—it's Jack Terry. I hear you did good in surgery." He sounded pleased. "I knew you weren't ready to give up."

The sound of ripping paper reached me, and the room filled with delicious smells.

"I brought barbecue."

November 7, Monday

"YOO-HOO, sweetheart, it's Winnie. And I brought Faridee with me. She's been busy because everyone wants her to tell them who will win the presidential election tomorrow!"

Oh, right. Tomorrow is Election Day. I'm into politics, but I have to confess, this is one race I haven't minded missing. Come on, friend, aren't you a little envious I've been in a coma all this time and you had to endure campaign season?

"But I haven't disclosed the name of the winner," Faridee sang. "It would be unethical to say something that could change the outcome of history."

A convenient cover line for psychic hacks.

"And Marigold," Faridee said, suddenly sober, "I'm so glad when we were here last time, the whiff of death I sensed wasn't you."

Yes, Faridee had freaked out a little and dragged Winnie out of here, leaving me to wonder if I was reeking of decomposition. Instead, the next morning, the nurses had found poor Jill dead in her bed. I think after Jill heard Audrey Parks deliver her grim prognosis if she lived, Jill had simply given up.

So Faridee had called that one. And I do have to give the woman props for snagging the sock-in-my-brain thing out of thin air—I mean, that can't be a coincidence. If her skills are growing sharper, maybe I'll try to send her a for-real message to relay.

But what, and to whom?

I have so many secrets to share, I'm fairly bursting.

"Your mom told me the surgery went beautifully," Winnie said. "You'll be awake soon, won't she, Faridee?"

"Why don't we let Marigold tell us?" Faridee said, seizing the opening for her act to begin.

"Shall I try to connect with her this time, too?"

"You can try. If you don't reach her this time, Winnie, you will definitely need to take another one of my classes."

Oh, brother.

"To help you make contact, I brought one of my special Thoughtwave Candles."

Winnie, you can't fall for that. She bought it at Bed, Bath & Beyond.

"That's nice of you, Faridee."

"Only twenty-nine ninety-five."

"I'll settle up with you later."

"Cash?"

"Yes."

"Okay. While I light the candle, close your eyes, Winnie, and rub the amulet."

"I noticed this morning the amulet chain is turning my neck green."

"That means it's beginning to work."

"Oh, wonderful!"

Mental eye-roll.

"Rub it, Winnie, rub it hard."

"I'm rubbing, I'm rubbing."

The scent of burning wax reached me. This is starting to sound and smell pornographic.

"Envision a path," Faridee said. "A path to Marigold. Walk the path, Winnie."

"I'm walking, I'm walking."

"Walk toward us, Marigold."

Okay, so I'm doing my part, envisioning a path and at the end of it, two rotund women in colorful caftans. One woman is intensely rubbing her fake amulet while the other woman is stealing her purse.

"Do you see Marigold, Winnie?"

"No. Do you?"

"Yes. I see her at the end of the path. She's waving. Hello, Marigold!"

Howdy or whatever. I decide it's time to bear down and try to send a message to Faridee. *Tell Jack Sidney tried to kill me. She was driving the car. I can hear what everyone is saying. Help me.*

"She's speaking," Faridee said. "Do you hear her?"

"No," Winnie whispered. "What is she saying?"

"She says to tell Sidney... no, tell *Jack*... Sidney is driving... her crazy."

"Well, that's no surprise," Winnie said, deadpan. "Sidney drives me crazy, too."

No! No! No!

"Do you smell something burning?" Winnie asked.

"Ack! My dress is on fire!"

Much flapping ensued. But not enough to keep the smoke alarm from sounding. Did I mention my hearing is more acute? *Ouch.*

The door flew open.

"What's going on in here?" Teddy shouted. "No candles in the hospital, ladies—out!"

He ushered them out under protest, then returned with a fan, muttering under his breath. The smoke alarm fell silent, but I am despondent.

My visitors had been bounced and once again, Faridee had gotten just enough of my message to make a bigger mess of things.

November 8, Tuesday

"COMA GIRL, you should be glad you're missing this freak show of an election."

Apparently, Roberta is relieving the stress of voting day with a half dozen pumpkin spice crullers.

"I mean, I took my lunch hour to go to the polls, and by the time I was through, I was so traumatized, I called my boss and said I'm taking a mental health day."

The crullers smell divine, down to the sugary glaze.

"People cutting line and pushing and calling each other names. And that's just in the parking lot. Inside my poll, it was like a rioting prison. And I vote in a *church*." She sighed. "People have lost their dang minds."

She hummed her way through another cruller while I snorted the aromas she unleashed when she tore off little pieces and fed them to herself. (I've seen how Roberta eats.)

"Girl, you're slobbering all over yourself," she said. "Let me wipe your mouth."

Hm, are the appetizing smells making my mouth water? That has to be a good sign. On the other hand, I'm turning into a drooling vegetable.

"There, that's better."

She downed another cruller before licking her fingers with some *mm-mmm, good* moans.

"Okay, so I'm pissed off at myself for leaving the only clue I have to your baby-daddy, that daggone San Antonio Spurs hat, the last time I was here. And no one here knows what happened to it. I'll tell you what happened to it—someone stole it, that's what. Someone with a big old head or a big old head of hair. It's my newest case, the Who Stole the Damn Hat Case."

Maybe I should've told Faridee the orderly Gabriel had stolen the hat right off my bed rail. But who knows how that message would've gotten garbled.

"I didn't know you were going to have another surgery," she said. "Since I gave your living will to Sidney, the least she could do was let me know you were going back under the knife. And to expect another flood of cards from all your nutty fans. I had to let the super cop a feel this time because he was so riled up over the bag of mail." She laughed. "It wasn't too bad, kind of reminded me of sixth grade."

When I was in sixth grade, I was still watching cartoons.

"Anyway, let me read you some of the sweeter ones." She dutifully described, opened, and read to me almost fifty cards that had arrived from all corners of the earth. "This one is from Pakistan. Now how did someone in Pakistan get your mailing address? And how did they know how many stamps to use? *I* don't even know how many stamps to use on something that's going across town, much less to Pakistan."

I missed Roberta, missed eating with her and laughing with her. She had her faults, but she's eminently good-natured and likable, and makes life tolerable.

"So besides the election, you know what else is happening this month, right?"

Duncan is getting married.

"Duncan is getting married." She sighed. "On the Saturday of Thanksgiving weekend. His fiancé came in again to check on the cakes for like the tenth time and she brought me an invitation to the wedding."

She shifted in the chair.

"So should I go?"

Of course you should go.

"I don't think I should go."

Of course you should go.

"On the other hand, you're carrying someone else's baby, so I'm thinking you're over Duncan, and maybe I should go."

Yes, go.

"I mean, they have been good customers of the bakery."

Go.

"And it would be a chance to wear the turquoise mohair cape."

Wait a minute—the turquoise mohair cape is *mine*. It's vintage. And mine.

"So maybe I'll go."

Go, Roberta, go! I'll be here, aching inside.

November 9, Wednesday

"GOOD MORNING, Marigold. It's Dr. Jarvis. I came by to see how you're doing and to check your responses. Gina's coming in soon to help me."

He came to stand by my bed and I can almost feel him studying me.

"Marigold, I know you're in there," he said, almost in a whisper.

The door opened and he stepped back.

"Are you ready for me, Dr. Jarvis?" Gina asked.

"Um, yes," he said. "Dr. Tyson will be conducting an MRI on Ms. Kemp later this week, and other tests to see how the wound is healing inside. I believe an ultrasound has been scheduled as well, to check on the baby's progress. Today I want to change the head bandage and see how Marigold scores on the Glasgow Index."

"I'll get the charts and the supplies."

When she left, he checked the iPod hanging on my bedrail. "How about some new music?" he asked.

Yes! Christina Perri, Jake Bugg, Bad Seed Rising—

"I just downloaded a playlist of over one hundred songs."

American Top 40? The best of Motown? Disco?

"The best of Russian classical music, distinctive for its tonal bell-ringing."

Gee, thanks.

"While you're listening to it, Marigold, I want you to count the bells. Got it? Count the bells."

Okay, but *only* because I don't have anything else to do.

Gina returned with the supplies. Dr. Jarvis began the Glasgow Index test by asking me to open my eyes.

I can't.

"Gina, to your knowledge, has Ms. Kemp ever spontaneously opened her eyes?"

"No."

"Okay, I'm going to check her eye response to pain stimulus. Can you watch her eyes while I press on her fingernails?"

"Yes, Doctor."

"Wayne."

"Excuse me?"

"My first name is Wayne."

"Oh... it doesn't seem right to call you by your first name."

"I call you by your first name."

"Well... okay, maybe when it's just... us."

"Good. Okay, I'm squeezing the nailbed. Any blinking, twitching of the eyes?"

"No, Dr.—er, no, Wayne."

"Okay, so she scores a one under the eye section."

I heard the click of a penlight. "Please note the pupils are fixed. Let's move on to verbal responses. Have you ever heard Ms. Kemp made any verbal noises—grunts, moans, anything?"

"No, none."

"Alright. Marigold, this is Dr. Jarvis. Can you make a noise for me? Any noise will do. Can you groan?"

I can't.

"How about speaking? Can you say the word 'baby'?"

I wish.

"Think about making the B sound, Marigold. *Buh... buh.* You can do it with your mouth closed, just push air through your lips. Try it. *Buh... buh.*"

I try, but I can't. Would they know if my vocal chords had been damaged in the accident?

"Gina, will you bend down to her mouth and listen while I apply pain stimulus. Tell me if you hear her make any noise at all. There—anything?"

"No."

"How about now?"

"No, Wayne, nothing."

"Okay, so she scores a one on the verbal section. One section left, Marigold, but the good news is motor response has been your strong suit."

I ready myself.

"Patient previously responded to generalized pain stimulus, so let's try that first. Anything?"

"No," Gina said.

"And she doesn't withdraw from pain stimulus to nailbeds. Okay, let's see how she responds to commands. Take her hands, please."

"Marigold, I need for you to move the fingers on your right hand, can you do that? Can you tell your brain to move your fingers, Marigold?"

I drew the little diagram in my head, where my brain tells my arm to tell my hand to tell my fingers to move.

"Nothing," Gina said.

"How about your left hand, Marigold?"

Again, I try. Again, nothing.

He asked three more times, then moved to my toes. After several rounds of commands, none of which I responded to, he heaved a frustrated sigh. "That's a one on the motor response section, for a total score of three."

In other words, I am just above a pumpkin.

"I'm sorry, Wayne," Gina said.

"So am I," he said. "But she's only a week post op, and we'll know more about the swelling in her brain after Dr. Tyson conducts more thorough tests." He tried to sound cheerful, but was failing.

He was quiet as he and Gina changed the bandage. I imagined a black scar in my shaved, bristly head. "Looks normal," he said finally. "Let's apply antibacterial cream and rewrap."

They finished and Gina left the room to discard supplies. Before he left, Dr. Jarvis turned the Russian music up a notch.

"Count the bells, Marigold."

I'd been so sure I was getting better, the disappointment is keen. To keep the desperation at bay, I begin to count.

One... two... three, four... five...

November 10, Thursday

TWO THOUSAND THIRTEEN... *two thousand fourteen... two thousand fifteen...*

The door opened and from the banging and the bumping, I know it's bath day.

"I heard Marigold didn't do so well on the Glasgow test yesterday," Teddy said.

"A three," Gina said on a sigh. "Wayne was so disappointed."

"Who's Wayne?"

"I mean—Dr. Jarvis was so disappointed."

"Since when are you and Dr. Jarvis on a first-name basis?"

"We're not," she said in a rush. "I slipped. Can you hand me the white sponge, please?"

"Here you go, Mrs. Jarvis."

"That's not funny."

"Yes, it is."

She laughed. "Stop. The soap, please?"

"Oh, come on, I can dream for you, can't I?"

"I have a boyfriend, remember?"

"Is that what you're calling Gabriel now?"

"I suppose," she said lightly. "We have a date tonight."

Ugh—I don't like Gabriel a little bit.

"It's got to be close to your no-nookie-for-ninety-days mark."

"Yes, today, in fact. We were both looking forward to our date, I think."

"Were?"

She sighed. "This morning Nature came calling."

"Jesus, Gina, you're a nurse, you can say you got your period."

"Since you said it, I don't have to."

"Hey, it's a new generation. Some guys are okay with period sex."

"Well, I'm not. And what could it hurt to push things off a few more days?"

"How do you think Gabriel will react?"

"I guess I'll see."

Whew, a reprieve.

"I say end things now before you go there. If Dr. Jarvis is interested, you'd be crazy to go with Gabriel over him."

"Because he's an orderly?"

"Yeah. And..."

"And what?"

"And he has a reputation."

"I know what people say," Gina said. "But Gabriel has been a complete gentleman."

"Okay, I'll say no more."

"Powder, please?"

"Oh, look, the baby is moving."

My heart squeezed. It is?

"How sad she's not awake to enjoy her pregnancy."

At the moment, pregnancy is an abstract concept. Because I can't feel my baby or see my body changing, I'm disconnected from the process.

"Wonder who the father is?" Ted asked.

"I don't know. And I don't think her family knows either."

"So somewhere out there a guy is walking around without a clue he's about to be a father."

"Maybe it was a one-night stand, or a sperm donor," Gina offered.

"Why do you say that?"

"If they were close, he'd know she's in here, and he'd know about the baby, right?"

"Yeah."

"Since he hasn't come around, it stands to reason the father is someone who doesn't care about Marigold."

Teddy sighed. "Except for the kooky aunt who almost set her room on fire and her roommate with the donuts, it doesn't seem as if Marigold has anyone who really cares about her."

Two thousand sixteen... two thousand seventeen... two thousand eighteen...

November 11, Friday

THREE THOUSAND SIX HUNDRED FOUR, *three thousand six hundred five*—

The knock that sounded was so timid, I thought I might have misheard. But a few seconds later, the door opened.

I don't recognize the shoes (dress) or the gait (tentative), but I recognize the perfume from 2008: Deseo by Jennifer Lopez. If my college buddy Joanna had been wearing it on previous visits, it must've been overpowered by the stink of rum.

"Hi, Marigold." She stepped closer. "It's me, Joanna, and don't worry, I'm not loaded."

That's a relief.

Her footsteps sounded and I realize she'd walked over to the window. "You have a nice view. I can't believe how much Atlanta has changed since I left. It's absolutely cosmopolitan compared to Allentown." She made a noise that sounded like homesickness. "It's such a pretty day. The leaves are changing in earnest now—all coppery and yellow."

I appreciate her description. Fall is my favorite time of the year. I'm one of those solid girls who is happy when shorts and tank tops give way to corduroys and sweaters.

"Fall makes you recognize how quickly life can change," she murmured.

She turned back toward my bed and settled into the chair quietly. I sensed something about *her* had changed since her previous visit.

"I've been a terrible friend, Marigold. Coming here and purging myself while you're lying there, probably confused and terrified about what's happening to you. I've been so wrapped up in my melodrama, I haven't even considered how much pain you might be in." She sighed. "If you can hear me, then I'm ashamed. And if you can't, then I'm heartbroken. Because you don't deserve this."

That's kind of Joanna to say, but I'm starting to realize that merit doesn't always matter in the randomness of life. Despite all the evil in the world, good things happen. And despite all best intentions, bad things happen. Although Sidney had been driving when our accident occurred, who's to say it wouldn't have been the same outcome if I'd been driving instead?

"I had an epiphany last night," Joanna said. "I realized I could've easily been the person driving drunk who put you in that bed. I've been so, so lucky I haven't hurt someone else or my kids." Her voice broke. "The twins are beautiful, Marigold, and they deserve a better mother." She sniffed. "Most of my misery is of my own making, and drinking has only led to more bad decisions, so I'm going to stop. I have a bag packed in the car. I'm on my way to a rehab center where I hope to start putting my life back together. I'm sorry I won't be here for you, but I'll be thinking of you every day."

From the scuff of the chair legs, I know she's standing.

"I've been so out of touch, I don't even know who the father of your baby is. Whoever he is, I hope he's a great guy, and I hope you're as crazy about him as you were that guy—oh, what was his name?"

Duncan.

"Well, anyway, bye for now. I hope you wake up soon, Marigold."

Three thousand six hundred six… three thousand six hundred seven…

November 12, Saturday

FIVE THOUSAND EIGHT HUNDRED THIRTY-SEVEN… Five thousand eight hundred thirty-eight—

"Dr. Jarvis, will you please turn down the volume of that so-called music?"

"Yes, Dr. Tyson."

The bells are silenced so quickly, I would've blinked if I could've.

"Standby for Dr. Oscar."

A couple of beeps sounded.

"Hello, Dr. Tyson, Dr. Jarvis. How's our patient?"

"Ms. Kemp is recovering well from the surgery, sir," Dr. Tyson said, "but her condition is unchanged. Did you receive the MRI and CT scans?"

"Yes, I've reviewed them. From what I can see, the surgery couldn't have been more successful. Well done, Dr. Tyson. You too, Jarvis."

"Thank you, sir," Jarvis said. "But we expected her responses to have improved by now."

"What's Ms. Kemp's Glasgow score?"

"Three," Jarvis said.

Dr. Oscar grunted. "How's her BP?"

"Perfect," Tyson said.

"Temperature?"

"Normal."

"White blood cell count elevated?"

"No."

"So no infection. And the fetus?"

"Twenty-four and a half weeks. An ultrasound this morning showed all is normal."

Far and away the best news of the day, in my opinion.

"So the fetus is viable."

"Barely," Tyson offered. "Survival rate at this stage is sixty percent. Another two and a half weeks will get us to ninety percent."

"Then that should be the short-term goal."

The blunt observation rendered my doctors silent: Keep me alive for two and half more weeks for my baby's sake.

For the record, I totally agree. But it still sucks.

"From my point of view," Dr. Oscar added, "you've done all you can do for Ms. Kemp. Keep her well-nourished and let her continue to heal. Maybe she will defy the odds."

"So just wait and see?" Dr. Jarvis didn't bother to hide his frustration.

"Yes," Dr. Oscar said. "Sometimes the best course of action is no action."

"Excuse me," Dr. Jarvis said, then his footsteps retreated to the door, which opened and closed with punctuated force.

"You'll have to forgive Dr. Jarvis," Dr. Tyson said. "He's become attached to the patient."

"I understand," Dr. Oscar said. "And it's refreshing."

"Thank you for your input, sir. We'll keep you posted."

"Please do. Signing off."

A beep sounded, then Dr. Tyson exhaled and began to gather up equipment. When her phone rang, she answered it with a brusque, "Yes?" After a pause she said, "Excuse me? Who is this?" She made a sound of disgust. "Don't ever call this number again."

After she ended the call, more tapping sounded.

"It's me," she said, her voice low. "Tell me you didn't take out a sleazy ad and list our *home phone number*? Have you lost your mind? I'm expecting a call on the landline, so I forwarded it to my cell. Imagine my surprise when someone named *Champagne* called."

Sounds as if her husband had moved full-steam ahead with his plan to have an open marriage. Poor Dr. Tyson—she must be mortified.

"I don't care. Fix it—now. And this evening, you and I are going to talk about the future."

She ended the call and stifled a sob. I feel like an eavesdropper.

Dr. Tyson sniffed mightily, then finished gathering her things. Before she left, she turned up the volume on the iPod.

And since I'm endeavoring not to think about Dr. Oscar's short-term outlook...

Five thousand eight hundred thirty-nine... five thousand eight hundred forty...

November 13, Sunday

"HI, MARIGOLD, it's Jack—"

"Hello, Detective Terry," Aunt Winnie said.

"Hello," he said warily.

Rightfully so, because the last time he saw her, she accused him of being the father of my baby.

"I come in peace," she said with a chuckle.

"If I'm interrupting family time, I can leave," he offered.

"Actually, I have a message for you."

"A message? Who is it from?"

"Um, it's from Marigold."

He made a strangled sound. "Not the psychic thing again."

"Just hear me out, Detective. It's a simple message and it doesn't make much sense to me, but it might to you."

I heard him sigh and rearrange his body. "I'm listening." I envision him with arms crossed defiantly.

"I wrote it down," Winnie said, then stepped toward him.

The crinkle of paper sounded.

"'Tell Jack Sidney is driving me crazy.'" He grunted. "What's that supposed to mean?"

"Other than the obvious, I don't know," Winnie said. "Sidney gets on my nerves, too."

I heard the sound of the piece of paper being stuffed somewhere—hopefully not in Winnie's mouth.

"I'll hang on to it," he said in a mollifying voice.

"Then my job here is done," Winnie said. "I'll leave you to... do whatever it is you do when you visit Marigold. Toodle-loo."

The door opened and closed.

Jack chuckled. "Interesting gal, your aunt."

Winnie means well. And Faridee *almost* got the message right.

"Funny she should bring up Sidney. Your sister sure spends a lot of money for someone who doesn't have a job."

Jack is tracking Sidney's spending habits? That's curious. But I'd heard her tell David she'd put diamond earrings on her credit card. Sid probably reasoned she'd be making a lot of money when she graduated law school, and could afford to go into debt now.

"The Falcons are playing today," Jack said mildly. "They're having a great season, thanks to Keith Young. Since he recovered from that beating, he's been playing better than ever."

The beating David Spooner, aka Dean Bradley, had something to do with.

"His image will take a big hit if he pleads guilty to the charges ADA Spence put in front of him. He has a lot to lose."

Although if Keith Young doesn't sign the papers and I check out, he'll be on the hook for much more serious charges... unless Sidney comes forward.

But if I'm gone, why would she?

And it hurts my feelings a little that Jack thinks I want to listen to the football game knowing how my life is entangled with Keith Young's.

"Which is why I thought with the announcement of the new MSL franchise of Atlanta United, now might be a good time to learn the rules of soccer." Jack groaned. "I can take it if you can, Coma Girl."

Inside I'm smiling.

November 14, Monday

TEN THOUSAND TWO HUNDRED TWENTY-ONE... *ten thousand two hundred twenty-two—*

The door opened. "Peace be with you, ladies."

Oh, no. *No, no, no.* What I do not need today is a visit from Sister Irene, the sadist nun.

"It's rainy and cold," she sang. "A great day to be cooped up inside."

In a cage, perhaps? That's probably where she had stowed her sister's killer, George Gilpin, whom she'd lured to her gingerbread house with the promise of easy handyman work. Or had she already skinned him and made slippers out of his hide?

"Hello, Marigold. I heard you had another surgery. I've been praying for you."

Thanks, Sister. Beggars cannot be choosers.

"What happened to your rosary?"

I'm pretty sure my sister used it to almost smother me. The two of you should meet for tea sometime and compare M.O.'s.

"I thought you might like an update on my houseguest."

Nope. Nada. *Nein.*

"Mr. Gilpin was recuperating nicely from his previous injuries, but he attempted to leave the bed too soon and I had to give him a shot."

Let me guess—with a nail gun?

"Just a little something to make him sleep."

Weed killer?

"And now he's back on the mend."

So you can dissect him again?

"I have to admit, I'm getting used to having companionship."

That will come in handy when you share a cell at San Quentin.

Sister Irene laughed. "He still doesn't know who I am. I told him my name is Ginger. It's my real name, you know. When I took my vows, I was given a more appropriate name to live by. So it only makes sense that I'd revert to Ginger for this task."

Is that how she's able to compartmentalize her actions, the praying and the slaying? Maybe she has a split personality.

Then she made a pensive noise. "Although, this undertaking has sorely cut into my time for visiting the sick, and for that I apologize, Marigold. As soon as I take care of Mr. Gilpin, I'll come around more often."

And with that cheery thought...

Ten thousand two hundred twenty-three... ten thousand two hundred twenty-four...

November 15, Tuesday

TWELVE THOUSAND SEVEN HUNDRED ELEVEN... twelve thousand seven hundred twelve—

The door burst open.

"All I'm saying is you could've parked closer to the elevator," my dad said, thumping inside on his crutches.

"And get my new company car dinged? No way."

Dad scoffed. "It's a Kia, not a Mercedes."

"You're jealous."

"That's ridiculous."

"You're jealous because I finally have my own career, and my own interests."

"I just think it's bad timing with... everything that's going on."

"What's that supposed to mean?"

Dad made an exasperated noise. "I mean we have a daughter in a coma, who's about to have a baby!"

"And I suppose you expect me to take care of Marigold, and her baby."

"I expect us to do it together, as a family."

"Oh, sure—while you're on the road all week, eating on your expense account and going to titty bars, I'll be saddled at home with two invalids in diapers!"

Technically true, but *ouch*.

My mother burst into tears. "I'm sorry. I shouldn't have said that."

Here's where you have to read between the lines—she's not saying she doesn't mean it, just that she shouldn't have said it.

"It's okay," my dad soothed. "We're all stressed to the max."

But I totally understand where she's coming from. Mom wasn't that into me when I was able-bodied and -minded. What the heck is she supposed to do with me now? And my unplanned child? Deep down I think she went along with Sid's encouragement to keep the baby because she thought by now I'd be awake and out of her life again.

"What if she never gets better?" my mom sobbed. "What if this is the only life Marigold is going to have?"

"Then we have to accept it," Dad said, ever reasonable.

And so do I. The realization hit me like a brick wall.

I've been lying here thinking my situation is temporary, that it's just a matter of time before I open my eyes and swing my legs over the edge of the bed and walk out of here. I've been letting Dr. Jarvis pull me along, mistaking his egotism for optimism, when maybe I'm simply never going to wake up.

Maybe this is how I'm going to live out the rest of my life—in my own head, listening, and being a well that other people pour themselves into. It's a function. It's not what I had in mind when I graduated college, but neither was being a carpet warehouse wrangler. Maybe this is God's plan for me. We don't all get to be bright and shiny. And conscious.

Twelve thousand seven hundred thirteen... twelve thousand seven hundred fourteen...

November 16, Wednesday

FOURTEEN THOUSAND THREE HUNDRED THIRTY-FOUR... *fourteen thousand three hundred thirty-five—*

The door opened quietly. I might not have heard it except for the fact that it's early and the hospital is only beginning to rouse.

"Good morning, Coma Girl."

It's the volunteer who reads to us often and exploits us occasionally. But at this point, what's another photo of me in my bed? I might be wearing a different headscarf and from what the nurses say, my baby bump might be showing, but otherwise, I'm a still life arrangement.

"It's chilly this morning," he said, blowing—I assume into his hands to warm them.

I believe I've forgotten cold and hot. When I think of the words, instead of sensations, colors pop into my head—pale blue for coolness, flame red for warmth. And I can conjure up images of ice and fire, but I can't recall what they feel like on my skin.

Audrey Parks had escaped the vegetable patch only to come back and torment the rest of us with descriptions of how horrible it was to try to adjust to living again. I suspect after a couple of years of nonbeing, a person would have to relearn everything about interacting with the world. No wonder she was having a rough go of it.

"A while ago I marked this Dickinson poem to read," he said, "but the timing never felt right. But today for some reason, it feels right, and I hope you like it."

Even the pages of the book sounded stiff as he turned them.

"It's called 'I Have No Life But This,' and I think it applies to everyone on this earth."

He paused to good effect, then began to read.

"I have no life but this, to lead it here, nor any death, but lest dispelled from there. Nor tie to earths to come, nor action new, except through this extent, the realm of you."

It's as if he's looking straight into my heart, as if he knows I'm struggling to accept this life. Part of the resistance is knowing what a burden I will be on my family, and especially my mother. But part of the resistance is plain old brattiness and wanting what I had before.

And even though the philosophy of the poem seems especially poignant for someone like me and Karen Suh, our volunteer is correct that it applies to everyone in all walks of life. As hard as it might be to understand, even a life of privilege comes with its challenges. Look at Joanna.

The door opened again, and I could tell the volunteer was startled by the way he jumped to his feet.

"Excuse me?" a woman asked. "The security guard told me I could come in? I'm looking for Marigold Kemp?"

My mind is racing to identify the voice—the woman sounds young, and she's an 'uptalker'—she ends every sentence as if she's asking a question.

"You're in the right place," the man said smoothly. "That's Marigold, with the flowered headscarf."

"Oh? Are you a relative?"

"A friend."

She sighed, then I heard the shuffle of papers. "I teach an evening writing class at Kennesaw State?"

Suddenly I recognized the voice, and I know what's coming.

"I've had a manuscript of Marigold's for months? I didn't know what had happened, she just stopped coming to class? And I didn't have a mailing address for her? Then one day, I heard her name on television, and there she was, in a coma? Anyway, I brought the manuscript?"

Holy God—what the disorganized uptalker left out is the supremely pertinent fact that it was a *therapy* writing class. The manuscript is basically one long bitchfest about my messed up family. And because it was supposed to be confidential, I even used their real names.

"Leave it," the volunteer said. "I'll make sure it gets to the right person."

"Thanks? You're a lifesaver?"

This can't be happening. A tell-all on Coma Girl's life story was just handed to the man who has TMZ on speed-dial.

Sure enough, after the woman left, I heard the zip-snap of a backpack being opened. "I'll take this for safekeeping," he said, almost to himself.

After a quick goodbye, he left whistling under his breath.

When I started recalling all the horrible things I'd written about everyone in my family, my mind began to spin. Because we had been encouraged to purge our demons in the assignment, I had bled my spleen on those pages with bitterness and scorn—even cruelty. If—when—it got out, my family would definitely cut ties with me. And worse, the manuscript might be the only thing of me my child would ever know.

When panic threatened to close in, I focused on the funereal music in my ear.

Fourteen thousand three hundred thirty-six... fourteen thousand three hundred thirty-seven...

November 17, Thursday

SEVENTEEN THOUSAND FIVE HUNDRED EIGHT... Seventeen thousand five hundred nine—

The door opened and from the banging and clanging, it's clear something is being moved inside.

"Got a new roommate for you," a male voice announced—Nico, I think.

"A fresh veggie for the patch," another voice snarked—Gabriel, for sure.

They rolled the bed inside and positioned it between mine and Karen's. Back is the wheezy rattle of a ventilator, like Jill had required. Whoever the patient is, she's behind the eight ball—and that says a lot coming from someone whose eyes don't dilate.

"Oops, dropped my hat," Gabriel said. "Fell out of my back pocket."

"The hat you stole from a comatose patient," Nico reminded him.

I believe the word you're looking for, Nico, is "ghoul."

"Do you see anybody asking for it? No. CG over there don't even know it's gone."

Uh, yes, I do. You're not only a grave-robber, but you stole the only connection I had to Duncan.

"At least leave it in your locker," Nico bit out.

"It's my lucky hat. I get lucky with Donna every time I wear it."

"Uh-huh. What happened to tapping Gina's honeypot?"

"Man, she lured me over to her place, then put me on ice. I'm done with that."

Nico laughed. "Remind me to congratulate Gina when I see her."

The door opened. "Did I hear my name?" Gina asked.

"Was bragging on you, baby," Gabriel said, his voice undulating like a song.

"It's 'Gina' at work," she reminded him.

"Got you a new cabbage for the garden," Gabriel said.

"What is the patient's name?" she asked crisply.

"Shondra Taylor," Nico responded. "Twenty-one, brain and spinal cord injury."

Gina made a mournful sound. "So young. What happened?"

"Playing a virtual reality mobile app with friends, and walked off a bridge."

Ugh—how is that even possible?

"The second patient this month, same thing," Gina said. "Luckily, the other one is only in a body cast. Who's her doctor?"

"Tyson."

"Okay, thanks, guys. I'll take it from here."

"See you, Gina."

"Later, Nico."

"Hey, Gina," Gabriel said, lowering his voice. "I was hoping we could have a date night *in* soon... you know, when the coast is clear, so to speak."

"I can't, Gabriel. I just signed up for double shifts through the end of the month. I need the extra money to give my boy a good Christmas."

"Okay, gorgeous, so maybe after that?"

"Maybe."

He made a clicking "gotcha" sound with his cheek and I'll bet a hundred dollars he had the finger-gun action going, too.

Yuck. I wish I could warn Gina. And get Duncan's hat back. And talk to Detective Terry. And let Karen Suh's ex-husband know she's still here. And retrieve that manuscript.

"Welcome, Shondra, to the long-term care ward," Gina murmured. "Better get comfortable, sweetie. No one in here is going home any time soon."

Seventeen thousand five hundred ten... seventeen thousand five hundred eleven...

November 18, Friday

TWENTY THOUSAND FOUR HUNDRED EIGHTEEN... twenty *thousand four hundred nineteen—*

The door opened and two sets of feet ran in—one with telltale flapping sandals. The door closed just as quickly.

"Did he see us?" Winnie whispered.

"Shh, I think I hear him coming," Faridee murmured. "Lean against the door."

The doorknob jiggled.

"Ladies," Teddy said from the other side. "I saw you. Open up."

They took their sweet time, but they finally opened the door.

Teddy came stomping in. "I saw you sneaking by the nurses' station holding magazines over your faces. Next time, make sure they're right side up."

"We wouldn't have to sneak in if you'd let me in to see my own niece," Winnie said in a huff.

"You're firebugs!" Teddy said. "And you're lucky I didn't call the police. Both of you, turn around, hands up."

"You're arresting us?" Faridee exclaimed.

"No. I'm patting you down for candles."

"But you're a man... and we're women," Winnie protested weakly.

"Unless you got a real roman candle under that tent, you're safe," Teddy said dryly. "Okay, you're good. But I'm watching you two."

The door opened and he marched out.

Faridee snorted her indignation. "Well, I *never.*"

"I did once," Winnie said with a conspiratorial giggle. "Actually, twice."

The women tee-heed, totally entertaining themselves. If Coma Girl makes it to Broadway, these two characters have to be written in as some kind of fairy coma-mothers.

"Hello, Sweetheart," Winnie called. "I'm here with Faridee."

Yes, I heard the commotion for the last ten minutes or so. Along with everyone else on the floor. You probably traumatized poor Shondra.

"Actually, we came to visit because Faridee has a wonderful idea for a business."

Okay, where is this going?

"You've heard of Wind Talkers," Winnie said.

"And Small Talkers," Faridee added.

"And Trash Talkers," Winnie ended with a flourish.

Okay, I've heard of maybe one of those.

"Now meet Coma Talkers!" they said in unison.

Oh, brother.

"Our idea is to go around to coma wards and transcribe what patients are thinking but can't communicate to their friends and family."

That will be a small disaster, but hilarious.

"But we need to practice more on you, Marigold," Faridee said.

"So when you wake up," Winnie said, "you can tell us how close we are."

Ah, the fatal flaw.

"Faridee is going to snort some vanilla Stevia because it worked so well that one time."

"It gave me such clarity."

A reminder that the Stevia-snorting session led to Winnie accusing Jack Terry of fathering my child.

"Here, I'll empty the packets onto this bed tray, Faridee. Why don't you open that straw—no one in here is going to use it—and snort it that way?"

"Much easier," Faridee agreed.

Uh, ladies…

"Oh! You should try this, Winnie. It's a rush."

"Don't mind if I do… Whew-we!"

I heard Teddy's whistle just as he opened the door. I'm sure Winnie and Faridee looked like two caftaned deer in headlights. With white powder on their noses.

"What's going on in here?" he thundered.

"We're snorting Stevia," Winnie said, just as if it made sense.

"Out!"

"But—"

"Out, out, *out!*"

He hustled them out and I could hear their raised voices as they rolled down the hall.

That scene is definitely going into the musical.

Where was I? Oh, yeah—*Twenty thousand four hundred twenty… twenty thousand four hundred twenty-one…*

November 19, Saturday

TWENTY-ONE THOUSAND ONE HUNDRED TWENTY-NINE… twenty-one thousand one hundred thirty…

I'm slowing down. Or maybe I'm just tired. Maybe the baby is restless… I wish I could feel *something.*

When the door opened, I assumed it's another visitor for Shondra.

Her young friends came in tearful droves, standing around her bed praying and singing and playing video games while narrating them to her. It's unimaginable that she'd landed in that bed because she simply wasn't paying attention.

Although, isn't that what happened to me? Because someone wasn't paying attention.

I'm waiting for word that the manuscript I'd written has been leaked to the highest bidder, but so far, nothing. If it happens and my family is too furious to talk to me, Roberta will burn a trail over here to clue me in.

"Hi, Marigold."

My ears tell my brain to go haywire before recognition kicks in. *Duncan.*

"I've been out of the country for a while, working. I had to come, though, and see for myself... "

How emaciated I look? Bald and pale and slack?

"You're really pregnant."

"She really is."

Roberta had slipped in.

"Hi, Roberta."

"Hi, Duncan. I guess you're back in town for the wedding."

"Right," he said. "But I wanted to see Marigold. How is she?"

"Still comatose. And pregnant."

"I just heard about that. Who's the father?"

I'm holding my mental breath.

"I think it's some guy she hooked up with on Tinder."

Wow, that hurt more than I thought it would... but it's for best, right?

"Oh," Duncan said.

Is that relief in his voice?

"So he's not in the picture?"

"No."

"Do I have something on my face?" he asked.

"I just realized what a tiny head you have."

"What?"

"Never mind. How are plans for the wedding? A week from today, right?"

"Right. Everything's... perfect. Trina's great at pretty much everything. Well, you met her."

"Yes. She invited me to the wedding. She seems great."

"She is great."

Great.

"You know," Roberta said casually, "I always thought you and Marigold would end up married someday."

"Marigold and I were always good friends. You know, dating messes up friendships."

"Yeah… or makes them better."

"Or worse," he said.

"Or better," Roberta said.

"Well, I have Trina now, and… all that.   So, what's Marigold's prognosis?"

He sounded concerned… or maybe he thought he needed to, for appearances.

"No one really knows."

"They don't know if she's going to wake up?"

"No.   She had a second surgery about three weeks ago, and the doctors were hopeful it would make a difference, but so far, it hasn't."

"Who's going to take care of her?"

"Her family, I guess."

"And the baby?"

"Same."

"Marigold isn't that close to her family."

"Yeah, they're all a little hinky, but I suppose when something like this happens, you band together."

"I guess you're right.   But what if she doesn't wake up?"

"That's possible.   That woman over next to the wall has been in a coma for over two years."

"Two years?"

"And people can live for decades in a coma."

"Do they know if Marigold can hear us?"

"There have been times when she responded to commands to move her fingers, but not for weeks now."

"So she might be able to hear me right now, but not respond?"

"Right."

"So she could be trapped in there?"

"I guess anything is possible.   The nurses tell me when it comes to the brain, it's a crapshoot."

Roberta has picked up some precise medical terminology since she started hanging out with me.

"Are you okay, Duncan?"

"Yeah… I mean, no, I'm not okay.   I'm angry that something like this happened to someone like Marigold.   She deserves… better."

"Won't get an argument from me," Roberta said.

But at the same time, is he thinking how lucky he is not to have me as a ball and chain around his neck?

"I have to go," Duncan said.   "Trina is… I'm expected to be somewhere."

"Go—you've got a busy week ahead of you."

He stepped closer to my bed. "Bye, Marigold. I'll be thinking of you."

Can you be more precise? Thinking of me when you need someone to help you lift a piece of furniture, or while you're walking down the aisle?

But as his footsteps retreated, I felt the life I'd dreamed of slip through my fingers.

"Duncan?" Roberta called.

"Yeah?"

"Just curious—how do you feel about professional basketball?"

Roberta, bless her, she had to be sure. This is my last chance to let Duncan know about the baby before he walked down the aisle.

"Total waste of time," he said.

Poof!

When the door closed behind him, a door in my heart closed, too.

November 20, Sunday

TWENTY-ONE THOUSAND SIX HUNDRED FORTY-NINE... twenty-one thousand six hundred fifty...

In between counting bells, I keep replaying Duncan's conversation over and over in my head, reliving the wonder of him walking into my room, and the agony of him walking out.

It's Sunday, so I'm waiting for Jack Terry to walk in and grouse about soccer and soggy pizza, but as the day wears on, it's apparent he's not coming. Maybe he's out house-hunting again today, or maybe he had to shop for the baby, or a hundred other little domestic things that are all probably new to Jack.

When ADA Spence had baited him about Liz Fischer, the mother of his child, he hadn't responded. I gather the women knew each other professionally. And he hadn't mentioned the other woman, Carlotta, for a while. But maybe he'd decided he'd never be able to build a relationship with Liz if Carlotta is uppermost in his mind.

The door opened, but instead of admitting Jack Terry, I realized Jonas Suh had returned to visit his ex-wife, Karen. Faridee had once "telegraphed" something from Karen onto a note for Jonas, proof she hears him and wants to communicate. But the note had been discarded before Jonas had seen it, so he's flying blind trying to decide whether to hold out hope Karen will someday get better, or if he should move on with his life.

Karen and I are in the same boat—bursting to communicate with loved ones, but trapped inside a body that betrays the mind.

"Hi, Karen. It's me, Jonas. How are you today? I brought you some mums I found at Pike's Nursery. Remember how much we used to love to go there? The blooms are a bright lavender, so pretty. You have a lavender silk dress that looks so nice with your dark hair."

But I can tell his small talk is forced. Underneath the false cheer, his voice is unsteady.

"I have some good news," he said. "The nursing home bed they found for you will be ready in late-December. That gives me some time to liquidate the furniture and get the house on the market. The agent I spoke to said it's a good time to sell, so you should get a nice price. And I start my new job in London January 1. So we have all kinds of reasons to celebrate, don't we?"

Poor Karen. I know she's listening and comprehending what he said, but she's powerless to respond.

I can't listen to him anymore. It's too heartbreaking. I have enough heartbreak for the whole ward already.

Twenty-one thousand six hundred fifty-one... twenty-one thousand six hundred fifty-two...

November 21, Monday

TWENTY-TWO THOUSAND TWO HUNDRED SIX... Twenty-two thousand two hundred seven...

The door opened and someone made their way inside with a limp— no, a cane. At first I thought my dad had graduated from his crutches, then I caught a whiff of feminine scented soap.

"Anyone in the vegetable patch awake?"

It's Audrey Parks, our former wardmate who had awoken from her coma only to find life outside even more harrowing. Our two previous reunions had not gone well. During the last visit Audrey had urged Jill Wheatley to give up and die, and Jill had done just that. Audrey had been so adversarial and cruel, hinting we each had serious ailments our doctors were keeping from us, that she had to be forcibly removed. I'm a little surprised Teddy had let her come in... but perhaps he wasn't working, or she had slipped by him.

"We have a newbie, I see," Audrey said, walking to stand between my bed and Shondra's. "I heard you did this to yourself playing a video game?" She gave a harsh laugh. "And I thought wrecking on water skis was lame."

Gosh, Audrey, give the girl a break. If she's semi-aware, she probably hasn't yet grasped the gravity of her situation.

She limped to the other side of the room.

"And Karen, you're still lying there curled up like an animal. Even if you woke up, they'd have to break your bones to straighten you out."

What, you couldn't find disabled kittens to kick across the room?

"And Marigold—or should I call you 'Coma Girl'? Our own little celebrity vegetable, like a Muppet. And you're pregnant with another little vegetable. Because you don't honestly think this kid is going to come out normal, do you?"

I strained to lift my foot for one good kick... just one... but no. Besides, bizarrely, it seems as if that's what Audrey wants—a physical altercation. To hit and get hit back. To feel pain.

"Well, not that I think any of you turnips are getting out of here," Audrey said, "but if you do, just know you're going to spend most of your life right back here in the hospital to fix all the little things they didn't even know went wrong until you wake up and tell them. Between not being able to work and all my medical bills, I'll be in debt the rest of my life. I have no friends, no social life, and I'm not allowed to drive because I could have a seizure at any time."

Why are you here, Audrey? Because you feel picked on by God, and you want to pick on someone, too?

"Anyway," she said, her tone and mood changing as if someone had turned off a switch. "I really just came to say... goodbye."

Okay, that was odd... maybe she's on medication?

She dragged the chair across the room to the little-used bathroom. I wonder if she plans to sit and glare at us all evening.

Suddenly I heard the chair squeak, then topple over, and the scrape of shoes and hands, then the grunts of Audrey gasping for breath.

With dawning horror, I realize she's trying to hang herself from the bathroom door.

And from the choking sounds she's making, if someone doesn't intervene soon, she's going to succeed.

I try to rally my resources to move or scream or anything I can do to raise an alarm, but my mind is racing, distracted by the noises of the gruesome scene playing out mere feet away, and I'm paralyzed.

The door opened.

Thank God—the cavalry!

"There were three empty parking places next to the elevator," my dad said, stumping in on his crutches. "Three!"

"Lazy people park next to the elevator," my mom said. "And lazy people ding other people's cars."

"Carrie, for God's sake, sooner or later, your car's gonna get dinged!"

"Well, it won't be today."

It wasn't until they'd both fallen into a sullen silence that the throes of death noises could be heard.

"What the—?"

My mother screamed as if her hair was on fire, then ran back to the hall.

My dad stumped over and from what I could tell, held Audrey up with his crutches until help arrived to cut her down.

So, my Dad finally gets to be a hero, and Audrey will live to hate another day.

But I'm horrified that this far along into my "recovery," I couldn't rouse myself from my deep sleep even when another person's life was in imminent danger an arm's length away. And if a life or death crisis won't jar my body out of its fugue state, then I'm afraid nothing will.

November 22, Tuesday

TWENTY-TWO THOUSAND SEVEN HUNDRED THIRTEEN... *twenty-two thousand seven hundred fourteen...*

The door opened, and it took me a minute to realize my Mom had walked inside because she's not talking on her phone or walking fast, or nursing the cup of coffee that has become her power accessory.

"Hello, Marigold."

She sounds wistful and tired and a little buzzed. I can smell the faint scent of the red wine she buys from Trader Joe's, so that means she drove here from home. Without my dad. The fact that she settled into the guest chair Audrey had used last night to climb to her suicide attempt without insisting on a replacement tells me she's on a mission. I can tell from her subdued mood that she wants to tell me something, and my first thought goes to what the doctors had said about keeping me alive until the end of the month, which is fast approaching. Is she going to tell me I'm dying?

"I don't know if you can hear me," she began, "but the doctors say to speak as if you can. I need to tell you something, and even though this probably isn't the best timing, I want to tell you before I lose my nerve."

Okay, now I'm worried.

"Before you were born, your father and I were having some problems—mostly money problems, but other things, too."

Around the time Dad had taken twenty-five grand from the safe to pay off gambling debts, and blamed the missing money on a burglar.

"Anyway, like I said, we were having some problems and... there was this man I met... and liked."

My mind is jumping all around and ahead, and I don't like where it's landing.

"We had an affair."

Holy chastity belt—*my mother had an affair?* I no longer believe the world is round, and I'm throwing that whole gravity thing out the window, too.

"And I became pregnant."

Wait—that would be *me.*

"Shortly after that, the man was killed in a tragic amusement ride accident."

What? How horrible. And... random.

"Your father never knew about the other man, and that's the way I'd like to keep it." She sighed. "But I look back at your childhood, Marigold, and I realize I might have taken my guilt out on you, and that was wrong."

So, those elusive feelings I had when I was young about being at the center of my family's discontent were valid. I felt like the outsider because I *was* the outsider.

"I want you to know I've always loved you just as much as Alex and Sidney—maybe more because you remind me of him. He was an independent thinker and marched to the beat of his own drum, and so do you. And if I ever made you feel less than Alex or Sidney, I'm so sorry. You should never feel inferior to anyone. You're as unique and special as the name I gave you, and I..." Her voice broke. "I love you so much."

I don't know what to think, or feel, except to marvel over her revelations and try to let them sink in.

Mom made an anguished noise. "I wish you could talk to me. I wish I knew what you are thinking. If you can hear me, I want you to remember how much your father adores you and loves you. Robert would be wounded if he thought you didn't consider him to be your father."

Of course he's my father. Dad is... Dad.

"Robert is such a dear man." She's crying again. "I haven't been fair to him. I blamed him all these years for being distant and driving me into the arms of another man, but I made that choice. I'm going to make things better at home, for all of us, including your baby."

A mental weight rolled off me because I've been feeling like the straw that was going to break my parents' marriage, when in truth, they'd both harbored corrosive secrets that had eaten away at their relationship. Maybe things could be better now.

But there's still Sidney to contend with.

And I'm so conflicted over everything that's happened, I just don't know how this is going to turn out.

November 23, Wednesday

TWENTY-TWO THOUSAND NINE HUNDRED FIFTY-EIGHT...
twenty-two thousand nine hundred fifty-nine... Twenty-two thousand nine hundred
sixty...

The door opened to small hard-soled shoes tapping and stomping on the floor to a tune in the head of the dancer.

Christina is back.

"Hi, Magic Lady."

She did another little dance punctuated by jumps I can only assume are spectacular.

"I came to say thank you."

More dancing, and some humming as a bonus.

"My mommy is all better and she's coming home tomorrow for Thanksgiving!" She clapped and jumped up and down.

Oh, the best news ever. Which I cannot take credit for, but will celebrate.

"We're going to have turkey and ice cream and cranberries and ice cream and gravy and ice cream and—"

She stopped.

"What will you eat for Thanksgiving? Will the doctors bring you turkey? And ice cream?"

It's sweet of her to be so concerned.

Cristina gasped. "Is that a baby in your tummy?"

She dragged the chair over and climbed up, I presumed, to get a better look.

"Yep, it's a baby, alright. It's wriggling all over."

Oh, I wish I could see it... I wish I could feel it. I'm starting to feel like a floating head, disembodied and listening from a dark corner.

"Is it a magic baby?" Christina asked in awe.

I guess you could say that, considering all the baby has survived.

"Can I come back and see it sometime when it's out of your stomach?"

I love how kids need no interaction to carry on a conversation. They can talk all day to a doll, or a dog, or a coma patient.

"Christina!"

"Gots to go," she said, then jumped down and pushed the chair back.

"Hey, Magic Lady, if you ever get sad in there, just think about dancing—that always makes me happy. Dancing and ice cream. Bye!"

She bounded out of the room and I shot a thank you to the Powers That Be for arranging for Christina's mother to be home on Thanksgiving with her family.

Mom and Dad are having a big dinner at home for Sid and some neighbors and some of their coworkers. I believe even Mom and Winnie have buried the hatchet long enough to slice a turkey and break bread. They're stopping by after dinner on their way to the Macy's tree lighting ceremony at Lenox Mall.

The weekend will be full of celebrations—sales, fireworks, the Turkey Trot run, riding the Pink Pig, Santa, festivals, lights, music, parties, brunches, dinners...

And a wedding.

Twenty-two thousand nine hundred sixty-one... Twenty-two thousand nine hundred sixty-two...

November 24, Thursday

TWENTY-THREE THOUSAND TWO HUNDRED SIXTY-ONE... twenty-three thousand two hundred sixty-two... twenty-three thousand two hundred sixty-three...

Dr. Jarvis came by this morning to wish all the staff and patients a Happy Thanksgiving, and while he was here, gave me a quick motor response test.

I failed.

So while I'm still counting bells, I confess I'm losing hope. Because no one can put their finger on why I'm not getting better. And at what point do I simply accept where I am? Is acceptance giving up, or is it acknowledging a plateau?

The door opened and at the sound of bootsteps, I first thought Jack Terry was making holiday rounds.

"Hi, Sis."

Alex. My hero brother. What a wonderful surprise!

"I thought I'd sneak in for a few days to surprise the folks. And I wanted to see you, too. I've been so worried. You look pale, but good. Your scars are almost gone, I see. And we both have buzzcuts now."

He could always make me laugh.

"You're so pretty, Marigold. I don't tell you often enough. You stand in Sid's shadow, and we both know she casts a long one, but in your own way, you're just as striking as she is."

I'm preening under his praise, even though I know he's being kind.

He chuckled. "Pregnancy obviously becomes you. Did anyone ever figure out who the lucky guy is? I gave Dad the name of a dude you mentioned in your letters, some guy who was in the Peace Corps... I think his name is Duncan. Hope that's okay. In your letters you said you were just friends but I kind of got the idea it might be more than that for you. Which reminds me."

He pulled the guest chair over and sat down. "I've been keeping something from you, Marigold, and the whole family, in fact."

Inside I scoffed. The only secrets Alex could have would be concerning his work with top-secret agencies, in and out of the military.

"After the accident and when I couldn't talk to you, I started thinking about all the things I didn't tell you, and one in particular stuck out. It's about your letters."

My letters?

"As soon as I was shipped overseas, you started sending me letters."

Almost every day—I remember.

"And I loved getting them in mail call—all the other guys were jealous. So I let my buddies read them... to me. Because I couldn't."

I'm confused. What was it Alex couldn't do?

"What I'm trying to say, Sis, is I couldn't read."

I froze. What? That's impossible. Alex is and always has been the smartest, most accomplished man I know—he went to college, for heaven's sake. Of course he can read.

"I know what you're probably thinking—how can that be? But it's true. I got by on listening in class and standardized tests and oral exams. Same thing in every job I've ever had. It wasn't until I started getting your letters that I wanted to get better. And I did. I worked with a couple of great tutors and did a lot of stuff online, and some of the guys in my unit helped, too. Now I'm almost where I want to be... and it's all thanks to your letters."

He's giving me way too much credit. I was only trying to keep him from being homesick. I teach reading myself—how did I miss the signs?

"Looking back, I just want to say if I ever brushed off something you were doing or didn't seem interested, it wasn't because I didn't care... it's because I was afraid you'd find out I couldn't read and think less of me. And your opinion has always meant a lot to me."

Wow... I'd misinterpreted just about every interaction of our teen years, had assumed Alex was too cool for my dorky science projects and spelling bees.

He cleared his throat. "Anyway, if something had happened to you, and I hadn't told you how much your letters had meant to me, I don't know if I could've lived with myself. I love you, Marigold."

I heard his kiss, although I didn't feel it. But I folded it into my heart.

"I'm going to head home and surprise Mom. I'll be back real soon. You take care."

I want so much to get up out of this bed and go with Alex so our family can be together for Thanksgiving.

But I can't.

Twenty-three thousand two hundred sixty-four… twenty-three thousand two hundred sixty-five…

November 25, Friday

TWENTY-FOUR THOUSAND SEVEN HUNDRED THIRTY…
Twenty-four thousand seven hundred thirty-one… Twenty-four thousand seven hundred thirty-two…

Since my family had all visited the night before, I don't expect any visitors on Black Friday. Besides, I'm now in the twenty-four hour countdown to Duncan's wedding, so I don't mind being alone to wallow.

Anyway, when the door opened, the last person I expected was Sidney. She and David Spooner had stepped into ICU after my recent surgery to visit, but to my knowledge, this is the first time she's been alone in my room since Halloween.

When she tried to kill me.

Let's just say I'm skittish.

"Hi, Marigold. I wanted to talk to you when no one else is around. I feel like there's a lot of unfinished business between us, but it's hard to tell when I don't know if you can even hear me or understand me." She sighed. "Ugh, this is hard."

Harder if you're the helpless one, trust me.

"Remember when we were little, and we shared a bedroom? We had two twin beds with matching pink polka-dotted bedspreads."

I remember. The beds had shelves in the headboards. Mine were full of books, and Sid's were full of dolls.

"There were shelves in the beds. Mine were stuffed with dolls and yours were stacked with books."

Shared memories.

"You read stories to me at night while I held my dolls."

No matter how many stories I read, it wasn't enough.

More, Mar'gol, more. Please?

And Sid hated sleeping alone.

Sid laughed. "But I hated sleeping alone, remember? I would whine until you'd crawl into bed with me and let me stroke your hair."

Mar'gol, let me pet your hair.

Twirl my hair was more like it. I'd wake up the next morning and my hair would be in knots.

"I loved sharing a room with you," Sid said. "It made me feel grown up. I was so upset when you convinced Mom to let you have your own bedroom."

It didn't matter. Sid still came in to my room most nights.

Can I scooch in, Mar'gol?

Then she would proceed to sprawl her little body over the entire bed.

"We used to be so close," Sid said. "When did that change?"

The age difference, and divergent interests... it just happened. A tiny part of me is resentful that my mother's choice to have an affair meant I don't have as much in common with my siblings as I might have otherwise.

"I was so jealous of you," Sid said.

Wait—what?

"Mother always trusted you, let you make your own decisions."

And I'd assumed Mother hadn't been interested in me enough to weigh in on my life.

"But she was always pushing me, like she didn't think I could make a good choice on my own."

I'm starting to think that Sid grew up in a different house than I did, because that's not how I remember it at all.

"Sometimes I'm afraid when I get my law degree, it'll have Mom's name on it instead of mine."

Wow—I had no idea Sid felt this way.

"You don't know how hard it is to live up to her expectations," Sid said, her voice cracking. "It's a lot of pressure. I've... done things I'm not proud of." She blew her nose. "And the things I've done to, um, hurt you, Marigold... well, I wasn't myself, and I'm sorry." Then she made a frustrated noise. "Can you even hear me?"

I hear her... and while I appreciate that Sid is sorry for what she did, is she going to make it right?

November 26, Saturday

TWENTY-FIVE THOUSAND ONE HUNDRED FIFTY-TWO... twenty-five thousand one hundred fifty-three... twenty-five thousand one hundred fifty-four...

The problem is, every bell I count today sounds like a wedding bell.

By my estimation, Duncan's wedding should be starting soon. The guests will be arriving. I had planned to be there in high spirits and bearing something appropriately unnecessary, like a soup tureen, then dancing at the reception like a fool, just as if I wasn't brokenhearted to see him marry someone else.

But I don't even get to do that. Instead I'm lying here with his progeny in my stomach, marinating in misery.

The door swings open and instantly I know it's Roberta.

"I couldn't go to the wedding," she announced. "I decided to come and sit with you and read you some funny mail to cheer you up. And I brought some white cupcakes so we can have our own celebration."

I love this woman.

"But first, there's something I have to get off my chest, and you're not going to like it." She inhaled deeply. "I was the one who took the money I was saving for you in freezer," she said on a long exhale. "There. But before you hate me, let me tell you why." She sucked in another deep breath. "I'm a kleptomaniac and I used the money to pay a therapist to cure me. Now you can hate me if you want."

I can't hate you, Roberta.

"Although when I described it all to you just now, I saw the irony in stealing money to cure myself of stealing. Okay, I need a cupcake."

The door burst open and Roberta gasped, choking on her cupcake. "What are *you* doing here?" she asked with her mouth full.

"The right thing," Duncan said.

Holy matrimony, Duncan is here?

He walked close to my bed.

"Marigold, I don't know if you can hear me, but I am possessed by you. I was standing in the church today and I felt empty because you weren't there, standing next to me. I can't marry Trina. I love you... it's always been you, I was too dumb to realize it. I can't stand the thought of you lying in this bed and me not being close by. Whatever happens, I'll be here. I know the baby's not mine, but I'll help you raise it if your family is okay with that. I know I'm rambling, but I'm shaking all over, and I just want to kiss you right now."

Is this happening? Because I might be hallucinating.

Roberta began to slow clap. "Since Coma Girl is in a coma and can't answer you, I'm going to answer for her—go on and kiss her, baby. That was a good speech. And I got it all on video so in case she didn't hear you just now, you can play it for her when she wakes up. I'm taping the kiss, too, just in case she pops up like Sleeping Beauty or something."

Sadly, I don't wake up like a Disney character, but I hear Duncan kiss me, and that's enough for now.

"We have cupcakes to celebrate," Roberta said. "I'm going to grab a Sprite from the vending machine so we can have us a toast."

The door opened and closed, but a few seconds later I heard raised voices in the hall—and one of them was Roberta's.

"What the heck's going on?" Duncan muttered.

Roberta burst back into the room. "You just try to take this from me, you jackass."

I'm at a loss, too, as to what's happening.

"I found the guy who stole the hat from your bedrail, Marigold! He was walking around with it hanging out his back pocket like he'd bought it or something."

"Hey, my hat," Duncan said happily. "Where did you find it? I've been looking for it everywhere."

November 27, Sunday

TWENTY-SIX THOUSAND THREE HUNDRED SEVENTY-TWO…
Twenty-six thousand three hundred seventy-three…

The door swung open, and booted feet sounded on the floor.

"Hi, Marigold, it's Jack—" He stopped. "I didn't mean to interrupt."

"No worries," Duncan said. "Duncan Wheeler."

"Detective Jack Terry, I'm working Marigold's case."

"Great to meet you—can you catch me up?"

"Um… I'm sorry, are you related to Marigold?"

"Not really. She's having my baby."

"You don't say? Well, nice to meet the father of Marigold's baby. I see you're a San Antonio Spurs fan."

"Uh, not really. A man I worked with in Haiti gave it to me. It was his favorite hat and he had no idea what it even said on the front. But I thought the world of him, so I like the hat."

"Great story. You like barbecue, Duncan?"

"Who doesn't?"

November 28, Monday

TWENTY-SIX…   THOUSAND….   THREE   HUNDRED….
SEVENTY…SOMETHING

"This is Sidney Kemp. I'm calling to transfer funds from a money market account for my sister's foundation into a cash flow account."

She rattled off an account number—I think. I'm having trouble with those ones and zeroes things today.

"Yes, ten thousand dollars. I'll hold."

You know, those things on your phone you push to call people. Num-something. You use them in math.

"That's impossible," Sidney said, her voice escalating. "According to my records, the money market account has close to a half a mmmwaahh mwaaaahh."

Something's wrong... some... thing's wrooooong—

"Marigold!"

November 29, Tuesday

ONE... EIGHT... twelve... seven... two... one... one...

"What's causing the seizures?" Duncan asked.

"We don't know exactly," Dr. Tyson said. "But this isn't good."

Since I can hear them, I must be between seizures. I'm terrified, but at least Duncan is with me.

"We're going to watch her through the night. If the seizures get worse, we'll need to deliver the baby by cesarean."

"And what about Marigold?"

"We'll do everything we can," Dr. Tyson said, her voice grim.

The Russian bell music ended abruptly. Dr. Jarvis has given up on me.

"I'm here, Marigold," Duncan whispers in my ear. "I didn't like that terrible music anyway. How's this?"

A lullaby begins to play. I'm instantly calmer.

But I'm slipping.... away...

November 30, Wednesday

CAT... PINK... shoe... shoe... shoe...

"The seizures are getting worse.... prepping a surgical suite to deliver the baby by C-section... need to prepare yourselves...very sorry."

So this is it. I'm dying. The doctors hit it just right—I've lived just long enough to deliver the baby. That I'm so happy about.

And I had ten minutes of happiness with Duncan, which is a gift. And just knowing he will be here to raise our child will allow me to die in peace.

My family is around me, I can feel them, can feel their love. Such a shame things were just beginning to gel, and now this. But perhaps it took this to get us to a better place.

I can hear Sidney's voice. She's crying.

"Marigold, you can't die... it's my fault... driving that night... phone..."

I'm floating… and there is a light, as bright as the sun… I'm hand in hand with a little girl. It's Sidney… no, it's my little girl… oh, it's so beautiful there… I want to go closer…

I'm being pulled through a tunnel, so fast… so fast… roaring in my ears… I can't resist it…

More, Mar'gol, more… Can I scooch in, Mar'gol? More, Mar'gol, more… please?

The light… I can't… bear… it's… searing me…

"Marigold?"

"Dr. Tyson, what's going on?"

"My, God… she's … *awake.*"

DECEMBER

I SLOWLY BECAME conscious of my surroundings—the muted chirp of the hospital's PA system, the stinging odor of disinfectant, the unfamiliar chill on my face.

The fact that I could feel my skin disoriented me at first, then the memories of the past few days came flooding back—the seizures, the sensation of being forced through a tunnel, the bright light I'd been sure was the combustion of life meeting death, then the stupefied declaration I was...

Awake.

Am I still, or had I dreamed it?

My heartbeat is pounding in my ears, fast and thick. I gingerly open my eyes and see cloudy grayness. I blink a few times for the sheer pleasure of moving my eyelids. I love my eyelids, I decide—they move beautifully up and down... up and down... up and down...

They push the liquid gathered in my eyes onto my cheeks, creating little rivulets down the sides of my face to my ears. My deprived corneas are reeling, trying to focus in the shadows of the room. Gradually I make out a dim recessed light bulb overhead and a grid of stained ceiling tiles. They are as beautiful as a piece of artwork. I soak them in, vowing I will never again take the gift of vision for granted.

Cautiously, I inhale, and when nothing bad happens, I pull more air into my lungs for the sheer joy of hearing and feeling my lungs inflate, then exhale slowly, experimentally. When it seems to work okay, I do it again... and again. I quietly thank my body for doing the basic things to keep me alive when I couldn't tell it what to do.

With a healthy influx of oxygen, all my senses scream to life and I feel assaulted trying to process all the inputs. I blink my eyes wider. I know I'm not in the vegetable patch because there are no windows and the noises are subtly different—perhaps ICU?

I slowly and laboriously turn my head a quarter of an inch—apparently my muscles are not bouncing back as quickly as my corneas. I'm immobile, but I can feel my feet—my right one is uncovered, so I take that as a good sign. Before I can absorb more of my surroundings, my stomach growls... no, wait—that was movement, not noise.

I froze. My baby?

There it is again—a sweep from one side of my abdomen to the other.

My heart took flight. *Hello, my sweet little baby girl. Your mommy is awake now! I can feel you inside me!*

A painful kick landed, and I feel my bladder yield. Since I don't feel any wetness, I assume I'm still wearing a pee bag.

I hope this is not a foreshadowing of my relationship with my daughter. If she's angry in the womb, there are rocky roads ahead.

I hear footsteps and the rustle of clothing and suddenly my view is blocked by a blob. When the blob splits into a toothy grin, I realize it's a face... of a man... whom I don't recognize.

"Well, well, Marigold, we meet at last. I'm Dr. Jarvis."

My heartrate spikes—my hero. He has curly dark hair, and kind eyes behind thick glasses. I can't get my vocal chords to move, but I feel my mouth spasm.

He grinned wider. "I'll take that as a smile. You, Miss Marigold, are a medical miracle. You're giving Dr. Tyson fits over how she's going to write up your paperwork."

In place of a laugh, I manage a squeaky little sigh.

"The feeding tube will make it difficult to talk," he said gently. "All I need to know is if you understand me."

I tried to nod, but nothing happened, and I can't squeak again.

"Marigold, blink twice if you can understand me."

I do.

He brought his fist to his mouth and seemed overcome with emotion. "Good girl," he said hoarsely. "Okay, then, you should know you were in a car accident and you've been in a coma for six months. Today is December first. You've been through a lot, but yesterday you opened your eyes. You're in the intensive care unit so we can monitor you... and your baby. You're pregnant, Marigold. Do you understand?"

I blink twice.

"Okay, good. You're in the last trimester, and the baby is fine as far as we can tell. We were afraid you might slip back into a coma during the night, but your condition seems stable. We'll be doing another CT scan soon, just to take a look at your brain. Your family was exhausted, so we sent them all home." He grinned again. "To give the staff a break."

I blink twice.

He laughed. "But I'm sure they'll be back soon. And the guy named Duncan? He seems devoted to you."

I blink twice.

"Okay, enough chatter for now. Can you move your fingers? Either hand?"

He clasps my hands into his big warm paws. I concentrate and my right thumb jumps.

"Good. Are you in pain?"

I conduct a quick survey. My head and back twinge, but honestly, I don't mind—I want to feel it. I blink once.

"No? I'll ask again—blink twice for yes, once for no. Are you in pain?"

I blink once.

"Okay, then. That's good news. I'll tell the nurses to ask you, though, each time they come in to check on you. Don't be alarmed that you can't move or speak—you'll just have to retrain your muscles."

When he starts to pull away, I make a desperate noise.

He looks concerned. "You're not in pain?"

I blink once.

"It's something else?"

I blink twice. And grunt through the pain, high, then low, then high again.

His grin widened. "Music. Music?"

I blink twice.

He laughed out loud. "I'll bring you some music. Meanwhile, get some rest. You're going to need it. The entire world wants to hear from you, Coma Girl."

December 2, Friday

"HER EYES LOOK GREENER," my Mom said, leaning over me.

She would die if she knew how unflattering her face looks at this angle.

"Her eyes look the same as always."

Dad is also leaning over me, still on crutches. He's aged in the six months since I've seen him.

Mom squinted. "Are you sure?"

"Yes, Carrie. She has my sister's eyes."

Not unless his sister is related to the man my mother begat me with, but I'm staying out of this.

My mother cast a worried glance at my father, then back to me. "Marigold, can you hear us?"

I blink twice.

"Is twice yes or no?" she asked Dad.

"Twice is yes. She wouldn't have blinked at all if she couldn't hear you."

"Maybe she read my lips. Marigold," she said, exaggerating her mouth movements like a mime, "do you know who we are?"

I blink once.

My mother gasped.

Ha—just playing with you, Mom. I blink twice.

"There—she does know who we are," my dad said, sounding relieved. "Do you know where you are, sweetheart?"

I blink twice.

"Yes? Good. I mean, not good that you're in the hospital, but good you know what's going on." He cleared his throat. "You're probably wondering how you got here."

"Do we really need to go into that now?" my mother asked.

"She deserves to know, Carrie."

"I suppose you're right," she conceded. "Marigold, you and Sidney were in a car accident Memorial Day weekend, and you received a head injury. Another car was involved—a Falcons football player named Keith Young."

"His Jaguar hit your Escort head-on," Dad said. "It's totaled," he added as a sorrowful afterthought. "And apparently Sidney was driving."

"That's what she said just before you woke up," Mom rushed to say. "But she was so upset, frankly, we're still not sure which one of you was driving."

"Carrie," my dad said sternly, "the detective found Sidney's DNA on the airbag."

Ah, so Jack Terry had been on to my sister and hadn't needed the garbled message Aunt Winnie had passed to him.

"As if it even matters who was driving," my mother said with a wave.

"You know it does matter," Dad said lightly.

"But Keith Young was driving drunk."

"Not according to his blood alcohol test."

"Whose side are you on, Robert? What if that tipster was right and the lab was paid off to say he wasn't drunk?"

"The fact that Sidney lied about what happened, and now all this mess with David Spooner embezzling from the foundation... none of it looks good."

"I never trusted that man. He took advantage of Sidney."

"And Marigold," Dad added. "When they find him, I'm going to kill him."

"You're not going to kill him, Robert. That would be murder."

"Then I'm going to make him wish he was dead."

"That, I will support," Mom said. "I'll hold him down while you beat him to a pulp with your crutch."

And then they kissed.

Kissed. On the lips and everything. It was just a peck, but was the first gesture of affection between them I'd witnessed in...

Wait—it was the first gesture of affection between them I'd witnessed, period.

"Sidney is busy, um, sorting things out," my mom said vaguely. "But she'll come to visit soon."

"And Alex had to go back to Afghanistan, but he's ecstatic you're awake. He said his entire unit celebrated."

I'm so glad. Alex had said such touching things when he'd visited at Thanksgiving.

"But there's something else we have to tell you," my mother said primly. "Somehow or another, Marigold, you became pregnant."

Somehow or another?

"And there's a young man hanging around who says he's the father," my dad said in a suspicious tone. "A Duncan Weaver?"

"Wheeler, dear."

"Whatever."

"Anyway, Marigold, do you understand you're going to have a baby?" Mom asked.

I blink twice.

"And is this Duncan person the father?" Dad asked.

I blink twice.

They looked pained for a few seconds, as if they were picturing me and Duncan procreating.

Mom sighed. "It'll be a stocky child."

"But beloved," my dad said warmly.

"Yes," my mom said.

And they kissed again! Who *are* these people, and will they please adopt me?

December 3, Saturday

"YOUR PARENTS grudgingly gave me permission to sit in when they talked to your doctors," Duncan said. "Do you want to know what's going on?"

I blink twice.

He laughed. "Of course you do."

I can't stop staring at him. His hand-rumpled hair is the color of brass, his eyes are deep brown. He's so earthy and handsome, rocking a gray corduroy shirt. I'm still marveling over the fact that he left his fiancée Trina at the altar to come to my bedside and say he loved me when it looked like I might never wake up, and when he thought I was having someone else's baby.

I mean, that's love, right? Big, fat love. The kind of love that Emily Dickinson wrote about… the kind of love that transcends all. Because it's hard to imagine Duncan and I will face anything more challenging than the circumstances of the past six months.

He grinned. "Did you know the baby is a girl?"

Only because I'd seen her in my mind just before I'd awakened. I blink twice.

"Wow, a little girl. I hope she looks like you."

Speaking of… I wonder what I look like these days. Is my face still a crosshatch of scars? Is my hair growing back from the last surgery? Without my regular nurses, I'll bet no one is bothering to cover up the bandage with a head scarf.

"They're going to move you into a room tomorrow."

Good—I could have regular visitors again. I wonder if they would move me back to the long-term care ward.

"Then you'll have physical therapy and speech therapy, and they'll wean you off the feeding tube. Does that sound good?"

I blink twice.

He smiled and nodded, then his face clouded. "Marigold, I owe you an apology."

I wonder if he can see my confusion.

"It's no secret I've made a mess of things. Trina is hurt and angry, and her parents are just plain angry." He made a contrite noise. "I've made selfish decisions that affected other people, including you. It occurred to me that even though the baby is mine, you might not want me here. When I barged into your room the day of the wedding and told you how I feel about you, I foolishly assumed you could hear me… and that you felt the same way about me."

No one had yet asked me if I was aware of what was happening around me during the coma… if I could hear and understand and deduce.

Depending on who asks, things could get tricky.

Duncan took my hand and squeezed it. "Do you want me here, Marigold?"

I blink twice, and for good measure, I squeeze his hand back.

"Hey, I felt that!" He exhaled and brought my hand to his mouth for a kiss. "I'm not going to ask how you feel about me. We can talk about that later. Right now you need to concentrate on getting strong, okay?"

I blink twice.

"Okay," he said, then smiled again. "I'm not trying to steal your thunder, but I feel like I'm the one who just woke up."

December 4, Sunday

THE DOOR TO MY ROOM opened and when I heard the bootsteps on the floor, so did my eyes.

"Hi, Marigold. I'm Jack Terry."

Holy Testosterone—the man is a specimen in jeans and a black fleece. Now that I'm back in the long-term care ward, my bed is slightly elevated, so I can see without people standing over me. And the tall, bulky detective is definitely a treat for the eyes.

Poor Carlotta.

He grinned. "I heard you woke up."

I try to smile and feel my mouth twitch. Under the covers, my toes are also curling.

"Those are some pretty green eyes," he said, coming to stand by my bed. He held up a potted red poinsettia. "I brought you a plant. The nicest Home Depot had, but not as nice as all the flowers you've received, I see."

The area next to the window was overflowing with plants and flowers from well-wishers, but none were more special than his gesture. The black-eyed Susans around his houseboat must be gone—or maybe the houseboat was gone. If Jack was spending time at Home Depot, maybe he'd bought a fixer upper.

"I've been warned not to stay long, that you have a physical therapy session."

But I needed for him to stay long enough for me to somehow communicate to him at this very moment, Sister Irene was holding a man captive at her home and torturing him. I wasn't as concerned about saving the life of the man who'd murdered her sister as I was about saving Sister Irene's life. If she killed him, it was so clearly premeditated, she'd probably get the death penalty. If Jack got to them before she killed the man, the most she would be found guilty of would be kidnapping and general bad nun behavior.

On the other hand, if word got out I'd heard everything being spoken, discussed, and confessed over my bed and in my room the past few months, how would my friends and family react? Jack himself might be uncomfortable knowing I actually remembered all the personal things he'd related about his own life.

"The nurses say you can understand me?" he asked.

I blink twice.

"That's a yes, I'm told."

I blink twice.

"Good. Has anyone told you what's going on with your case?"

I blink once.

"I thought so. Okay, so your sister finally admitted she was driving your car the night of the accident, not you. I suspected as much, but the forensics hadn't come back yet, and I was hoping Sidney would come clean first. And to her credit, she did."

I blink twice.

"She could be charged with filing a false report and obstruction of justice, but I doubt the D.A. will prosecute. But the drugs..."

My heart skipped a beat and he must've seen the alarm and question in my eyes.

"Ah... you don't know about that either?"

I blink rapidly, so shocked, I can't stop at a single blink.

He sighed. "Sidney had a side business on campus selling amphetamines, in part to pay for her own addiction."

My mind raced, sorting through disparate pieces of information. Sidney's phone had been confiscated after the accident, yet she'd had a phone all along—an extra, for her business? The call she hadn't been able to ignore the night of the crash, the cryptic conversations I'd overheard about a "project," her occasionally manic moods, the slurring of her speech the night she'd tried to smother me... and her remarks about feeling so much pressure to excel at school—at life in general. Apparently it had all been too much for her.

"Sidney was arrested this morning with possession and intent to distribute. But I arranged for her to turn herself in to try to keep it as quiet as possible. Still, the media will know soon enough."

My heart squeezed for Sid. She must be humiliated and my parents, devastated. Tears gathered in my eyes and spilled over. Little whimpering noises came from my rusty vocal chords.

"I know," Jack said simply. Then he pulled a folded white handkerchief from a back pocket of his jeans and dabbed at my tears. "I'm sorry, too."

December 5, Monday

"GATHER AROUND bed three," Dr. Tyson said. "Move some flowers if you have to."

I've previously wondered about the faces of the eager young doctors on their rounds to discuss the more obscure cases. I'd even been perversely flattered to be one of the hospital's more provocative patients. But I confess under the gaze of so many white lab-coated people, I feel a bit like a frog on a high school science table.

A very pregnant frog.

"Patient is a twenty-nine-year-old female brought to Brady approximately six months ago with a traumatic brain injury received in a car collision. The patient is approximately twenty-eight weeks pregnant. She underwent two surgeries to relieve pressure on her brain, but remained in a coma until last Wednesday. Questions? Statler, go."

"How is Coma Girl's baby?"

Dr. Tyson frowned. "Please don't refer to the patient as Coma Girl."

"Why not? She's famous."

Dr. Tyson frowned harder. "For one thing, as I said, she's no longer in a coma. And as far as we can tell, the baby is normal. Kwan, do you have a question?"

"Is Coma Girl's baby a girl, or a boy?"

Dr. Tyson pursed her lips. "Not that it's particularly relevant, but it's a girl."

A few aw's sounded.

"If she's no longer in a coma, why is she back in the coma ward?" Kwan asked.

Back with my previous roommates Karen Suh and Shondra Taylor.

"For the record, it's called the long-term care ward," Tyson said. "And for the next phase of her care, I thought it would be better to keep her with nurses who are familiar with her circumstances. Goldberg?"

"Why is a security guard posted outside the door?"

Dr. Tyson looked irritated. "As Statler alluded, there's intense media curiosity about the patient's condition. For that reason, the family has requested limited access to the patient. Phillips?"

"Coma Girl's sister was arrested. Turns out she's a drug dealer and she was driving the night of the accident, not Coma Girl."

Dr. Tyson arched an eyebrow. "Was there a medical question in there somewhere?"

"No, just… fyi, it's lit."

"Lit?"

A few titters sounded.

"Lit up on social media," Kwan offered weakly to back up Phillips.

Dr. Tyson turned a lethal glare on the young doctors. "If the next question isn't a legitimate medical question, you can all find somewhere else to do your residencies. Tosco, *go*."

"Um… how are the patient's cognitive abilities?"

"The patient is communicating yes and no through eye blinks, and appears to recognize family and friends." She looked down at me. "Hello, Marigold. Am I Dr. Jarvis?"

I blink once.

"Good. Am I Dr. Phillips?'

I blink once.

"Good. And thank God," she added to the chagrin of Phillips.

Laughter chorused through the group.

"Am I Dr. Tyson?"

I blink twice.

"Very good, Marigold. Thank you." She looked back to her audience. "She can also identify common objects, colors, and shapes. What else would you test, Kwan?"

"The patient's senses."

"Good. Her senses have been tested and are functioning well. Goldberg, go."

"How is the patient's mobility?"

"There's no paralysis, but her mobility is limited to moving fingers and toes and she can turn her head a few degrees. What do you suggest?"

"Physical therapy, neuromuscular electrical stimulation, massage, acupuncture."

"Good. Dr. Jarvis is utilizing all those methods. Gaynor?"

"Is Coma Girl—er, is the patient able to speak?"

"Not yet. But we're not pushing her until we remove the feeding tube, which should be soon. Phillips?" She gave him a warning look.

"Why did she wake up after six months?"

Dr. Tyson took her time responding. "Clinically, I would say the pressure in her brain was relieved after the second surgery to remove blood debris. But in truth, we don't know exactly why she woke up. You're bound to encounter situations in your medical training that defy clinical explanation."

"How are we supposed to handle something like that?" Kwan asked.

"With humility and appreciation," she said, her voice earnest. "Let's move on…."

As the group left, I tried to get a peek into the hallway through the opening and closing door, a glimpse into the world outside my room, the world that, according to Phillips, was abuzz with my family scandal. I dearly wish someone would put a television or radio in the ward... but I fear the reason no one has is to protect me from what's being said about me and my family.

I'm worried sick thinking about the tell-all manuscript my dotty therapy-writing teacher unwittingly gave to my volunteer poet whom I suspect has been leaking photos of me to TMZ. Now would be the perfect time to reveal dark details about how I felt about my dysfunctional family. And since the volunteer hasn't been back, I suspect he cashed in on a big payday and made a hasty retreat.

My intestines are in a knot... because over the past six months I've come to realize the way each of my family members treated me had little to nothing to do with me, and everything to do with secrets they each harbored. If I could, I'd set fire to the manuscript.

But of course, I can't. And even if I could talk, I can't reveal its existence without causing more grief.

December 6, Tuesday

"GIRL, I DIDN'T think I'd ever see your eyeballs again. Let me get a good look at you."

I am so happy to see Roberta, I feel tears gathering in my eyes as she studies me.

"Oh, no, no, no. No tears," she said, shaking a finger. "We got too much talking to do, and since the nurses say you can only blink yes or no, this could take a while." She held up a white bakery box. "I brought a dozen chocolate chip muffins to keep us company, but I had to leave six at the nurses' station and dole out two more to the security guard to get through your door, so that only leaves four for us. And since you're still wearing a feeding tube, by 'us' I mean 'me.'"

She laughed heartily and I tried to smile.

"First things first, do you know me?"

I blink twice.

"You do? Good." She opened the box and removed a muffin. "Do you know what day it is?"

I blink twice.

"Good. It's Tuesday, by the way. And Christmas is less than three weeks away. I mean, how did that happen?"

It occurs to me I need a blink for "I don't know."

She sighed. "I was really sorry to hear about Sidney being arrested and all. Did you know she had a drug problem?"

I blink once.

"Well, now I feel horrible for giving her the papers I found where you gave her control of your healthcare decisions. I mean, what if she'd wanted to get rid of you so you wouldn't wake up and tell everyone she was driving?"

I fastidiously didn't blink.

Then Roberta laughed at herself. "Forget I said that. I think I'm letting this private investigator thing go to my head. I mean, Sidney might not be the squeaky clean girl everyone thought she was, but she wouldn't want you dead, right?"

I blink once.

Roberta stopped mid-chew and leaned closer, her eyes as big as jelly-filled donuts. "Was that 'no'? No, Sidney wouldn't want you dead, or no, I'm not right?"

I stared straight ahead, then up, down...

"Marigold, did Sidney try to hurt you?"

I blink once... and pondered a second blink.

Roberta laughed on an exhale. "Of course she didn't... I'm sorry I even brought it up. You have more important things to worry about—like who's going to take care of your Coma Girl social media now?"

Again, I need an "I don't know" blink.

"I can do that if you want me to."

I blink twice.

"I'm on it like a pogo stick."

There's a mental picture to enjoy.

"You know, that reporter is still calling me about a book deal. We should think about it now that you're awake and all."

Not that again.

"At least let me tell him we'll think about it."

I blink once... then relent and blink twice.

"Oh, good! And the baby! Are you happy about the baby?"

Relieved at the change in subject, I blink twice.

"Of course you are. Do you know if it's a girl or a boy?"

I blink twice.

"Is it a girl? Oh, it has to be a girl."

I blink twice.

She clapped her hands, then reached for another muffin. "Do you have a name yet?"

I blink twice.

"You do? Okay, how do we do this? Blink twice when I get to the first letter. A? B? C?"

I'm excited for a new way to communicate. I wait until she reaches the letter "L," then blink twice.

"It starts with an L—hm. Laken? Lottie? Lorelei? Lacey? Ladonna? Lola? Leslie? Lily? Liberty?"

Damn—those are all good names. Maybe I settled too soon.

"Okay, second letter. A?"

I blink twice.

"L-A. Laticia? Latoya? Lavender."

I squint.

She shrugged. "Okay, third letter—A? B? C?"

Getting all the way to "U" was painful, but we make it.

"L-A-U... Laura? Laurel? Lauren?"

I blink twice.

"Lauren. That's a pretty name, Marigold." She sighed. "I'm so glad you woke up, girl. I've missed you."

I tear up again.

"Okay, none of that," she said, knuckling away her own tears. "If I start bawling I'll never get through all these cards and letters I brought to read. You're getting a dang bag of mail a day. You know how much mail I get? Past due notices from the cable company and postcards from Peter Glenn's ski shop from when I entered a contest for a free trip to Aspen six years ago. Have never snow skied in my life and I don't ever plan to, but man, they are persistent. You, on the other hand—"

I was blinking like mad because right now there was something I wanted more than to hear from well-wishers.

"What's wrong?" Roberta asked. "Do you want to tell me something?"

I blink twice.

"Okay. Does it start with an A? B? C?"

When Roberta got to "M," I blink twice.

"Okay, M. Second letter A? B? C?"

I stop her at "I." Then "R."

"M-I-R," she murmured. "Are you trying to say 'miracle'?"

I blink once.

"Not miracle... mir-something... mirror?"

I blink twice.

"You want to see a mirror?"

I blink twice.

"You haven't seen yourself since you woke up, have you?"

I blink once.

"And of course you want to know what you look like. I've got a mirror in my purse."

She wiped chocolate off her fingers, then began to empty the contents of her purse on my bed. Phone, makeup bag, Kindle, brush, phone charger, bottle of water, another charger, toothbrush, nail polish, a tube of lotion, a condom, flip flops, a remote control—

"Well, dang—I've been searching everywhere for that remote control."

—half a club sandwich, one glove, a pair of scissors, a bottle of perfume, a wine cork—

"Aha! Here it is."

She pulled out a hand mirror and came to stand behind me. My heart raced as she held the mirror so I could see myself. It takes a few seconds to register the face looking back at me is mine. I've almost forgotten what I look like.

I'm startled by the sheer starkness of my features—my brows and eyes and mouth stand out in relief against my pale skin. A thin white feeding tube is inserted in my right nostril. Across my left cheek is a crosshatch of fading scars. My regular nurses have resumed covering the head bandage with scarves—today's headwrap is a holiday design of red, green, and gold. My dark hair peeks out where the scarf meets my forehead. I sigh in abject relief. I'm not horribly disfigured. Aside from the faint scars and the feeding tube, my reflection looks much like it ever did.

"See?" Roberta said. "You're still pretty, Coma Girl."

Not pretty… but what had my sweet brother Alex said when he visited? That my face is *striking*. I'll take that.

December 7, Wednesday

"HELLO, MY DEAR."

Aunt Winnie floated into the room in a flowy garb of blue and yellow. I am so happy to see her, want to tell her how much I appreciated her visits over the past few months, Faridee's garbled messages notwithstanding.

But I can't speak yet. Dr. Jarvis promised me during a particularly grueling physical therapy session this morning if I continued to improve, my feeding tube could be removed as early as Saturday. I am ecstatic because that means when and if Jack Terry visits Sunday, I can tell him about Sister Irene. After Roberta left yesterday, I kicked myself mentally for not telling her to contact Jack while we had the spelling communication thing going. But even if I had, it would be next to impossible to explain what I thought was going on one guessed letter at a time.

Which was why I am so eager to see Faridee—she can "translate" my thoughts for me, and I can autocorrect her with yes or no affirmations.

Winnie came to my bed and leaned over to hug me. I can't hug her back, but it's nice to feel her warmth around me.

"I knew you would wake up," she said. "And so did my psychic Faridee. Do you remember her?"

I blink twice.

"We came to see you several times while you were in the coma. Faridee connected with you mentally, with some very accurate translations."

That's not how I remember it.

"Do you recall connecting with her telepathically, Marigold?"

I blink once.

"Oh, well, you probably just don't remember. But look at you, awake and on the road to recovery."

She clasped my hands, then hugged me again.

"I'm sorry I couldn't come sooner. Faridee has been so ill, and I've had to stay with her, poor dear, and take her back and forth to the doctor. She has Psychic Syndrome."

Oh, brother.

"She fell ill the very day you woke up, in fact. She's bedridden, says it's something all psychics get occasionally, and it just has to work its way through her system."

Like bad mental sushi?

"But what's all this about Sidney being arrested for selling pills? Carrie left a voicemail and said it was all a misunderstanding."

Mom and Faridee—the great spin doctors.

"Goodness, it seems like there's a lot happening all at once," Winnie exclaimed.

Agreed. And I'm so frustrated. I'm bursting with questions to ask and information to exchange. And the one time I truly need Faridee to intervene, she calls in sick.

And then it hits me—it's no coincidence that Faridee fell ill the same day I woke up—the old fraud doesn't want to face me because she's afraid I can debunk her claims.

December 8, Thursday

THE DOOR TO THE ward opened and a tall slender blonde walked in. I don't recognize the face, but I do recognize the clackety-clack of the high heels.

"Hello, Marigold. I'm ADA Spence. We haven't met, but I'm handling your case."

So she assumes I can't remember our previous encounters. Fair enough.

She pulled a chair closer to my bed and sat heavily, resting her briefcase on her lap. "What a difference a few days makes. First, let me say how glad I am you're awake. And I understand you can respond to questions by blinking twice for yes, once for no?"

I blink twice.

"Good."

She opened her briefcase and took out a thick file folder.

"Are you aware of the circumstances surrounding your accident?"

I blink twice.

"That Memorial Day weekend, your tan Ford Escort collided with a yellow Jaguar F-Type coupe driven by a man named Keith Young?"

I blink twice.

"And that Keith Young plays for the Atlanta Thrashers professional hockey team?"

I blink once.

She nodded, satisfied she hadn't tripped me up.

"I meant to say the Atlanta Falcons professional football team."

I blink twice.

"And the only occupants of your vehicle at the time of the accident were you and your sister Sidney?"

I blink twice.

"You're aware your sister changed her story from the original accident report to say she was driving your car when the accident occurred?"

I blink twice.

"And you confirm Sidney was driving?"

I blink twice.

"Okay. Just so you know, your sister reported smelling alcohol on Keith Young at the scene. His blood alcohol level originally came back just above the legal limit, but when it was retested, it came back at the legal limit."

I blink twice.

"Last month I convinced Keith Young's attorneys you were going to testify and you would be a sympathetic witness. I was trying to get him to plead to a lesser charge so you would have a chance to get a civil judgment.

I blink twice.

"But since your sister who now admits to driving the night of the accident was arrested last week for possession and intent to distribute amphetamines, our case has been gutted. I'm here to tell you the DA's office is dropping all charges against Keith Young."

I blink twice. It's only fair.

"But we're prepared to prosecute Sidney for conspiring with David

Spooner to embezzle from the foundation that was set up to pay your medical bills."

I blink once.

"No? I think Sidney used money from your foundation to fund her drug business and her own addiction, and if we lean on her hard enough, maybe she'll give up Spooner's whereabouts and some of the money can be recovered."

Again, I blink once.

Her phone rang. She glanced at it, then closed her eyes briefly.

"Excuse me just a moment." She punched a button and held the phone to her ear. "Hi, Dad. I'm in a meeting. What's up?" She listened for a few seconds, then sighed. "I'm sorry, that's not going to work for me. Yes, the office is closed Christmas Eve and Christmas, but I have to be in court the morning of the twenty-sixth, and I'll need to prepare. Right. Maybe I can come up for New Year's. I'll check my schedule and let you know. I promise. Okay, bye."

She ended the call, then heaved another sigh. "Where was I? Oh, the embezzling. You should know I don't need your permission to bring charges against your sister, but it would help if you testify against her."

I blink once.

She tapped her finger on the file folder. "So there's no animosity between you and Sidney?"

Is she trying to trip me up again? Does she have in the file a copy of the lost manuscript I'd written? If so, she has everything she needs to prove there was discord between us sisters.

"Marigold, is there animosity between you and Sidney?"

Defiant, I blink once.

Slowly, ADA Spence returned the file to her briefcase and unfolded from the chair. "We'll chat again when you can actually talk, Marigold. Meanwhile, I certainly hope your sister deserves your support."

When the door closed, my stomach was churning. I can't help but think about Audrey Parks, my former ward mate who had awoken from her coma but had found her return to life so unbearable she had attempted to hang herself in the coma ward. If my parents hadn't bumbled along, she'd be good and dead right now instead of recovering in the psych ward.

I'm starting to understand what she meant. Returning to the world meant returning to hard choices. Audrey had a valid point in asserting there was something comforting about simply keeping one's eyes closed.

December 9, Friday

"HI, SWEETHEART. Are you sleeping?"

When I open my eyes, I'm pleased to see my Dad sitting in the chair next to my bed. From the expression of relief on his face, I realize he thought I'd slipped back into a coma versus snagging a nap between physical therapy sessions.

To show him how I'm improving, I flutter my right hand in an uncontrolled wave.

He grins. "That's great. That's really great, Marigold."

I notice the crutches are gone and the cast has been replaced by a brace he's wearing over his pants leg. When he pulls a hand over his mouth, I realize how haggard he looks.

"You heard the DA is dropping all charges against Keith Young?"

I blink twice.

"It kills me to know he might've been responsible for the accident, yet getting away scott free because of mistakes Sidney made."

I blink twice.

"He's probably out tonight partying and congratulating himself for gaming the system."

I hope not.

Dad made an anguished noise. "Sidney is in serious trouble. Your mother and I are trying to help her as much as we can. And as strange as it sounds, it's been good for our relationship, has made us closer."

The silver lining of a very dark cloud.

"Which is why... "

He stops and heaves a sigh so labored, I'm worried what's coming next.

"Marigold, when you were in the coma, could you hear things that were being said to you? You know, conversations or... stories? Because you might have overheard things that would be best forgotten."

Things such as early in my parents' marriage, Dad had taken twenty-five thousand dollars from a home safe to pay gambling debts and told my Mom the money had been stolen?

"Could you, Marigold?" he pressed. "Could you hear the things we said, the things *I* said to you?"

I weighed the fallout of my response. I blink once.

"No?" he asked, sounding relieved.

And involuntarily I blink again.

"Yes?" he asked, sounding panicked.

I rallied my resources and channeled them into a single physical response.

"No," I squeak past the feeding tube in my throat.

The fall of his shoulders in abject relief makes the lie worth it.

December 10, Saturday

"PEACE BE WITH YOU, ladies."

I don't want to open my eyes. I'm afraid Sister Irene will smother me if she thinks I might squeal on her. Which I totally plan to do. If Dr. Jarvis makes good on his promise to remove the feeding tube today, tomorrow I can unload on Jack Terry and let him handle the nun.

"Hello, Marigold," she whispered near my face. "I know you're awake. I'm on Facebook."

Miserably, I open my eyes to meet her gaze, and I'm shocked by how petite and innocent she looks. Google 'nun' right now and the first image that comes up in standard black and white habit with her hands clasped in prayer is Sister Irene.

"God has answered our prayers," she sang with an angelic smile. "You woke up... and your awakening was my awakening, too."

She raised her arms and I winced, sure she was going to plunge the big knife she bragged about buying right through my chest.

"Praise be to God," she said, holding her hands high. "Through Him all things are possible, including absolute forgiveness."

She lowered her hands and I winced, sure she was going to put her tiny fingers around my throat and use her super-human evil strength to choke the life out of me.

"I nursed my ailing guest Mr. Gilpin back to health and he returned to his own home. Only God can judge him for what's in his heart, right, Marigold?"

I can't blink, can only wonder if she's telling the truth or spinning a story to dissuade me from spilling my guts.

"Let us pray," she said, and bowed her head.

Sister Irene prayed for mercy and goodness, for her sister's soul, and for the grace of forgetting—that last one was aimed at me, no doubt.

It seemed more than one person was regretting their decision to unburden themselves onto Coma Girl.

December 11, Sunday

THE DOOR OPENED and Jack Terry strode in, carrying a bag of food.

"Hi, Marigold."

"J….kuh," I manage past a throat that feels as if it's lined with broken glass.

He came up short. "You talked. Hey—the feeding tube is gone."

"Liz… zen." I swallowed painfully, then glanced at the cup of warm broth sitting on my bed tray. Teddy had been letting me sip on it, but had been called away with the promise to return.

"Do you want a sip first?" Jack asked.

To save my throat, I blink twice. He held the thin straw to my mouth and guided it between my lips. I sip a tiny amount of the broth, then swallow.

"Liz… zen," I repeat.

"I'm listening."

"Mun… maahn."

"Man?" he prompted.

I blink twice. "Jor… jah."

"Georgia?"

I blink once.

"Man… George?"

I blink twice. "Guh… puhn."

"George Gullpin?"

Close enough, I hope. "Puh… row."

"Puh… row? Puh… row. Parole?"

I blink twice.

Jack held the straw to my mouth for another tiny soothing sip. "You're trying to tell me about a man who's on parole?"

I blink twice. "Dan… juh."

"Dan.. juh," he repeated. "Dan… danger?"

I blink twice.

"Did this man threaten you?"

I blink once.

"No. Then who's in danger?"

"Jor… jah."

"George? He's the one in danger?"

I blink twice, practically limp with relief.

"Do you know this man George?" Jack asked, pulling out a notebook.

I blink once.

"No. Did you overhear something?"

I blink twice.

"Okay." Jack scratched his temple, then reached for his phone. "I'm

270

putting out an inquiry on parolees name George Gullpin." He punched several buttons, then set down his phone. "Anything else you want to tell me now that you have your voice back?"

I blink twice.

"I'm listening."

"Spuhn... r."

"Spuhn... r. Spunner... Spooner? David Spooner?"

I blink twice.

"What about him?"

"Dee... nuh... Burrd... lee."

"Deena Burdlee?"

"Maahn."

"Man. Deena... Dean?"

I blink twice.

"Dean Bradley? The guy connected to the assault on Keith Young?"

"Ye...sssssss," I hiss.

"David Spooner and Dean Bradley... they know each other?"

I blink once.

"No. They don't know each other?"

My throat is on fire. I lift the fingers on my right hand a fraction of an inch and put the first two fingers together.

"They're together?" Jack asked.

I grunt.

"David Spooner and Dean Bradley are together?"

I grunt louder.

"They're... the same person," he said, as realization dawned.

I blink twice, exhausted, but triumphant.

December 12, Monday

"READY FOR A BATH?" Gina asked as she and Teddy rolled in a cart.

"Uh-hmm," I murmured.

"Look at Coma Girl, talking," Teddy said, sounding pleased.

"And moving," Gina added. "Both hands and feet, plus she can turn her head and nod."

"And she's eating. A cup of broth this morning and a protein shake for lunch."

Gina turned to me. "The more you swallow and retrain your muscles, the sooner you'll be on solid food."

"And Duncan will be glad you can swallow again," Teddy said, wagging his eyebrows.

I tried to laugh, but it hurt.

"Don't be crude," Gina chided.

"It's a joke," Teddy said. "For lovers."

"How do you know they're lovers?"

"Hello, can you see this big baby bump?"

Gina laughed. "Yes."

"And it's obvious the guy is crazy about our Coma Girl."

"But what if she isn't nuts for him? Love can be one-sided, you know."

"Like your love for Dr. Jarvis?" Teddy teased.

"Stop it. *If* I had a crush on Dr. Jarvis, it wouldn't get me anywhere. He hasn't asked me out."

"That's because he's been working days and you've been working nights."

"Whatever. I needed a date for my neighbor's Christmas Eve party... so I invited Gabriel."

"Please don't start that up again," Teddy said.

"I've been putting him off while I worked overtime during the holidays and he's been a gentleman about it."

"Nooooo," I croaked.

Gina frowned and looked at me. "Did you just say 'no,' Marigold?"

I blink twice.

"Why?"

"Dahn... nuh."

"Donna?" she asked. "What about Donna?'

"Gay... bruh.. Dahn... nuh."

"Gabriel and Donna?" Gina asked. "What about them?"

Teddy guffawed. "Come on, Gina. Does she have to spell it out for you?"

"Sesssss... eeee.... sesssss," I provided.

"Sex," Teddy translated.

"They're not having sex," Gina insisted. "Besides, how would Marigold know?"

"Woom," I said.

"Womb?" she asked.

"She said *room*," Teddy corrected. "Did Gabriel and Donna have sex in this room?"

I blink twice.

"Ew," Teddy and Gina said in unison.

"That settles it," Teddy said. "You can't go out with Gabriel now."

"No way," Gina agreed. Then she sighed. "Guess I'll go to the holiday party alone."

Teddy tore off a piece of bandage tape and secured the nurse call button where I could reach it.

"In the meantime, Marigold. If anyone starts up any shenanigans in here, just push this button, okay?"

I blink twice.

December 13, Tuesday

"HO, HO, HO, Merry Christmas, Marigold!"

Santa Claus is standing just inside my room. I recognize my boss, Percy Palmer, within a split second, but I'm so gobsmacked, I'm rendered speechless. The man I worked for was anti-social to the point of being awkward—where did this jolly fat elf come from?

He pulled down the fake white beard. "It's me, Marigold. I heard you done woke up."

I lift my head and manage a shaky smile in his direction. "Hell-o, Per-cy. L-look at... you."

He stepped closer to my bed. "I know—who would've thunk it? But I'm having a great time cheering up the little ones here at the hospital. It was Sophia's idea."

The woman who had thanked him in person for donating new carpet for the hospital waiting rooms and invited him to lunch. Ah, so she was the source of the twinkle in Saint Nick's eye.

"Good," I said. Mr. Palmer deserves companionship.

"Is the baby healthy?" he asked.

I nodded. "It's a... girl."

He grinned. "I have just the thing." From his pack he removed a fuzzy pink teddy bear and set it on the pillow next to me.

"Thank... you."

"I should be thanking you, Marigold. I wouldn't have met Sophia if not for you."

I don't have a short response, so I simply shook my head to deflect the credit from my comatose-ness.

"It's true," he insisted. "And now you're awake and getting well. Everyone at the office is so excited... well, except for the person I hired to fill in for you."

Oh... yikes.

"But she's finally getting the hang of things, so I'll find something else for her to do around there. You can have your old job back as soon as you're ready."

I wasn't sure when that would be, but eventually I would have to earn money again, so I gave him a grateful nod.

Being incapacitated has allowed me not to worry about the financial burden my condition has created. But now that I'm improving and can foresee a day I might go home, I wonder what the final tally will be... and if the foundation funds aren't recovered, if I have sentenced Duncan to a life of servitude.

December 14, Wednesday

"HELLO, DEAR, It's Mom."

I guess Mom has forgotten I can see now.

"Hi... mommmmm."

She seemed surprised and pleased to hear me speak. My speech is still slow and I tend to run my words together, but I'm making good progress most days.

"Loooook." I slowly lift my right arm until my hand is over my head, and do the same on the left side.

"Very good, Marigold. Good job." She gave me a little smile. "Now that you're awake, it's hard to remember all that time when you... weren't."

Not for me... but I know her cues. She wants to talk about something.

"What was it like being in a coma?"

"Empty," was the only word that came to mind.

"Empty," she repeated. "So... could you hear the things that were going on around you? Could you hear people when they, um, talked to you?"

You mean when you told me I'm the product of an affair you had on Dad in retaliation for him not being there for you?

"I'm just wondering because it stands to reason... that is, one might assume the unconscious person they're talking to isn't really listening... and won't be able to tell any tales."

She was nibbling on a nail.

"Do you understand?"

I nod slowly. "But... I did not."

"You don't remember hearing anything?"

I shake my head.

"Oh, good," she gushed. "I mean... it's not good or bad... It's just better if we all get to hit the reset button at the same time, don't you agree?"

I do, actually.

December 15, Thursday

THE DOOR OPENED and admitted a young blond woman who seemed vaguely familiar. My mind raced to identify her—someone from my burlesque class? I don't think so. The instructor who passed my tell-all manuscript to a stranger? I remember her being dark-haired. Perhaps she is a visitor for Shondra Taylor, the unfortunate woman in the bed next to me whose hordes of visitors had dwindled over the past few weeks.

But when she walks directly to my bed, warning flags go up—more of them when I realize who she is.

Trina, Duncan's ex-fiancée.

How did she get past my security guard?

"Remember me?" she asked. "I was the woman who was going to make Duncan happy. I was nice to you, Coma Girl, because I felt sorry for you. And I still feel sorry for you."

I focus all my efforts on moving my fingers over, over, over until I touch the nurse call button. I depress it and, to my immense relief, a buzzer didn't sound. Instead, behind Trina, a light came on over the door.

She stepped closer. "Because you don't honestly think he's going to stay with you forever, do you? Why would a man want a vegetable for a wife?"

She bent over my bed and put her face close to mine. "You're just Duncan's charity project du jour."

The door opened and Teddy strode in. "Who are you?"

Trina straightened. "I'm... just leaving."

"That's a good idea. And don't come back."

Trina marched from the room. Teddy looked back to me and I imagine my expression reflects the whiplash I feel.

"Are you okay, Marigold?"

I nod.

"Should I call someone? Duncan?"

"No," I croak. "I'm... good."

Teddy nods, then leaves the room.

But I'm not good. I'm not good at all.

December 16, Friday

NORMALLY I would've been asleep when Dr. Tyson slipped into the dimly lit ward. It was the end of a long day of physical therapy sessions in a long week of successive days of physical therapy sessions. I know I'm gaining ground, but it is punishing to my weak body, and you'd think I'd be happy to close my eyes.

But tonight I'm fighting my old demon insomnia. My mind has been in a constant churn since Trina's visit. I don't blame her for being angry with me—in her eyes I'm the person who interfered with her life plan. If not for me, pitiful pregnant Coma Girl, she'd be well into the season of hosting holiday parties with her handsome husband Duncan by her side.

I watch Dr. Tyson walk to Karen Suh's bed and check her position, her vitals, and the equipment around her bed. The doctor's movements are purposeful and unhurried before she moves to Shondra Taylor's bed. Since Shondra is on a wheezing ventilator, there are more items to check.

By the time she gets to my bed, I'm sure Dr. Tyson is tired and ready to go home, yet her movements seem just as methodical.

"Hi," I croak.

"Oh, hello, Marigold. I'm sorry to wake you."

"You... didn't."

"Ah, you can't sleep either?"

"No."

"You must be antsy to leave the hospital and get out of here. Dr. Jarvis says you are progressing at almost unbelievable rates. He's been your champion all along." She sighed. "I'm sorry I wasn't more optimistic, more encouraging."

I don't know what to say, so I remain silent.

She gave a little laugh. "I used to be just like Dr. Jarvis, always the first person to try something new, to believe the impossible. You, Coma Girl, have been a wake-up call for me. Because you showed me just how much I've changed—and not for the better. I don't know what happened to my life. Somewhere along the line, I traded in hope and curiosity for apathy and status quo." She made a rueful noise in her throat. "And not just in my professional life."

She leaned into the bed rail and steepled her hands. "Tell me, Marigold... do you remember any conversations that took place when you were comatose?"

She was probably referring to her confession that her husband had asked for an open marriage... or perhaps the phone call she unwittingly took from a call girl prompted by an ad her husband had taken out on an adult website.

I have a choice to make. As a doctor, Sigrid Tyson needs to know some comatose patients can hear everything happening around them. But as a woman, she needs to feel she can keep her private humiliation private.

"No. I don't... remember... anything."

Her relief is palpable. "Good to know. I want to say goodbye, Marigold. I'm leaving Brady and Atlanta to take a position on the West Coast. I'm going to start over. But I'll leave you and my other patients in the very capable hands of Dr. Jarvis. He's a fine physician. Good luck, Marigold. And thank you."

Dr. Tyson slipped from the room and I sent good thoughts after her before turning back to my own fears.

What's keeping me awake isn't the fact that Trina came by to vent her anger on me. I rather wish she'd pointed out the obvious—that I'm not as pretty as she is, or as well-educated, or as well-employed, and those inadequacies would leave Duncan wanting.

Instead what she'd said about me being a project for Duncan had the awful ring of truth.

December 17, Saturday

"HEY, SIS! Look at you—I can't believe you're sitting up and talking to me."

I'm Skyping with Alex on a touch screen computer in the physical therapy room. A helper is within sight in case I need assistance, but once the connection is made, there isn't much to do except to keep the conversation going.

"I'm... making... headway."

"I'll say. It's hard to believe a few weeks ago you were in a coma and unable to communicate. How's the baby?"

I patted my rounded abdomen. "Active."

He laughed. "That's good. How's Duncan?"

"Fine... good." Obligated? Nursing a damsel in distress fixation?

"He seems like a great guy, Sis. I'm looking forward to getting to know him better."

"He... likes you... too."

"The important thing is that he likes *you*."

I try to laugh, but the sound that emerges is more like a wounded bird.

Alex sobered. "Have you heard from Sidney?"

"No."

"Me neither. I get the feeling she's hunkered down with an attorney trying to hash through things. I had no idea she was hooked on uppers.

Did you?"

He's asking the girl who didn't notice he couldn't read. "No."

"But looking back at some of her behavior when I visited at Thanksgiving, it makes sense. Sid was pretty manic at times. I just thought it was Sid being Sid—high strung and high maintenance." He sighed. "How are the folks?"

"Okay, I... think."

"Good to hear. You know having a family secret aired like this is Mom's worst nightmare."

"Uh-huh." I try to tamp down the panic that rises a little every day the tell-all manuscript doesn't come to light. Everyone would be scorched by it. I have a bad feeling whoever has it is biding their time for the perfect window of opportunity to use it.

Did I mention I'm not sleeping much these days?

December 18, Sunday

"AREN'T YOU A font of information?" Jack Terry said in a suspicious tone, flipping pages in a small notebook.

I'm on pins and needles to hear what he uncovered.

"I made a few phone calls about the parolee you said was in danger. I found a George Gilpin who was paroled a few months ago here in Atlanta. Was convicted of a pretty brutal murder of a young woman—the only reason he got parole is prison overcrowding and he'd served seventy-five percent of his sentence. Even this guy's parole officer said he's bad news— no way he's in any kind of danger."

Jack leveled his inquisitive gaze on me.

"So here's where things get squirrely. Gilpin missed an appointment with his parole officer, so the P.O. puts out a warrant for his arrest. Imagine his surprise when Gilpin shows up two days later, looking like he's been used as a target for knife-throwing practice. *Begs* to be put back in prison to finish out his term."

I nod. "Okay."

"Okay? That's all you've got to say? How did you find out about this?"

"Um... I, um... "

He held up his hand. "Don't tell me it's another one of your aunt's kooky psychic encounters."

"Okay. I... won't tell you... that."

Jack's expression turned sour. "It sounds like Gilpin is back where he belongs, so how about let's both forget it?"

"Forgotten."

He ripped the page out of his notebook and crumpled it for trash. "Moving on. You were right that David Spooner uses the alias Dean Bradley. We can connect him to the Keith Young assault. How did you know that?"

"Overheard Spooner... talking on... the phone."

Jack squinted. "When you were in the coma?"

I nod.

"Let me get this straight—when you were comatose, you could hear what was being said around you? Everything?"

Panic flashed in his eyes. Is he trying to recall all the personal information he'd shared with Coma Girl?

I'm enjoying this immensely.

But we're interrupted by a knock at the door and the appearance of ADA Spence. She gave Jack a sardonic smile.

"I thought I might find you here, Detective."

"What's up?"

"David Spooner was arrested in Key West, trying to board a catamaran headed for the Bahamas."

Jack gave a fist pump. "Yes."

"He should be back in Atlanta tomorrow morning. Good luck with it." She walked back to the door.

"Wait—are you off the case?"

"Off the payroll actually. I quit the D.A.'s office. I'm moving to Minnesota to be closer to my father."

Jack wrinkled his nose. "Minnesota?"

"Yep—where the weather is lousy, and you can't buy liquor on Sunday. The things you do for family, right?" ADA Spence made pointed eye contact with me, then walked out.

Truer words were never spoken.

When the door closed, Jack linked his hands behind his head and leaned back in the guest chair. "Good work, Marigold. I owe you one for the lead on David Spooner."

"Okay. I'd like... to collect."

"Already?"

"Yes. Write down... this name: Jeremy... Hood."

He whipped out his notebook and wrote in neat block letters. "Is he a criminal?"

"Sort of. He's bullying... a friend of mine."

Jack frowned. "I'll take care of it."

December 19, Monday

"GOOD EVENING, Marigold."

Dressed casually in jeans and a sweatshirt, Dr. Jarvis looks handsome and approachable, but he's walking and talking doctor-fast.

"The service said you needed to see me right away. I got here as quickly as I could."

He pulled out his stethoscope.

"Are you feeling okay? Is there a problem with the baby?"

I give him my most apologetic smile. "I'm sorry... Dr. Jarvis. The service... misunderstood. This could've... waited until... tomorrow." I nodded toward the silent iPod hanging on my bedrail. "The battery... is dead."

His smile was good-natured, as usual. "No worries. Mine is charged up. I'll just swap them out and swap them back tomorrow. How do you like the new playlist?"

"I do. Rap is... helping me... get back into... the rhythm of talking."

"That's the idea." He clapped his hands together. "If there's nothing else..."

I eased my hand toward the nurse call button and pressed it.

"Actually, while you're here... I can't think... of a better time... to say thank you... for all... you've done. You are... my hero."

He blushed under my praise. "That's very kind of you, Marigold, but I'm only doing my job."

"More than... your job. The music therapy... saved me."

He smiled. "It was more than the music therapy, but I'm glad you think it helped."

"It did."

"Good."

"Immensely."

"Well, you're welcome. If that's all, I'll be going now."

The door opened and Nurse Gina came in. "Oh, hello, Dr. Jarvis."

"Hi, Gina. And it's Wayne, remember?"

"Wayne." She pulled her gaze away from his to face me. "You called, Marigold?"

I sighed. "I don't know... what's wrong... with me... this evening. I must... have pressed... the button... by accident. I'm sorry."

"It's no problem." She smiled and reset the button.

"You're working nights now?" Dr. Jarvis asked Gina.

"Double shifts, just through the holidays."

"Makes for a long day."

"Yes," she said, massaging her neck. "I'm getting ready to clock out now."

"I'll walk you out," he offered. "If that's okay with you?"

"Sure," Gina said.

I watched them walk out together and smiled, pleased with myself.

December 20, Tuesday

"THAT MAN NURSE almost didn't let us in!" Aunt Winnie cried when she and Faridee fell into the room. "And he practically mauled us patting us down for contraband."

"Did he... find any?" I asked brokenly from my bed.

"Those bath salts were for baths," Faridee declared. "And I keep a can of spray paint with me at all times for protection."

"Against rust?" I asked.

"Poor Faridee is just now recovering from her bout of Psychic Syndrome," Winnie said.

Indeed, Faridee looks a little worse for wear. She's obviously wearing a black bun wig because it's askew. And her sandals are on the wrong feet.

"But doesn't Marigold look wonderful?" Winnie asked, preening. "She's awake and talking, and the baby is getting big."

"Yes," Faridee gushed. "So beautiful."

But she's not making eye contact. In fact, she's inching toward the door like she might make a run for it.

"Aunt Winnie... my throat is... so sore... would you... step out... and ask Teddy... for a cup of... warm broth?"

"I can do it," Faridee offered.

"I'd rather... my aunt... handle it."

"Of course."

As soon as the door closed behind Winnie, I narrowed my gaze at Faridee. "Look... we both know... those gewgaws and classes... you peddle to my aunt... are worthless crap."

Faridee tried to look outraged, but wound up cowering. "I'm just trying to pay the mortgage like everyone else."

"You also have... some legitimate talent."

Faridee brightened. "I do?"

"Yes—some. More often... than not... you get your... wires crossed... and things... come out garbled."

"Such as?"

"When I... tried to tell you... the father... of my baby... you got...

the 'spurs' part right... but the clue was... San Antonio Spurs... not a cowboy."

She whooped. "But that's close!"

"Sort of."

"What else did I get right?"

"I asked... you to tell Jack... that Sidney... was driving."

"We did! I told Winnie and she told Jack."

"You said... Sidney was driving... me crazy."

She winced, then shrugged. "That's pretty darn close."

"No... it isn't. But you did... pull a random thought... about a lost sock... out of my head."

"I remember that!"

"And you... sensed death... before my... roommate Jill died."

"I did indeed."

"Although... it's a coma ward, so...."

She made a rueful noise. "I see your point."

"But... you seem to... connect with... Karen Suh... my roommate... by the wall."

"Yes, she's talking to me now. She says I need to hurry, they are running out of time."

"I want to... offer you... a deal."

"What kind of deal?"

"I won't... expose you... as a fraud... if you will... translate between... Karen and Jonas Suh... for free."

"How about thirty percent off?"

"Free."

"Half off?"

"Free. And no more... taking advantage... of Winnie."

Faridee sighed. "Okay." Then she brightened. "But this is the best day of my life! I am the real deal—I'm psychic! Thank you, Marigold."

She grasped my shoulders and kissed my forehead, then she pulled back.

"You're a true lucky charm, Marigold. You improve everyone else's good fortune." Then her expression darkened. "But as far as your own luck..."

"What about my own luck?" I pressed.

Faridee loosened her grip, then gave a little wave. "It's... fine." Then she turned her head toward Karen Suh. "I'm coming, I'm coming."

December 21, Wednesday

THE DOOR OPENED SO QUIETLY, I wonder if my poet volunteer has returned to sneak in and out again.

Instead Joanna Fitz walks inside, her footsteps tentative. She's dressed for warmth, not style. Her hair hasn't been styled and her makeup looks pared down from what I remember.

"Hello, Jo," I said from my bed. But I confess I'm worried she's been drinking, or has brought alcohol with her. Or both.

"Hi, Marigold. So it's true—you're awake. And talking."

"Awake... and getting better... at talking. But not... mobile yet. My doctor says... I can try... to walk soon."

Fear crosses her face and I think she's going to turn and run out of here.

"But I can raise my arms."

I lifted my arms toward her and she gives me a gentle hug.

"You won't... break me," I said, laughing.

"I might. I've been working out."

"You look good," I hedge, unsure how much she thinks I know about her. Does she even remember the things she said when she visited?

"Lifting weights and running are part of my recovery program."

I just nod. "Where are you in the process?"

"Fairly early, lots more to hash through." She squinted. "Do you remember me visiting before?"

"I remember knowing you were here."

"So you don't remember anything I might've said?"

When I see the utter humiliation hovering in her eyes, I decide Joanna has enough to rebuild without worrying she said something that would make me think less of her.

"Sorry... but no."

Her expression instantly eases. "Ah. Well, I've screwed up my life and I'm hitting the reset button."

"Ah. Well, I've been in a coma for six months, woke up pregnant, and I'm hitting the reset button."

Joanna laughed. "Who's the father?"

"Duncan Wheeler—do you remember him?"

"I do. You were crazy for him."

I nodded. "Still am."

"So when did it happen for him?"

"When I was in a coma and he was about to marry someone else."

Joanna squinted. "Isn't that the plot of a telenovela?"

We laughed.

"How far along are you?"

"About thirty weeks. It's a girl."

She smiled wide. "You'll love having a daughter." Her face crumpled, but she regained her composure. "I love having a daughter, and a son. They're both different, and special."

"Do you have pictures?"

She nodded and proceeded to show me pictures of her beautiful children. "I'm on my way to the airport to pick up Stuart and the kids. They're visiting for a week to see how things go."

"I hope it goes well."

"So do I," she said, then exhaled. "I've done a lot of things I'm not proud of."

"I think if given the chance, most people would choose some things they'd go back and do differently."

"One thing I wouldn't do differently," she said, "is having you for a friend."

"What a sweet thing to say."

"You got me into recovery, Marigold, and you didn't even realize it. But I drew on your inspiration every day I was there."

I made a face. "You mean when things got bad, you told yourself, 'at least I'm not in a coma'?"

"When you put it that way it sounds bad, doesn't it?"

I purse my mouth and nod.

We both burst out laughing.

December 22, Thursday

MY ARMS AREN'T yet strong enough to operate a rolling wheelchair, but I've become proficient enough with a motorized scooter that if Teddy or Duncan or Dad are around to lift me into the chair, I can strap myself in and zip to and from physical therapy sessions.

Today when I get back to my room, I find someone has crawled into my bed and is taking a nap.

Christina Ann Wells.

As much as I'd love to let her keep sleeping her deep little girl sleep, I'm sure someone, somewhere is looking for her now or will be soon. So I sit in my scooter and gently shake her awake.

She rouses slowly, then opens glazed eyes to stare at me for a few seconds and whispers, "Hey, Magic Lady."

"Hey, Christina."

"You can talk."

"Yes, I can. How's... your mama?"

"She's good. She had to come back today for tests. I went for a walk because I was afraid they might make me take a test, too, and I didn't study."

"Good thinking. But won't... your mama... be looking for you?"

"She'll put my name on the God speaker."

"The God speaker?"

She pointed to the ceiling. "The voice you can hear all over the hospital."

"Oh. Right."

Her eyes got big. "Guess what happened in school yesterday?"

"What?"

"A tall policeman came to tell all the bullies to stop it! Stop calling people names and stop putting gum in my hair and stop making fart noises when kids walk by."

"Oh, that's good."

"It's very good because Jeremy Hood gots scared and now he doesn't call me Fatso or Fathead or Fatface anymore. Or Fatbutt."

Nice going, Jack.

"I like your music," she said.

"Thanks. I like it, too."

"Why are you in that scooter?"

"Because my legs aren't strong enough to walk yet."

"Why?"

"Because I've been asleep for so long."

"My legs get numb when I sit on the floor and play jacks. Is it like that?"

"Sort of."

She sat up and grinned. "Do you wanna dance?"

"But my legs don't work."

"You can stay in the scooter and I'll stand up. Then we'll be the same amount of tall." She scrambled down from the bed. "See?"

"Okay, but you have to be careful."

"My meemaw gots a scooter, so I know how to dance with it."

In the fearless way kids are, she reached over and expertly turned up the volume on the iPod, then started swinging her shoulders and hips and arms in front of me.

"Wave your arms around," she instructed. "And now do this with your head. Now clap."

I try to keep up. "You're better than I am."

"I'm a good dancer," she agreed.

We danced until the end of the song, then Christina gave us a big round of applause.

"Christina Ann Wells."

We both looked up to see a woman standing there, eyeing Christina. "What are you doing?"

"Hi, Mama!" Christina ran over to hug her waist. "This is Magic Lady I told you about. She's the one who made you better."

I winced. "I'm just Marigold. It's nice to meet you finally."

"I'm Nora. And I'll take all the magic I can get. I'm sorry if Christina was bothering you."

"She wasn't. She was teaching me how to dance."

"Well, little girl, it's about time to dance on home."

"Did you do good on your test, Mama?"

Nora smiled. "An A+."

"Yay!" Christina said as she went out the door. "I think we should stop and get some ice cream on the way home..."

December 23, Friday

THE DOOR BURST OPEN and Jonas Suh skidded into the room. "Karen?" He rushed to her bed. "Karen?"

"Mr. Suh?"

He turned his head and glanced at me, shocked, I assumed to find someone in the coma ward talking.

"My name is Marigold. I'm the person... who called you."

"The message said you had news about Karen."

"I said I... wanted to... talk to you... about Karen. I didn't mean... to alarm you."

He looked confused. "How do you know Karen?"

"I don't actually. Except for... lying in this bed... for the past six months. I'd like to help... you and Karen. What I'm... going to tell you... might sound... a little strange... but please... bear with me."

"I'm listening," he said.

"A few months ago... I overheard... a conversation... you had with Karen... about some work you'd done... around the yard. In particular... you mentioned a pear tree... you'd had to take down."

"I remember."

"Sometime after that... a well-meaning relative... brought in a psychic... to talk to me... in hopes of establishing... some kind of communication. That was a big fail... but on the way out of the room... the psychic said... Karen was calling to her. I thought... the same thing... you're probably thinking... that it was a scam. The psychic wrote down...

a message from Karen... and it was to you. It said... something to the effect of... 'I never liked that pear tree.'"

Jonas looked confused.

"There were three people... privy to that conversation... and two of us... were in a coma. So the only way... the psychic could've known... about the pear tree... is if you told her."

"I didn't," he said. "But why didn't I get the message?"

"Someone tossed it... in the garbage... before you could see it. So when I woke up... and could communicate... I asked the psychic... to come back... and talk to Karen." I extended a sheath of ten sheets of paper. "This is what... she transcribed."

Jonas crossed to my side of the room, and when he reached for the papers, his hand shook. As he began to read, he gasped and made noises of exclamation.

"This is impossible... this is incredible. No one could know this information except me and Karen." He looked up at me. "She's in there. She's in there and she can hear me."

I nodded, smiling. "I know. But you're going to... have to help... convince the doctors. The psychic's name... is on the back... if you wish to contact her. She is prepared... to translate between you and Karen... at no charge."

"You're an angel," he said, his eyes brimming with tears.

But I'm not. I'm just someone who was in the right coma at the right place and the right time.

December 24, Saturday

"I THOUGHT DUNCAN might visit Christmas Eve," my Mom said, her voice chiding.

"We talked... about this, Mom. Duncan has to work... either Christmas Eve or Christmas... at the Peace Corps office. This way... when you're in Savannah... with Aunt Winnie tomorrow... Duncan will be here... to take me... to physical therapy. And don't forget... he's still working... to get his house... retrofitted for... a wheelchair."

"How much money does Duncan make?" Dad asked.

"I'm not sure," I admitted.

"It couldn't be much working for the Peace Corps."

"Probably not," I agreed. Surprised by the sudden tension, I decided to change the subject. "Mom, it's nice of you... to accept Winnie's invitation... for Christmas dinner."

"Siblings are important. When your father and I are gone, it'll be up to you to make sure you and Alex and Sidney are always close."

"Me?"

"Yes, you. You're the strong one, Marigold."

"I'm the pregnant one... in the hospital... in a scooter."

"You know what I mean. Don't be sassy."

Wouldn't dream of it.

"Still no word... from Sid?" I asked lightly.

"No," Dad said. "Her attorney assures us she's taking the steps necessary to deal with her problems. How is Duncan going to support you and a baby?"

"I'll be... going back to work... as soon as I can. We're resourceful adults, Dad. We'll figure it out."

"But how are you going to pay your medical bills?"

"I have insurance."

"Not enough. And you might need care for years to come. And then there's the baby—"

"I know. But the foundation money—"

"Sidney said David Spooner took it all."

"Now that... he's in custody... maybe some of it... will be recovered."

"I hope so, because it's going to take everything your mother and I have to help Sidney out of her mess."

"This isn't a nice topic for Christmas Eve," Mom cut in. "Let's try to count our blessings." She nodded toward the inert figures of Karen Suh and Shondra Taylor for emphasis, and passed out ginger ales.

"You're right," Dad said, giving her a contrite kiss. "Sorry. What should we toast?"

A rap on the door sounded. Dr. Jarvis lifted his hand in greeting. "I might have just the news. Marigold, your rehabilitation is so far ahead of schedule, I've decided to release you to go home New Year's Eve."

My heart bounces high at the unexpected news. I know I still have a lot of outpatient physical therapy ahead of me, but being discharged is a huge step forward.

"That's the best gift ever!" Mom said, leaning over to give me a hug.

"Yes, indeed," Dad said, pouring Dr. Jarvis a plastic cup of ginger ale. "Let's toast to Marigold going home!"

"Cheers!"

The ginger ale is fizzy and cool in my mouth as I toast my own good news. I thought the day would never come... and now it's happening so fast.

December 25, Sunday

"MERRY CHRISTMAS," Duncan said. Then he kissed me.

I kiss him back, but he must've detected something is... off.

He lifted his head. "What's wrong?"

"Duncan, I need... to tell you something."

He is instantly concerned. "Is it the baby?"

"I'm sorry, I didn't mean... to scare you. The baby is fine, and so am I... considering."

"Then what is it?"

I winced. "Trina came to see me."

"What? When?"

"About... ten days ago."

"Why didn't you tell me?"

"Because I was ashamed."

"Of what?"

"That I let her get to me."

"What did she say?"

"She said I was your project *du jour*, and you would get tired of me."

He picked up a lock of my hair. "Wow... and you believed her?"

"I'm sorry to say I did a little. My medical bills—"

He quieted me with a finger to my lips. "Sweetie, one thing my job gives me is a perspective of most of the problems we have in this country compared to problems people have in other parts of the world. Medical bills for bringing you and our baby through what you've been through, are still First World problems."

"And that... is why... I love you," I whispered.

He kissed me again, this one a lingering promise of our life together. The baby kicks hard between us. I am simply the luckiest woman in the world.

When bootsteps sounded on the floor, I'm surprised. It's Sunday, but I'm sure Jack Terry has someplace better to be.

"Just passing through," he said, extending a manila envelope. "Trying to get all my cases updated before I take some time off." He winced. "I wish I had better news, but Spooner had already spent all the cash he siphoned out of the foundation. The D.A. will try to get some of it back, but it might take years."

Disappointing, but not unexpected. "Thanks for the update, Jack."

"Sure thing. Hey, congrats—I hear you're going home New Year's Eve."

An involuntary smile split my face. "Yes."

"Good… I need my Sundays back." He gave me a wink. "Send me a picture of the baby."

"Right back at you," I called.

At the door he turned back. "By the way, I found something of yours I thought might come in handy and stuck it in the envelope, too. Cheers, Coma Girl."

Intrigued, I looked inside the envelope. I flipped past the pages of statements from the foundation accounts showing overdrawn balances. Behind the statements, I noticed a thin slip of paper, and pulled it out.

A lottery ticket. I scanned the date and time and realized with growing incredulity it's the lottery ticket I'd bought the night of the accident. Jack must have found it in my wrecked car.

"Will you pull up the lottery website on your phone?" I asked Duncan. "And check these numbers."

"Give me the ticket—I can scan it with the app to see if it's a winner."

He waved the ticket barcode over the app, and a bell sounded.

"It's a winner," Duncan said with a chuckle.

"How much?"

"It's still loading…. Here it comes."

He stared at the screen, then turned to look at me.

"How much?" I asked.

He turned the screen in my direction. *Winner: $77,000*

December 26, Monday

WHEN THE DOOR opened, the last person I expected to see was the person I wanted most to see.

Sidney. She looked thin and sallow, with dark circles under her eyes.

I burst into tears. "Where have you been?"

She came over to hug me, and held on tight, the way she used to when she was little.

"I've been getting well. I've been in a rehab program to prove to the prosecutor I want to kick my addiction."

She sounds different. Humbled, but also calm and peaceful.

"I'm so sorry, Marigold, for making such a mess out of everything. It's probably my fault you're even here."

"Don't go there. I'm better and I'm being released New Year's Eve."

Her face lit up and I saw hints of the old Sidney. "That's the best news of my life."

She gave me another long hug, then pulled back.

"Marigold, I have to ask you… when you were in the coma, could you hear what was going on?"

I stalled. "What do you mean?"

She wet her lips. "I mean, were you aware of what was happening around you?"

Did I remember that she'd tried to smother me? Yes. But did I want to relive it for the rest of my life? No.

"Oh, no… I couldn't hear anything. When I woke up, it was like I'd lost six months of my life."

Her eyes welled, and she puffed out little exhales. "Good," she said, her voice cracking. "Because I don't think I could live with myself if I thought you remembered some of the things I did to you. Even though you don't remember them, Marigold, I do, and I'm so, so sorry. I love you so much."

She pulled my face against hers and our tears mingled for long minutes. When I pulled back, I brushed her hair back from her face. "What happens next for you?"

"I have to complete another more intense cycle of rehab. My attorney thinks it will reduce my jail time by half. But that will have to wait until I can earn the money. I sold my car and my jewelry and everything else I had of value. But it's still going to be a chunk of change."

"Mom and Dad said they would help you."

Sid shook her head. "No. I'm not going to take money they've worked hard for all their lives to pay for my mistakes. It just means things will be on hold for a while."

Sidney was paying dearly for her mistakes. Practicing law was off the table. And she'd always have a drug charge on her records.

"It's okay," she said, squeezing my shoulder. "I'm clean for the first time in years, and even though everything sucks right now, I feel free. And long-term sobriety—that's worth the wait."

"A friend of mine just went through a program here in Atlanta." When I mentioned the name, Sidney nodded.

"It's one of the best, but it's also one of the priciest, like fifty grand— no way can I afford it."

I clasped her hands. "If I could get you in, would you go?"

"Absolutely, I'd go tonight."

I smiled. "Pack your bag." I'd rather put the lottery money toward Sidney's future than my medical bills. The bills would wait.

And I knew Duncan would understand.

December 27, Tuesday

I LEAN OVER SHONDRA TAYLOR'S BED, close to her ear.

"Shondra, my name is Marigold Kemp, and I'm your ward mate, code name Coma Girl. I've been lying in bed three in the vegetable patch for six months, and I'm going home soon. And you can, too. I know you're in there. I know you can hear me. You have so many friends and family members visiting you, so many people rooting for you. You're young and you're strong. You can wake up, just like me. I want to give you something to latch on to. Trust me on this—it works."

I hang a new iPod on the bedrail near her head, and turn on the playlist of classical music.

December 28, Wednesday

I STEER THE SCOOTER down the hall, looking for a specific room number. When I find it, I pull to a stop at the door and gently work my way inside.

Inside the room is dark. I buzz over and pull the curtains aside to let in some daylight. The patient in the bed rolls her face toward me.

"Time for our walk, Audrey. Are you coming?"

She nods and slowly swings her legs over the side of the bed. Once she stands, it takes her a few minutes to push her feet into house shoes and find a warm housecoat to put on over her pajamas. But by this time, she is looking forward to the walk.

"Where would you like to go today?" I ask. "The garden? The plaza? The cafeteria?"

She lengthens her stride to keep pace with my scooter. "Anywhere but home."

"Okay, Audrey. We can do that."

December 29, Thursday

"THANKS FOR SEEING US, Dr. Jarvis."

"Always happy to see my number one patient," Dr. Jarvis said with a wide smile. "What can I do for you?"

"We're just trying to get out in front of the paperwork before Marigold is discharged New Year's Eve," Duncan said. "I don't want to run into any snags—I'd like to get her home as soon as possible."

Under the desk, his hand clasps my knee. I appreciate the comforting gesture.

"Smart," Dr. Jarvis said, "since it'll probably be a busy day. But there's really not a lot to do. I'll have the discharge papers ready to go by nine am, and bring them to you myself. I know the staff will want to say goodbye. Then we'll put you in a wheelchair and take you down to the front and you can pick her up. Easy peasy."

I wet my lips. "And when will we receive the final hospital bill? Should we be prepared to pay something on it before we leave?"

"I don't know what you mean," Dr. Jarvis said. "I have a letter here from accounting that says your hospital bill has been paid in full. In fact, there's a credit balance."

I feel my eyes boing open. "How's that possible?"

"I'm not a CPA," Dr. Jarvis said. "But it looks like it's been covered by TMZ?"

"The celebrity website?" Duncan reached for the letter. "How can that be?"

The bottom falls out of my stomach. Did TMZ get their hands on my tell-all manuscript, and to appease their guilt before leaking it, sent a big, fat check to cover my medical bills?

"May I see the letter?" I can hear the tremor in my own voice. After all my family has been through in the past few months and for us to emerge stronger and better, I can't bear the thought of all of the banked goodwill and love being torched by a thoughtless manuscript I wrote before I even knew what made my family tick.

But when I glance over the list of checks, I realize the first payment was deposited shortly after I arrived at the hospital, and checks regularly thereafter.

The sound of a camera phone shutter comes to me. The poet volunteer I had suspected of leaking photos to TMZ... had his conscience gotten the better of him and he'd decided to share the proceeds?

December 30, Friday

"COMA GIRL, I WAS BORN to do this job."

I sat back in my chair. "I'm impressed, Roberta. You've grown the subscription numbers more than the company Sidney was working with."

"That's because I know you... and when I post entries, they're personal, and they're good."

"Well, keep up the good work. At this rate we're going to grow the foundation by leaps and bounds."

"That's the idea," she sang. "Oh, by the way, this package came for you this morning, special delivery."

"What is it?"

"I don't know because it says right on the front it's only supposed to be opened by the person it's addressed to."

I arch an eyebrow at her.

"Hey, I'm cleaning up my act."

I'm still laughing when I open the package, but the contents tear a gasp from me.

My missing manuscript. And a book of poems by Emily Dickinson. On the manuscript is a sticky note.

Coma Girl... I wanted to keep this safe until you woke up... but then I couldn't get close to you again. Have a happy life.

There was no signature.

My relief is complete.

"Roberta, do you have a lighter in your purse?"

"Girl, what color?"

I zoom my scooter to the bathroom and turn on the exhaust fan. Then I set each page on fire in the sink, and watch the hateful words I'd written burn and blow away.

December 31, Saturday

"GOODBYE... GOODBYE... GOODBYE!"

The staff on the floor send me away with tears and flowers and a sack of colorful head scarfs. I will miss Gina and Teddy the most. And Dr. Jarvis, of course.

But I'm going *home*.

While I sit in the lobby in a wheelchair waiting for Duncan to pull around and pick me up, I am so excited for my new life to begin, I am overwhelmed with gratitude, and brimming with love.

The coma took everything from me, and gave back to me tenfold. I am a lucky, lucky woman.

A sound captures my attention and I involuntarily smile. It's the unmistakable silken voice of my poet volunteer. I turn in my wheelchair, eager to finally meet him...

Only to realize the sound is coming from a rather large television in the corner. On the screen, my poet volunteer is fit and handsome, dressed in business casual clothes, conducting an interview. I had wondered if he had a career in broadcasting.

But as I wheel closer, I realize he isn't conducting the interview, he's the person being interviewed.

Nearby stands a man watching the interview, rapt.

"Excuse me," I said. "Can you tell me the name of the man being interviewed?"

The guy does a double-take. "Lady... are you kidding? That's Keith Young, star receiver of the Atlanta Falcons. Dude is football royalty. Where have you been—in a coma?"

He walks away and I sit there in awe.

Keith Young has been visiting me the entire time, leaking pictures of me to cover the cost of my medical bills—because he knew he was innocent and wouldn't be charged? And he'd kept the damaging manuscript safe until I recovered. He didn't have to get involved, had risked a lot by sneaking in and out of my hospital room... caring.

Life is truly awesome, friend.

I'm going to go live it.

-The End-

A NOTE FROM THE AUTHOR

Thank you so very much for taking the time to read my story COMA GIRL. I hope you've enjoyed Marigold's story—I've certainly enjoyed writing it! This story is special to me because it's a concept I've been carrying around in my head since a grade school teacher of mine shared with me that years previously she had been in a coma after a car accident, and she had been aware of everything going on around her. While I suspect my teacher didn't have as many confessors visiting her as Marigold, I'd like to think she'd be pleased with the way the story turned out.

Reviews are so important to authors and our books. Reviews help me to attract new readers so I can keep producing more stories for you. Plus I really want to know if I'm keeping you entertained! If you enjoyed COMA GIRL and feel inclined to leave a review at your favorite online bookstore, I would appreciate it very much.

If you'd like to sign up to receive notices of my future book releases, please visit www.stephaniebond.com and join my email list. I promise not to flood you with emails and I will never share or sell your address. And you can unsubscribe at any time.

Thanks again for your time and interest, and for telling your friends about my books.

Happy reading!
Stephanie Bond

ABOUT THE AUTHOR

Stephanie Bond was seven years deep into a corporate career in computer programming and pursuing an MBA at night when an instructor remarked she had a flair for writing and suggested she submit material to academic journals. But Stephanie was more interested in writing fiction—more specifically, romance and mystery novels. After writing in her spare time for two years, she sold her first manuscript; after selling ten additional projects to two publishers, she left her corporate job to write fiction full-time. To-date, Stephanie has more than seventy published novels to her name, including the popular BODY MOVERS humorous mystery series. Her romantic comedy STOP THE WEDDING! is now a Hallmark Channel movie. For more information on Stephanie's books, visit www.stephaniebond.com.